THE
ENGLISHMAN

By David Gilman

THE LAST HORSEMAN

NIGHT FLIGHT TO PARIS

THE ENGLISHMAN

Master of War series

MASTER OF WAR

DEFIANT UNTO DEATH

GATE OF THE DEAD

VIPER'S BLOOD

SCOURGE OF WOLVES

CROSS OF FIRE

Dangerzone series

THE DEVIL'S BREATH

ICE CLAW

BLOOD SUN

———

MONKEY AND ME

THE
ENGLISHMAN
DAVID GILMAN

HEAD
of ZEUS

First published in the UK in 2020 by Head of Zeus Ltd

9 7 5 3 1 2 4 6 8

A catalogue record for this book is available from
the British Library.

ISBN (HB): 9781838931391
ISBN (XTPB): 9781838931407
ISBN (E): 9781838931421

Typeset by Divaddict Publishing Solutions Ltd

Printed and bound in Great Britain by
CPI Group (UK) Ltd, Croydon CR0 4YY

MIX
Paper from
responsible sources
FSC
www.fsc.org
FSC® C020471

Head of Zeus Ltd
First Floor East
5–8 Hardwick Street
London EC1R 4RG

WWW.HEADOFZEUS.COM

CONTENTS

THE
ENGLISHMAN

For Suzy

In any man who dies there dies with him his first
      snow and kiss and fight...
Not people die but worlds die in them.

Yevgeny Aleksandrovich Yevtushenko
(1932–2017)

Prologue

Russian Federation
October 2019

The road was long and straight, and the dark forest pressed on to the verge on both sides. Heaped snow, ploughed from the previous winter, was still frozen and had become an even higher bank from the fresh snowfall. He lengthened his stride and ran faster towards the rising sun.

He dared not stop.

The sun had reached the top of the trees either side of the chill, sunless gulley of a road. His laboured breathing muted the sound of the first vehicle. Instinct made him turn. Another vehicle was travelling behind that, its headlights weaving. There were probably twenty men in pursuit.

He leapt over the snow ledge on the side of the road and ducked beneath the overhanging branches. A slender track channelled between the accumulated snow and ice on the side of the road and where the tree trunks barred his way into the forest. He heard the engines change pitch. They were slowing. He ran; branches caught his face and he raised an arm. A rattle of gunfire cut the air above his head. He cursed his own stupidity. By brushing the branches away from his face he had disturbed the snow lying on them and the fine powder left low on the tree had been seen. He kept running, ducking lower, avoiding the branches. The thwack of bullets hit the trees where he had been moments before. They were shooting wildly. Ripping through the air. A storm of treebark and snow.

His breath came hard. The cold air raw in his lungs. And then he ran out of track. He plunged into the low branches. Felt them them whip his face. Searing pain scorched his thigh. He stumbled as another bullet tore into his side. Ignoring the pain he ran on. He was leaking blood. Leaving a trail. The distant sound of dogs echoing through the forest. His foot caught a root, tumbling him into deep snow. He slammed into a tree, the wind knocked out of him. He needed a moment to draw breath. He shook clear the pain and the sweat from his eyes. He could hear them now. Voices calling to each other. Fearful. Of him. He dared to close his eyes for a moment. More gunfire.

And he remembered what had brought him here.

PART ONE
WEST AFRICA

1

French Foreign Legion Operating Base
Republic of Mali
February 2013

The temperature was already nudging fifty degrees Celsius and as well as their combat gear and weapons each man carried in excess of thirty kilos of supplies and ammunition. Their destination was the harsh mountainous terrain where Salafist Tuaregs and Al Qaeda ethnic militias had surged across the border from Algeria. These tribal fighting men knew their ground and it was up to the elite 2e Régiment étranger de parachutistes to dig them out and stop the Islamic militants' advance.

United Nations Resolution 2085 had backed France's military intervention in the French protectorate of the West African country of Mali, a landlocked area the size of Texas. The world had applauded when the French and Chadian army liberated Timbuktu, but more brutal fighting was soon to take place hundreds of miles away in the desolate Ametettaï valley, in the heart of the mountainous massif of Adrar des Ifoghas in northern Mali, on the border with Algeria. It was an area controlled by criminals, terrorists and warlords, men who trafficked arms and drugs with brutal efficiency to fund anti-western organizations. The combined ground and air operation to clear the villages in the valley and the nearby caves already promised to be a tough fight. French Special Operations Forces had flown several hundred kilometres from their base in Ouagadougou, Burkina Faso, and seized Kidal prior to the assault on the mountains. The President of France and his politicians wanted this fight, the generals wanted it and the boots on the ground were happy to oblige. France's honour was at stake.

Caporal-chef Serge Sokol ushered his sniper platoon into the Puma helicopter's oven-hot interior from where he and the other eleven men would fast rope down once they reached their landing zone. A month before, when they had parachuted into Timbuktu and secured it from the terrorists, they had had the upper hand, but the rough terrain of boulder-strewn ground here favoured the defenders. Limited access towards the caves funnelled troops into narrow choke points. Easy targets for ambush. The snipers were going in by helicopter and would then slog across the broken ground and establish their own fire positions. Their long-range rifles would give the attacking legionnaires a better chance of advancing.

'Bird!' a voice hailed Sokol.

The Russian's face, lined from twenty years' service in every eye-squinting theatre of war that Africa could throw at the Legion, creased further into a grin. In the Slovak language, Sokol was a bird of prey – his new identity given to him by the recruiting captain at the barracks in Marseilles on the day he had joined. The immaculately dressed Foreign Legion officer told the gangly, unkempt and malnourished youth that it suited his hawk-nosed face. And that if he survived the weeks of training and made it through to the Legion's parachute regiment the captain would pay for a falcon tattoo out of his own pocket. It was the first sign of comradeship the runaway youth had ever known and it spurred him on. And now there were so many falcon tattoos across his muscled torso his skin looked like a damned aviary.

Sokol's close friend, Dan Raglan from the Legion's parachute commando group, jogged towards him. Sokol cupped a hand to his ear against the Puma's roar as Dan shouted: 'The target's moved. He's in another cave.'

The caves were refuge to Abdelhamid Abou Zeid, one of the world's most wanted terrorists, commander of Al Qaeda in Mali and the 2nd Foreign Legion Parachute Regiment's target. Their task: to capture Abou Zeid alive and retrieve terrorist intel hidden in the caves.

Sokol grimaced. Last-minute changes could cost lives. The briefing had been precise. As the Legion's paras fought forward the regiment's commando unit would abseil down from the clifftops and strike into the caves that held the terrorists and their leader. 'Moved where?'

The commando shoved a folded map into the Russian's hand and traced a line across the contours on the map. 'Here. Cave Thirteen.' He grinned. 'You think that's unlucky?'

'Only to idiots like you who expose their arses sliding down a cliff face on a rope. Who's made the change?'

The younger man turned to face the cluster of officers standing in the background with two civilians. One civilian wore an eye patch that barely concealed the welt of a scar. These were British and French intelligence officers who had laid out the plan to capture the wanted man. A third spook, an American, had left two days before. It was obvious to anyone with half a sun-baked brain that this operation was all French despite international support. If there was a cock-up it would only be French blood that was spilt. Though not all French. Not for those who served in the Legion. Those who went in first.

'Intelligence,' the Russian said derisively. 'I don't know who Sinbad the Sailor is,' he said, nodding towards the French intelligence officer with the eye patch, 'but those wankers get their intel out of their dicks.'

Raglan gripped his friend's arm. Other than his slightly different array of combat gear and helmet he looked the same as any of the other lean, burnished men. 'You have to open the door for us, Bird, or we are screwed. Your boys need to get in position and take out those defending the caves.'

Several hundred insurgents stood between the legionnaires' jump-off point and the cave entrances. Every cave had to be cleared but the one holding the Al Qaeda leader would be the more heavily defended.

The Russian looked again at the map. 'If this is my position then it's a longer shot than they told us. I reckon eight hundred and fifty plus and the wind will sweep across those cliffs.' The snipers needed to be in place at the right time – every man depended on the other to do what was expected – but getting into position in the mountains to cover those abseiling down to enter the caves while fighting a stubborn enemy would take time. 'First we have to fight our way forward.'

The younger man grinned. 'Then you'd better get a move on and not drag your arse, otherwise we're all going to see the seventy virgins promised by the terrs.' He slapped the Russian's arm and ran to where his own men waited.

The legionnaires were fighting in sweltering heat, in a soon-to-be forgotten conflict, but the desire for war is why the men had joined the Legion. That and the desire to escape whatever lay behind them. Their combat fatigues already clung to them with sweat and the weight of their equipment dug into their flesh as they sprinted towards the choppers. That was nothing new. No one complained. The roar of the Pumas' blades beat down their thoughts of what might lie ahead. No matter how heavily fortified the mountains might be, the legionnaires were hungry for the fight. New recruits who had recently qualified through the relentless selection programme were keen to be blooded; while those old sweats who had spent their time fighting in the deserts and jungles knew full well how tough and well equipped their opponents would be, and that success would take skill, determination and a mind focused on one thing: to inflict as much violence on their enemy as possible and to kill them before they killed you. It was a simple equation that even the newest member of the Legion understood.

Sokol tucked the map beneath his webbing and shouldered the padded canvas bag that carried his beloved sniper's rifle. He spat. Men in suits. He settled his backside on to the Puma's floor, wedging himself between his men's legs. Sokol's feet dangled in space as the twin Turbomeca C4 engines powered the battlefield helicopter into a sky undiluted by cloud or haze, whose diamond-bright clarity was suddenly speckled as the raptors thundered their way heavenward at 147 knots.

Raglan watched as Sokol's helicopter lifted. Hundreds of jihadists were waiting to fight to the death against these ground troops who would labour against their resistance before the legionnaires could reach their objective. It was time to throw the full weight of the Legion's elite into the saw-toothed mountains.

He looked at his squad of men.

He could think of no better place to be other than among them.

For Dan Raglan the legion was family.

The terrorists were prepared for any assault. Gun positions and snipers were dug in, concealed across the cliff face and valley floor, directing heavy fire and rocket-propelled grenades on the advancing paratroopers. They were well armed – after the fall of Libya abundant weapons had been there for the taking. French generals feared the terrorists had air-to-air missiles and that restricted their use of combat aircraft in the area. French artillery fire from forty kilometres away pummelled enemy positions but they could not dislodge many. It would take grim determination, relentlessly skirmishing across the valley floor, for the men to get close enough to kill them.

The caves were supplied with enough food and ammunition for months of siege. The turning point came when the legionnaires took the village of Ametettaï, the source of the terrorists' water supply. From then on it was a fight to the death with no escape for the Salafists, who were pushed back into those caves where their last reserves of water were stored. The Legion had fought in Afghanistan and gave these Al Qaeda fighters and their Tuareg allies their grudging respect. They were more determined and more skilled than the Taliban.

Raglan and a company of commandos traversed the mountaintop and attacked from above. He blinked sweat from his eyes as he and a dozen others used fire and manoeuvre to get closer to the well-concealed fire positions protecting the heights above the caves. The ankle-twisting ground was a tougher terrain than the pancake-flat plains below and made speedy movement impossible. Clawing their way forward took as long for the men on the valley floor as those who had gained a foothold on the treacherous slopes above them. Both attack groups had suffered some casualties. The lack of cover from the barren, rock-strewn ground was a gift for their enemy. Raglan's team were three hundred metres from the cliff edge from where they would abseil into the caves' openings when, suddenly, the jagged-toothed silhouettes in the distance shimmered with movement. Figures loomed from behind boulders worn smooth by thousands of years of desert winds. Bullets crackled through the air.

Raglan heard the bullet strike the man a couple of metres away. The thud of rounds hitting his Kevlar body armour knocked him back on his heels but the sickening sound of metal tearing into flesh was unmistakable. They were outnumbered at least six to one as the swarm of terrorists rose up and advanced. Aggressive training and instinct made the legionnaires stand their ground and return sustained fire. And then they strode forward a metre at a time, laying down effective fire as Raglan's men picked their targets, some firing their under-barrel grenade launchers. Their coordinated counter-attack made their enemy falter. Now it was they who knelt or lay on the broken ground. Raglan signalled for the men to take cover. They couldn't stay silhouetted against the skyline. The enemy showed no sign of having air-to-air missiles on the mountain plateau, but an RPG could just as easily bring down an attack helicopter. Amid the heavy crackle of gunfire, Raglan shouted their coordinates and called in an air strike. French helicopter pilots were some of the most daring he had ever encountered. The strike was confirmed. Two minutes. One hundred and twenty long seconds to keep the attackers at bay.

The helicopter attack was dangerously close to where he and the others were pinned down, so orders were called and the men worked in pairs: fire and movement saw them safely to the few raised boulders that offered some shelter. Once the Tiger choppers came in low and fast their laser-sighted cannon and rocket fire would plough the ground and if ricochets didn't scythe the air stone fragments would.

Raglan bent down, pushing his face close to the wounded man who lay unmoving, eyes wide. 'Sammy, hang on, *mon ami*,' he shouted above the constant chatter of gunfire and explosions.

'Dan... sorry... don't stop. Keep going,' his friend said through gritted teeth.

Raglan kept one eye on the terrorists, who were keeping their heads down, but that wouldn't last for much longer. He checked the sky. There was no roar from the attack helicopters' engines. As he comforted the wounded man he quickly dragged rocks to form a protective shield around him. One of the other commandos was ducking and weaving under covering fire towards them.

'Plenty of time, Sammy. Too many of the bastards for us to move forward. Choppers are coming,' said Raglan as he pulled aside the downed man's webbing that held his ammunition pouches and slipped his hand beneath his body armour. Blood swathed his hand. Somehow a round had punched through his midriff.

The commando ran the last twenty metres and took up position next to Raglan to cover his exposed comrades. Empty brass cartridge cases bounced on the rocks as he poured fire towards the terrorists.

'Milosz!' Raglan warned him, pointing to a handful of Al Qaeda fighters who rose up and rushed them. The Polish-born commando shifted his arc of fire and brought them down.

'Can't feel my legs, Dan,' said their wounded friend.

Milosz spared a quick glance at him. He smiled. 'Sammy, that's because you're a malingering bastard.

You'd better stay put while we sort these fuckers out,' he shouted, dropping an empty magazine and seamlessly reloading another. The weight of suppressing firepower far outweighed the legionnaires' few numbers.

'Fuck you too. Everyone knows you Poles can't run for shit anyway. I could crawl faster,' Sammy answered, sucking in his breath from the pain.

Raglan pressed his hand behind his friend's back. There was no exit wound. Pulling open the wounded man's medical pack he took out a blood-clotting gauze dressing. Tearing it from its packet he pressed it beneath the wounded man's close-fitting body armour. 'Keep your hand pressed tight,' he shouted.

'Listen... don't leave me here... not like this, eh? You know what they'll do to me. Do what you have to do, yeah?'

Raglan had no intention of either killing his friend or letting the enemy take him. Neither was an option for these close-knit fighting men. Before he could answer Milosz yelled a warning.

'Dan!' The Pole fired a forty-millimetre red smoke grenade into the enemy position as moments later the wind at their backs heralded the clattering blades of the helicopter approach.

Bitter experience from previous operations stopped the commandos from pre-warning the pilots what colour smoke they would be using. The enemy could monitor transmissions and pop their own smoke drawing helicopters to land in an ambush. Raglan pressed the transmission button.

'Identify smoke.'

'I have red smoke,' answered the pilot.

'Roger that,' Raglan confirmed and covered the wounded man with his body as the terrifying power of cannon fire ripped ground and enemy apart. The devastation was staggering. As the downdraught pummelled them Raglan and his men pressed themselves flat. Stone fragments whirred from the unfolding scene of slaughter. The daring Tiger pilots had come in low and fast and locked on to the enemy position. With devastating violence, human bodies became ragged pieces of flesh hurtled this way and that, staining the rocky ground. The killing was swift and efficient. Raglan heard the crackle in his headset asking for confirmation that the enemy position had been neutralized. Answering in the affirmative Raglan requested a casevac. Now that the mountaintop plateau was clear the wounded man would be airlifted to safety.

The raptor choppers swooped away. The legionnaire commandos quickly got to their feet and moved forward. Raglan watched them step across the killing ground. If any Al Qaeda had survived the slaughter they would soon be dispatched.

He undid the wounded man's helmet strap and reached once again for his medical pack. 'Now we're screwed if any of us get hit. You're the bloody medic,' he said as he fumbled for the painkiller in the pack. Each man was trained to administer medical aid but it was the team medic who carried the lifesaving supplies.

The injured man grimaced in agony. Adrenaline had fled his body, leaving the door open for biting pain. 'Trick is,,. don't get bloody hit. Jesus... come on... mate...'

Raglan shook the small clear liquid bottle, inserted a syringe and then tapped it free of air bubbles. 'Casevac's on its way, Sammy. Hang on in there, this'll give you happy dreams.' Raglan injected fifty milligrams of ketamine into his friend's thigh muscle. Ketamine was preferable to morphine as it did not cause respiratory depression and the heart is stimulated rather than suppressed. He heard the whirring blades approaching. As urgent as the Tigers' but at a more sedate pace. He wrote the dose and the time it had been administered on his friend's forehead and then popped a green smoke canister to identify his location. Once again Raglan had the pilot confirm the smoke colour. With a final tap of farewell on his injured friend's shoulder, he gave a thumbs up and ran to where the men waited to abseil down into the caves. There was no denying the regret he felt at seeing a friend wounded. They had been lucky so far on this mission. In the past, so many had been killed. Concern filled the men's faces; they needed no words to express their feelings. They had been together for years. Raglan readied the rope. The casevac helicopter's blades swept the canister's smoke across them.

If they were to snatch the terrorist leader and secure the intelligence material, they needed to abseil to the mouth of the caves. Their lives were now in the hands of the snipers. They launched themselves into the void.

2

'Bird' Sokol wiped the sweat from his eyes. His ghillie suit of tufted hessian stitched over his disruptive pattern combat uniform made shooting even more difficult in the oppressive heat. His sniper rifle was balanced, its thirty-pound weight supported by the boulders that gave him and his spotter cover. The full length of the weapon was fifty-four inches from its stock to its box-shaped muzzle break at the end of its 27.6-inch barrel, which was wrapped in sacking. Shooter and his weapon were well concealed, their outline broken against the rock-strewn terrain. The rifle fired a .50 calibre round over 2,000 metres at 850 metres per second. Sokol had shot that distance but the most effective range was 1,800 metres, and even though the paratroopers' assault had secured the ground approaching the lower slopes there was still a several-hundred-metre stretch to clamber across to the cave's entrance. The legionnaires had killed hundreds of terrorists and the survivors had withdrawn into their mountain stronghold. An enemy belt-fed machine gun with an effective 1,500-metre range was sited in the cave entrance and swept the ground to Sokol's front. The jihadist machine-gunner was protected by a sangar of rocks beneath the cave's overhang, which kept him safe from mortar fire, and neither the Russian sniper nor the spotter at his shoulder had declared a clean shot. Time had run out. The legionnaires on the ground needed to press their attack now that he saw the commandos abseiling down the cliff face, but if he could not make the shot a lot of men would die the moment they dropped into view.

Sokol had been at his fire position long enough to establish his wind and range markers and now the wisps of dust that sheered across the mountain face settled. He had already killed the enemy snipers and neutralized camouflaged pickup trucks with mounted twin-barrelled cannon, now he needed to make the machine-gunner break cover. He recalculated, turning the settings on his telescopic sights to adjust elevation. A bullet never travels straight; it flies on a parabolic curve, gaining height before gravity makes it drop. Sokol had the range he needed to correct his scope and compensate for the bullet's flight. He pressed his cheek against the stock keeping his eye on his telescopic sight and saw a movement across the face of the cave. Belt-fed machine guns had a voracious appetite for linked ammunition and he saw a terrorist shuffle across the face of the cave to resupply his gunner. Sokol's spotter had barely called the target when Sokol aimed in front of the man's strides and fired. Rule of thumb said a thousand-metre shot would take a little less than two seconds for the bullet to reach its target. He had barely counted those two seconds before he saw the splash of blood as the heavy-calibre round tore into the terrorist's leg. He'd soon be dead from shock and blood loss. Sokol cycled the bolt action, chambering another round from the magazine. He fired again into the rocks that gave the machine-gunner cover. In the seconds it took for the round to strike and shatter some of the rocks from the man's protection, another round was already loaded. Now Sokol relied on his instincts. To kill effectively meant thinking what the enemy might do next in the time it took for the sniper's bullet to reach its intended target. The machine-gunner needed ammunition and Sokol expected him to risk everything and go for it – he had helped make up the gunner's mind by killing his loader and then pounding his protective cover. Sokol changed his aim and risked laying off to where the loader had been shot. Sokol steadied his breathing. The crosshairs in his telescopic sight caught the movement. He squeezed the trigger. If he missed then the machine-gunner would have no difficulty turning his weapon on the dozen men who were moments away from swinging down into the open mouth of the cave. The terrorist stretched forward and the bullet took him in his head.

No sooner had the man gone down than two or three more fighters emerged from the shadows, but they were too late. The commandos swung down, tossing stun grenades into the cave. The explosions echoed across the valley floor, quickly followed by staccato gunfire. Sokol lifted his eye from the telescopic sight. The commandos were inside.

Raglan and his men cast aside their ropes and swiftly killed the few stunned gunmen. They split into pairs, chose a tunnel and moved forward tactically. Speed was of the essence now they had breached the cave. The deeply hidden terrorist base held vital intel and Abou Zeid. The first thing Raglan noticed was the cave's symmetry. The walls were ribbed like a whale's skeleton, the bone-like curves etched as if hand dug over a thousand years, which probably they had been. The initial cave was big enough to drive a truck through. The legionnaires who would already be clambering across the ground towards the caves now that it had been breached could secure these big caverns; it was the smaller tunnels that the commandos were tasked to search. Raglan had Milosz, the Polish commando, two paces behind him, weapon at his shoulder, scanning left and right. Both men steadied their breathing after their exertions. Cables ran the length of the tunnel walls; light bulbs flickered. There must be a generator somewhere far below.

The tunnel narrowed. They crouched, edging forward. Suddenly, a gaping black hole. At first it appeared to be a large recess but it was an opening into an antechamber. A scuffle alerted them; they swung their weapons round. Raglan quickly raised his arm to stop Milosz from pouring fire into the confined space. A dozen young faces stared back at them in deepening shadow. Children, huddling in terror. The terrorists used them as runners between the caves and the villages. Raglan beckoned them to stand, wary that they might have been booby-trapped with explosives. The terrorists had no compunction about wiring kids with Semtex. He tugged each one past him. The wide-eyed boys, for there were no girls among them, couldn't have been older than eight or nine. And through their fear or their training none made a sound, not even a whimper.

'Milosz, take these kids to the entrance. If they make a run for it they'll be targets.'

'Leave them here is better. We go down the tunnel together.'

It was a sensible point the Polish commando made, but if the troops coming in behind them used grenades to clear their way before they ventured too far into the labyrinth then the children would still die.

'No. Take them out. Hand them over and then get back. I'll keep on down this tunnel.'

The decision was made. Milosz nodded and gathered the children like a primary-school teacher and had them hold hands in a daisy chain. As he led them away Raglan followed the tunnel. After another fifty metres, it twisted left and then right. It became narrower. The dangling lights fewer. The shadows deeper. Raglan stooped and edged around the bend. A sudden burst of gunfire tore fragments from the rock face. Raglan drew back, pulled free a grenade and rolled it down the gentle uneven slope of the tunnel floor. The gunfire fell silent as the rattling grenade made the man look down. Raglan turned the corner and fired. The gunman was less than five metres away. His body jerked as the rounds hit him, his AK-47 assault rifle clattered against the wall. Raglan stepped quickly forward, kept his weapon covering the passage ahead and bent down to pick up the grenade he had deliberately not armed. Concussion waves from an exploding grenade at such confined quarters would have killed the gunman but would also have harmed him. The pin was still tight. He tucked it back into his webbing. His breathing quickened and muscles tensed as he stepped gingerly forward across the fallen man. Now he saw that the tunnel burrowed ahead for thirty metres, widened slightly and looked as though it made another turn away from the lights. One passage left, the other to the right. He moved slowly, reached the dark corner, saw that light bulbs had failed in a few places and then flickered again. He heard the gentle hum of a generator. The main command cave was close.

Had the shadow that loomed forward twenty paces down the passage on his left not cried out *Allahu Akbar* he would have had time to detonate his suicide vest. Raglan fired two rapid head shots. No brain, no neurological reflex. And no guarantee if the suicide bomber had a dead man's trigger. This one didn't. Raglan's ears rang from the gunfire but he still heard distant echoes of other gunfights in other tunnels. The man's impetus had carried him forward close to where Raglan stood. He stepped back warily. Makeshift terrorist laboratories mixed a lethal explosive cocktail of triacetone triperoxide, commonly known as TATP, and even when inert it was dangerous. His caution in stepping away from the headless terrorist nearly cost him his life. Metal scraped on rock behind him. He spun around. A muzzle flash flared from a gunshot fired by a crouching terrorist further back in the shadows. The bullet struck the rim of his helmet, knocking him back on his heels. He slammed into the wall. Three more scattered pistol shots followed. Raglan threw himself to one side. His weapon fell from his hands. Reaching for his chest holster he yanked free the 9-mm pistol and fired instinctively into the shadows. Bullets thudded into flesh. Raglan crawled forward, desperately reaching for his rifle. His hands touched the shooter's body. He slowed his breath and listened. He felt a moment of disbelief as he tugged the body over. It was a boy who looked to be ten or eleven years old. Anger and disgust flared in him. The fresh-faced child stared sightlessly at the man who had killed him, eyes wide and jaw slack in shock and surprise.

And then what lights remained went out. He reached for the pouch holding his night vision goggles but felt the ragged tear from where one of the other bullets had torn through it. Like a blind man feeling his way in an unknown environment, he pressed his palms forward. Somewhere in the distance low reflected light from what must be another room seeped into the tunnel. Letting his eyes adjust, his fingers explored the rock face. The passage narrowed. A grown man could not get through. The tunnel's junction gave access from the left-hand passage for the suicide bomber, but this way was too tight and the terrorists had sent a boy to kill him. If he backtracked then Raglan thought the other way could lead into a deeper labyrinth. If he could get through the narrow entrance then the dull glow ahead promised a widening of the tunnel. He realized that if he pushed his assault rifle through the gap the sound of it scraping on the tunnel floor might alert anyone further down the tunnel. Raglan stripped off his webbing and body armour, pulling free his combat knife. With pistol in one hand and knife in the other, he belly crawled into the narrow space.

His shoulders pressed against the low ceiling. He squirmed and wriggled until he felt the pressure on his body ease. Crawling forward on hands and knees, he listened for any movement ahead. There was barely enough reflected light touching the rough walls to distinguish if there were any other side tunnels. But he smelt water, a damp chill as you would experience in a grotto. A sheen of water, no more than a sliver, glinted on a jagged piece of rock ahead of him. He stopped. He heard the hollow drip of water drops falling into a pool or well. The humidity in the tunnel was oppressive. Men lived deep in these caves; their bodies and cooking stoves gave off heat. Raglan went forward, senses alert for any movement. The dull glow ahead seemed illusory. A curved glow of reflective light on the tunnel roof disappeared as he got closer. Then it appeared again, creeping into crevices, exposing the walls' ribbed curves. He crouched, and saw that it depended on his position in the tunnel as to where the light showed itself. A waft of air freshened his face. Chances were he had come close to an air shaft. He lost his footing as his boots slipped on a slimy surface. He fell hard, one leg dropping away into a void. It was a natural well in the rock floor eroded by a thousand years of running water. The pistol slipped from his grip. He swore, found dry rock and hauled himself upright. He had lost his weapon. A moment of panic fluttered in his chest. The darkness and fear were as much a threat to him as an unseen enemy. But Raglan was the gatekeeper of his own emotions and he pushed the fear away. Mind over matter was the key to survival. His probing hand told him he was in a full-height tunnel again. Using his left hand as a guide he gripped the combat knife in his right and went forward. His heartbeat threatened to deafen him. He stopped, slowed his breathing and realized that somewhere ahead was a voice, reduced to a whisper. Another voice answered the first. The murmur had to find its way through the crevices and turns of tunnels that lay ahead, just as did the elusive glimmer of light. And then he heard another voice, urgent despite its distance. It sounded like a name being called. The boy. Whoever had sent the young gunman was calling for him. The demand was issued again and then he saw a shadow block the shimmer of light as a man stepped into the tunnel. Instinct borne of years of fighting a guerrilla war made the man stop. Now his voice lowered cautiously. 'Faisal?' he called.

Raglan held his breath. He kept his left hand pressed against the rock wall, feeling for some purchase that would help propel him forward. He held the knife at an angle between stomach and chest. He was balanced, ready to push off with his rear leg. He heard the man mutter a curse beneath his breath and saw him fumble for something in his belt. The man had yanked free a torch and its beam suddenly swept the tunnel. Raglan powered himself forward, short sharp steps, body held straight, careful not to lunge which would give the man a chance to sidestep. As the torch beam danced towards

Raglan he saw the man's teeth bare in a snarl behind his thick beard. He was bigger and heavier than Raglan, but with a knife in his hand Raglan had the advantage. The terrorist did not turn away; instead Raglan saw the glint of a blade in his hand. Knife fighting was part of the man's culture.

There was little room to manoeuvre although the torchlight showed Raglan that this end of the tunnel was much wider. The man tried to blind him with the beam but Raglan was ducking and weaving his head and shoulders as the man tried to position himself for the knife fight. The blade slashed forward, Raglan stepped inside the lunge, turned his back, grabbed the man's muscled forearm with his left hand and rammed his elbow hard into his sternum. The rank smell of sweat and bad breath filled Raglan's nostrils. His winded assailant still had the strength to bang the metal-cased torch against Raglan's helmet with his free arm. It was enough to throw the commando off balance. The torch fell to the floor and cast dancing shadows against the walls. Raglan spun away and thrust quickly, concentrating on the man's knife hand, wanting to slash tendons or fingers and force him to drop his blade. The man had sidestepped, anticipating the strike. Raglan regained his balance before the man could counter-attack. Raglan's knife blade was in line with his knuckles. Wherever he struck the cutting edge would make contact. In contrast, his opponent's wrist was loose, cutting the air in rapid figures of eight, his free hand palm out to deflect any strike against his neck. It wasn't a trained defence; it was something that looked good in the movies. The man could take a cut to arm or shoulder but if Raglan's blade reached his neck he was dead. Raglan ignored the fancy knife-wielding exhibition and took two fast tight strides and slashed diagonally; the man blocked the strike but the tip of Raglan's knife caught his arm. It was not a debilitating wound. His opponent grunted, twisted his wrist, counter-struck, aiming for Raglan's armpit. The blow would have put Raglan down, but his attacker was too slow. Raglan saw it coming. Muscle memory was quicker than any thought process. The jihadi jabbed repeatedly towards Raglan's face and neck. His reach was short and Raglan looked beyond the blade, trying to see the man's eyes and gauge his body language.

Raglan jabbed diagonally left and right, fast, stabbing and crisscrossing the blade in a small, tight area in front of him, forcing the man to try and break through the impenetrable attack. He was no coward. Hatred fuelled him. He took too big a stride forward. Raglan changed his stance so that the man facing him was in the one o'clock position. In that instant, the man's eyes told Raglan that the man knew he had made a mistake. Raglan's downward slash cut into the man's leg. The wound was deep. Tissue, fat and muscle parted as neatly as if a surgeon had made an incision. The leg could not support the man's weight. He pitched forward and as he did a lucky strike caught Raglan's lower leg. Raglan's adrenaline negated the sudden burning pain; he reversed his wrist and stabbed his blade beneath the man's beard into his throat.

Raglan yanked free the knife before the man's face hit the floor. Wiping the sticky blood from his hand he moved towards the source of the light. Sweat stung his eyes. He sucked the fetid air and took a moment to slow his heartbeat. There was a turn in the tunnel, and within a few paces that too curved to the right. Now the light was brighter. He edged forward, peered around the corner and saw the opening into a cave as high as a double-storey house. A steel ladder was bolted to the far wall ascending to another level – a dark gap in the rock face told Raglan there was another way in and out of this main bunker. A line of trestle tables bore cans of food and a camping gas stove. Filing cabinets boxed in a desktop computer. Two laptops partnered each other married by a cable. Weapons were laid out with loaded magazines next to them. Easy for the man thirty paces away, who had his back to Raglan, to reach. A low-frequency handset was cradled between the man's ear and shoulder. The Al Qaeda fighter pulled a briefcase from the filing cabinet drawer as he shouted into the handset, temper rising, words poisoned by desperation. Raglan heard what sounded like final instructions to keep fighting even though the caves were breached. He called the French *les chiens* to whoever was on the other end of the radio, probably in another cave. His back was still turned to Raglan, who moved as quietly as he could towards the weapons. If he could reach one of the AK-47s or automatic pistols he had a chance. The bearded fighter turned, caught by surprise, but Raglan recognized the man they hunted. Abdelhamid Abou Zeid had a suicide vest strapped to him. He was never going to surrender. Raglan was ten fast paces from the table and the weapons. He hurled the knife to buy vital seconds.

Those seconds were denied him.

Abou Zeid's eyes widened. His mouth opened in a final defiant scream. '*Allahu Akbar.*'

Raglan's luck ran out.

PART TWO

EUROPE

3

Bedford Park
London W4
September 2019

Bedford Park is a select residential quarter of west London: a designated conservation area with proximity to the nearby Underground station giving easy access into the city, making these tree-lined roads a highly desirable location. Woodstock Road is a leafy street occupied by people in the media – actors, film directors – lawyers and families who are considered 'old money', those who have enjoyed the privilege of professional status and wealth for a couple of generations.

Jeremy Carter, a 49-year-old City banker, lived in one such house in Woodstock Road with his wife, his adopted thirteen-year-old son, Steven, and his daughter, five-year-old Melissa. Carter had embraced the boy as his own since marrying Steven's mother Amanda, and, as on every Saturday since the rugby season began, this morning he would be accompanying him to his team's rugby fixture across the River Thames at the private St Paul's School in Barnes and urging him on from the touchline.

The persistent ringing of the telephone inside the five-bedroomed house made no impression on the running argument between Carter and his wife. She was a tall woman, several years younger than him with well-cut shoulder-length auburn hair framing a handsome face. Her good bone structure and exercise regimes at the tennis courts and swimming baths made her look even younger than her forty years.

'You said the twenty-seventh was fine,' she insisted.

'And I told you I have to go to Zurich,' he countered with more equanimity than his irritated wife could muster as he followed her through to the utility room where she bundled an armful of bedsheets into the washing machine. Her domestic help had been off sick for a week and the additional household chores added to her bad temper.

'You said that was the seventeenth. I've planned this dinner party. Everyone's accepted.'

'For God's sake, I'm hardly likely to—'

She raised a hand to stop his self-defence and picked up the phone's handset. 'Hello?'

Carter ignored her gesture and continued to fight his corner. '—make a mistake about a business trip. It's been planned for months.'

Amanda Reeve-Carter flicked an angry glance at him as she pulled a length of hair from her face and spoke into the phone. 'Helen, no, I won't be able to get there before three. Look, can I phone you back? Well... yes...'

Her friend Helen was not an easy woman to silence. Carter shrugged and walked back through the kitchen into the entrance hall. He called up the stairs. 'Steve! Ready?'

A moment later the boy thundered down the staircase carrying a kit bag and a rugby ball tucked under his arm.

Amanda pushed the phone against her chest to smother the chattering as she ruffled her son's hair, wished him luck and glared at her husband. She turned her back and climbed the stairs to remake the bed, putting the phone back to her ear. By the time she reached the front bedroom she had dealt with her friend's demands and looked down across the garden as her husband and son climbed into the car. Steven turned and waved. Carter did not.

She wished she could overcome her irritation. It was unreasonable, she knew. It was only a dinner date that had to be changed. She would make up with her husband. They always did. It was too good a marriage to let pettiness sour it for too long. As the car turned down the street she was distracted by her five-year-old.

'Mummy?'

She picked the child up and immediately felt the tightness around her heart diminish. 'What, my baby?'

'Daddy went away without kissing me bye bye.'

She stroked the child's fair hair and kissed her cheek. 'He was in a hurry so he asked me to give you one instead.'

Carter and his son settled in the back seat of the Jaguar XJ as the driver levered the indicator, checked his mirrors and swung across Woodstock Road into Rupert Road.

'Ready to give 'em a run for their money then, Stevie?' said Carter's long-serving driver, Charlie Lewis. He had been with Carter for six years and watched the young Steven grow into a fine, well-balanced lad, despite his near-constant mobile use: the ubiquitous phone culture endemic in youngsters. In all the years the boy had known his father's driver, the man had always dressed in a dark suit, white shirt and regimental tie with highly polished shoes – a result of the well-groomed 53-year-old having served twenty years in the Irish Guards. No lilting brogue softened his south London accent, however, and nor was it likely to, given the mix of men who served in the regiment. Once retired, Staff Sergeant Lewis had applied to and was accepted by the Rochester Crawford (Private) Bank as chauffeur to the bank's Risk and Compliance Director, Mr Jeremy Carter. A bonus for Lewis was that the British-owned bank had foregone the slightly more ostentatious S-Class Mercedes and 7 Series BMW in favour of the British-made Jaguar for their directors. It was felt that the marque and styling made a more appropriate statement to their client base. And it was a fast, well-balanced car much loved by those who drove them. All in all, Charlie Lewis was more than content with his lot in life.

The hours Lewis worked were long because Carter often worked late at the bank but it was time paid for, as were the Saturday mornings usually spent happily ferrying father and son to various sporting events. In fact, Charlie Lewis barely thought of what he did as employment because the friendliness and mutual respect between the two men made for a comfortable relationship.

Steven barely lifted his head from texting on his phone. 'Hard and fast, Charlie. Knife through butter. No pain, no gain. There to win not to whimper,' he said, happily repeating some of the ex-soldier's clichéd mantras.

'That's the spirit,' said Lewis. 'Happy for me to wait, Mr Carter, so I can see the game?'

'Beth'll know you're skiving off the Tesco run,' Carter answered.

It was a conversation that took place virtually every Saturday morning. It cemented their routine. 'Have to have a bit of relief from the wife after thirty years, Mr Carter. Besides, no point in trying to get back through all this traffic to fetch you.'

'You'd better stay, Charlie. We need all the support we can get,' Steven added, finally switching off the screen.

'One of these days I should bring some of my mates down. A right raucous lot, they are,' said Lewis.

'Not a bad idea,' Carter said. 'Raise the roof and shout down the opposition.'

The car edged along the narrow street, stopped at the junction with Bath Road and turned right. As Carter chatted to his son about the tactics of the game, Lewis effortlessly took the car into traffic, swung left in Turnham Green Terrace and then soon after left again into Chiswick High Road. The traffic was murder on any day of the week and even though most of the 'white van man' tradesmen were elsewhere on a Saturday it was easier to get off the High Road and avoid ending up in the logjam before the Hammersmith roundabout. Carter and his son's voices murmured quietly behind him. Chit-chat about home, the winter holiday and Melissa's next birthday. He drew the car to a standstill soon after the High Road merged into King Street and waited in the middle of the road, indicator quietly flicking to turn right as he waited for the approaching cars to present a gap so he could turn into Weltje Road, a short rat run on to the A4 and the quarter-mile drive down before turning off left before the Hammersmith flyover.

Weltje Road is a one-way street with terraced houses on either side. Like many roads in the overcrowded city, parked cars on both sides make it even narrower. There's usually little pedestrian traffic as it leads only to the residents' houses and there is no destination beyond the head of the road other than the fast-moving traffic on the A4 arterial dual carriageway travelling down towards the Hammersmith slip road or the Hammersmith flyover. A centre barrier separates the four-lane traffic. Lewis steered the Jag into the queue of cars that slowed to a halt. Ahead the road twisted in a slight S bend and at the furthest corner on the right-hand side before the road merged on to the A4 stood a box-sided Transit van with the name of a contract company emblazoned on its side beneath the red and yellow chevrons declaring it was for Highway Maintenance. Looking past the stationary cars, Lewis saw two road-construction men in hi-vis jackets working outside a yellow plastic barrier. One of the men was wearing ear defenders and leaning on a jackhammer; a third labourer manned a Stop/Go lollipop board. The first two men were digging out and filling in a pothole with tarmac. Lewis sighed. Was there ever a time that the council wasn't filling potholes? Even on a Saturday. 'Shouldn't be too long, Mr Carter,' Lewis assured him.

Carter's thoughts were elsewhere. The trees in the street were already starting to turn. Autumn beckoned. They would go skiing again this year. Steven sat behind Lewis, giving Carter an unobstructed view of the road ahead. He looked to where one of the men abandoned his tarmac duties and put a hand to his ear. Most likely listening to music on a mobile phone, Carter thought as the second man walked to the van where a fourth sat on the passenger side, facing away from the waiting cars. The earphone worker looked towards them. Carter glanced behind to see if there was a problem. Perhaps the cars had backed up too far on to the High Street? There was only one small car behind them. Carter looked back and saw the lollipop turn from Stop to Go. A couple of cars got through; the queue edged forward. Lewis pulled up behind it. The Stop/Go board turned again. In the gap between the four cars in front of them, Carter caught sight of the man's boots. His overalls were tucked military style just above the ankle. Black laced-up boots. Thick rubber soles. Military all the way. By now the second man had pulled something from the floor of the van and turned. The face in the Transit's passenger seat turned to look in Carter's direction.

'Charlie! Back, back, back. Get us out of here!' Carter shouted.

Lewis hesitated; then he saw the danger. One of the approaching men lifted a semi-automatic rifle; the other raised a handgun. Lewis pushed the gear lever into reverse and pressed his foot down hard. The Jag slammed into the car behind. Steven fell forward, saved by his seat belt. He looked wide-eyed at his father whose face was pressed close to his. His mouth yelling something at him as he reached across, unbuckling the seat belt. Telling him what to do. Where to go. His urgency frightened the boy. The crash. The fear. More instructions. Did he understand? his father insisted. The boy nodded, his father's words penetrating the terror. The Jag's power heaved the smaller car metres back, but then it jackknifed, blocking any chance of escape. Carter pushed open the passenger door, forcing his son to run as Lewis, seeing that he could not drive back any further, changed gear and accelerated at the men running at them, weapons aimed and ready to fire. Half a dozen holes punctured the windscreen, followed by the jarring sound of gunfire. Three bullets struck Lewis in the chest, two passed between him and Carter as he threw himself flat, desperately trying to kick open his door, but the parked cars blocked it. The sixth bullet struck Charlie Lewis in the head. Blood and brain splattered across the rear seat. The open door was suddenly filled with the man wielding the assault rifle. He flipped it, struck Carter on the head with its butt, reached in and dragged the unconscious man out into the street. The man was strong enough to haul him to the van. The back doors were already open and they threw him in face down, pulled a sack over his head, bound his ankles and wrists with plastic ties. The van lurched off the kerb and accelerated into the fast-moving traffic.

The assault, murder and kidnap had taken twenty-seven seconds.

4

Eddie Roman's life of crime had ended twelve years before, when he was nabbed for driving a gang during an armed robbery. It was an old-fashioned smash-and-grab style heist. Simple and stupid. He'd been doing old mates a favour: old cons who thought they could run as fast as they used to but were ignorant of twenty-first-century technology that had them tracked, identified and nicked in record time.

Eddie served his prison sentence and when he was released promised his wife of twenty-eight years that he was on the straight and narrow. It did not last long. Promises were a fluid commitment as far as Eddie was concerned and there was no money in being a regular van driver. Not with zero-hour contracts. He kept the small delivery jobs to himself; the less his wife Shelley knew the better. To her, he was doing the Amazon delivery run most days. It stopped her worrying and if there was one thing Eddie regretted it was causing so much grief to a woman he had loved since the day he had met her. She was in the same house in Brentford that they had bought soon after they were married and finally, at forty-eight, he was content.

Eddie had had ambition once: youthful aspirations to be a racing car driver. He was fast and proficient but when he realized how much money he'd need to buy into the race game he was persuaded by the local crime families to drive for them instead. His reputation grew and so too did his profile with the Metropolitan Police. Since last being a guest of Her Majesty's Prison Service he had sold his skills to the foreigners who ran the sex and drug business in the West End. He delivered their product and dirty cash from A to B with no diversion in between. He was trusted. He never skimmed. Even if he had wanted to he wouldn't dare. Serbians had controlled much of the trade, until the Albanians, who were even nastier, pushed them aside. Violent bastards, the lot of them. In the old days Eddie had seen men being beaten and coshed, and then the sawn-off shotgun boys had appeared: all that was part of the world he used to live in; but now, these foreigners used violence without a moment's hesitation. Real ugly stuff. In truth, it offended his sensibilities but he had learnt not to make any comment. Head down, do the driving and take the cash. Two weeks ago a Russian club owner had approached him and introduced him to a hard-looking man with a scar that looked permanently raw across his eyebrow and cheek. The scar-faced man's English was perfect but Eddie couldn't place the accent – maybe French, with a touch of Russian? Whatever – he didn't care. The good thing about Europe having no borders was that it brought high-paying employers into the business. He was to drive the man and his crew around west London. That was easy work for Eddie. His house in Brentford was just off the A4 and he knew Chiswick and Hammersmith blindfold. This crew were a humourless lot. Not a smile among them. Real sullen foreign types. Round and round they went, through all the avenues of the area looking for an ambush site. It was Eddie who showed them the choke hole on Weltje Road and what an easy escape it would be. That did the trick: they liked him for that. And when he showed them where the sub contractor's yard was, stealing the van and equipment was child's play. The money being offered was enough to buy the holiday of a lifetime for him and Shelley.

And then the shooting started.

'Drive!' said the crew's leader. The command was sharp but lacked any sense of panic. Eddie knew where he had to go: the route had been planned in advance. But the killing? He hadn't bargained for that. That wasn't part of the deal. A dead man slaughtered behind the wheel and a bound and gagged hostage in the back of the van. A kid running down the street and Eddie didn't even know whether they had gunned the lad down. The game had escalated big time. The scare factor was up 100 per cent. The part of the human brain that had controlled man's instinct to survive since Stone Age hunters fought mammoths kicked in. He did what he was paid to do and accelerated fast, expertly getting into the traffic. In less than two minutes he bypassed the slip road to Hammersmith and carried on for the flyover. He shifted the gears, causing no fuss to other drivers by cutting in. He was just another van driver in a hurry. The traffic cameras would pick them up soon enough: in five hundred yards, when Eddie would earn his money. He changed up a gear. No one spoke. No sound came from the injured man. The van stormed across the flyover. His instructions had been to head in the opposite direction to the ambush but he couldn't do that from the ambush site because of the median barrier. The skill to get the van travelling in the opposite direction was what Eddie was being paid for.

The A4 continued over and down the raised roadway and became Talgarth Road. The next junction, in the dip of the road, allowed no right turn to the Barons Court Underground Station, so to go back the way Eddie had come on the opposite side of the dual carriageway would have meant turning left at the traffic lights into Gliddon Road, stopping, turning round and then taking the van back across the junction to legally turn right on to the A4 and drive in the desired direction. That would take time.

As he came over the brow of the flyover he saw the traffic lights flick to amber. Cars sped across the junction not wishing to be caught on a long red light. The amber turned red with no waiting cars on the start line. Eddie's concentration was intense. He slipped into a mental zone where nothing else existed. The men, the ambush, the guns and the fear: none of that mattered any more. He was as steady as a plumb line. The man next to him cast a quick glance to check that the driver was not frozen in apprehension. He wasn't. Eddie had many variables to consider. He needed a few vital seconds to swing the cumbersome van in a tight U-turn and not collide with anyone or anything. He had weighted the back of the van with strapped-down bags of cement to give the rear wheels traction. The men in the rear of the van knew what to expect because he had briefed them. They had strapped themselves to the van's metal struts.

He slowed to forty miles an hour, kicked in the clutch and brought the van down to third gear. Checking his mirrors both sides, he saw there was enough distance from the following cars. Praying the lights would not change now and bring the traffic head-on, with a final smooth drop of the gear lever into second, he pressed his foot flat on the accelerator, pushing the rev counter past the 3,500 mark. With the engine protesting, he gripped the steering wheel with his right hand at the nine o'clock position, swung hard all the way around to six o'clock while at the same time his left hand heaved up the handbrake. The rear wheels locked and the van tail-ended towards the traffic lights. For a few heart-stopping seconds, it seemed as if the van would roll. As rubber gripped and squealed, Eddie let in the clutch and gave the engine its power. Smoke poured from the tyres but then the van was heading west. Now he put his foot down because traffic cameras would have caught that stunt and there would be calls being placed to traffic police and the one thing a Ford Transit van could not do, even this one with its modified engine, was outrun a BMW police pursuit car.

The man next to him had the good grace to exhale and swear at the same time. The killers in the back laughed and said something in a language Eddie didn't understand. But it felt good nonetheless. For that brief moment, he deluded himself that this tight-knit crew of hardened men had accepted him.

On the other side of the road, the journey's waypoint loomed into view. The star-encrusted blue dome of the Russian Orthodox Church in Chiswick meant he was getting close to his turn. Eddie knew it well. The Cathedral of the Dormition of the Mother of God and the Royal Martyrs was a constant sight on his daily travels to and from the city, and it told him he needed to get across into the left-hand lane. The start of the M4 motorway lay ahead and his instructions were to get down the slip road before it and avoid the next set of cameras. He flipped the indicator, the van slowed into the tight left-hand bend. It picked up speed once on to the wider A205 road heading towards Kew Bridge and as he approached a railway bridge he swung the van into a narrow lane on the right-hand side. An industrial yard of blue-stacked self-storage containers was set back, its mesh wire fencing obscured by overgrown bushes. The lane was a perfect place to swap vehicles. On the opposite side, an overgrown embankment tumbled down to Kew Bridge Station, which meant no one would see anything untoward because they were below the road. The nondescript white Renault van was parked facing down the lane where it had been left at six o'clock that morning. Eddie swung into the yard's gates and quickly reversed. Two of the men jumped out, opened the rear doors of the Renault and then the three ambushers clambered inside, roughly manhandling their captive, by which time Eddie was in the Renault cab. The Russian gang leader, for that is what Eddie had determined his nationality to be, twisted a timer device on a large plastic container full of petrol, threw it into the Transit and slammed closed its doors. Fifteen seconds later, as the Renault drove out of sight down the lane, they heard the rush of air and explosion as the Transit burst into flames. A shortcut led them back on to the A4 dual carriageway. Eddie's heart skipped a beat. They were passing Brentford and he thought of Shelley who would be putting the kettle on about now and sneaking out the chocolate digestives from the fridge door. He smiled to himself. Almost home, love. Almost done with this crew. And then they'd be off. There was no rush now. The van glided into the roundabout traffic and turned towards Heathrow Airport. After two and a half miles the second waypoint appeared in the form of the Syon Clinic on his left. Eddie swung into the opposite feeder lane, waited for the lights and then turned the van back in the direction they had come. Two hundred metres further along he turned down a narrow industrial track, so narrow it was barely possible in places to squeeze the van past the big parked trucks that hogged the roadside. It was appropriately named Transport Avenue. Straight ahead was a cement factory and nearby a scrap-metal recycling yard. It was noisy and he suspected that would help mask any sounds the captured man would make. Of one thing he felt certain. That poor bastard had something these men needed and they were going to hurt him to get it. He stopped the van next to some locked gates that, once opened, exposed a boarded-up semi-derelict brick building that was part of a disused industrial area. The large contractor's board declared: 'MALCOLM & SONS DEMOLITION. DANGER – KEEP OUT. CONDEMNED BUILDING UNSAFE'. Alongside the warning was more modest signage stating it had been 'Sold (subject to contract)'. Once the van rolled into the abandoned yard and the gates were closed no one outside would see or hear anything.

Eddie Roman let the men haul their victim away. He lit a cigarette and noticed that there was a slight tremor in his hand. Home was less than fifteen minutes away. He asked the God he had never believed in to protect him long enough to return there.

5

Within an hour of Lewis's murder and Jeremy Carter's abduction, the well-rehearsed standard operating procedure for a Major Incident swung into place. Following the pattern established in London and many other world cities that had experienced terrorist attacks, the events in London W6 would, privately at least, until the investigation proved otherwise, be treated as terror-related. Three cordons had been established. The first secured the immediate area surrounding Carter's car in Weltje Road and the crime scene. They established a second cordon extending from the start of the road. The third and outer cordon nudged into the A4 approach lane and at the other end of the ambush site at King Street, where traffic was stopped and forced through a diversionary chicane. The entrance to Weltje Road became the cordon access point. All parked cars on the road were quarantined, no public pedestrian access was permitted and the residents were confined to their houses. Borough police commanders were briefed as scene-of-crime officers erected a white tent covering Carter's car and the dead man who still lay sprawled in the driver's seat. Empty cartridge cases were identified and marked as evidence. With an efficiency born from years of experience the Forensic Investigation Specialist Crime officers, experts in major incidents such as terrorist attacks, murder and armed robbery, plied their trade while uniform and plainclothes officers conducted door-to-door interviews. The media was herded away behind barriers at the entry point to the ambush road.

An official-looking car passed a police outrider blocking access to Weltje Road from traffic approaching along King Street. The man who sat in the back showed his credentials and was waved closer to the edge of the cordon. The car had barely stopped when an agitated police officer gestured it to move on. The moment the stuttering blue light was flashed behind the car's radiator grill the officer stepped back and, like the policeman before him, checked the passenger's proffered identification. The man in his fifties who alighted from the car had the look of a career politician. His wiry grey hair was groomed, the standard-issue politician's charcoal suit hung well on a slim athletic frame, the similarly coloured overcoat was casually unbuttoned. He strode confidently and with an easy graceful gait towards the borough police commander and investigating officers. At first they did not recognize him but when he extended his leather-encased identity card the uniformed borough commander's brow furrowed. Such an incident would normally be of immediate interest to MI5, the Security Service, not a suit from MI6, the Secret Intelligence Service.

'Mr Maguire, Commander Pickering is at Bedford Park with a firearms team.'

Maguire nodded; Pickering was the counter-terrorism commander and the two men had already spoken by telephone. Maguire's eyes scanned the scene of police tape cordons, the flood of uniformed officers and the white-suited forensic officers. Photographs were being taken and blue-boiler suited Met policemen were conducting a fingertip search of the ambush site.

'What information do we have?' said Maguire.

'A van was parked just beyond the curve in the road,' said the senior officer, pointing to the choke point. 'The shooters were dressed as highway maintenance workers. The vehicle and tools were stolen from the company's north London yard two days ago. There are no CCTV cameras on this road but we are checking traffic cameras on the approach along the Chiswick High Road and their escape route down the A4.'

'Is there a CAP?' he asked.

The borough commander extended her arm towards the inner cordon and the common approach path. 'This way.' Like every crime scene, this one had restricted access allowing only essential personnel to cross the inner cordon. A young female police crime-scene manager nodded as her senior officer approached with Maguire.

'Ma'am.'

Maguire signed her ledger as she booked the time he entered. When he left she would book him out. Time and personnel control was essential to the effective running of a crime scene. Maguire stepped towards the white-tented area. A forensic officer greeted him.

'Can you show me?' said Maguire.

The officer turned his tablet around and swiped long shots and close-up images of the bullet-punctured windscreen, the dead man and the items discovered in the car. A blood-smeared rugby ball and a mobile phone lay in the rear seat well. 'Given what we could see on the mobile phone it appears to belong to the boy and with the rugby ball it indicates that the child was in the car at the time of the shooting.'

'Nothing else?' said Maguire. 'Any sign of the boy being shot? Any blood down the street?'

'No. And initial tests indicate we have only the driver's blood and a smear on the floor of the car behind his seat which might belong to the abducted man.'

Maguire knew that whoever had staged the attack would not have given a second thought to killing a child. Carter's son had either escaped or been taken.

'Ballistics?'

'We'll know soon enough but 5.56-mm empty cases are everywhere.'

That suggested an assault rifle, and if the rounds were the enhanced variety with a hardened steel core then they had been expecting the car to be bulletproof. They weren't taking any chances. 'Enhanced rounds?' said Maguire.

'The lab will tell us soon enough,' the man replied.

Maguire nodded his thanks and turned to the borough commander. 'No sign of the boy?'

'Nothing. He must have been terrified. We'll have his photograph on all the news along with that of his father.'

'Stepfather,' Maguire corrected her. He cast an experienced eye over the ambush site. The choke point was as near perfect as you could expect. Blocked cars, narrow street, bend in the road. No way out for the victims. Assault rifles probably meant specialist weapons. Determining what rifles and exact ammunition were used might help to find what country the killers hailed from. Taking his leave of the borough commander he felt one thing was certain. The operation had been carried out with professional expertise. They knew their target and they had taken Carter for a specific reason. It was no random grudge killing of a banker. Jeremy Carter had information his abductors wanted. And that was what worried Maguire.

❁

Maguire's driver retraced the route Carter, his son and Lewis had probably taken from Bedford Park. At the house a strong police presence was obvious. The junction of Woodstock Road and Rupert Road was blocked and a cordon extended three hundred metres in all directions. The threat level had been increased on the orders of the senior officer in charge of the Counter-Terrorism Branch and a half-dozen CTSFO armed officers stood strategically placed. Two of them barred entry to the crossroads as a more lightly armed Met officer checked the identity of the car that drew to a halt. A third officer checked Maguire's credentials. A tall, suited civilian carrying a police phone was standing nearby with three senior uniformed officers as he briefed them on the situation. Commander Tom Pickering saw the car draw to a halt and excused himself from his briefing. He waved the car forward and waited in the driveway to Carter's house. Maguire climbed out of the back of the car and extended his hand in greeting. He needed no special clearance.

'Hello, Tom,' said Maguire affably, glancing at one of the heavily armed CTSFO officers who stood with another at the rear entrance to the house. A quick look upward told him a sniper team was in place on the roof and were he a betting man he'd have put a hefty wager on there being more than one. If this was a concerted terrorist attack and a suicide bomber attempted to break through the cordons at the end of the streets they would be dead before they made it halfway. There was unlikely to be anything the counter-terrorism commander had failed to cover.

'Mr Maguire,' said Pickering in greeting. 'The commissioner said you were on your way. Everything here is locked down. Five is on the case.'

The Security Service, known as MI5, is the nation's key counter-intelligence service. Collecting and analysing covert intelligence lies at its heart. Maguire needed them onside because of his own connection with the abducted Carter. He had already spoken to his opposite number at MI5, who'd offered complete co-operation. In the current climate of terrorist threats, inter-agency collaboration was vital, but Maguire was a different breed of intelligence officer. He was the keeper of a treasure trove of secrets and not always as forthcoming as his counterparts would like. However, he had sufficient authority to give them the official version of the two-finger salute. And he didn't kid himself. Turf wars still existed. But what outsiders did not realize was that the Service was not as bureaucratic as they imagined. In reality it was a collegiate meritocracy. People depended on each other and secrets were hermetically sealed. Maguire was an ex-army officer and his exploits when he served in special forces many years before made him feel at home in MI6, where those responsible for operational territories are still referred to as 'robber barons' – an old-fashioned sobriquet that suited Maguire rather well.

He recalled one astute observer of the Service referring to the members of its arcane and layered organization as sorcerers who knew the secrets of its Kabbalistic demonology.

Pickering accompanied him to the entrance. 'Your people are inside with Mrs Reeve-Carter. There's a police family liaison officer with her and her family doctor, and there's a friend from across the road. I insisted, in the gentlest terms, that the civilians leave the area but she is adamant that the friend stays. As far as we can see, sir, there is no immediate threat but given your association with the family I would appreciate it if you could convince her about the friend.'

Maguire nodded. 'Are you giving media interviews yet?'

'They've already blocked the end of the road. We'll get a Noddy to deal with them later.'

Maguire smiled at the patronizing reference to the uniformed police. 'All right, Tom, let me get started in there.'

He took his leave and went into the house, past the policeman at the door who booked him into the house, checking his name off against a list of personnel. The place was locked down. Like a crime scene. Which it might be, Maguire thought to himself. The nagging doubt was that Carter might be the guilty party.

6

Amanda Reeve-Carter was one of those women who had a knack for creating a beautiful home without it looking like an interior designer's death-wish fulfilment. It was her taste, her imprint and Jeremy Carter had been happy to pay for it. Yet she did not spend money for the sake of splashing out. The artwork hanging on the walls was more likely to be from art college students rather than from overpriced and, to her mind, self-indulgent, pretentious 'names'. Maguire had always liked Amanda's practicality. She had been an army wife before she married Carter and kept her late husband's name as part of the new.

Tony Reeve had been a major in the British Army, awarded the George Cross, the highest award for gallantry below that of the Victoria Cross. Seven years ago, Major Reeve, a bomb-disposal expert, died in Afghanistan defusing several improvised explosive devices that threatened the lives of a half-dozen wounded men already caught in an ambush. The men were evacuated as Reeve stood out in the open alone, coolly working through the intricate set of wired devices. The booby trap that killed him was triggered by a child probably no older than his own son. Jeremy Carter had insisted that the hero's name live on for the boy and there were plenty of pictures of Steven's father in the house. Maguire paused by the bank of family photographs and wondered whether a double tragedy might be too much for even the strong-willed Amanda to bear. One husband dead, one husband abducted and the possibility that her son had been taken. If there was a God, Maguire thought to himself, He knew how to wreak havoc in someone's life. He glanced up as raised voices reached him from the rear of the house.

He walked through to a bright modern room: a glass-panelled coach-house-roofed extension that housed the kitchen, dining and family day room; beyond glass doors spanning the breadth of the room lay the walled garden. Amanda Reeve-Carter was sitting on a sofa with a much younger woman. Maguire knew she had no other relatives so this had to be the friend from over the road. An older man, who presumably was the doctor, stood in front of them. Amanda held a glass containing what looked to be a generous helping of whisky. She was insisting that she did not need a sedative of any description and that she was not prepared to abandon alcohol. The ever-patient doctor was equally insistent that by nightfall she would need medication and implored the woman next to Amanda to ensure that she ate a meal as soon as she could be convinced to do so and then took the prescribed sedatives. He placed a small bottle on the table.

Maguire glanced along a corridor to his right where members of his team were systematically searching Carter's study. One of them saw him and stepped outside bearing a handful of files.

'Well?' asked Maguire quietly.

'Nothing yet, boss.'

'It's here somewhere. Find the bloody stuff before we all go down the pan,' Maguire told him. He carried on into the family room as Amanda Carter looked his way. He could see that she was stoically holding down her fear. She had clearly realized that offices of the state were now involved and whatever was going on in her home was procedure. Seated near to her was a woman in her forties. Her lined face suggested to Maguire that she was the police family liaison officer, a woman who had spent too many hours sitting with grieving relatives. She would have been trained to use specific words to try and ease trauma and grief. By the look of her, Maguire guessed she was a mother and wife who probably threw half the counselling advice down the pan. Woman to woman, she would have found the words needed.

The fifth person in the room was one of Maguire's

junior officers, Abnash Khalsa. She wore jeans, trainers and a casual leather jacket over a finely knit mohair sweater. Her hair was cut to the nape of her neck, short enough to be cared for easily and long enough to attractively shape her face, a face that unlike the family officer's was still unblemished by life's vicissitudes. As he stepped closer she gave him a brief smile of greeting and an almost imperceptible shake of her head. Amanda Reeve-Carter had revealed nothing of interest in her general conversation.

'She needs more than booze, Abbie,' said Maguire.

'I'll put the kettle on,' the young woman answered.

'You're not here to serve tea,' he said quietly. 'I need you working in the study.'

She nodded. 'I know, sir, but they'll fetch me if there's anything I need to see in there. I thought a bit of support out here was appropriate.'

'Fair enough,' said Maguire as he walked past her. 'Amanda,' he said in greeting, 'we are doing everything we can.'

She frowned. 'Are you?' she said bluntly. She'd had a drink too many.

'I know this is a difficult time but we should get some food inside you.' He nodded in acknowledgement towards the doctor.

'You don't control me. This is my house. You're supposed to be out there finding my husband and my son.'

'Of course,' said Maguire, impervious to her antagonism, which was more than understandable given the circumstances and the fact that she and Maguire had never had an easy relationship, especially not with what he had asked her husband to do in the past. 'That's exactly what we are trying to do.'

'Try harder.' The edge to her voice bore sufficient pain to make the doctor look concerned.

'Mrs Reeve-Carter, please let me help you, you are bound to feel increasingly upset.'

She swallowed the last mouthful of whisky. 'I'm not in the habit of becoming hysterical. I've gone through the bloody hoops before.'

The doctor looked perplexed.

'Thank you for your concern and help but I think it's time everyone left,' said Maguire. The moment's hesitation shown by the doctor and liaison officer was quickly dispelled when he added firmly: 'Now.'

Amanda's friend half stood from the shared sofa. 'Not you, Helen,' said Amanda, placing a hand on her friend's arm.

Maguire nodded. He needed to appease the grieving woman – momentarily at least. 'You can stay. Where is...?'

'Melissa?' said friend Helen. 'She's at my house with our au pair and my two children. The man outside has some of his men in our garden. I do hope this won't be for much longer, for everyone's sake.'

Maguire smiled. His voice softened. 'I'm sorry, I don't know your name.'

Amanda's friend reacted to what was a barely disguised charm offensive. 'Oh. Helen Metcalf. I live across the road at Woodlands.'

'Mrs Metcalf, does Melissa spend much time with your own children?'

Helen Metcalf nodded. 'Oh yes.'

'Then rather than me send one of my officers across to... Woodlands, was it?'

Once again the chatty friend nodded, her head bobbing like a small bird dipping into a water bowl.

'Rather than have one of my officers see that she is not in any distress with everything that is going on here and in the street...' He sensed that she felt calling her upmarket suburban road a street was a slight. '... perhaps you would see that all is well.'

She flourished her mobile phone. 'Oh, I can just...'

'No, Mrs Metcalf. Go and see for yourself, would you?' Maguire's tone of voice left no doubt that it was not a request. Maguire didn't give a damn that the woman looked crestfallen at being dismissed. Amanda Reeve-Carter understood perfectly well that Maguire needed to speak to her in private.

'Go,' she said. 'See she's all right.'

Helen Metcalf hugged her friend and then Abbie escorted her from the room.

Maguire pulled a dining-room chair around and sat

facing the grieving woman. 'He's alive, Amanda. I know that much.'

'And what is it they want then? He is not in the Service any longer. Hasn't been for years, so what dirty little secret is he hiding from his past? Or is it from your past? Is that why your people are taking apart his study?' She crossed an arm over her chest and then one leg over the other, folding in on herself, keeping Maguire at bay, protecting the inner place that resisted the unbearable pain. For the first time, he saw her fight back the tears that welled up. 'And Steven. My boy. Whatever you have done my son is paying the price as well. Damn you and your dirty games, Maguire. I thought we were shot of you and the Service.'

Maguire remained unperturbed. His voice softened again. He needed to soothe her. 'I believe they are both alive and both of them are resilient.'

'He's thirteen, for God's sake.'

Her retort made Maguire realize there was little point in sympathetic platitudes. 'Did Jeremy ever speak of having a safe deposit box anywhere? Would there be anywhere else that he might keep information?'

She frowned as the question took its time to lodge in her scattered thoughts.

'He was with the Service for nigh on twenty-five years. If there were any secrets they were locked away here,' she insisted, touching her temple. 'He's a banker, Maguire. There's nothing hidden here; there are no safe deposit boxes. If there are problems with the bank look there.'

Maguire's team had already swooped on the bank and raided his offices with the help of the Metropolitan Police. Whatever Jeremy Carter had that others wanted so badly, there was no evidence – so far – of it on his work or personal computer or in any paper files. And Maguire knew in his heart that there wouldn't be. Not from an old pro like Carter. She was right. It was in his head. And that's the safe the killers wanted to crack. There was nothing more to be gained by questioning her. She was superfluous to his investigation and he saw no point in feigning sympathy. He stood abruptly and walked out as Abbie carried a tray towards Amanda.

'Finish up here and get back. I've a job for you,' said Maguire and then made his way back outside.

Amanda stood and watched him approach Commander Pickering in the garden as Abbie placed the tray on the coffee table.

'It's better if you have something,' Abbie said.

Amanda ignored her and kept her gaze on the two men. 'They're talking about Jeremy. Wondering how vulnerable he's made you people.' She looked at the girl who waited patiently. 'Are you married?'

'No.' There had been offers, of course, but the wistful smile on Abbie's face gave rather too much away. She had made the sacrifice because she was at the start of her career and wanted more than a marriage.

Amanda Reeve-Carter saw it, knew the look, understood immediately. She sat down and allowed the attractive young woman to pour her tea. 'Difficult in this line of work, isn't it?'

'We all make choices,' Abbie said.

'Don't leave it too late,' Amanda said, accepting the mug of tea.

'For?'

'Children.' Amanda watched to see whether that touched a nerve. Abbie showed no sign that it had.

'I want to get ahead,' she answered, seeing Maguire's car pull away.

'Ah. Yes. God, how I hate dedicated soldiers and ambitious spies.' She sipped her tea and looked into space across the rim. 'I've been married to both. My first husband was a bomb-disposal officer, but you probably know all that. And now Jeremy. He and Steven... they're really like father and son. Formative years, I suppose. Male bonding. Insidious, isn't it? Or haven't you noticed yet?'

She had, but she wasn't going to be drawn into the woman's bitterness. Abbie stepped back. 'I'm sorry.'

Amanda tipped what was left of the whisky into her tea. 'So am I.'

7

It had taken two hours flying from London to the pink stone city of Toulouse in southern France and then another hour on the A61 in a hire car to reach the outskirts of Castelnaudary. The journey gave Abbie time to absorb the information that Maguire had given her when she returned to his office after leaving Amanda Reeve-Carter. The MI6 man's desk was bare except for a telephone, his two fountain pens sitting parallel to a desk blotter and a beige file with a double slash of red across one corner that showed its contents were, as the letters indicated, *Top Secret*.

Abbie was security vetted to see its contents, but Maguire had not yet made the final decision about Abbie's suitability for the task. She was not an operational field officer; she was a linguist, and it was that skill that her boss wanted, whether to read documents or hear conversations in the various languages she was expert in. He had a duty of care towards his staff. Risk was their business but his proposition could make the young woman vulnerable. She waited demurely until he asked whether she was prepared to consider undertaking the task he had in mind. She could not calm the pulse that beat rapidly in her neck but she answered in the affirmative.

His forefinger slid the file towards her with the instruction to not open it yet. There was a man he wanted her to contact whose whereabouts were known only to an intermediary who was a retired legionnaire in Castelnaudary, south of Toulouse, where the Legion's basic training was conducted for new recruits. Many of the old guard retire in the area around the base. The people he was sending her to were men who had been at the sharp end of danger. Was she still prepared to go? Again she nodded her assent. Maguire let her open the file. There was barely any information listed on the sheet of paper stapled to its parent folder. The man's description was missing. There was no photograph. She looked over the file to Maguire.

'Who is he?'

'He doesn't exist as far as we are concerned. Part of the agreement we had with him was that there should be nothing recorded officially. He's done work for us in the past.'

'And we kept to that agreement?' she said, knowing full well that such a concession meant the man was off the books, unaccountable, which gave Maguire a free hand.

'We did. And we will continue to do so.'

A brief one-page single-spaced summary listed the basic information about the man she was to find. As she read Maguire gave her further details of the man's background.

His father had been a military attaché, so he had been exposed to different languages all his young life. British military surgeons are the best in the world when faced with serious battlefield wounds but they aren't so hot on spotting ovarian cancer; the boy's mother died when he was eleven. He was sent to a boarding school where he flourished. The teachers at the school channelled his grief into physical sports and he became an accomplished boxer and excellent rugby player. And he was academically bright, earmarked as a future rugby blue. It seemed likely that he would follow in his father's footsteps and go to the University of Oxford. When he was a teenager, however, his father was killed in a car crash. The second tragedy hit the boy hard and his studies went to the wall as many times as a boxing opponent went to the mat. Basically, he went off the rails. Looked for trouble wherever he could find it. It seemed the more he got physically hurt the more he was determined to fight back even harder. He was getting a reputation with the police as a troublemaker and, for a while, it looked as though the only place he would be heading was prison. He was saved by his housemaster at school, and his wife, who took him in and treated him like one of their own children. It was risky: their teenage daughter was also still at home, but by all accounts they were soon like brother and sister.

One night the young man was returning home after boxing training when he tried to stop a street gang attacking a black teenager. He beat off two of the five and the teenager escaped but as he grappled with a third the thug produced a knife; the attacker was stabbed and died. The gang members told the police the kid from the nearby boarding school had stabbed their friend to death. His teachers spoke up on his behalf, convincing the police that his father's recent death was still affecting him deeply and he should not be held in custody. When released on bail he must have thought the evidence against him was too great, that they would arrest him eventually and, with his record, not believe him. He ran, taking a cheap flight to Marseilles. At first he worked as a farm labourer. Six months later he walked into the Foreign Legion recruitment office at Aubagne. Meanwhile, CCTV footage and the black teenager's testimony had proved his innocence but by then no one knew where he was.

Despite public misconceptions, the Legion doesn't take wanted criminals, but as there was no warrant issued for his arrest, he was sent to Castelnaudary for basic training after initial assessment. The best recruits got their pick of regiments within the Foreign Legion. Months later he volunteered for the 2nd Foreign Parachute Regiment. Five years later he was a corporal – the highest rank possible unless he took French citizenship.

His potential was recognized when he passed selection for the Groupement des commandos parachutistes. These commandos were tasked with covert operations against terrorists and enemies of the state. After fifteen years he left the Legion following an incident in Mali and was recruited by the French Counter-Intelligence Service, Direction générale de la sécurité extérieure. His language skills and contacts from God knew how many nationalities from his time in the Legion made him a valuable asset as a freelancer. He and others like him are expert hunters of men.

Two years later he came home when a joint operation in Africa brought him into contact with an MI6 agent he had previously worked with. Maguire used him because the agent had been Jeremy Carter. It was a suitable arrangement that kept British hands clean. Then a job went wrong when a client's family were killed after ignoring the asset's instructions; following that, he disappeared. Cooperation between French and British intelligence services gave Maguire information that tracked him down through an intermediary legionnaire in Castelnaudary, near the Legion's induction training depot. Only he knew where the man was. By the time Maguire finished his account and she closed the dossier,

Abbie knew she was being sent to a remote place that harboured tribal men whose loyalty to each other could not be challenged by outsiders. To fetch a trained killer.

Abbie swung the car off the main route south, trying to conjure up an image of the man in the skimpy intelligence dossier. There had been no official name, and no address shown, not even a country where he might be residing. Maguire insisted he was in France and when she found him all she had to do was tell him what had happened in London. He would know what to do. Uncertainty and trepidation had mingled within her when she sat opposite Maguire and they persisted now as she switched on the car's windscreen wipers against a rain flurry. How would she recognize him? she had asked.

Maguire had taken the folder back and explained it was likely he had changed his appearance since Maguire had last used him. If she ever got close and he agreed to see her she might be surprised to find that he was no stereotypical shaven-head thug with scarred knuckles. He was intelligent and well read. But, he insisted, she must not let his quiet demeanour fool her. She was to ask only for the Englishman.

8

The smooth-surfaced road purred beneath the car's wheels as Abbie drove through Castelnaudary heading south-east on the D33, Route de Pexiora. After a couple of miles, she drove on to a slip road signposted 'Quartier Capitaine Danjou'. It would soon be dark and it had been a full-on day since the events in London earlier that morning but she wanted to see the training camp where men with dreams or a desire to escape from their past went to find a new life. She stopped outside the camp gates and the sign denoting that she had arrived at 'Légion Étrangère Quartier Capitaine Danjou'. A hundred metres beyond the open camp gates a concrete sentry box sat between the entrance and exit barriers. There was nothing about the low-rise buildings that suggested the torturous regime that lay waiting for new recruits. Beyond the gates and low buildings, she saw the fringe of the parade ground where squads of men dressed in pressed khaki with red epaulettes and white kepis were led, six abreast, by a military band marching at an almost hypnotically slow pace. A sentry appeared and began walking towards her stationary car. She smiled and waved at the grim-faced legionnaire and turned the car back towards the town. Before she found the guesthouse and a place to eat she needed to find her contact.

She parked beneath the trees in a nearby parking area and walked down the narrow Rue Gambetta where she found the small *tabac* next to an estate agent's window smothered with photographs detailing properties for sale. The windows above the shopfront were closed with weather-beaten wooden shutters. As she entered the small shop she smelt the pungent scent of tobacco mingling with the tantalizing aroma of confectionary. It brought back childhood memories of a corner shop, long gone since her neighbourhood had been gentrified. A woman behind the counter raised an eyebrow and asked how she might help. Abbie asked to speak to the owner. The less said the better. Abbie presumed the woman was the shop assistant and not the owner's wife as she had no wedding rings on her finger. She muttered for Abbie to wait, went behind a bead curtain and called. A tall muscular man with cropped hair and a beaky nose came through the curtain. He wore a black round-neck sweater over his jeans. Was he the owner? Abbie didn't think he looked like someone who ran a *tabac*; he was too cool – as if he didn't give a damn about anything. He seemed to sense that Abbie was not there to buy a packet of Gauloises and dismissed the woman. The bead curtain swished behind her as she left and Abbie saw a tattoo peek out from the man's sweater: two glaring eyes and the open beak of a bird of prey.

'*Oui?*'

Abbie dragged her eyes away from the raptor's glare back to the man. His eyes were as hard as the raptor's. 'I wish to speak to the Englishman.'

The man's gaze snapped past her to the street. It took only a second to see she was alone. He asked where she was staying; she told him the name of her modest lodgings and he nodded: a dip of the head that said the conversation was already over. Awkwardly, Abbie turned at the door. 'It's about London,' she said.

He made no acknowledgement and when she closed the door behind her and looked over her shoulder the hard-looking man had gone and the woman was back behind the counter. By the time she had found her room, showered and eaten at a small bistro, it was eleven o'clock. She slid gratefully beneath the crisp white sheets and blankets. A mere fourteen hours had passed since a man had been murdered, another kidnapped and a boy had gone missing.

Abbie was so tired she fell asleep without turning off the bedside light.

★

When she awoke and dressed she saw a note had been pushed beneath the door. It gave her instructions to drive north off the A61 towards the Montagne Noire and head for the town of Mazamet on the D road. Five kilometres south of that commune was a small unmarked gravelled road on the right next to a ruined stone barn. That road led into the foothills. Abbie checked the route on her mobile. It was under two hours away. No town or hamlet was named on the instructions as to where she might meet the Englishman. She phoned Maguire and confirmed contact with the intermediary. The man they sought was close.

He had assured her her phone signal would be tracked, but as she turned off the road at the ruined building an hour and a half later and drove through the forests she lost the signal. Driving deeper into the foothills she felt the rugged countryside press in on her. This was a wilderness in which it would be all too easy to disappear. As she turned a corner and saw four rough-looking men loitering next to a parked pickup truck, rifles and shotguns slung on their shoulders, the first real sense of fear overcame the tingle of excitement she'd felt before. The bearded men looked like brigands, reminding her of pictures she had seen of partisans who'd fought in the war. A couple of hunting dogs barked as she slowed the car. The men watched her approach. Then one of them stepped forward and gestured her to stop in front of him. The wild man bent his face down to the window and tapped gently on the glass with a nicotine-stained finger whose nail hadn't seen soap and water for a while. She lowered the window, feeling the thudding beat of her heart. He grinned.

'Young lady, do not be frightened. You are safe here.' He looked down the road from where she had travelled. 'We like to make sure you were not followed. Please, go ahead. It is not far now.' His gentle voice belied his appearance. She almost gushed her thanks but nodded instead, just a little too vigorously. He smiled again and stepped back.

After a couple of kilometres, the narrow track widened into a hamlet of houses with dwellings scattered either side. There was a bar next to small shop. As Abbie stopped the car, wondering where to park, a woman came out of the shop and strode across to her. 'The man you are looking for is at the end of the village at the school's playing fields.'

Abbie thanked her. The whole village must have known she was coming. There had been no sign naming the village and an unkind thought lurched into her mind. Perhaps these people were the French equivalent of hillbillies or outcasts from society who chose to live a survivalist lifestyle. So what? she told herself. She knew what it meant not to fit into mainstream society. Having a Sikh father and a Scottish mother, schooldays had been a challenge, and when she became an adult speaking with a south London accent people often didn't know how to place her. She sounded rough, looked beautiful and had a keen questioning mind, which confounded others' preconceived ideas.

Following the woman's directions she passed a small village school. A kilometre on, the road led to where a sports field spread itself across a plateau, a broad expanse between the rising forests. Two groups of young schoolchildren were being coached on the pitch, one group being versed in attack, the other in defence. The two teachers were lean, muscled men, athletic-looking. Scruffier perhaps than the teachers of her childhood, with their stubbled faces. A casually dressed man about the age of the one she was meant to meet sat in a chair next to the old-fashioned wooden pavilion. His mop of hair fell into his face as he bent his head, reading the book in his lap. Abbie glanced around. A whistle blew. The coaches looked her way and then ignored her. The book-reader raised his head as she approached. *He even looks like an Englishman,* she thought.

'Hello,' she said in English.

The man met her gaze but didn't move from the chair. Placing a finger to mark his page, he closed the book and looked up at her. He was handsome, slender, his tanned face glowing in the sunlight. Blue eyes studying her. 'Hello, yourself,' he answered, definitely English, though she couldn't quite place the accent. She settled for southern England, the inflections altered slightly by living in France.

'I'm so pleased to meet you,' she said, feeling clumsy, over-formal. A bit too *Dr Livingstone, I presume*. 'My name is Abnash Khalsa.'

'Abnash,' he repeated, raising his eyebrows with a questioning look. 'Don't know that one.'

'Everyone calls me Abbie.'

He smiled. 'Then why should I be any different? Abbie it is. You meet the blokes on the road? The ones who look like a bunch of bloody outlaws, which I'd say they are but not to their face. They're tough, not rough.'

'Yes, I... Look,' she said hesitantly. 'I'm not too sure how to go about this...' She faltered. 'I have something very important to discuss.'

She was suddenly aware of one of the coaches from the pitch standing near her. He must have approached from her blind side. He was lean-muscled, about six-three or -four, with a few days' stubble on a weather-beaten face. The loose-sleeved T-shirt did little to disguise his impressive physique. He looked like a trained athlete, one who would feel at home on any field of conflict, whether a rugby pitch or a battle zone. He spoke in French. 'Have you had lunch?' he asked her.

'Er... no. No, I haven't,' she answered, just as fluently. The man bent and with effortless strength gathered up the book-reader, lifting him into his arms. 'Come on, Sammy, stop chatting up the hired help,' he said in English. He looked directly at her. 'I'm the man you've come to see,' he said. 'I'm Raglan.'

9

Back at the hamlet, once Raglan had taken his friend
Sammy out of one of the cars and lowered him into a
wheelchair, Abbie realized for the first time that there
were boardwalks connecting the houses and the bar,
and ramps had been fitted so that the wheelchair-bound
veteran had unfettered access. It looked like a town from
a Wild West film. The bar turned out to be more like a
clubhouse diner with a dozen scattered tables covered
with chequered plastic tablecloths. Men and women
were already seated, including the tough-looking men
who had stopped her on the road. There was no sign
of their weapons. Carafes of red wine stood on every
table and the *plat du jour* was ratatouille with chunks of
fresh bread.

Raglan sat opposite her at one table. She quickly
explained events in London. Raglan remained silent
until she had finished and then asked about the boy, and

the kidnapped man's wife and daughter. She confirmed the mother and daughter were safe and under guard. Her urgency and agitation contrasted with his calmness. He poured her a glass of wine and encouraged her to have some food. There was no point trying to get back to London in a hurry. There were only two flights a day and they needed to eat. It was a practical assessment of the situation and she realized that he was correct. The food smelt good and the women who served it flitted back and forth to the kitchen where a brutal-looking hulk of a man was clearly the chef. Raglan caught her stare.

'He's South African. He served with me in the Legion – as did all the men here. They are all veterans.'

She looked more closely at the various pictures and military insignia framed on the walls of the diner. Squads of men in posed photographs, heavily laden paratroopers freefalling from the rear of transport aircraft, some images taken during combat, in rugged terrain. Incongruously, the atmosphere in the room was more like a village hall social than a gathering of tough war veterans. She had never been in the company of soldiers before, apart from Maguire, who she knew had commanded British special forces before he came over to the Service. These men had obviously known deprivation in the field and done their fair share of killing, but there was no sense of bravado among them, and some of the women who shared their meal had young children with them who were not yet old enough for school. It felt like an extended family. She finished the last of her wine. It was good and added to her sense of well-being.

Raglan poured more crimson wine into her glass and then one of the women brought two bowls of ratatouille to them with a smile for Abbie. 'When we left the army some of us bought this place. I mean the whole village. It had been abandoned years before so we got it at a knockdown price. We all wanted a place where no one would ask too many questions about who we were and what we'd done and where we could still trust the people around us.'

She glanced at the motto on the wall. *Legio Patria Nostra*. It was an unambiguous statement: The Legion is our Home. Abbie felt the rush of being so close to fighting men and that, coupled with her hunger, was making her eat too quickly. It had been a long morning and her stomach growled. The food was delicious, so too the wine. Raglan refilled her glass again. She was about to refuse, thinking of the drive back, but she was on unfamiliar ground and didn't want to come across as an ungrateful guest.

'From what you've told me you've been on the go in trying circumstances,' Raglan said. 'And, as you said, you're not an operational officer so you're out of your comfort zone. The body needs fuel. Adrenaline can do that. Make you ravenous. Need to feed it. What is it you do for Maguire?'

So far she thought she had played it cool. Her brief was to listen because Raglan spoke several languages and if he used any of those she was familiar with then she could report back what Raglan was discussing with others. Forewarned and all that, Maguire had said.

'I work in admin. It's boring but I'm OK with that for now.'

Raglan seemed only mildly interested as he tore a piece of bread and mopped the sauce on his plate. 'I wouldn't have thought Maguire would send someone from bog-standard admin.' He chewed thoughtfully. 'What kind of admin?'

Her cover was flimsy – after all, she was only a messenger – but she'd known she was bound to be asked and Maguire had instructed her to be vague. She shrugged. 'Data analysis,' she lied. 'That kind of thing. I was going to look at Carter's computer at his house. That's why I was there.'

Raglan wiped the plate clean with a piece of bread. The girl was flushed, two large glasses of wine before the meal arrived and another one during it had made her tipsy. He nodded as if he believed her. 'I'll phone Maguire and get a sitrep,' he said. 'We use satellite phones here. There are no landlines and there's no chance of a mobile signal. We're too far down the valley. Sammy's got a spare room in his house across the road so I suggest you get a couple of hours' kip and we'll catch the evening flight. That OK with you?'

She nodded and disguised her relief at not having to turn around and head straight back to Toulouse. 'That would be great, thanks.'

'Look, I don't want you feeling isolated here. Finish up and I'll take you to my friends' table. Talk to Sammy and his wife while I make the call. You've already met the other two with him on the road in. You feel OK with that for a while?'

'Sure. I should really speak to Mr Maguire myself, though.'

'Of course. I'll arrange it.'

Raglan was old-school polite. He stood and pulled her chair away for her. She mumbled her thanks. None of the men she'd dated had ever done that, nor had they stood when she approached the table where they sat as did the 'bandits' when Raglan escorted her over.

'You must excuse me,' said Sammy, smiling at her. 'I let the others do my legwork.'

Raglan made the introductions. Sammy's wife's name was Didianne and the two 'wild' men from the roadblock were Ansell and Baptiste. They made a fuss of her, with Didianne insisting she sit next to her so she could hear about London and the current trends in fashion and celebrity gossip. Ansell and Baptiste loudly proclaimed they wanted the privilege of having such a beautiful girl seated between them. By the time Abbie looked up after the effusive welcome, Raglan was gone.

The next hour passed quickly, and so too did the next.

No one spoke of the Legion, or of war, or how Sammy became a paraplegic. No matter how often she slipped Raglan's name into the conversation to learn more about the man they always gently guided her probing away. The men became more raucous, the room loud with laughter as personal insults were thrown back and forth with a teasing familiarity. The men paused, looked her way and raised their glasses in salutation as every other man stood and began singing. She recognized the words of their regimental song.

> La Légion marche vers le front,
> En chantant nous suivons,
> Hérltiers de ses traditions,
> Nous sommes avec elle.

The chorus and following verses mellowed, rose and broke in a final impassioned confirmation of their pride at having served with the Foreign Legion's 2nd Parachute Regiment. As the men fell silent the women rose as one to their feet and applauded their men. Abbie spontaneously joined them, a lump in her throat. Tears threatened to sting her eyes at any moment. Too much wine, she told herself. But a pang of envy stabbed her. It was, she realized, the privilege of being allowed to witness their tight-knit camaraderie.

Sammy saw her reaction. 'It's all right, Abbie. It gets to us all.'

The ex-legionnaires had somehow drawn her in and she did not understand how. They were a family and it was clear from what she heard in the conversations around her that this closed fraternity had a bond that no outsider would ever break.

The men at the table charged their glasses and broke easily into Arabic.

'God knows why such a doll comes all the way here to chat up Raglan,' said Ansell.

'Maybe they had something going he hasn't let on about,' said Baptiste. 'He's a dark horse is Raglan, the randy bastard, and who wouldn't want to keep her a secret? Give me half a chance.'

'I'd keep her under lock and key and keep the wine flowing.'

Sammy told them to cool it and brought her back into the general hubbub of conversation. The laughter and bonhomie returned. The wine tasted even better with such convivial company and by the time Didianne escorted her to a brightly coloured, warm room whose shutters were already closed, she sank gratefully on to the comfort of the bed. Her final thought before falling asleep was that she was grateful not to have been plunged into danger but, instead, welcomed by Raglan's friends.

She awoke with the chill of the evening when the sun had already slipped behind the mountains. Her mouth was clammy from the wine and she stumbled her way to the small en-suite bathroom. She splashed cold water on her face, pulled a brush through her hair, and stepped out of the bedroom into the living room where Sammy was sitting with a girl of about ten years. They were doing homework together.

'Hey. You sleep OK?' said Sammy.

'Yes. Too long it seems.'

'Didianne is in the kitchen. This is my daughter, Cadice.'

Abbie introduced herself, but sensed that something was wrong. She should not have slept away the afternoon. They had to get back to London.

'Listen, Abbie. Take it easy, yeah? Don't throw a wobbly. Raglan's gone. He took your car. He'll be in London pretty soon. He'll speak to your boss.' Sammy shrugged. 'It's the way he is. He doesn't like chaperones. He works alone.'

Abbie felt the pit of her stomach drop. 'Christ, I'm in trouble.' She sank into one of the chairs, glanced at the child, saw the crucifix on the wall behind her and regretted her careless blasphemy. 'I am sorry. Forgive me.'

The child shrugged and picked up her books. 'No problem. Papa says much worse things when he thinks I cannot hear him. I will see you at dinner, madame.'

Abbie stared at the ceiling. Raglan had conned her. 'Can I phone London?'

Sammy's face was a picture of regret. 'We'll get you on

the morning flight. Didi will sort you out with anything you need. You have to let Raglan do his thing.'

Abbie knew she had no choice. She was a prisoner made welcome.

Legio Patria Nostra.

10

The British Airways flight from Toulouse to London Heathrow landed ten minutes overdue at 6 p.m. Raglan had no luggage, not even a holdall. He had no need of clothes where he was heading so he got through passport control and was out of the terminal long before any of his fellow passengers. The cabbie had an effortless run down the M4 and in just under forty minutes dropped him off outside Marks & Spencer in King Street, Hammersmith, less than a ten-minute fast-paced walk to Weltje Road and the ambush site.

Raglan paid in cash. He had no intention of contacting Maguire until he'd determined what had happened to Steven Carter. If he had survived the ambush and not been abducted then there was one place he might be hiding – the odds were his father would have sent him to a safe place. Raglan crisscrossed the street twice, stopping now and again to look into the small shopfront windows, using their reflection to check for any watchers. There was no sign of anyone staking out the building he was heading for. He was certain that no one except Jeremy Carter knew of his one-bedroom flat in the two-storey block whose unassuming passage door was scrunched between a hair salon and a funeral care shop. The modest-looking brick-faced building had been renovated ten years before: two apartments separated by a common landing on the first floor. Raglan had bought one of them furnished, modern and functional, from a young city trader who had burnt his fingers on a speculative trade. He walked down the street on the opposite side of the entrance door and when traffic came to a halt in the narrow road he dodged between the vehicles and disappeared from view into a convenience store. He bought milk, bread and a bag of sugar.

Raglan checked the street again and moved to the entrance to his building. He waited in the low-lit passageway to be sure that no one had followed him. A dozen strides further and he punched in a security code that opened the main hallway door. At the top of the stairs, he could hear his neighbour's television. He pressed his ear against the door to his apartment. Silence. His fingers traced the door frame, found the narrow split between frame and wall and let his fingertips tell him that the hidden key had been taken. Using his own key, he turned the lock slowly and stepped silently inside.

The kitchen cupboards had been raided, tinned food opened; empty soft drink cans and packets of spilt potato crisps revealed someone's hunger. He walked quietly to the bedroom door. The curtains were closed but there was sufficient light for him to see the curled, sleeping figure beneath the duvet. Raglan retreated to the kitchen and prepared two mugs of tea, spooning two measures of sugar into one of them. The violent attack and murder had happened less than thirty-six hours ago. The boy would still be in shock and sleep was the best thing for him, but he'd need his glucose level boosted. Raglan put the two mugs on the bedside table and squatted next to the sleeping boy, whispering his name, increasing the volume of his voice so it gently penetrated the boy's consciousness. Steve Carter's eyes flickered open and he gaped at Raglan's smiling face close to his own. He squirmed upright, grappling with a sudden onslaught of confused emotions. He stammered, gasping for air.

Raglan reached out to place a comforting hand on the boy's shoulder. 'Hello, mate. I made a cuppa.'

Steve Carter reached for him and held him tightly. Raglan waited, letting the boy's shock subside and, in his own time, Steve released him. He handed the mug to the boy.

'Dad said you'd come. He said they'd find you,' Steve blurted, hands embracing the mug's warmth.

Raglan nodded. 'Drink some of that and we'll talk.'

The boy grimaced at the tea's sweetness. They never had sugar at home.

'You need it,' Raglan insisted, sipping his own tea, his eyes checking the boy for any sign of injury. There were no blood splatters on him, which was a good sign. It meant the boy had escaped before the killing had taken place. 'Did you phone your mother?'

Steve shook his head. The tea seemed to be working; the kid's hands had stopped trembling. 'I dropped my phone in the car and Dad said not to. Said to wait for you. Said you'd come. Said I should wait two days before going home or until you came. Why wouldn't he let me go home?'

'In case there was an attack.'

There was a surge of panic in his voice. 'Are Mum and Melissa all right?'

'They're fine. I'd have known if they weren't. Your dad wanted you here so you'd be safe.' Raglan knew there was a reason for it that went beyond the boy's safety. Carter would have relayed information through the boy. Now wasn't the time to press the distressed kid. He'd wait. The youngster would get to it soon enough.

The boy's lip quivered but he bit it, squeezing closed his eyes to dam the tears that threatened. 'Did they kill Dad?'

'It's not good, Steve. You know that. No, I don't think he's dead but Charlie Lewis was shot. He didn't make it.'

The news of Lewis's death had a numbing effect on

the youngster. He fell silent and then whispered: 'It was terrible... I was really scared. I was so scared I ran and left Dad.'

Raglan calmed him. 'It's what you were supposed to do. You did exactly right. If they had taken you they would have used you against your dad and then the bad guys would have got what they wanted because he would never have let them hurt you.'

'I didn't think anything like that could happen. I feel such a coward, Dan.'

'Hey, I've been there plenty of times with really tough blokes. Being scared is good. It keeps you sharp.'

Steve's lukewarm smile was a candid admission of a shared experience.

'Listen, the police and other people will want to talk to you. I'd rather you told me everything. Everything you can remember. Maybe we'll find something you've forgotten. OK? Our own debrief. With your help, we'll get the men who did this. Why do you think your dad told you to get away? He relied on you. You did a hundred per cent.'

'Really?' said Steve, a glimmer of hope that he had, after all, done the right thing.

'Absolutely,' said Raglan, and saw that his compliment lifted the boy's spirits. 'I bet you haven't had a hot meal. How about I get us a pizza delivered? I'll phone your mum and tell her I'll have you home later. We'll eat and then we'll talk.'

The boy was definitely calmer now, though he would need counselling for the trauma. But for the moment he was more settled.

Steve's brow furrowed as he reached for a thought in the turmoil of his memory. 'Dad gave me a message... a name...'

One of Maguire's men knocked on his office door; Maguire beckoned him in.

'There's still no signal from Abbie's phone,' said the young man. His clothing made him look as tough and streetwise as any of the other twentysomethings on the streets of a sink estate. He wore the suit hanging in his wardrobe only when intelligence-gathering in the business world demanded it.

Maguire felt the press of doubt. Had he made a huge error after all, sending an untrained young woman into a place of danger? He immediately dismissed the thought. Negative emotions destroyed clear thinking. Abbie was intelligent enough to know what to do. 'And the airports and points of entry?'

'No record of anyone named Raglan coming into the country in the last twenty-four hours.'

'I didn't think there would be. He'll come, I'm sure of it. If Abbie found him he'll use another passport to get here. Have them check who was on the flights from Carcassonne or Toulouse.'

'No flights from Carcassonne and one late afternoon from Toulouse.'

'Run down all thirty-something males on that flight. He's here. I know he is. Raglan is the kind of man who will not do what we expect. He'll move quickly with or without Abbie.'

A young woman knocked and walked in without waiting to be invited. 'Sir, we have intercepted a call on the Carters' home phone.' She handed Maguire a transcript. 'We couldn't trace it.'

Maguire felt a glow of satisfaction as he scanned the typewritten account of the brief conversation Raglan had conducted with the abducted man's wife. 'Of course not. Raglan knows the game. And if he is going to take her son home then he's somehow found the boy, God knows how. But now we know he's here.' He placed the sheet of paper neatly on his desk. 'As I thought.' He nodded his dismissal to the female communications officer.

'Shall we intercept them?' said the scruffily dressed agent. 'Before Five gets to him? We aren't the only ones with a tap on her line. They'll want to debrief the boy. Be better if we did it first.'

'Five aren't interested any longer. This doesn't have the hallmark of a terrorist attack: it's a murder and abduction so it's a police matter. Let the boy and his mother have their reunion. The Met's family liaison officer is still in place. She won't let the police talk to the boy without social services present. Whatever information the boy has, Raglan will have it by now. We'll get what we need before the Met interrogates Carter's son.'

'Then we do nothing?'

Maguire looked out across the Thames and the darkening city. The days were drawing in as autumn made itself felt. Street and office lights glistened in the cold clear air. Jeremy Carter was hidden where these fairy-tale lights did not twinkle with a false promise that all was well. He was alone in darkness and in pain. Maguire caged his desire to get out on to the streets and take direct action. Old habits, old emotions were now channelled to organizing a rescue plan once they tracked down the abductors or they made a ransom demand. Providing Jeremy Carter was still alive. He shook his head in a belated answer to the question.

'Be patient. Raglan will come to us.'

11

Eddie Roman shivered. Now that the buzz of the fast drive had left him, he felt sick to his stomach. He regretted getting involved with this heavy crew. He dragged deeply on his cigarette and averted his eyes from their victim, tied to a chair. The bastards were savages. They didn't give a toss about anyone or anything. When they'd killed that poor sod in cold blood those high-velocity rounds could have punched through walls and snuffed out an old lady watching morning telly. No, no, this was not what he signed up for, but was he going to say anything? Not on your life. These cold-hearted killers would slit his throat and then go back to the sandwiches they were eating. What the hell was an old lag like him doing getting mixed up with hard-porn violence? he muttered to himself, cursing profusely under his breath.

This place was getting to Eddie. He had done enough time in solitary to always carry the heart-crushing need to see the sky, but the windows in the abandoned building had already been boarded up before they arrived so there was no likelihood of any light from the arc lamps they had set up escaping into the night. He was caged again. All he wanted was to slip away the couple of miles home to Brentford and Shelley. He'd told her this job would only be for a couple of days and if he didn't phone her she'd be getting worried. Please, God, she didn't get worried enough to call the police. He glanced around at the dingy surroundings. The place was filthy except for the area they had cleared, deep inside the building, where the two harsh arc lamps, ones that could be bought in any builder's yard, scorched their glare on the man who sat, head slumped, dried blood from the blow on his head. He reckoned these blokes were so well organized they had been preparing this attack for weeks. This was a perfect site, just a spit away from the concrete yard and metal-crushing plant. It offered security and soundproofing, but it was also a good defensive position. He could see that. Anyone trying to assault the place would be cut to pieces getting over those gates and into the yard, and as for the detritus-filled gully behind the yard, which he knew to be a tributary of the River Brent, even crack-hot SAS troops would get caught up in the rusting shopping trolleys and fly-tipped junk there.

Two of the gunmen were posted at strategic parts of the disused factory, each with a view through a small, uncovered window tucked away at each wing. The other three killers rotated on sentry duty. There was one man extra who had not been involved in the ambush and was waiting at the site and who had quickly opened and closed the gates when they arrived. They were cool and relaxed as they monitored the darkened yards, wedging themselves on to windowsills, submachine guns slung over their shoulders. One pressed his two-way radio, its transmission squelch answered by the other gunman confirming that all was clear. It was useless for Eddie to try and pinpoint their East European accents. He had asked them where they were from but they had smiled and ignored him. Eddie had no purpose other than to wait for further instructions, and be ready to drive wherever the gang's leader wanted to be taken.

They had bound a naked Carter with duct tape on his legs, arms and chest in a chair, its back to the area where the men would relax, eat and sleep. A bloodstained pillowcase covered his head. The gang's leader had complained that their victim had been struck too hard with the rifle butt: he had slipped in and out of consciousness for an hour after being seized, then he'd been too groggy to answer questions. If the kidnapped bloke could only remember what these men wanted to know then the job would be done and Eddie could get himself home. The leader had dribbled water into the battered man's split lip and made a cursory check on his dilated pupils. In other words, Eddie Roman told himself, this evil bastard knew what he was doing and just how far he could go. He was a trained torturer.

Eddie gave the injured prisoner a wide berth and moved to the far end of the room, where it seemed the gang had been staying before the kidnap. They had arranged a worn old sofa and a couple of battered armchairs in a circle on an old piece of carpet, probably retrieved from a builder's skip. Cot beds and sleeping bags were gathered around a propane gas heater, the beds shared as two men at a time took their turn at being on guard duty. A small fridge stood between two folding tables. One bore cans of food, an electric kettle and bottled water next to the makings for instant coffee; the weapons and ammunition clips were arranged on the other. These were additional weapons to what the men carried, oiled Hechler and Koch MP5s. Handguns and four grenades lay next to the same number of canisters. Eddie wasn't sure, but he had watched enough Hollywood thrillers and war films to think they might be smoke canisters. The longer he stayed in this small fortress with what were obviously professional mercenaries the more determined he was to make a run for it when the opportunity presented itself.

The interrogator dragged a wooden chair closer to his captive, his face right next to the pillowcase where the man's laboured breathing sucked and blew the cloth back and forth.

'This is not the time to fall silent, Jeremy, my dear old friend,' he said, his words laden with sarcasm. 'Your educated tones were always pure joy to my mongrel ear. Let not your voice quieten now.'

Carter made no answer.

'I don't want to hurt you... but I will. And, if I'm honest, I'll take some pleasure doing it.' He pulled the pillowcase off the man's bruised face. 'The skills we learn, eh, Jeremy?' He lit a cigarette and looked up at the gunman who stepped forward.

Carter was going to get hurt.

12

At Woodstock Road, the approach to Carter's house was still cordoned off by armed police, much to the annoyance of some residents expecting dinner guests. The taxi inched slowly towards the intersection as the uniformed police officers flagged it down. Raglan saw two armed officers stationed at each corner. They would catch anyone attempting to break through the cordon in a crossfire. Raglan showed his genuine passport. Once the officer was satisfied with Raglan's identity he contacted the house, and then signalled a fourth officer standing at the crossroads who withdrew the stinger from across the road. Raglan knew the investigation would have been downgraded from a serious terrorist threat. There was no sign of armed counter-terrorism officers and the stinger's line of spikes was only a slowing device for cars and bore no comparison to the Talon road mesh that could stop a lorry from ramming a target.

Once Raglan and Steve were ushered past another uniformed officer at the front door, Amanda and her son embraced. She began to cry with relief.

'Thank God. Thank God,' she whispered through her tears, before quickly regaining control. She wiped a palm across her cheek and threw an arm around Raglan, burying her face into his neck. 'Thank you.' Her words carried more than gratitude. It was a greeting, a surge of hope that, now Raglan was involved, the world might soon be a less frightening place.

'Let's get you to bed,' she told her son.

The boy was resilient, but his mother's emotion had triggered his own tears. Like her he quickly dismissed them.

'Mum, I couldn't help Dad. He told me to run.'

'Of course he did,' she assured him. 'Everything will be all right. How about a hot bath?'

'I want to see Melissa first. Dad always reads to her. I'll do it tonight.'

A look of uncertainty crossed her face. How much would the boy tell his young half-sister about what had happened?

'Mandy, he's right. Let him do what he wants,' said Raglan. 'He knows how to handle it.'

Amanda still looked uncertain but she kissed her son and told him, 'She would like that. She's very upset.'

'I'll sort it, Mum,' Steve said. 'Dan. Thanks. You know... for everything...' The boy's words faltered, wary of expressing too much in front of his mother. With a final hug from Raglan, Steve moved away.

The family liaison officer stepped into view from the sitting room where she had been discreetly waiting. She keyed a number into her phone. 'I'll have a doctor come and look at him, Mrs Carter, and then the investigating officer will want to question him.'

'Not now, surely?' said Amanda.

'The sooner the better,' the FLO said.

'Forget it,' said Raglan. 'I've already done that.'

'I don't know who you are,' said the woman.

'That doesn't matter. Your bosses will have the audio download tomorrow. There's a government agency involved and they'll clear everything.'

The FLO turned away, pressing her phone to her ear.

'I can't tell you how relieved I am that you're here,' said Amanda.

'Steve's eaten. He'll be OK, up to a point, but he'll need professional counselling after what he experienced. Kids are tough but let's make sure there are no hidden time bombs tucked away that'll go off in ten or twenty years' time.'

She nodded her understanding.

Raglan asked the question he had so far avoided. 'Jeremy?'

'Nothing, not yet.' She wanted to believe that he would be returned home to them all safely. Hope was all she had. 'My God, where *have* you been? You'll stay with us? Sleep here?'

'No, I've things to do. You go on up to the kids and see they're OK. I picked up a new phone at the airport.' He reached for a pad next to the house phone and wrote the number down. 'You call me whenever you need to but they'll be listening.' He embraced the woman whose parents had taken him in at boarding school when he was orphaned. He and Amanda were as much brother and sister as were Steve and Melissa, their bond as strong as any blood tie.

She gave him a final embrace and kiss and stepped wearily upstairs.

Raglan pressed a speed dial on his phone. The voice that answered had the same deep timbre and no-nonsense tone he remembered.

'Where do you want to meet?' said Raglan.

'The bank,' said Maguire and killed the connection.

Raglan smiled. Maguire always had to be sure to have the last word.

The bank was a code name to throw anyone who might be listening in. It did not refer to where Carter worked but the old Midland Bank building whose magnificent edifice, designed in 1924 by Sir Edward 'Ned' Lutyens, had been stylishly converted into a hotel and was more commonly referred to as the Ned. Situated a ten-minute walk across London Bridge into the business district from the south side of the River Thames, the vast building became a watering hole and eatery for the young gods and goddesses of finance and trading. Raglan walked up the steps and into the entrance that separated the internal restaurants and lounges on both sides. The noise was deafening. A couple of thousand people were drinking and eating. It wasn't that far removed from a vast railway station, Raglan thought. Bright young PR-greeter things welcomed him, hosts and hostesses, smiling warmly, chosen for their perfect teeth and youthful exuberance, twenty-something cherubs ushering him into hostelry heaven. *You have arrived in Nirvana.*

In front of him was a raised bandstand where a jazz quartet played. They were good, but from what Raglan could see not one of the multitude was listening, hunched as they were in conversation. It was a waste of fine music. One of Charlie Parker's covers 'Out of Nowhere' drifted over him as he turned left for the bar. Its title seemed appropriate. Raglan looked left and right. Maguire would be somewhere he could be seen. Green upholstered booths nestled next to one of the bars. That would be a good place. Far enough away from the mainstream; near enough to catch a waiter's eye. Raglan saw the back of Maguire's head. There had been a time when he thought it made a tempting target. He didn't know what section in MI6 Maguire ran these days. The last time Raglan had worked for them Maguire was C/CEE, which gave give him responsibility for Central and Eastern Europe. Who knew what Maguire was running nowadays? Odds were Raglan wouldn't be told. He didn't care. He slid on to the bench seat opposite him. A bottle of chilled Hitachino Nest Red Rice beer was already on the table. Maguire nursed a large whisky.

'Where's my girl, Abbie?' said Maguire with a sour look.

'I'm well, thanks,' said Raglan and sipped the cold beer. It tasted sweet, like strawberries. Raglan raised a hand. The waiter was two strides away. He bowed down so he could hear the order. 'A single malt, thanks.'

'Any preference, sir?'

'You choose,' said Raglan. A place like this wasn't going to serve anything that tasted like drain cleaner. 'She'll be on the morning flight,' he told Maguire. 'She's unharmed, but you knew that. You sent an untrained woman into what could have been a dangerous situation, Maguire. That wasn't very gentlemanly.'

'I needed an innocent. Any of my operational people might have bristled at your lot. Preferable that she didn't know better. She was no threat and your people would have known that.'

The waiter settled the malt whisky on the table. Maguire nodded. It was on his tab.

'How did you find the boy?'

'Did you trace my call?'

'You know we didn't.'

'I have a place.'

Maguire raised an eyebrow. 'I didn't know.'

'Jeremy did.'

'And he sent the boy there. Naturally.'

Raglan nodded. 'He holed up, which means Jerry knew you'd send for me.'

'First choice. You know him. You're family.'

Raglan watched Maguire. The man's brain was racing but his eyes were as steady as the hand that took the drink to his lips. He was an unflinching man, was Maguire. Raglan had dug out some of his past from people he knew in their shared business. Maguire had been at the sharp end. Had bled. And caused others to bleed. But one thing came out of it all: he looked after his own people. He did not risk their lives needlessly. That determination went back further than his time in special forces and remained now that he was at MI6. That was one credo Raglan shared with Colonel Ralph Maguire.

'Why Jeremy?' Raglan asked.

'I don't know. Yet. What did you get out of the boy?'

'The recording's on my phone. There's nothing much. A couple of names,' said Raglan, not yet ready to divulge what he had learnt.

Maguire waited. Names were what he wanted.

Raglan let the intelligence man stew a moment and

then gave him a titbit. More than. It was enough to chew on and digest. 'Serval,' said Raglan. 'Remember Mali? The Ametettaï valley in the Adrar des Ifoghas. I know you had people there. When we went into the mountains the French HQ had British and American intelligence officers with SAS advisers in tow. The French played everything close to their chests but when the rumble started the British and Americans were nowhere in sight. So why did Jeremy give his stepson the name of the operation?'

'I'm not sure,' said Maguire. But his tone had softened and Raglan knew that Maguire had information that might link to the anti-terrorist operation those years before: Operation Serval.

'Was he there? Did you have Carter in place? If he was your man on the ground did something happen back then that's come back to bite you?' said Raglan, watching for any flicker of deceit in Maguire's eyes. Yet the man was too much of a pro for that. Maguire could sell the nation's nuclear codes on the back of a napkin and make the sales pitch thoroughly convincing.

'What else?' said Maguire, ignoring Raglan's question.

Raglan finished the whisky. 'Have the police shut down the crime scene?' he said, playing the same game.

'There's nothing to see there.'

'Humour me. I'd like to see it before forensics clean up.' And then in answer to Maguire's question he threw a bargaining chip on the table. 'Then you get to hear the recording I made with the boy.'

Maguire suppressed a sigh and checked his watch. 'Everything is already being cleared.'

'Then there's no time to lose,' said Raglan, sliding out of the booth. He would be glad to escape the cacophony of the braying herd. Maguire shrugged and took a few banknotes out of his wallet, tucking them beneath the empty whisky glass. He pointed out the payment to the waiter and pulled on his overcoat.

They walked past the greeting committee, who nodded and smiled. Pearly whites. Expensive dental work. PR work was getting more costly. 'Why send for me?' said Raglan. 'It wasn't only because of my connection to the family.'

'That's part of it,' said Maguire as they hovered on the Ned's steps. Maguire raised a hand to signal his driver, who appeared as if by magic, given that parking was so heavily restricted.

'What's the rest of it?'

Maguire half turned so he could face Raglan. 'You worked with Carter in the past. The woman you consider to be as much a sister as a blood relative is married to him. I wanted to see whether you would respond when I sent you the news.'

'Like I said, why?'

'Because you have a network of contacts. Some of them unsavoury. I wanted to convince myself that you were not involved in his kidnapping.' He stepped to the kerb as the Ned's doorman opened the car door. 'If you were involved, then you wouldn't have come.' He smiled. 'And here you are.'

13

Police lamps illuminating the crime scene created a flickering sheen of wavering droplets as the breeze swirled the fine rain. It made no impression on the white-suited forensic officers moving ghost-like as they lifted aside the tented shroud that still covered Carter's gunshot car.

'Everything is bagged,' said Maguire, tugging his collar up around his neck. His breath billowed in the falling temperature. Raglan was impervious to the cold and rain. His waxed jacket was a second skin, and anyway the first was waterproof. A police transporter's ramps were down, its chains attached to the car's grab points, ready to haul the damaged car away for further scrutiny at the forensics garage. As the car was dragged up the ramps, the rear door swung open.

'Hold it!' Raglan shouted.

The operator stopped winching as Raglan stepped

forward to close the door. Steve's rugby ball lay half wedged on the floor beneath the driver's seat. Raglan bent in, retrieved the ball and slammed shut the door.

'All right!' Maguire called, signalling the operator to continue.

As the winching restarted a scene-of-crime officer stepped forward and pointed at the rugby ball. 'There's blood on that. The forensic lab will need it.'

Raglan spat on the dried blood and wiped it clean. 'There's enough blood in the car, they don't need this.'

The white-suited officer was about to object when Raglan turned his back and walked further along the ambush area. Maguire raised a hand, his authority absolute. 'It's been a tiring time for us all. I'll cover for you if it comes to it.'

The SOC officer shrugged and turned away. The incident would go in his report. His pay grade did not give him authority to challenge the suits. Maguire joined Raglan, who studied the curve in the road. The perfect choke point.

'You don't need a PhD to see it was professional,' Raglan said, seeing the ambush go down in his mind's eye.

'They drove on to the A4, and swung back once across the flyover. A traffic camera picked up the van. It never got as far as the next camera before the M4 so they must have turned off. A burnt-out van was found. After that, nothing.'

Raglan turned to Maguire. 'All right. You sent for me. Now tell me about Carter's involvement.'

'An international jewellery manufacturer buys gold through a London merchant bank that has a branch in New York,' said Maguire.

The first connection was easy to figure out. 'Through Jeremy's bank and Jeremy controlled the account,' Raglan said.

'Correct. And he's the financial compliance officer. So he scrutinizes everything. Once that's done the transactions are credited to the New York account of the bank which electronically transfers those funds to accounts all over the world. It's more complex than that but in a nutshell, it's a money-laundering operation. Gold into dollars, or vice versa, or bloody bitcoin for all I know, but one way or another the cartels are washing their money and Carter had the information,' Maguire said as they walked towards the waiting car. 'And by following up those bank accounts we and the American DEA have arrested and closed down drug manufacturers and dealers. Some of them at least.'

Raglan tucked the rugby ball under his arm. 'So you had a pipeline straight into their operations. How much?'

'More than a billion dollars over the past four years.'

'That's what I call winning the lottery.'

'We had much the same feeling.' Maguire wiped a hand across his wet face.

Raglan scuffed some broken glass. 'Tell you one thing: it wasn't South American cartels who did this.'

'How do you know?' said Maguire.

'Not enough blood.' For once in his life Maguire's emotions betrayed him – Raglan could see the MI6 man was conflicted. 'There's something else, isn't there?' said Raglan.

Maguire grimaced. What he said next obviously pained him to admit. 'He had his fingers in the till.'

Raglan placed a restraining hand on the intelligence director, halting his walk to the car. 'Not a chance. Jeremy Carter is a straight arrow. I'd bet my life on it.'

'Everyone at the bank is under scrutiny. So far the only person who had access to anything connecting these elements was Carter. This is a complex operation – layers and layers of operatives, contacts, supergrasses... Carter has hidden vital information. He could expose us all and what we are doing. Blow the whole thing out the water.'

'I've worked with him. You can't toss a man's life away.'

'Men turn, Raglan.'

'Not him.'

'Anyone can be bought. He's either staged this whole thing himself or someone in the drug cartel has traced the operation back to him. How, I don't know.'

There was no doubt in Raglan's mind about Jeremy Carter. Raglan's instinct told him there was more to the killing and abduction than drug lords snatching a banker, no matter how much information he had on them. They would have killed him outright if he were blackmailing them and take their chances with the authorities penetrating their cartels. It was part and parcel of who they were. Risks were factored in. Despite his place of authority at the bank, Carter was still too small a fish in the eyes of the cartels. They had many people on their payroll. Perhaps they had tried to buy him and failed? None of it made any sense at the moment. What was important was finding him before he died. Raglan had information from debriefing Steve that showed a clear link to the war in Mali and the fight against terrorist insurgents funded by drug money. He needed another piece of the puzzle.

'A former intelligence officer, now a respected banker, has been snatched. His driver murdered. This isn't security service or foreign intelligence matter, it's a police investigation,' said Raglan.

They reached the car. 'Is that what you think?' Maguire said. 'That Carter was retired? He was active. He's still on the payroll.' Maguire felt an instant of satisfaction to see that his comment had momentarily surprised Raglan, like showing a strong poker hand. But such small victories are easily vanquished by a player holding aces.

'Then I know who's taken him,' said Raglan.

★

Maguire and Raglan sat in the car beyond the cordon. Maguire remained silent. The boy's voice faltered on the audio recording of the debrief.

'... there were two, no... three men, yeah, definitely three... in the street... They were just doing the road... and then Dad shouted, really shouted and told Charlie to drive, to get us out of there. I didn't know what was happening... and then we smashed into a car. Dad grabbed me, he got hold of me and shook me and said to run like hell, to come here, to find you... And... and said tell you... Serv... Serval... Yes, that was it... and then JD, to tell you it's JD... He shouted at me, he really shouted, he scared me... and then the men came at us... They were shooting... It was like fireworks going off... I just ran.'

Raglan switched off the phone. 'There wasn't much more he could tell me.' He tugged a photo from his pocket. 'I found a photo album in the boy's bedroom when I was at the house. This was in it.' Heavily armed, unshaven men, including Raglan, stared back at Maguire. Two others wore loose-fitting tropical suits and were non-combatants. One of the men was Carter; the other wore an eye patch.

'JD,' said Raglan, pointing out the one-eyed killer. 'We were in West Africa taking out drug-distribution bases. At first we thought he was French, but then reckoned he was a mongrel, some kind of Russian expat. The Americans had used him. He was a freelancer and an asshole. He wouldn't tell us his name, but his initials were JD, so we called him John Doe.'

Maguire studied the photograph. The man referred to as JD had a cigar gripped between his teeth. 'No name?'

'We never found out. We didn't care. It wasn't important. He had this pseudo way of talking. He liked to get in on a kill if it was operationally possible. Months after that photo was taken we were on Operation Serval. I figured Carter was back in London and that JD had something to do with intelligence liaison because he was there all the time.'

'I'll have his face enhanced and get copies out on the streets,' said Maguire.

'Don't let a street copper get taken out. Advise extreme caution. He's armed and dangerous. He's a psycho. But an intelligent one.' Raglan tapped the photograph. 'We didn't want him anywhere near us. He was over the edge. Carter used him for special jobs.'

'What kind of jobs?'

'You don't know? Carter is your man.'

'Operational officers use various people on the ground. I don't know this man. He has never appeared in any report or any financial audit. So he was below the radar. An asset who was off the books,' Maguire said.

'About a month after I was in hospital after the Serval op, John Doe was in a chopper that was shot down in the jungle. The remains of four bodies were found. The two pilots, John Doe and the American liaison officer.'

'DNA?'

'Not out there. It was a given. There was no flight plan. I heard it was an undercover job. An assassination. Some tribal leader.'

'On Carter's orders?'

Raglan shrugged. 'Who knows? But if he's the man Carter saw here, then JD's come back from the dead.'

Maguire flicked the photograph with his thumb. There were never many certainties in his line of work. 'Or Carter arranged the whole charade – blaming this John Doe to throw us off the scent.'

'You can't take that chance. If he's been lifted, the clock's ticking.'

Maguire raised the photograph. 'If I publish this, it will panic him into finishing off Carter.'

'He doesn't panic. But you're right, you can't publish it in the media. It'll tell him we're on to him. Make it tougher for Carter.' He watched the rain dribbling down the window.

'How long do you think Carter can last?' said Maguire.

'He hasn't been at the sharp end for a few years. Tonight perhaps. Maybe tomorrow. Best hope is the day after. JD will get what he wants out of him. No one holds out forever.'

Raglan's gaze stayed on the blurred light beyond the murder scene. A red traffic light reflected on the rivulets trickling down the window. The red light flickered. Raglan's memory unfurled. Images concertinaed. Blood rain.

14

Back in those caves time ceased to exist, swallowed by the thundering noise and dust cloud that billowed after the explosion. Terrorists blundered through it and grabbed the semi-conscious Raglan. They knew their leader Abdelhamid Abou Zeid had martyred himself but the legionnaire had survived the explosion, saved by the low rock formation in the middle of the underground chamber. Blood trickled from the legionnaire's nose and ears but he was alive and that gave them a hostage. A part of Raglan's mind knew he was being dragged away. It urged him to fight but his body was unresponsive and failed him. One of his eyes was already puffed and closed. He did not know how long it took for the blows being rained on him to shock him back into consciousness. He was on his knees, bound, the glare of bright lights blinding him. Voices cursed in Arabic as another fist broke more teeth. Raglan spat blood. Adrenaline surged and focused his mind. This was not the time to retreat into the safety and darkness. An unseen assailant punched him in the kidneys.

The red eye watched. Silently recording everything.

He knew he had been taken from the caves. The room was square. Adobe walls. Dirt floor. Dust rose from the men's scuffling feet as they danced around him choosing where to strike next. He was naked. Humiliation was part of the process. He knew that. Had endured it before when his training demanded he be subjected to interrogation techniques. That had lasted a week. How long had he been in this room? He tried to recollect how many beatings he had taken. After every session, they dragged him into a darkened room with a heavy wooden door. Before they beat him they gave him water. There was no food, but water would keep him alive. No light penetrated the room and when they came to drag him away again it was into a narrow passage with an overhead light and then once again into the interrogation room. Time and again they hurt him, always under the watchful red eye of the camera. He gave snippets of information away. Capture and torture was no time to show bravado. Keep your eyes low. Don't challenge them. Whatever information he gave them was already out of date but it showed willing.

The first time they put the blade across his throat ready for the ritual beheading he thought it was over. He was determined to fight his way to his own death but as

he willed his weakened body to prepare itself for a lunge,
the knife was withdrawn and the terrorists laughed.
Three times over as many days they repeated the threat.
On another day they hauled his arms above his head on
to a pulley attached to the roof beam and forced a yoke
of wood between his ankles. His splayed legs offered
no protection and when the terrorists ushered in half
a dozen veiled women he felt the sickening lurch in his
stomach, believing that one of the women would castrate
him. It was another attempt to break his will with further
humiliation. One of the men handed a blade to a woman
and pointed at Raglan's genitals. She stepped forward.
His heart raced. He struggled against his bonds and then
bellowed and spat a curse. A guard punched him and
then slapped him hard across the side of his head. Raglan
sucked in air but kept his eyes firmly on the woman, who
seemed to hesitate. His ears were ringing so he could
not hear what the woman said to his tormentor but she
handed back the knife. The man smiled and nodded. He
turned to Raglan and repeated what the woman had
said. She thought his private parts were too small to cut
off. Raglan almost laughed with relief. All the men who
served with him had endured the scorn of female staff
when they underwent their interrogation training. That
was their ritual. Men were taunted, badgered, threatened,
beaten and waterboarded. They were as prepared as
they could be to face the possibility of being seized and
tortured. One of his captors suddenly levelled a kick into

his balls. There was no food in his stomach to vomit but bile spewed from his throat and he passed out.

They left him alone after that. He did not know how much time passed as he lay face down in his cell. Instinct dragged him back to consciousness when he heard his captors' raised voices preparing for his execution. This time they would do it.

Raglan forced his back into the corner and pushed himself upright, determined to attack the first man who entered and do everything he could to kill him. An explosion floored him as rapid gunfire swept through the air.

He would learn later that the legionnaires had been searching for ten days. They had stopped a goatherd and noticed the combat boots he wore that could have only come from a dead or captured legionnaire. The men had their own methods of persuasion and discovered where Raglan was being held.

As they stretchered Raglan to the waiting helicopter Sokol walked alongside and held his friend's hand, just as Milosz, the big Polish commando, did on the other. Raglan was slipping away into a pain-free world from the injection the medics had administered and the beating hum of the chopper's blades almost drowned out any spoken words. In those final moments, he strained to hear what Sokol was saying.

'You look like shit,' said the Russian.

15

When the child spoke to him his whispers kept sleep
at bay. Raglan wedged a chair into a corner of his flat,
pulled a light stand close and opened a book to read.
The light comforted and the book distracted him. His
back against the wall made him safe. It was not the fear
from when he was tortured and minutes away from
being beheaded that tormented him. Nor was it the
years of violence and killing. It was the fixed stare of
the dead boy's brown eyes. The boy he had killed in the
cave. Reaching out, even in death. Asking why Raglan
had killed him. The look in those eyes as Raglan's
bullets snatched him into darkness bored into Raglan's
mind. It was not accusatory, but filled with shock and
surprise. There had been a time when alcohol blurred
the child's face, but not the words. They kept whispering
throughout the night. Raglan, held in regret's vice-like
grip, had tried to answer, wanting to know the boy's

name, wanting his forgiveness. But the boy never gave him absolution. Raglan had crawled out of the well of alcohol years before. Had kept that monster at bay ever since through sheer willpower.

Sometimes lights triggered the flashbacks. Like those down at the kidnapping scene: the angle of them as they exposed the carnage. The terrorist's knife at his throat. Their laughter. Their taunts as they took him to the edge of the abyss. The dead child led him into their arms. He had long ago reconciled himself to the thought that his torture was the boy's revenge. Raglan could go months, even a year without the haunting, and then it would return. He had learnt how to deal with it: with wakefulness and distraction. The small bookshelf in his apartment held a couple of airport thrillers from times he'd come back to London on leave. Often as not he wouldn't tell Amanda he was in town. The apartment was his own desert oasis. His quiet retreat from the pursuit of death.

Other books stood spine straight at attention, but none tempted him. There was an eclectic mix of classics, novels, biography and travel. The thriller he had chosen was set in the snow-laden north of Europe; the ambience was too cold to hold his interest. He slipped it back into place on the lower shelf. His eyes scanned other books and realized there was a gap in the tightly packed volumes. He fingered their spines, searching his memory for what was missing. Then he remembered. An old favourite. A

1940s pocket hardback, in Arabic, about the Tuareg. He had picked it up in Algeria years before on an operational tour, an insight into the culture of the nomads which helped him understand how the desert shaped them and showed him how to fight an enemy adept at being at one with their environment. His eyes scanned the room. It lay in plain sight on top of the low side cabinet, where no one would notice it except Raglan. Who had moved it? Hardly likely to be Steven. It fell open on a well-read passage and a slim bookmark slipped free. He reached to pick it up and saw it was a boarding card. First class, for Hamad International Airport, Doha, the capital city of the natural-gas- and oil-rich Qatar. It was dated two weeks ago; the passenger name was Jeremy Carter. Had he been expecting something bad to happen? If it did, he knew Maguire would send for Raglan. And he knew that Raglan would go to his flat, and being the kind of man he was would notice when something was out of place. And that's where Carter had left a message.

Qatar. Middle East Gulf States had severed diplomatic relations with Qatar when it was accused of supporting and funding terrorism. Now there was a direct link between an MI6 officer and the suspect state. And two weeks after that visit Carter was taken. Yet Maguire had not mentioned the trip, had raised no causal effect between the visit and the kidnap. Why not? Was he trying to keep Raglan out of the picture? Was the visit legitimate? Or did MI6 have a rogue agent?

The book and its content served their purpose. Raglan was distracted.

Less than a twenty-minute drive away at the demolition site the night's rain swallowed the old building. The warehouse behind the heavy gates was nothing more than a blackened shape in the darkness. Inside the lights were as harsh as those at the snatch site where Maguire and Raglan had stood on the street. The light's glare accentuated the agony of the man strapped to the chair. It highlighted the sweat dripping from Carter's face on to his heaving chest and crystallized his tears as he wept with pain. His tormentor sat close by and examined the glowing end of his cigar. He glanced at his watch and waited patiently for his victim to snort back the phlegm and recover his breathing to something that might resemble normal. Normal if agony from every nerve ending wasn't already tearing into his pain-specific neural pathways.

Carter buried himself deep inside his mind, trying to blank out the agony. The torturer's words pierced the darkness.

'Somewhere, old friend, you have hidden a list of names. A long list. Long as my arm, as you Brits say. Why do they say that, Jerry? Eh? Your list is much longer than my arm. And that list is worth serious, serious money. And I have a client who has very deep pockets.

You have hidden the magic key to those hundreds of names. Important names. Secret names. Bank accounts. Contacts. Agents and informers. What a cornucopia it must be. A gourmet's menu of delights. And I really, really need it. I bet it's encrypted somewhere. On a flash drive maybe. Or...' He raised his eyes to the ceiling. '... perhaps it's on the Cloud. Do you think the Almighty guards it? The good Lord is no firewall, Jerry. He does not give a fuck about you and me and what happens to the great unwashed. It's a game. Now, the information I want cannot be in your head. You're not that clever. Clever enough to know the pain is going to get worse though. Hey, Jeremy? A lot worse.' With a weariness borne of tedium, he blew out a column of blue smoke. Carter had slipped into unconsciousness. JD sighed and accepted the plate of food delivered by one of the gunmen.

Eddie Roman was hovering far enough away not to make himself too obvious, but his body language left no doubt he wanted to speak to the gang leader who had begun spooning food into his mouth.

'What is it, Eddie? Come over here.'

Eddie shuffled forward. At one time in his life, he would have shown more courage, but age and fear now made him subservient. 'I agreed to sort out the vehicles and gear – I did that, didn't I?'

'And a good job you made of it too.'

'I didn't know nothing about no kidnapping or

shooting at kids or any of this... stuff... this kicking the
shit out of him.'

'There is a point to all this?'

'Thing is, boss, I'm on parole, I got to report in, I didn't
know it was gonna be anything like this. I'm gonna end
up back in the nick if I don't get back to my routine and
the wife.'

'Parole was never mentioned when I employed you.
My contacts said you came highly recommended.'

'This is a high-risk gig. Bigger than I'd thought.'

'And you're being well paid for your local knowledge
and skills. Yes?'

'The money is brilliant but, tell you what I'll do, I'm
prepared to give it back. All of it. Just so I can get back
home. I want out. This is too heavy. I won't say nuthin',
that's not my style. Ask anybody. They'll all tell you
the same.'

JD finished eating and tossed aside the paper plate. He
pulled the tab on a cold drink can and raised it to his lips.
Once he had savoured the taste and run a tongue over
his teeth he levelled his gaze at an increasingly nervous
Eddie Roman. 'I think it might serve all our interests
better if you stayed,' he said flatly.

Eddie knew when a veiled threat was being made. He
nodded in surrender and turned away.

JD relit his cigar and looked at the nearest gunman
over the flame. With a nod of his head, he directed the
shooter to follow Eddie, who had made his way outside.

Then he turned his attention back to his victim. 'Wakey, wakey, Jeremy.'

Outside Eddie sheltered from the rain and drew deeply on a cigarette. It wasn't the night's cold air that made him shiver. He pressed his phone to his ear.

'Listen, girl, I can't tell you nuthin',' he whispered. 'I'll be home soon as I can... I'm all right, things have just taken a bit longer than I thought... I'm not far from home so don't fret, I promise. I'm all right.'

The gunman stepped into view. Eddie turned, aware he was being watched. Fear-riven guilt made him switch off his phone.

16

There was nothing more Raglan could do to find Jeremy Carter until Maguire fed him progress reports and Raglan had tested the water about Carter's trip to Qatar. The city had swallowed a victim and until it spat him out Raglan needed to be patient. His only other source was Abbie. He doubted there was much she could add to what he already knew but if she had picked up on something that had seemed irrelevant when she visited Carter's house or had sight of a document that Maguire had not mentioned then it was worth a couple of hours with her. He instructed the taxi driver to follow the route the police suspected the kidnapper's van had taken towards Heathrow and then turn off on to the slip road and industrial estate next to the railway line. The scarred road surface told him where the burnt-out van had been discovered and since removed by the authorities. Back on the main road, he could see how easy it was for the killers to escape. They had the choice of going in multiple directions. After going twice around the Chiswick roundabout so he could get some sense of where they were and what routes led off it, he instructed the driver to head for the airport.

The flight from Toulouse landed five minutes ahead of schedule. Raglan shadowed Abbie as she walked out of the arrivals hall at Heathrow's Terminal 5. When he allowed himself to be seen she stopped. The scowl on her face told him all he needed to know.

'I owe you an apology so I thought the least I could do is buy you breakfast and a cab ride to the office.'

She brushed past him, obliging him to step away from the wheeled case she dragged behind her.

He fell in step. 'I don't blame you for being irritated but I had to make the move so I could see what had happened for myself. I didn't need a minder.'

'Thank you for your offer,' she answered coldly. 'I phoned Mr Maguire as soon as I got out of the valley.'

'Did Sammy and Didi look after you?'

She nodded.

'Good. Then let me make it up to you for your unplanned stay with my friends.'

They reached the taxi rank and it was a long queue. She snorted in frustration. He knew she had been up since the early hours so her irritation was understandable. 'I came in a taxi. He's waiting and the meter's running.'

'Then this has been an expensive journey for you,' she said.

'In-flight breakfast is a joke. Let's grab a bite.'

'I'm not going to the office. I'm going home to shower and change.'

'So why stand here? Come on. I'll get you home.' Without waiting for her reply he grabbed the case and walked away. He ushered her into the waiting taxi and she relented, giving an address in Southall. The taxi driver told her traffic on the M4 was slow, an accident had closed down two lanes, and so he planned to use the Parkway route. Raglan wasn't familiar with the area but the exchange between the cabbie and the young woman told him she knew her way around. The driver leant his head back, listening as she gave him an alternative route to get to the address and once he got within a couple of miles to avoid certain streets. Her fluid instructions clearly impressed the driver and he and Abbie struck up a friendly conversation while Raglan sat as a silent passenger. She explained that her father had been a London taxi driver and when he'd taken to the streets on his scooter all those years ago to learn the multitude of routes before sitting the examination he'd brought his only child with him on the pillion. The cabbie laughed and congratulated her. If ever she needed a job he assured her she would walk the test without breaking sweat.

The two continued to share their street knowledge

until the driver pulled up outside a 1930s semi-detached house in Southall. Most of the owners in the street had paved over their front gardens to accommodate cars, but this house had a brick wall surrounding well-planted flower beds, small but colourful. Any thoughts Raglan had of questioning the girl had disappeared. He had been studiously ignored throughout the forty-minute journey. Abbie fussed in her handbag, then swore beneath her breath in frustration as she searched her pockets for her door key.

'Lost your key?' said Raglan. 'I'm fairly handy at breaking and entering.'

She cold-shouldered him and said her goodbyes to the driver. Raglan watched her ring the front doorbell. So this wasn't her own house – probably shared, given the price of accommodation in London. Raglan saw where she got her looks from when a handsome white woman in her fifties opened the door and hugged her. Mother and daughter shared a common beauty. So, she was still living at home with her parents. Raglan ignored the driver's request for his next destination and told him to wait. Abbie's mother asked her something but Raglan did not hear what, or Abbie's answer. With an anguished look, Abbie half turned to face his way. Her mother smiled and gestured Raglan to join them: home-grown hospitality frustrating Abbie's desire to get away. He paid the taxi driver, with a generous tip, and stepped on to the pavement.

Abbie introduced him to her mother through near-clenched teeth. The older woman's quiet dignity impressed him as she clamshelled his hand between her own and dipped her head in greeting. Her lilting Scottish accent made him feel even more welcome. Abbie made her excuses and heaved her case upstairs. Her mother, perturbed by her daughter's sudden departure, guided Raglan to the sitting room where a heavy-set bearded man wearing a black turban sat in a wheelchair. Despite the blanket draped over his lap it was obvious he had no legs. He lowered the book he was reading to greet the surprise guest.

'I heard Abnash's voice,' he said in honey-rich tones, glancing from his wife to the stranger in his home and then back to his wife again.

'She's here and she's brought a friend,' she said.

Raglan stepped forward, extending his hand. 'I'm Raglan,' he said.

'I am Abnash's father, but you have guessed that already. My name is Jal and you have already met my wife, Jean.'

'I don't mean to disturb you,' Raglan said by way of apology. He could not help feeling he was intruding.

Abbie's father raised a hand stopping any need for an apology. 'Please, it's not often we get visitors. You're welcome. Sit, please.' He turned off the radio. 'Jean, where is she?'

'She's having a quick shower, she'll be down in a

minute.' Abbie's mother turned to Raglan. 'You'll have tea with us?'

'I'm all right, thank you. Please don't go to any trouble.'

She smiled. 'Oh, no trouble at all.'

The two men sat in silence, neither of them wishing to initiate small talk. After five minutes Jal Khalsa's desire to be hospitable obliged him to break the ice. 'I don't know what's keeping her.' He sighed. 'How long does it take to boil a kettle?' There was no answer from his guest. 'So, you are a friend of my daughter's?' he went on, fixing his eyes on Raglan. 'A good friend?'

Raglan didn't mind being gently interrogated by the girl's father. The man was probing. Fair enough. Why wouldn't he? 'We only met recently. We work together.'

Mr Khalsa nodded. 'So you too are in administration at the Department of Transport?'

Abbie obviously had a cover story for her family. 'Yes. I spend a lot of time on the road.'

'Did she ever tell you how she got such an important job? It was because when she was a very young girl I used to take her on my scooter when I did the Knowledge. Do you know what that is, Mr Raglan?'

'Yes, sir. I do. It's an amazing feat of memory learning.'

'It is. I drove a taxi for twenty years. I told her, "Listen, my girl, you can earn a very good income from driving a black cab in London. You should sit the test." But she is an independently minded woman who would rather do what she thinks is the right thing for her. I don't blame her, of course. It is how we brought her up. To think for herself.' He settled his gaze on Raglan. His voice lowered. 'And we have no problem if she wishes to marry someone who is not of my religion or race. It is difficult, we know that.' He gave a nod towards his absent wife. 'When we fell in love the community turned against us. It was hell for a long time. Death threats even. But after some years they accepted us. And I refused to move away from here. This is our home.'

Raglan heard the note of defiance in Mr Khalsa's voice. A Sikh marrying a white woman thirty years ago could not have been an easy journey. 'That's very commendable, sir. But, as I said, I don't know your daughter very well. We are work colleagues. I only met her a couple of days ago.'

'Oh? No romantic inclination then?' he asked bluntly.

'No, sir.'

Raglan suspected there was a hint of regret. Maybe he wanted his daughter married off.

Abbie towelled dry her hair, dragged a broad-toothed comb through it and quickly dressed. She had left Raglan alone with her father for too long. A lot could be said in twenty minutes and anxiety added urgency to her actions. Pulling on her sweater she clattered down the stairs and heard men's laughter coming from the lounge.

As she reached the room she saw her father smiling broadly, clearly pleased to have male company for once. It was obvious her mother had deliberately left them alone so the two men could talk.

'Where did you meet?' her father was asking Raglan.

Abbie's entrance interrupted Raglan before he could answer, which was just as well because if the girl's parents did not know where she really worked then odds were she had not told them that she had gone to deepest darkest France in search of an ex-legionnaire. Where had she been? She glanced at Raglan, gave a barely perceptible shake of her head, then bent and kissed her father.

'My girl, there you are. At last. I was just telling Mr Raglan how you got such an important job in the civil service.'

'Let's not bore Mr Raglan, Daddy. I have to get to the office. I brought Mr Raglan down from Manchester with me.'

Raglan was thankful he hadn't had a stab at it.

Her mother entered with a tea tray. Raglan quickly got to his feet and took it from her. She instructed him to set it down on the coffee table.

'Mother, I must get back to work,' Abbie protested.

'There is always time for a cup of tea,' her mother chided her. She smiled at Raglan. 'Sugar?'

17

Eddie Roman's stomach lurched. The noise from the nearby metal-crushing plant muted the cries of the tortured man, now bent double in the chair. Despite the cold, sweat sluiced from him. He sucked lungfuls of air to subdue the pain and focus his mind. When he threw back his head and bellowed in defiance Eddie could take it no longer. He went to the door. One of the gunmen stopped him.

'Mother of God,' Eddie hissed, 'this is inhuman. Inhuman.' He shook his head unbelievingly. That he was a part of this sickened him.

'Relax, Eddie,' said JD. 'We'll be moving soon. Have you checked all the vehicles?'

Eddie trembled. The stone-faced man next to him showed no trace of emotion and the torturer chewed the last bite of a juicy apple, wiped his hands on his jeans and tossed away the core. Eddie nodded.

'Check them again,' said JD. 'We want everything to run smoothly. It's all about timing. The police will find this place sooner or later. All right, Eddie? Are you OK with that? This unpleasantness will soon be over. We're depending on you, you know that. You've done a great job so far. Hold your nerve a little longer. Yes?'

Eddie felt as though he was the family pet that had been patted on the head and given a treat. The man's voice held nothing but contempt for him even though he had tried to disguise it. Eddie nodded. What else could he do? He was thankful to leave the fetid confines of the room and get back outside to check the car he had stolen the previous week. It was an old turbo-charged Saab, a hefty bit of metal that could shunt lesser cars aside if needs be, and a doddle to steal.

Jeremy Carter shook the sweat from his eyes. 'How long... have I been here?'

'You have plans?' JD reached out and wiped his victim's face with a cloth. True to his skills and temperament, the torturer was impervious to the pain he was inflicting.

'How long?' Carter insisted.

'For what difference it will make, two days.'

Carter struggled to find some spittle in his mouth; it was dry with congealed blood. 'I saved your life once... you've betrayed me.'

JD edged his chair closer. 'And I owe you. Which is why, when you give me what I want, we'll finish it quickly. Promise. But betrayal? No, no, that implies loyalty. I was never loyal. I was employed.' Then he stood and wheeled over an intravenous drip stand with a clear bottle hanging from it. 'Now, I'm going to hook you up to an IV because I need to keep you alive a while longer. What's going to happen to you is brutal. No, worse than that, old friend, it's medieval.' He found a vein in Carter's arm, inserted a cannula and then attached the drip-feed tube. 'Two days is really too long for you to hold out. In truth, I didn't expect you to last twenty-four hours. So you can see my predicament. Time is against us both. Hang on in there, Jeremy, but start talking.'

He hovered a switchblade below Carter's damaged eye. The jocularity was gone. 'When an eye is that swollen it's best to cut into it and release the pressure. Jeremy, I need to know what I need to know.'

Carter desperately tried to hang on to his courage as with a terrifying gesture of intent his tormentor de-cored a fresh apple.

'All right... all right...' he whispered. 'There's a place...'

Abbie swung her small city car expertly through the traffic, cutting down side streets as she circumvented known areas of traffic jams.

'So you noticed nothing unusual in Carter's house during the search?' said Raglan. 'No documents that might suggest his involvement in anything out of the ordinary?'

She had agreed to drive him back into town. Her parents' generosity had given her no choice. 'You know I can't talk to you.'

'Maguire won't mind. Why do you think he sent you? One of the reasons was he knew that at some stage, either then or now, I would ask. If he hasn't briefed you on selling me a given set of answers then he knows that you know nothing. Are you really a technical analyst?'

'Of course,' she answered a bit too defensively.

He noticed the brief look of panic in her eyes and her knuckles whitened on the wheel. A rush of guilt from a woman not used to lying. Definitely not an operational MI6 officer. Certainly a desk jockey of some description. Likely to be a woman with inherent skills needed by the Service. But computers? His instinct told him otherwise. She could be useful once he found out more. Peeling away secrets always revealed a more attractive truth than that being offered on the surface. It was worth appealing to a different side of her nature.

'Why don't you help me in all of this?'

She glanced at him and then looked back to the traffic. 'Sammy said you don't work with anyone. That you are some kind of a loner who works out the problem and gets a result. Why would you want me to help you?'

'You came to France; you did what was asked of you. Now you're driving me back to town. Isn't this better than sitting staring at a screen all day? This place has gone nuts since I was here a couple of years ago. All this construction and the weight of traffic. I don't know how anyone manages. I need a driver.'

'Mr Maguire would never allow it.'

There it was. That note of hope. A brief spark in her mind that her boss might let her in on an operation. Raglan knew he could reel her in.

'Maguire needs my help. I need yours. If you want it, I'll ask.'

He sensed part of her came a step closer. A nervous fawn approaching a concealed trap. 'I don't want you asking any more questions about me or my family.'

'Of course. I simply need you to navigate London for me.'

She said nothing for a few moments. Then she nodded. 'All right. If Mr Maguire says it's OK, then I'll be your driver.'

A car hooted behind them, as someone cut in. He saw that the cut and thrust of the traffic distracted her.

'*Allah yarham waldik,*' he said, thanking her.

'*Walidina u walidik,*' she answered without hesitation.

It took a couple of seconds for her to realize he had tricked her into speaking Arabic. She darted a glance at him.

Raglan smiled. 'Just checking,' he said.

'You're more devious even than I took you to be,' she said bitterly.

'Abbie, we're trying to find the man. He's got a family. It's no good those of us searching for him having an agenda. You're a linguist. French, Arabic. What else? Any Russian?'

She checked her mirrors, clicked on the indicator and swung the car down a side street. 'Some Russian. Not much.'

'And the Arabic?'

'My grandfather served in the army in North Africa during the war and he taught my father – and he taught me.'

'And Maguire wanted you to keep listening to me and my friends because of where the Legion spent a lot of its time. If we said anything interesting between ourselves you were to report back.'

'Yes.'

'We're old hands at being spied on by outsiders. Did we say anything interesting?'

'A few complimentary comments they thought I couldn't understand.' Her game was up so there was no point feeling sore about it. 'They said some nice things. I could've pulled. There were some good-looking blokes there.'

Raglan grinned. 'Dating ex-legionnaires can spoil a girl's reputation.'

'Who said anything about dating? I don't need marriage proposals to have some fun,' she said with a straight face. 'All right. Where to?'

★

Amanda Reeve-Carter appeared calm despite her obvious fatigue. Her red-rimmed eyes looked as sore as the rawness in her heart. Raglan dropped the holdall he was carrying and embraced her. Amanda nodded politely to Abbie. Before the grieving woman could ask, Raglan shook his head. There was no word. Not yet. The armed police were still in place outside the house and inside additional panic buttons had been installed. The family could still be targeted, their safety used as a threat against Carter.

'There's coffee,' she said. 'I'm still clearing up after Maguire and his people turned the place upside down.'

'Where's Steve?' said Raglan.

'In his room.' Amanda looked wearily from one to the other. 'If you're here to commiserate, don't. The line of work you and Jeremy are in doesn't leave much room for sympathies.'

Her bitterness was understandable, but he wanted to distract her by doing something positive. 'Mandy, I brought Abbie with me to help you tidy up things in Jeremy's office. Sometimes there are obvious things that people miss when they don't know what they're looking for.'

He saw a flicker of hope in her eyes at the lifeline he had thrown her. 'Have you discovered something?'

'Only that Jeremy went to Qatar a couple of weeks ago.'

The cloud of uncertainty settled again. 'No, he went to Europe for a banking conference.'

Raglan placed his hands on her shoulders. He would uncover the lies one by one. 'He went to the Middle East and I want to find out why.'

Her grief forced her frustration to boil over. 'You men and your bloody stupid egos. It's not a game! Can't any of you see that? Selfish bastards! You too. You left without a word when you were a kid. You had a future. A bright shining star of a future and you ran off because of what happened. You didn't have the courage to stay and see it through.'

'I was on the wrong side of the tracks by then, remember?'

Amanda softened. Her hand touched his cheek. 'You broke my mother and father's heart, you know. They grieved for you.' She wiped a hand across her tears. 'But they were always proud of what you achieved.' She shrugged. 'I'll be here if you want me.' She turned and walked away into the living room where there were still piles of books and pictures stacked on the floor that had been taken down when Maguire's people searched the house.

Raglan picked up the holdall. 'See if you can help her,' he told Abbie. 'If she prefers to be alone, grab a coffee and wait for me in the kitchen, but check out the study again.' He jogged upstairs and moments later she heard him knock on a door and call the boy's name.

Raglan sat down on the end of Steve's bed as the boy turned from where he sat at his desk. 'Homework?' said Raglan.

Steve nodded. 'Trying to keep myself busy. I wish I could get back to school.'

'You can't. Not yet. Even if I arranged armed protection we daren't risk another attack. If they get you or anyone else in the house it's leverage against your dad.'

The boy nodded, shoulders slumped. 'I know I can't. Not with Mum and Melissa alone in the house.'

'Your mum is a tough lady, but she's got a lot to deal with and Melissa doesn't understand any of this so that's where your mother's attention needs to be. The cops will want to interview you. You can handle that. You've already been debriefed by me, so you can keep it simple with them. They lean on you; you walk away. Call me and I'll sort it.' Raglan opened the bag and took out the cleaned-up rugby ball. 'I know your dad gave you this, so I figured it was special and that you'd like it back.'

The boy was subdued as he sat down on the bed next to Raglan and cradled the ball. 'Have you heard anything?'

'No. And I promise you will be the first to know when I do.' He studied the boy's body language. The athletic young man seemed diminished, his body folding in on itself. 'We should go for a run sometime. You and me. Get some air in our lungs. What do you say?'

Steve raised his chin and nodded bravely but Raglan could see he wouldn't be able to hold on to his composure much longer as tears welled in his eyes. Such sorrow would take a long time to ease and by the look of it he had been holding it together for the sake of his mother and baby sister. Raglan hesitated for only a second. Either the kid had to tough it out and suck up the pain or he needed a safe place to release it. Raglan put an arm around him and pulled the teenager to him. 'Let it go, mate. Trust me. It's OK.'

Steven finally released the bottled-up tension and sobbed into Raglan's shoulder. His body shuddered as he clung desperately to the veteran legionnaire, seeking refuge in the strong man's embrace.

18

Nothing stays the same. The Watergate at a corner of the Victoria Embankment Gardens next to the River Thames was built in the early seventeenth century by the Duke of Buckingham as an entrance to the river. The mighty river's waterline has receded over the centuries and now the gate sits a hundred metres from the water's edge. Intelligence operations shifted more rapidly. Maguire sat in one of the deck chairs in front of the bandstand where a Salvation Army brass band played a mournful rendition of 'Abide with Me'.

Those who walked through the park were muffled against the crisp autumn air and chill breeze off the river. Maguire wore an overcoat over his suit. 'You've a damned neck on you, Raglan. She's a bloody linguist, not your personal taxi driver,' he complained.

Maguire had called Raglan at the Carters' and they had arranged to meet. Raglan had left Steve Carter in better shape than when he had found him. The cathartic release of pent-up emotions had given the boy the focus he needed.

'She's useful. I don't know the city that well and if I need to get somewhere fast then she can find the quickest route.' Raglan waited for further complaint. Abbie and Raglan had found no further clues in Carter's study, but he had seen how efficiently she worked. He wanted to keep her onside.

Maguire scowled. 'I have other assets who can do that. She'll get in the way.'

'I don't care whether or not you give her to me but your field officers are put to better use chasing down Carter's kidnappers. Any leads?'

'No. We are tracing all known associates since he worked in the bank—'

'You need to go back further,' Raglan interrupted.

'—and further back,' continued Maguire, irritated. 'Whatever he's done is in plain sight or so hidden we could never find it. And there's another complication. I've had a meeting with a police liaison officer for Europol. There's been an approach from the Russians.'

'Their security people?'

'No. Moscow CID.' The final chords of 'Abide with Me' faded. Maguire got to his feet. 'Russian police officers are not permitted to make direct contact with any European police force. Most embassies in Russia have a police liaison officer. It cuts corners. Helps find a way through red tape. Supposedly. Sometimes it does, more often not. These people usually have more than one role to play. They're required to be experts in PR, legal and, of course, spying. We lost our liaison privileges in Moscow when we demanded the Russians turn over those blokes who poisoned Litvinenko back in 06. This is a strange one, though. Their police made the request through the Dutch; they, in turn, contacted our Met counter-terrorism people.'

'And they've come to you,' said Raglan.

'Yes, but with the restrictions placed on the Russians, any contact has to first be cleared by their Ministry of the Interior, and the MVD is not known for speedy action. Makes our bureaucracy seem like private enterprise by comparison. But this had a priority clearance.'

They reached the garden's cafe. Maguire ordered and paid for two takeaway coffees, tucking the receipt away in his wallet. That said a lot about being a government employee. He turned to watch the people coming and going in the gardens as Raglan played waiter, sugared the coffee and handed the paper cup to Maguire.

'So what's the connection?' said Raglan.

'Obviously, something to do with our kidnapper, I would have thought. The Russian police departments are highly competitive. They jealously guard their patch because the more arrests they make, the more they get paid. But this might be more than we suspect. It is not unusual for the Russians to use Europol to hunt down people they want. Easy enough to declare someone a major criminal or terrorist and, with our help, have him tracked, detained and deported right back to whoever wants them dead.'

'So they might want JD as a criminal?'

'We'll soon find out. They've sent a major from Moscow CID. Until they feel more comfortable with us they prefer a meeting outside. Somewhere it's less likely they can be recorded.' Maguire sipped his coffee. 'It's a gesture, of course.' He glanced up at the buildings rising above the trees. 'They know I have people up on those roofs watching and listening.'

'The meet is here? Am I going to meet this Russian cop?'

'No, you're not. Not yet anyway. Not until I know what's going on.'

'Hell might freeze over before that happens, Maguire.'

Maguire had the grace to smile at the sarcasm. You don't spend the better part of your life as a soldier and not give and take insults. The armed forces don't breed snowflakes. Maguire screwed up his face at the taste of the coffee, poured it away and dumped the paper cup into a bin. 'Sit your arse on that bench and wait ten minutes. I'm meeting her and the Met boys—'

'Her?'

'Major Elena Sorokina.'

★

The coffee was strong and sweet. Raglan liked it. It was the way he used to drink it in the souk. He watched two men and a woman approach Maguire, who sat on another park bench fifty metres away. The men wore jeans and leather jackets over hooded fleeces. Pretty much standard dress for cops who worked the streets. The woman, by contrast, wore a tailored charcoal suit over a white blouse. She made no concession to the chill breeze. It was probably high summer compared to Moscow, thought Raglan. Her hair was coal black and she was as tall as the men. Long legs, firm body. She didn't smile when she extended her hand to Maguire. This wasn't a social occasion. Business all the way. Raglan saw the unmistakable shape of a semi-automatic pistol in a black clamshell holster on her hip. That meant she had special clearance. Top-drawer special. The two counter-terrorism Met officers backed off and left the MI6 section chief and the Moscow cop alone. Maguire sat on one end of the bench, the Russian on the other. Raglan could see that Maguire was listening. He was good at that. Absorbing the flow of information, filtering fragments that were less important, ignoring any political smokescreens, but this conversation seemed to be direct and to the point. After a couple of minutes, the Russian cop stood up and extended her hand again. Maguire got to his feet and as their hands clasped, she looked right past Maguire to where Raglan sat. She'd clocked him. The woman was no fool.

Raglan waited for Maguire. 'Well?' he asked. 'Am I in on this?'

Maguire fussed the scarf at his neck. It looked as though he was deciding. 'I have to check this out first. I don't trust Russians.'

'I don't even trust you,' said Raglan. 'And how come she's armed?'

Maguire ignored the slight. 'She has Home Office approval and the man she's after is a killer. That's why counter-terrorism is working with her as well as the Met's CID. And I'll let you know whether you're in on this,' he said, turning away. He still held the whip hand.

Raglan called after him. 'What about Abbie?'

Maguire turned. 'I'll give her a pool car. Keep her in the driving seat. Nowhere else. Anything goes down she's to be kept out of it. Understood?'

Raglan nodded. Small victories were always welcome. Win one, win them all when the time was right.

19

The entrance door to Raglan's building was ajar. There was only one other resident in the building and her door was across the landing from Raglan's apartment. Raglan saw her body lying just inside her door. Her head lay at an awkward angle. She must have buzzed in her killer. He stepped warily inside. The radio was playing classical music. A mug with a tea bag and a plate with two chocolate biscuits stood untouched next to the kettle. Raglan touched it. It was still warm. As warm as her body. She hadn't been dead long. She hadn't been expecting guests; the mug and biscuits were for her and the intruder buzzing from the main entrance had interrupted her. She'd have gone to her door to meet whoever it was. A bogus delivery most likely. And she had been killed quickly and efficiently. Her rooms were untouched. No sign of a burglary. The killer had not come to terrorize or rob an elderly actress;

he had come to gain access to Raglan's apartment opposite.

He pulled free a seven-inch Sabatier knife from the block in the kitchen and stepped over her body towards his own front door. He listened but heard nothing. Raglan spread his fingertips across the door and pressed gently. The door was locked. He traced his fingers around the frame, feeling for the hidden key. It was missing. The intruder had been told where the key was hidden. Raglan stepped back on to the landing and aimed his kick at the lock. The door burst open. He barged rapidly into the room as the man who was bent over the books on the floor staggered upright. Regaining his balance, the intruder flung a book at Raglan, who swatted it aside. The killer was quick on his feet. He half spun, crouched and suddenly had a knife in his hand. Raglan saw the automatic pistol tucked into his waistband. It told him he was an efficient knife fighter and did not wish to risk the sound of a gunshot. Raglan did not slow his attack. His left arm covered his body diagonally, protecting vital organs. The intruder lunged straight for Raglan's face and throat; Raglan pushed aside the strike and rammed his own knife forward. The man's reflexes were quick and with a counter-defence knocked aside Raglan's knife hand. Neither man hesitated and the killer struck forward again with three rapid slashes at Raglan, who blocked, swerved, attacked again and then stumbled on one of the fallen books. The knifeman did the opposite of what most amateurs would have done. He held back. Bending over and going in for the kill would have exposed the weight of his body to the downed man. Raglan rolled away, regained his footing, jabbed for the face, blocked the counter-attack, pushed hard with his free hand, forced aside the muscular knife-wielding arm and smashed the pommel of the knife and the side of his fist behind the man's ear. It would have stunned most men but this one absorbed and ignored the pain and danced on his toes away from Raglan's impending follow-up strike. Neither man had gained the upper hand and the killer never took his eyes off Raglan's.

Raglan took fast short steps like a boxer, jabbing so rapidly the man could not block all of his blows, yet he managed to slip his blade beneath Raglan's defensive arm, and Raglan felt its edge cut into the flesh on his waist. The strike carried the man's weight on to his left foot and Raglan pushed hard with his free hand, forcing the man's body away from him, and then plunged his knife beneath the man's raised arm, burying the blade into his armpit. He bellowed in pain and dropped his weapon, but spun quickly around, toppling on to the sofa. His left hand grappled the gun in his waistband as Raglan followed the attack through and levelled a kick against the man's head. Bones snapped. His body slumped. He was dead. Raglan tested the small gash in his side and stepped into the bathroom to find a dressing.

*

By the time the police and Maguire arrived Raglan had attended to his wound with antiseptic, closed it with butterfly strips and taped a dressing over the three-inch cut. He had checked the man's weapon was fully loaded and tucked it into a holdall along with the one change of clothes he kept in the flat. It was unlikely Maguire would ever let him go armed on the streets of London, but now Raglan didn't need to ask. The polymer and steel GSh-18 held eighteen rounds and was often used by Russian special forces or SWAT teams.

'Any reason you were targeted?' asked Maguire.

'Carter is alive,' Raglan told him.

Maguire looked at the sprawled body. 'He told you that?'

Raglan shook his head. 'Carter has held out longer than he should have. He told his son to stay here and wait for me. If I didn't show he was to go home after two days. That gave Carter every chance that I would be here to deal with things. He wouldn't have given up this place if he thought his son was still here. Carter has just bought himself more time by giving up some information.'

Maguire stepped around the body again, looking at the scattered books and the floor splattered with blood. A dark stain had seeped into the sofa's upholstery. 'And he was looking for what exactly?'

'Nothing,' said Raglan. 'Carter was throwing them a bone, drip-feeding information until we could find him.'

'Which we could have done if you hadn't killed this one.'

'He didn't give me any choice. I found a boarding pass in one of the books. Carter must have planted it here days ago before I even got here.'

'For where?'

'Qatar.'

Maguire showed no surprise. 'You think that was what they were looking for?'

'No, I told you, Carter bought himself some respite by sending them here. The boarding pass was meant for me to find. His wife has no idea that he went there. What's the connection, Maguire?'

'That's on a need-to-know basis.'

'I'm either in on this or I'm not. Tell me or I'll walk now and do my own investigation.'

Maguire hesitated but Raglan saw the decision being made. 'Not now, later when more of the pieces come together. You have my word.'

Raglan knew it was not the time or place. He nodded. Now there was a better understanding between them.

'Any identification at all?' said Maguire, turning his attention back to the dead man.

'Nothing. His jacket has a German label. The boots are American army. Probably got them at a US Army PX in Germany.'

'We'll check what we can but it won't be worth anything. He'll be ex-military.'

'Probably special forces. He knew how to use a knife and take a hit.'

'We'll run him through the system. See what connections we can make.'

'He'll be the hired help. One of them at least.'

One of the detectives appeared in the doorway. 'Sir, I need my people in here.'

Maguire nodded. 'We're finished here, inspector. Thank you.' He glanced around the flat. 'Nice place, Raglan. Until now at least. You can't stay here; it's a crime scene. Grab yourself a change of clothes and I'll put you in a room somewhere.'

Raglan grinned. 'I can find my own fleabag hotel.'

'I need to know where you are. You might end up in a police custody cell unless I get clearance for you to walk away from this. This is London, not the fucking desert. Killing people in your own flat will take some explaining.'

'Who said this was my place? I came to see an old friend across the hall. I found her body, saw this guy in here. He attacked me.' He stared down Maguire. 'There's no record of me owning this flat. If there was a change of clothes there aren't any more. I guess the police will discover that it's owned by some French guy. That's who pays the bills.'

Maguire's phone rang. He turned to Raglan. 'You need to get to the medics and have that wound looked at.'

'I've done that. No need.'

'Basic stuff, Raglan. You need a tetanus shot.'

'All up to date. You never know when you might stand on a rusty nail.'

Maguire sighed. 'All right. Give them your statement. I'll wait.' He made his way through the gaggle of police officers and the forensic team who were shuffling around the two apartments and landing.

Thanks to Maguire's influence it took only an hour for Raglan to be questioned and to give his statement. They quickly saw it to be self-defence and allowed him to leave pending further investigation. Carrying the small holdall, he joined Maguire in the street below. Both men knew the flat was of no use to him now. The main road had been cordoned off, creating an almighty traffic jam. Police cars, outrider motorcycles and an ambulance shared the narrow street. Two unmarked cars full of armed response officers completed the cut-off area. He saw Abbie standing next to a pool car in the taped-off perimeter twenty metres away from where Maguire stood with two younger men. They wore an agent's street uniform. Leather jackets, jeans and trainers. Similar to Raglan, except he preferred weatherproof trail boots, lightweight and with rubber soles for purchase that gave him a kicking advantage in a fight. One of the two men sported a quilted gilet beneath the leather jacket. Bystanders were being moved on as uniformed officers and detectives began questioning shopkeepers. There would be CCTV footage somewhere showing the killer arriving. There wouldn't be any of him leaving.

Maguire beckoned Raglan to him. 'We've got a break. An elderly resident at the kidnap scene on Weltje Road approached the men in the van before the shooting started. The driver was reading an old edition of a daily newspaper. Several days old. Our witness asked if he could have the paper when he'd finished. He uses old papers for his cat's litter tray. The driver handed it over.'

Raglan waited for the punchline. An old newspaper taken from the ambush didn't seem to offer much information. 'Did the cops get to it before the cat?'

'Apparently, they did.'

'It can't be as simple as having the address written on it for the paper delivery from the local shop.'

'No, a bit more complicated than that. Some newspapers, including this one, print a unique number on each copy that can be used for competitions for reader loyalty and reward programmes. This number identifies the print site, what time that copy was printed and the lorry that took it to the wholesaler.'

'I'm guessing there are more than a few copies printed,' said Raglan.

'Yes, initially that was a problem, forty to fifty thousand copies in this case and the paper wasn't prepared to give out any more information than that. They identified the wholesale depot, which wasn't much help, but then the coppers promised the paper a scoop on this story so they rifled their files. If a customer used their unique number to enter a competition or take up an offer of any kind then their name and address would be known. What we needed was a breach of data security but arm-twisting and promises go a long way.'

Then you have an address?' said Raglan.

'Yes, they wrote in for a dozen packets of seeds at half price. The house is in Brentford.'

20

Eddie Roman's wife was defiant.

Her Eddie was on the straight and narrow. And no she didn't know where he was. Not right now. Not this minute. He was on a job. He did delivery work these days. The police warrant gave them the authority to search the modest three-bedroomed house. A police inspector handed her a folded newspaper encased in a plastic evidence bag.

'Eddie's not been around for a while has he, Shelley? Not like him to miss a Saturday night down the pub, which he did last Saturday. This is your house number and this is the newspaper that's delivered here every day. Is that correct?'

Shelley Roman's face sagged. She nodded and sat heavily into an armchair.

The inspector turned to the two men waiting in the

doorway behind him. Maguire nodded. He'd take over the questioning now.

'Thank you, inspector. See what your search turns up. Mrs Roman, I am a government official. Make no mistake as to the seriousness of our investigation. A man was murdered, another kidnapped. You have seen the news and read the papers. This newspaper was taken from the van driver where those events took place.'

The colour drained from her face.

'When was the last time you heard from your husband?'

Shelley Roman was torn between telling the truth and fearing that her answers would further implicate her husband. 'Eddie? He phoned me… last night. It was last night.' She nodded. 'He said he couldn't talk but that he'd be home soon.'

'That's all he said?'

She nodded dumbly. Her hand trembled as she reached for a pack of cigarettes and lit one. 'Jesus, Eddie, what have you done.'

'Mrs Roman, your husband is known to the police, he is on parole and in the past has been a driver for various robberies. Is there anyone else he would have confided in?'

'No. Eddie kept himself to himself. He never gabbed to no one. That's why people trusted him to work with.'

Maguire watched her for a moment. Taking a brief pause during interrogation allowed extra doubt to creep into the mind of those being questioned. 'He is not a violent man, we know that—'

'Eddie wouldn't hurt nobody. It's not in him. He's a driver is all,' she blurted.

'But the men he is with are... brutal.' Maguire let the word hang. 'Your husband is likely to be in extreme danger himself.'

She gasped. Her hand trembled.

'Did he say anything at all that might help us locate him?'

She nodded. 'Said he wasn't far from home... that's all. That there'd been a complication, that things were taking longer than expected.'

Maguire reached for the mobile phone on the coffee table. 'On this phone?'

She nodded. Maguire turned to the police inspector orchestrating the search. 'He'll no doubt be using a pay-as-you-go. See what you can trace from last night. We might get the nearest tower and location.' He turned back to Eddie's wife. 'The police'll caution you. Do you understand what that means?'

Again, she nodded. This was familiar territory for the wife of an ex-con and local villain.

'What legitimate work has he done over the past few months?'

She shrugged. 'This and that.'

'Specifically.'

'Did a newspaper drop, and then picked up delivery work. He spent a few months driving for the road people, y'know, the highway maintenance gangs, but he didn't fancy that much so he thought he might go back to being a porter at the hospital. Especially with winter coming on.'

'When did he work at the hospital?'

'Last year.' She ground out the cigarette. 'He never told me nuthin' at all about his business. He tried to go straight a million bloody times but he just couldn't help himself. Stupid. Bloody stupid.'

Raglan followed Maguire outside. He had remained silent during the questioning. 'That explains how they got the maintenance vehicle. And a local villain would know local places. Check the hospital. If they're going to move Carter they might have used her husband's inside knowledge to steal an ambulance.'

'Good thought,' said Maguire and beckoned one of his team over.

Raglan turned towards Abbie and her car. 'Pass on whatever you get. I'll have a sniff around the area. The burnt-out van is ten minutes from here. What if they stayed close to home?'

'You suspect anything, call it in. I don't want you playing fast and loose.'

'Then why bring me in? I'm off the books. I'm unaccountable.'

★

Abbie eased the car along the narrow lane where the van had burnt. She had not spoken of the incident at his flat. Maguire had told her what had happened and asked if she wanted to be excused duty. She had put a brave face on it and said she would stay as Raglan's driver. Maguire almost pulled her off the job but knew that if anyone could get Raglan around the city in a hurry it was Abbie.

As she drove a part of her shuddered at the thought that the man who sat calmly at her side had been involved in a fight to the death. She knew it had injured him, but he gave no sign of being hurt. The contrast between the man's self-control and what had gone on a few hours earlier confused her. She acknowledged she would never understand what made men and women throw themselves into danger. Raglan asked her to stop, got out of the car and walked into the container storage yard. A packing crate stood next to the nearest twenty-foot shipping container. Raglan used the pallet to clamber on to the roof. He scanned the horizon. A helicopter patrol would have been of more use, but they could not waste police resources hovering over different parts of London on guesswork alone. He had no sense of where they could have hidden Carter. Everything had moved fast over the past forty-eight hours but he didn't know the city well enough to make even an educated guess. Which, he acknowledged, was why JD had paid Eddie Roman for his expertise. One thing was certain. Where Carter was being held wasn't a house and it wasn't somewhere that would have any kind of security patrols near or around it. It would be in plain sight where everyday life went on. Somewhere run down where rough-looking men wouldn't look out of place. A narrow road like the one he gazed over now would have been the kind of place he'd use. It was a nowhere road. There was no traffic using it. It had to be a similar place that the killers had chosen. He let himself down and went back to the car.

'You have a smartphone? Mine's only a burner.'

She handed him her phone. Raglan keyed in their location and brought up a map of the area, zooming in on narrow streets, searching for anywhere that looked desolate.

'If the driver was close to home then we'll start from here.'

Abbie put the car in gear. 'It's a wild goose chase, Raglan.'

'Then go back to your cubicle and stare at a screen and chase down terrorists posting on social media. You wanted this; don't pretend you didn't.' He could see she didn't enjoy being reprimanded. 'This is for grown-ups. It's not something you read about or watch on the news; it's happening and you're part of it. We can bitch and moan later when it's done. I want to find Carter alive and discover what he and Maguire were up to. Is that clear enough? Make your mind up.'

She drove smoothly, without anger. 'They were wrong about you, Raglan. They told me you don't say much. You must have just used up a whole year's worth of conversation.'

Raglan kept the smile of satisfaction to himself. Abbie wasn't going to be cowed, which was exactly what he'd needed to establish.

She drove in and out of the various small lanes that led off the Great West Road dual carriageway. The areas they entered were too exposed for the killers to remain undetected for any length of time. 'We're not that far from your parents' place,' said Raglan as he checked the map. Southall was due north of their location. 'If we had the time we could call in for a cup of chai.'

'Did my mother's Indian brew come as a shock? It's an acquired taste if you're not used to it,' she said as she swung back on to the main road.

'No, I've had it before.' Raglan didn't mind her loosening up – it would make her feel closer to the heart of the operation – but it wasn't the time for idle conversation. He was concentrating on his immediate surroundings and searching ahead for anywhere they might be holding Carter. 'Where are we now?'

'Hounslow,' she answered. 'There are a lot of industrial units around here. Where next?'

He looked at the busy road. If Eddie Roman had told his wife he was close to home was that simply a figure of speech? He scoured the map again. The Syon private hospital was a few hundred metres further along the road and would be ideal if they had injured Carter in the attack. Could there be any way JD had got his people into the private hospital? The killers had torched one van. There would be another, but if JD was planning a quick move to another location he'd need fast cars. Raglan felt a growing sense of desperation. When he had been kidnapped and tortured his men had worked day and night to find him. And they had found him moments before his death. 'Go back in the direction we came,' he said.

She gave him a questioning look.

'Just do it. This doesn't feel right. Get across the other side of the dual carriageway. There are two narrow lanes into an industrial estate.'

His phone rang. It was Maguire. 'They tracked the phone signal. There's a private hospital on the A4—'

'I'm there now,' said Raglan, raising a hand to stop Abbie from driving forward.

'That's the base tower, two more in the distance ahead. He's somewhere there. I'm sending backup.'

Raglan pointed. 'Get across there now. Fast. Cut across the traffic. Ignore the lights. Go. Go.'

She fluffed the gear change but quickly did as he told her. Once across the dual carriageway, she flicked on her indicator to turn left.

'Not this one. The next.' Raglan never ignored instinct. His was a sixth sense honed over the years. An early warning system that had saved lives, including his own.

Abbie took the curve and then braked as the road narrowed. They drove slowly along what was an unimportant route for heavy goods vehicles; the area was very overgrown – the bushes couldn't have been cut for years. She pulled over as a ten-metre-long heavy haulage lorry took precedence on the narrow lane, its company name telling them it was hauling stone aggregate. Raglan saw the ribbed structure of what looked like a stone-crushing plant rising above the treeline. The road ahead fish-tailed. Left to the plant and right to a scrap-metal-recycling unit.

'Stop here.'

Abbie looked around the desolate area.

'There,' said Raglan, pointing to the closed gates of the abandoned factory. 'That's where I'd go. Hidden behind those gates but with quick access out on to a fast dual carriageway. Stay here.'

Raglan was out of the door before she could argue. She watched as he tugged out a weapon from the back of his belt. Her heart skipped a beat. She had no idea Raglan was armed. It was no longer the kind of anxiety she had felt going into the French hamlet; this was fear.

She picked up her phone from the seat and called Maguire.

21

Raglan skirted the fencing, saw enough to convince him that there was no one in sight and clambered over the fence. At a crouching run, he went to the main building. Two doors were open on the other side of the yard exposing empty garaging. He knew that the killers had already gone. There was always the chance that a rearguard had remained behind so he edged along the main building, found a side door and pressed down the door handle. He burst in, not giving anyone inside time to react. He levelled the semi-automatic, sweeping the abandoned room, watching for any shift in light that would show movement from a hidden gunman. Then he skirted the room, ignoring the detritus that had been left behind. He checked the doorway into another side room; the stench of a blocked toilet led him to a small annexe where a bucket sat next to the toilet pan. The men who had been here would have taken water from the river at the back of the yard for the bucket latrine.

Raglan lowered his weapon but kept a firm grip on it. A trail of blood led across the floor to the outside. He checked the yard again and crossed to the open garages. The blood smear widened as if they had laid a body down, then it trailed again towards the mesh fence at the rear of the yard. Somewhere in the distance police sirens wailed. The cavalry was on their way. Raglan pulled aside the wire, which had already been cut, and stepped through the crushed undergrowth towards the riverbank. The shallow water was full of junk. Snagged in the tangled mess of branches, supermarket trolleys and old window frames was a man's naked body.

Forensic investigators dragged out the corpse as the police pathologist was ushered across the now cluttered yard. Police vehicles and unmarked cars from some of Maguire's people sealed off the narrow road. The body was missing its hands and the face was unrecognizable from the gunshot fired into the back of the head. Raglan went to the gate where Abbie waited uncertainly.

'Go home, Abbie. There's nothing here for you.'

'I'll wait and take you back to town.' Her eyes flitted past his shoulder to where the men were pulling what was left of the man in the river. Raglan stepped in front of her to block the gruesome view.

'Maguire's waiting for me inside. Go on, get going. I'll square it with him.'

Her smile was a mixture of gratitude and regret. She averted her face when she glimpsed the corpse.

Raglan held her shoulders, turning her so she faced the street. 'Say hello to your folks for me. You don't need any of this lodged in your mind.'

'I'll pick you up tomorrow. Where will you be?'

'I'll phone you.'

He watched her leave and then joined Maguire inside as the search teams went about their business. The two men stood amid the detritus in the factory's main room. It was plain to see where Carter had been kept and tortured. An empty saline IV bottle, a used blood-transfusion bag, hypodermic needles, dried blood on the floor, bottled water and tins of food shared the space with bloodied and dirty hand towels and a soiled pillowcase stained with vomit and blood. In the background someone was retching. Maguire glanced at the young constable from the search team who was sheepishly wiping his mouth.

'They cut out Carter's eye,' said Raglan. 'Forensics have it in an evidence bag.'

Neither man hid their disgust. 'They chopped the hands off the corpse. Pretty crude way to stop us identifying him,' said Raglan. 'They used hollow-point rounds which blew his face away. If there hadn't been so much junk in the river the body would have probably ended up in a sewer, never to be found.'

Maguire wrinkled his nose at the stench of the place. 'At least we know Carter might still be alive.'

'And Eddie Roman isn't,' said Raglan.

Maguire made three telephone calls to set up a meeting as his driver weaved his way back into the city. Several times they were caught in traffic and Maguire had to ring back and say he'd be later than planned. Raglan wished Abbie was driving.

'How many boroughs does London have?' Raglan said as he studied a map taken from the driver.

Maguire hesitated and then pulled the answer from memory. 'Thirty-two not counting the City of London which isn't technically a borough.' Maguire shrugged. 'If you want to be pedantic.'

'We need to find any abandoned buildings up for sale. Places earmarked for demolition would be my first port of call. Can you get the police to move on that?'

'That's exactly where we're going now,' Maguire said.

When they pulled up on the Victoria Embankment and Maguire instructed Raglan to follow him, the ex-legionnaire knew he was about to be given the information previously denied him. The MI6 section chief led him past a lorry-proof stone-clad concrete barrier that protected the curved glass entrance of the Metropolitan Police HQ at New Scotland Yard. Maguire showed his identification at the desk, both men signed in, and then waited to be escorted deeper into the 1930s building that loomed behind the modernized entrance.

Raglan and Maguire followed their escort through corridors showing open-plan areas where police officers worked. It was nothing like Raglan had imagined the main police headquarters to be. There were glass-fronted meeting rooms where briefings were taking place and he wondered how any secure material would be kept on a need-to-know basis given the open-plan desk stations – until their escort led them to a closed door that was anything but open-plan. As they entered Raglan saw two suited men, a senior uniformed female police officer and Major Elena Sorokina of the Moscow CID, as smartly dressed as she had been when he saw her in the park.

Introductions were brief. The uniformed police officer was the Met's Assistant Commissioner Joan Beaumont. One of the two men was Commander Tom Pickering from counter-terrorism; the other Phil Sheridan, the UK liaison officer from Europol. Raglan nodded a greeting to each of them and sat at Maguire's right hand. Major Sorokina headed the table and was clearly chairing the meeting. Maguire had introduced Raglan as an undercover officer working for his department and when the Russian asked for a situation report it was Raglan that Maguire turned to.

Raglan gave a crisp no-nonsense summation of the events of the day up to and including the discovery of where the kidnapped banker had been held and the murder and mutilation of a small-time crook who, it seemed, had supplied and driven vehicles needed in the attack. He made no mention of the attack in his apartment and the death of his assailant. Nor did he mention Carter's trip to Qatar. Whatever Maguire and Carter were involved in was an intelligence matter. He finished by suggesting that the police should begin looking for abandoned buildings in the London boroughs. It seemed the logical step to take given that Maguire believed the kidnapped man was still alive and had been moved to a new location. AC Beaumont told him that the order had already been given and that there was a team of thirty detectives working on the murder of Charlie Lewis and the abduction of Jeremy Carter and would now include the latest victim in their inquiries.

Major Sorokina listened attentively, her gaze fixed on Raglan throughout his report. He took stock of her features. It felt as though her cold, grey-blue eyes were staring into his soul. Looking, perhaps for any sign of subterfuge, hidden agenda or downright lies. Given the corruption in her country it would be something she would have to deal with on a daily basis. Her dark hair framed a face unlined by the biting cold of the Russian winters or what must be the tireless demands of her job. The eyes stayed on him even when she sat down. No warmth there, he thought. Not much chance of humour either. No laugh lines. He bet himself that she would be a hard woman to seduce even if a man had half a chance. More likely she would make the running. It must be tough for a woman to make a professional career in a place like Moscow, never mind reach the rank of major. Not so much breaking through a glass ceiling as punching through the polar ice cap. His thoughts contradicted themselves. Historically, Russian women had fought alongside their men in time of war and he imagined Elena Sorokina came from the same gene pool. Tough, determined, no-nonsense and not one to suffer fools.

Maguire poured himself a glass of water from the jug provided. 'General Sergei Ivanov is head of Moscow CID.' He glanced towards the Europol officer. 'He's worked with our European colleagues before and sometimes we have shared information through Commander Pickering's office. When General Ivanov reaches out we acknowledge it to be a matter of urgency and we welcome Major Sorokina's involvement in this matter that now presents itself.'

It was idle flattery and everyone in the room knew it. When it came to the political relationship between the agencies of the Russian Federation and the United Kingdom there needed to be some soft pedalling to ease general suspicion between the two of them. Maguire added a footnote. 'From what the major has told me in our previous meeting this matter is purely a police matter. It's an investigation set up by the Moscow police who are hunting a killer. A cop-killer.' He looked to the

Russian. 'Major, please brief us so we might see how to proceed.'

A screenshot of JD appeared on the wall behind her. It looked to be a typical police arrest picture. 'This man is Jean Delacorte. He is registered as a French national. He was also an agent for the French intelligence service, the DGSE. His real name is Yegor Kuznetsov, a Russian used by the Russian Security Service as a freelance operator.'

Raglan barely hid his smile. She noticed. 'Mr Raglan, you find something amusing?'

'Kuznetsov translates as blacksmith. Seems to me that even that might not be his real name but as a literal translation it might be appropriate, after the hammering he's given our kidnapped banker.'

'You understand Russian. And you speak it,' she said, turning that cold gaze on him again.

Raglan shrugged. 'Enough to swear and defend myself from insults,' he answered in Russian. He was gratified to see the corner of her mouth twitch. A smile in the offing. Almost.

From the folder in front of her she passed a sheet of typed notes to everyone. 'Our investigation concerns only the killing of four Moscow police officers. Two detectives and two uniformed officers went to arrest Kuznetsov six months ago and he shot them dead. He then disappeared from Moscow.' She hesitated, choosing her words carefully. 'There is no evidence that the Russian FSB aided his escape. Help has been provided by Europol because of the suspicious death of a German police officer two months ago. We believe the killings to be related as that is most likely the route chosen by Kuznetsov to enter the Eurozone.'

She glanced at Raglan as if expecting him to ask questions. Raglan remained silent. He was a guest and there was no point in stirring the pot. No one in the room had made any mention of Carter's involvement. Offered any connection to explain why he was a target. And no one had even whispered anything about Qatar. Maguire was expressionless. No hint of him having any knowledge of the wanted man. If Raglan had been sent for and was now sitting in on a need-to-know meeting then Maguire was desperate.

Sorokina said, 'The Moscow CID wants this man and we have judicial backing to take him back for trial.'

Tom Pickering was a man with few resources. Chasing a Moscow gangster who freelanced for different intelligence services was of little interest to him unless it was likely to impact on his operational effectiveness. 'Is this fugitive likely to be involved in or instigate any terrorist activities while he is in the UK?'

'He is armed and dangerous and has already murdered one man and kidnapped and tortured another,' said Sorokina.

'Major, with all due respect, this is a criminal investigation. Assistant Commissioner Beaumont has armed response officers available should they be needed.

My people have higher priorities and those demands mean I must excuse myself from this briefing.'

Pickering slipped his notes into his briefcase and left the room. Major Sorokina showed no emotion at Pickering's withdrawal from the operation, even though Britain's counter-terrorism branch worked with the National Crime Agency and the security service, MI5, and their street contacts could have proved useful in capturing Kuznetsov.

Maguire stepped in quickly. 'Major, I have an interest in finding your man. We'll work with you. I'm sure Assistant Commissioner Beaumont will brief her officers accordingly and that Europol will also lend all assistance possible.' Maguire stood up and draped his overcoat across his arm. 'Co-operation between Russian and European police forces is a positive step in the right direction and we all welcome it. And as far as my department is concerned we are at your service.' It sounded glib, rolling off the tongue like any diplomatic pat on the head.

Raglan looked at Sorokina. She didn't seem too upset or disappointed at the outcome of the meeting. She had asked for help from the key elements of British policing and had received little more than a nod of acknowledgement to her request. Raglan realized Maguire had stage-managed the meeting. This was nothing more than a courtesy call to the police and counter-terrorism people. That's why Raglan was there.

Maguire wanted his face seen. That was all. *This is my man*, was what Maguire was stating. Maguire knew there would be nothing sensitive discussed in the meeting so Raglan would not be privy to anything that he shouldn't. The charade was a done deal. Maguire wanted to control the operation. There was a barely noticeable glance from Sorokina to Maguire.

That's what the meeting in the park had been about.

Raglan knew they were both in on it.

22

Raglan had begun to wonder whether Maguire had an office of his own or whether he conducted all his business at the Ned.

'I'm a member,' said Maguire, reading his thoughts as he escorted Raglan and Sorokina into the basement of the hotel. The massive steel vault door was two metres wide and weighed twenty tonnes. Its impressive thickness was exposed as the circular opening served as the entrance to the Vault, the hotel's private club. The thousands of security boxes added to the impression that this was once a place of great wealth and secrets. And might still be. It was obvious that Maguire would never allow Raglan or a Russian national into the Secret Intelligence Service building at Vauxhall Cross. Not only would that pose a breach of security but this was off-the-record business. And this was one place where there would be no listening devices.

Raglan sipped beer from the bottle, Sorokina drank neat vodka and Maguire stayed with a whisky. The room was empty except for a couple in the far corner who bent forward face to face, hands clasped as if the boat was about to go down and these were their final moments.

'Tell him,' said Maguire.

She settled her eyes on Raglan over the rim of her glass without giving Maguire a questioning glance. If the MI6 officer wanted this rough-looking man involved then it meant he was trusted.

'Yegor Kuznetsov or Jean Delacorte, whatever name you know him by, has been a valued asset for the Russian intelligence services for many years. His parents escaped the Soviet Union thirty-five years ago when he was eight years old. They were part of the expatriate Russian community in Paris. He did his national service in the French army, excelled at university and was recruited by the DGSE, where he betrayed certain key operatives and their operations to our intelligence services almost from the start. Several years ago he was in Africa working with French forces to stop the terrorist infiltration from Algiers into Mali. He was reported killed in a helicopter crash.'

It was obvious that Maguire had not told her anything of Raglan's background and that he knew of the crash. If she had known she would not have bothered telling him about JD's involvement and reported death in

Africa. 'And he then went full-time freelance,' said Raglan.

'Yes. He had many contacts, and he became involved in organized crime that included international arms smuggling and the execution of dissidents. He was protected.'

'By the FSB and/or military intelligence,' said Maguire.

'Of course,' she said. 'When Putin came to power many criminal gangs thought they would face a crackdown. But he cut a deal with them. The state was the biggest gang in town and provided the mafia did nothing to challenge it then they were allowed to carry on – and then when the state wanted something from them they would comply. They became businessmen. The Kremlin uses organized crime to do their dirty work. You have to understand that the criminals on the streets are nothing. They are petty thieves compared to these people. You want to know who uses cyber warfare against the west? It's organized crime. Who facilitates weapons to terrorists? Organized crime. They are a useful tool that keeps our politicians' hands clean. They do not have blood on them. You understand all of this, what I am saying?'

'And you think you have a chance to arrest him for the murder of four Moscow police officers,' said Raglan.

Major Sorokina placed her glass down carefully. She knew her quest to capture the killer was at the least improbable and, with the fugitive being protected by the

Russian state intelligence services, probably impossible. 'I have just confirmed what you already believe: that my country's government is corrupt and considered by many to be a criminal state, but the Moscow Police Department has judicial backing to apprehend criminals.'

'Why?' said Raglan. 'Russia is run by the biggest crook of all.'

'We have to be seen to be taking murderers and criminals off our streets. We are given a great deal of freedom with the support of the Ministry of the Interior. Our CID operations are as removed from political interference as possible. This is because our public wants every serious crime committed against them by murderers, paedophiles and rapists solved and the perpetrators arrested, tried and convicted. So put aside your disbelief. We catch criminals. And I want this one more than any other.'

'Because he killed your fellow officers.'

She nodded and held his gaze. 'One of them was a judge's son. That's why I know I can get him.' She swallowed the last of her drink. 'Forgive me. I am tired. It has been a long day.' She stood up and tied the belt on her overcoat. 'A judge's son, and my brother.'

Maguire escorted her to the door and the Ned's doorman hailed her a taxi. As a visiting cop, her hotel would never be five-star luxury, but even Raglan winced when

Maguire told him she was staying at a down-at-heel place near Paddington railway station. 'She's Russian,' said Maguire, 'she probably thinks it's luxury.' He sipped his drink. 'But you can see how motivated she is and if she pulls in any information about JD then it benefits us.' He sighed. 'And now you'll want your own bedtime story.'

'Qatar,' said Raglan. 'All of it.'

Maguire settled back into the chair, giving an almost imperceptible shrug. 'When you were in the Legion and fighting in Mali you worked with three intelligence agencies. The French, us and the CIA. They were the ones feeding information for your strike teams.'

'And they pinpointed the caves where their Al Qaeda leader was operating. And that's how we got to Abdelhamid Abou Zeid,' Raglan said.

'How *you* got to him,' Maguire corrected him.

'I was close enough to smell his stench, but he killed himself before I could.'

'He was a very valuable target. Job well done all round.'

'We lost good men in that war and I don't need any patronizing bull from you. If JD was selling out the West then he was selling out me and my men on that operation.'

Maguire gave a cautious look around to see there were no waiters hovering ready to step forward when they saw an empty glass. 'No, you're wrong. JD knew that

Abdelhamid Abou Zeid was in that cave. He wanted him alive because that would have been a scalp for him and his masters. If Abou Zeid had been taken alive then he would have ended up in Russian hands, not ours or the Americans. No, Raglan, it was not JD who put you in danger, it was us.'

'This doesn't make sense.'

'We intercepted radio traffic from the caves. We knew Abou Zeid would martyr himself but we couldn't pass that on because we needed him to be the focus of the operation.'

Raglan's memory spooled back quickly. The briefing, the attack, the changed location. All fed through French intelligence, which meant that JD, the Russian double agent, would have scooped the prize of having Abou Zeid and the information he carried. Raglan thought it through. There was more Maguire hadn't yet revealed. If they knew the terrorist leader was prepared to kill himself then what else had been happening when he and the legionnaires went into the caves? 'There was an SAS advisory team for the French. I remember. You used them?'

'We used them.'

'For what?'

'Our real target. The bag-carrier.'

'The money man?'

'Yes. A Qatari. He funded several terrorist organizations using Middle East money and an international network of drug smuggling that generated even more funds into the terrorists' coffers. Much of it comes through the Middle East and into Europe. We snatched him. He was a mine of information.'

'And Carter ran him after that.'

'It was his operation and when we got Carter into the bank he traced every dirty deal because our Qatari gave us all the information for all the people and all the money and every undercover deal that he funded. That's who Carter controlled. And Carter had more than... more than we admitted. We had a... special fund. And then it went bad.'

'You kept dirty money for black ops.'

Maguire smiled. 'We're in an age of austerity. The government thinks we do what we do with what they give us.'

'I don't do politics, Maguire, but even I know you got extra funding from the Treasury.'

'It's never enough.'

'And what happened when Carter went to Qatar?'

'We don't know what he was doing there. Money went missing. The Qatari was killed. Carter became a suspect.'

'It wasn't him. I told you that.'

'There was a leak. Someone told us he was doing a deal on the side.'

'And you believed this unknown source?'

'We had to take it seriously. Until the kidnapping. Then we knew it was a set-up.'

'JD.'

'Or, as our lovely ice maiden Major Sorokina has said, his friends in the Kremlin. Misinformation strategically placed. The Russians had somehow learnt what Carter was doing. The Qatari was knifed outside a nightclub. It was put down as a robbery.'

'By?'

Maguire shrugged. He returned Raglan's enquiring look without answering, seeing if Raglan came to the same conclusion that he had now reached himself.

'If it was the Russians, why kill him?' said Raglan. 'They wanted what he had.' If indeed JD had had the Qatari killed it was because he was past his sell-by date. He had given everything he had to Carter. It was Carter who had burrowed deeper and linked the information together. 'If they killed him, it was to put suspicion on Carter because money went missing and the Qatari was the one person who knew who Carter really was,' Raglan went on. 'Odds are he went to Qatar because his asset sounded the alarm. Something had gone wrong. The Russians had contractors out there. Guess who.'

Maguire nodded and sipped his drink. 'And so it looked as though our man was covering his tracks because money was unaccountable.'

Raglan shook his head in disbelief. 'Slush funds are never accountable. You were conned. Somehow JD put the pieces together that Carter was running his asset, that he had all the information and that's why they came for him. And when you put Carter under investigation that drove a wedge between you. So JD is after the money and the drug running?'

'There's more. The Qatari banker drip-fed us every hidden enemy asset here, in Europe and in the States, and that was what Carter has concealed. Every time someone reached out to the banker for funding then we played them and shut down the threat. If someone else gets their hands on it all they can run it any way they like. They can activate paid terrorists, hold them back, bury them deeper. For God's sake, if an enemy gets that information then it's open sports day for international terrorism. And if our slush fund is exposed then it's bloody curtains and I'll be growing roses on an enforced early retirement.'

Raglan swallowed the last of his beer. He tapped the bottle on the table to emphasise the 64-million-dollar question. 'So, this whole disaster isn't about drugs at all. If it comes down to it, what are you prepared to lose? The money or the hidden assets?'

'The money. With the hidden terrorist cells known to us I can protect the nation and stop them.'

'Right answer. Then we need to recover that information.'

'And Carter. I owe him that much.'

23

Raglan had accepted Maguire's offer of a safe house flat and let him drop him off outside the entrance. The moment Maguire's car had gone from view he turned back on to the street and found a hostel two streets away that rented rooms by the day. It was usually used by women of the night plying their trade but it suited Raglan. He paid cash for three nights. Once in the room – small, with its bathroom and toilet added on with stud walling – he stripped, washed, pulled on a zip-neck sweater and unfolded the only half-decent jacket he possessed. He concealed the illegal handgun behind an air vent. By the time he had travelled across town the light rain had stopped and the chill wind from the river had abated.

Raglan waited opposite Sorokina's hotel. She might have had a busy day but it was far too early in the night for her to excuse herself claiming tiredness. Besides, she didn't look like the kind of woman who would tire easily. The hotel was in a back street halfway between the main rail station at Paddington and Hyde Park. It was a typical low-end tourist hotel, the kind of place he would have chosen, anonymous and cheap and with a clear view of the arterial road that served as a rat run towards the park and all routes into town. Raglan had phoned the hotel, establishing that she was in her room by hanging up when she answered the call. He waited an hour, keeping a constant eye on her building. He had checked the rear to see if she could leave without being seen, but there were enough fire regulation violations to stop anyone getting out of the back door on to the fire escape. Bags of waste and an old mattress blocked the exit door. If she was going to head out into the night it would be by the front entrance. He studied the street and the cars parked either side. The passing traffic helped obscure his movements as he cut back and forth across the road, double-checking that her hotel was not under observation by anyone. The street was cluttered with empty parked cars and no one loitered in any of the pillared entranceways to the many small hotels that ran the length of the road. Satisfied that he was the only one interested in Elena Sorokina, he took up position again. He was soon rewarded as she emerged from the hotel. She looked up and down the street. He stepped back into shadow, watching as she stepped to the kerb and hailed a cab. It drove past her, a fare already sitting in the back. She waited a minute longer. This time of night cabs were busy ferrying people to and from theatres and restaurants. She tugged her coat collar around her neck and strode towards the nearest Tube station. Raglan followed her. She tried a couple more times to hail a cab, without success, before reaching the Bayswater Road, which ran between her and Hyde Park. She went down into Lancaster Gate Underground Station. He was now less than a hundred paces behind her and as soon as she disappeared from view he quickened his stride. Scanning the passengers who came and went to the station platforms he saw her study the wall map showing all routes. She bought a ticket and headed down towards the Central Line. Raglan followed her and saw her standing on the platform. Within a minute the train arrived and he stepped into the next coach along. After four stops and ten minutes, she got out at Tottenham Court Road Station. He followed her up to the street level. It was obvious she was heading for the bright lights and noisy bars of Soho.

The downstairs club she entered was guarded by two bouncers and by the look of them they were not the usual dark-suited locals who were often ex-armed forces or moonlighting police officers. These guys looked Eastern European. She went past them without being challenged – probably, he thought, because she was an attractive well-dressed woman who might have been a high-end prostitute or who knew someone in the club.

Raglan thought his chances were slim, dressed as he was in jeans and jacket. But it was worth a try. He walked to the entrance and one of the men extended his muscled arm, blocking his way. The doorman shook his head. This establishment was not for the likes of Raglan.

'What?' said Raglan.

'Not tonight,' said the unsmiling bouncer.

'My wife's inside already. She left me back there to get the car sorted.'

The two men looked at each other. 'What does she look like?' said the bouncer's opposite number.

Raglan described Sorokina. One bouncer nodded to the other. The arm came down. A curt nod gave Raglan permission. He went down a dimly lit stairwell, the sound of a small jazz band and a woman's voice getting louder the closer he got to another door at the bottom of the stairs. He noticed the closed-circuit lens following him. Pushing open the door he stepped into a room whose size belied the narrow entrance. It looked as though it extended beneath two or three of the buildings on street level. He adjusted his eyes to the dim lighting. The place was filled with a mix of people. Younger city types with their women, or women with their younger city types. As he took it all in he realized that the women were most likely escorts. At least that was the polite way of describing them. They were no doubt run by the club owner. There were some older men huddled in one corner, hair long, a sprinkling of velvet and corduroy jackets: musicians probably. A few tables of couples seemed genuine. Champagne was a common tipple; the waitresses were already collecting empty wine bottles. There was much evidence of hard liquor too, which meant the champagne was at a premium price. You needed some decent folding money to be here and enjoy the music.

The singer finished her set, acknowledged the smattering of applause, stepped down and let the band carry on without her, three men and a long-haired blonde woman on sax. The place felt good. A good old-fashioned boozy dive of a jazz club. All that was missing was the fug of cigarette smoke that would have once engulfed the patrons. Jazz and booze without smoke. Nothing was the same any more. He rested a foot on the brass rail below the bar and leant in to order a bottle of beer. It came in a glass. He sipped and watched. The set was good. Mostly Thelonious Monk. The old standard 'Ruby My Dear'. The girl on the sax played it sweet and easy.

He looked past her and saw a booth at the end wall where Sorokina sat, her coat shrugged from her shoulders. She wore a simple black dress. Easy to pack but something that could be worn for any occasion. The man she sat with was ugly. Plain ugly. A bulbous nose sat on a pockmarked face. He was old enough to be her father. At least. His silver hair, brushed back across his scalp, touched his shoulders. His pudgy hands cradled a glass with clear liquid. She sipped from a champagne glass. The waiter who stood a few respectful paces away wasn't just guarding the ice bucket. The ugly man shook his head. Sorokina looked disappointed. Raglan had been watching them for too long. The music came to its gentle end. That meant for near enough six and a half minutes he had been observing her, trying to interpret what was going on. He had barely touched the expensive beer. A man stepped in close and blocked his view. A minder. Another had pressed close to the bar counter behind Raglan. Either had the ability and confidence to hurt him. If the man behind him was as big as the one in front then he was a head taller than Raglan. At least that gave him a fighting chance. Know your enemy. This looked more like an invitation to leave.

'You should finish your beer. Time to go,' said the man in front of him in a thick-tongued accent.

'I like the music,' said Raglan.

'They've stopped now,' answered the man behind him. Raglan guessed he said it without a smile because the one in front of him was tight-lipped. Jaw clenched. Eyes narrowed. Signals that he was getting ready for violence. Chest-beating an optional extra.

There was no sense in causing a scene. Raglan raised the glass to his lips. Perhaps the minder was trying to impress his boss because he grasped Raglan's left arm in a walnut-crushing grip. He was surprised to find the muscle in Raglan's arm didn't yield. It was a stupid mistake. Had they let Raglan finish his beer no one would have been any wiser that a threat had been made and he would have left. But not now.

Raglan whipped back his head, catching the man behind him on his lower jaw. His lip split, his teeth cracked, he stumbled back. Before the blood filled his mouth Raglan had pivoted and thrown the beer into the other man's face, forcing him to rear back his head, release his grip and attempt to raise his arm to protect himself. Raglan didn't let him. He twisted his left hand, gripped the man's wrist, pulled him forward, forcing him on to his toes. He was off balance when Raglan's elbow connected with the bridge of his nose. Raglan spun around and kicked beneath the second man's chin as he tried to scramble to his feet. Somewhere in the background, hardly acknowledged by Raglan, a woman screamed, men swore, glasses broke, then a flood of noise told him the panic came from the few tables nearby. Perhaps the band was used to the occasional ruckus because they hit a fast number that drowned out the commotion.

Raglan couldn't recall the title.

24

The stairs down to the club were too narrow for the hefty doormen to descend side by side, but they were halfway down one behind the other as Raglan started up.

A voice behind him called out. '*Nem. Hadd menjen.*'

Hungarian. Raglan half turned as the bouncers stopped in their tracks. A lithe man in an expensive suit, about the same age as Raglan, stood in the doorway behind him. He was no thug. 'Safe journey. Better you do not come back. Yes?'

Raglan knew Sorokina had spoken for him. He nodded at the well-dressed man and made his way out into the cold night air. He passed the two guardians, who had returned to their posts, and crossed the street to wait for her. She took another half-hour, by which time he knew she was letting him know of her displeasure. When she finally came out she spotted him immediately.

Experience had taught him that when Russians get mad it's best to let their blood cool from boil to simmer.

'You followed me! You stupid oaf. You fight in a place where I went for information. Information! Do you know how desperate we are to find help? Your police will only do so much. It will take time. Too much time. I have a contact here and you...' She spewed insults in Russian, some of which he caught. Most of them were a fairly accurate description of who he was and what he had done. Maguire was wrong. She was no ice maiden. She swore at him once more and turned on her heel.

'I'm not the marrying kind,' said Raglan calmly.

She turned again. He hadn't moved, hands in pockets. 'What?'

'I thought you'd just asked me to marry you in Russian. The bit about seeing me in my grave or some such thing. In English, they say "until death do us part".'

She looked confused for all of five seconds. 'You are a stupid man,' she said, the cold edge back.

'Buy me a drink then. And I'll forgive you.'

Her neatly plucked eyebrows arched.

'For saying you wished I was dead. I'm the forgiving kind.'

'I said you are lucky not to have been killed tonight. That is what I said.'

He smiled. 'My Russian is rustier than I thought. How about that drink?'

*

He ushered her into a nearby bar, giving her little chance to express her anger any further. The place was crowded and noisy and she retreated into silence. He helped her off with her coat, his hands briefly touching her waist where she had worn the pistol in its speed rig. There was no gun there tonight. He settled her coat neatly on the back of her chair and brought her a double chilled vodka because it was going to be difficult to get back to the bar to reorder through the crush. The clamour of raised voices made it impossible for them to converse. He watched her as she surveyed the room. The buzz swirled around them. He thought she liked it. And then she smiled. She bent her head and put her mouth close to his ear.

'You are clever. There can be no fighting here. No argument, I mean.'

He leant forward too. 'No need to argue. I didn't start that fight in front of your friend. They did. I finished it. They gave me no choice.'

To anyone watching them, they seemed like a couple with their faces pressed close together, sharing intimacies.

'Not my friends. People I knew. We rubbed each other's back.'

'You mean scratched each other's back,' he corrected her.

'Yes. They are Hungarians. They are not good people,

very violent, but they owe me favours. They have many contacts here, better even than Maguire's. They run prostitution and drugs, they clean their money through casinos and by buying property. They have heard nothing of Kuznetsov but he would not have used his own name here, so I ask him to look for Delacorte or anyone else leasing old commercial buildings for short-term rental. It is where your friend will be held. I am certain.'

'If he's still alive,' said Raglan. He struggled to dispel the thought of a tortured Carter out there somewhere in the night. There was little comfort in knowing that every agency available was searching for him and now that Sorokina had brought in her underworld contacts there might be a quicker result. She certainly was not the kind of woman to hang about. She was a huntress. Respect where it was due, he thought. Without a doubt, she was attractive, and the fitted black cocktail dress and her slim frame belied her strength. Her toned arms and legs were surely the result of frequent physical workouts. He had already checked her slender fingers. Russians wear their wedding ring on their right hand but he noticed that she wore no jewellery except for a small crucifix at her neck. Single, divorced or widowed?

The warmth of the room gave her face a gentle flush. Her eyes glistened. She had noticed. 'I lost my husband,' she said. 'Ten years ago. He was an engineer. There was an accident.' She took his hands in hers. 'No woman in your life who lies awake worrying if you will return home alive?'

'No one will have me,' he said.

She pulled a face. 'Not ever?'

'Once.'

'Ah.' She let his hand go.

He put his lips close to her cheek and smelt the subtle scent of perfume. Her elbows rested on the table, her bare arms raised, cradling the last of the vodka. 'I'm hungry,' he said.

There was no disagreement. She finished the drink. He eased on her coat and turned his shoulder towards the door and the crowd. He extended his arm towards her so she would follow close behind him through the press of people. He felt her fingers curl into his palm as she took his hand.

It was a good sign.

25

They found a hole-in-the-wall Italian eatery. Homely, family-run, the food freshly cooked. Thankfully, there was no piped muzak. Not even Italian opera. People were there to eat, not be entertained. Raglan ordered a bottle of basic red. It was business all the way. Nothing personal. Just the way Raglan liked it. He teased out her background, his questions always sounding like professional interest in her police career but exploring below the tough surface she projected. He learnt enough to know that she had had no easy ride through the ranks. Shot twice, demoted once and promoted again. She was bright. Not your standard plod who read the book and applied the rules. She had a keen mind, having studied law with the intention of following in her father's footsteps in the judiciary, but the prospect of working even higher up in the corrupt system made her change her mind. At least on the street, she could face down the criminals; if she had gone up the greasy pole and become a lawyer the odds would be more heavily stacked, because more often than not the crooks were in charge. Her father and a handful of judges fought behind the scenes to exercise justice but their hands were tied. Big-brother love convinced her she had made the correct decision to remain a police officer. He had been a brave cop and put many of the really bad guys away but when he and his men raided Yegor Kuznetsov or, as she had heard Raglan refer to him, JD, they were ambushed. Someone higher up the chain had learnt of her brother's investigation. Maybe he had even been betrayed by his own colleagues. It made no difference who was guilty; they walked right into an ambush and were cut down by intense gunfire. Their bodies were so badly shot up they were only identifiable by their personal documents and DNA.

She laid down her fork from the plate of antipasti and dabbed her mouth. The memory had soured her appetite. Raglan ordered grappa despite the waiter's look of surprise at him ordering the 60-per-cent-proof drink in the middle of the meal. It soon dulled her pain. No more questions. Once the food arrived, who could get the most spaghetti on to the fork soon became a competition until he managed the biggest mouthful, a feat which would have made his army friends proud. She laughed and reached across to dab the sauce from his mouth. After that she conceded defeat.

'Do you always have to win?' she asked him.

Raglan didn't answer.

When the taxi pulled up outside her hotel Raglan needed no invitation to come inside, and the night porter slumped behind the small and ineffective reception desk did not even rouse himself when Sorokina reached for her key. Her room was so basic there was barely space to fit in a double bed. Her suitcase was in one corner and the hanging rail sported day-to-day attire. The size of the room meant that the act of undressing was an intimacy in itself as they both disrobed quickly, their bodies nudging until she turned into his arms and pulled him to her. He lifted her on to the firm mattress, tugging the bed cover over them both to keep the chill of the barely heated room off their skin. She showed no sign of feeling the cold: her skin was not puckered; only her nipples were aroused. They explored each other's scars, marks sketching a life lived in danger. Sorokina lay full length on top of him, pressing herself against him, luxuriating in his firm body. She began to straddle him, eyes locked on to his, but he twisted her down so she was beneath him. She was strong and resisted, but only in play, and he spent time stroking and teasing her, letting his tongue and lips and hands arouse her until she began to whisper her frustration in Russian. He ignored her insistence that he make love to her and continued his deliberate teasing until she shuddered with the first of her orgasms, her legs drawing up, her back arching. He nuzzled her neck, listening to her shallow breathing as she let the surge within her subside. Then she drew his face to her and kissed him, a long demanding kiss that made her tremble as he pressed himself between her legs. Her eyes opened and closed as he moved slowly inside of her. When he lowered his face to her breasts he felt her tighten around him, a small gasp that grew louder as the intensity of her arousal increased. Her mouth opened in a silent, held breath, not yet released, trapped within the pleasure of what he was doing to her. When her cry forced itself to the surface she let its release explode. Their bodies were slick with sweat. He felt her spasms until she sighed and with a final breath of delight focused on him as if she was seeing him for the first time. He kissed her tenderly. She smiled and pushed him away so she could roll on top of him.

'My turn,' she said.

Raglan was gone when she awoke. At first, she wondered whether he had gone out for breakfast and would return bearing fresh coffee, but after she had stepped out of the cramped shower and he was still not there she realized his actions made sense. It would serve no purpose for Maguire to find out that they had slept together and

if Raglan's driver had been called to her hotel then it
would have been obvious. As she dried her hair her
phone beeped. A text message from Raglan telling her
she would be picked up in an hour. The night was over;
she was back on duty. With any luck, they would corner
the man she hunted. She knew that there was a strong
chance he would escape justice if taken back to Moscow.
No matter how hard her father might try and influence
the outcome, Kuznetsov had friends in high places.
She hoped the tough man who had given her so much
pleasure the night before would be the first to corner
him. Kuznetsov was a hardened fighter, though, and even
if Raglan got to him first she could not be certain who
would walk away from the confrontation. She promised
herself that if she got close enough and had a clean shot
she would kill him herself.

She took the semi-automatic pistol in its clamshell
holster from the room's safe. It was a standard-issue
Makarov but it was not the gun of choice for the police,
who had been promised the much improved Yarygin
Grach, which was usually kept for special forces. The
Makarov had been in service since the fifties, three
decades before she was born, which meant there were
thousands of them available. It was a mass-produced,
robust and reliable weapon; she was used to its weight,
had used it in anger before now and understood
its limitations. When she went to the academy her
small-arms instructor told her it had a fifty-metre

range but she would have more success if she threw it. Twenty metres was the limit. When she had killed with it in the past she had moved even closer. Better to make sure.

After Abbie had picked Raglan up he asked her to stop at a takeaway sandwich bar where he bought three coffees and a couple of sandwiches. As she drove he stripped out the ham from one sandwich and placed it over the cheese in the other. She didn't ask why. Raglan did things his way, but he didn't eat it. They sat across the street waiting for the Russian to emerge from the hotel. When Major Sorokina came out she was wearing a more workmanlike hip-length jacket and jeans. Abbie flashed the headlights. Sorokina climbed into the back as Raglan turned and handed her one of the coffees.

'I guessed milk and two sugars,' he said. Russians usually liked their coffee sweet in the morning, something he had learnt from Sokol, the veteran legionnaire. 'No kolbasa,' he told her as he handed over the doctored sandwich. 'We don't get sausage in a sandwich here so I made up cheese and ham.'

Abbie watched her in the rearview mirror. The brief smile of thanks and the touch of her hand on Raglan's shoulder was barely noticeable. Abbie was surprised at her own reaction. A twinge of jealousy stabbed in her stomach. Something had happened between Raglan and the Russian cop.

She engaged gear. No one would look that pleased with the world just because of a cheese and ham sandwich.

26

Jeremy Carter was still alive. That the man had endured so much pain did not surprise JD; in fact, he had planned for it, which was why he had set up three places where he and his crew could hole up with their prisoner. Each of the buildings was surrounded by either industrial estates or condemned buildings awaiting redevelopment. Money had changed hands months before when Eddie Roman had identified the best locations and secured them from funds that had been sent through by couriers. JD had visited London several weeks previously and conducted his own reconnaissance to establish Carter's routine and then, having decided on the ambush, he had planned his escape routes. Time would always be against him and eventually the police and security forces would get close.

The first location gave him the opportunity to get out of sight quickly after the ambush; had he gone any further on the roads cameras would have traced the van. Now he had different vehicles and a new location which would be good for a few days; and then, if Carter survived, there was always a third. They left nothing to chance, which was why his fixer, Eddie Roman, had had to be removed from the equation. He had broken the golden rule of no phone usage during the operation, which is how this had been planned, with military precision. The likelihood was that if the police found the first location they would not be able to identify the dead man, or not very quickly at least, and that gave him another time advantage because JD could not see how any connection could be made between the petty criminal and himself. There was no trail for the authorities to follow.

What concerned him now was the loss of one of his men, Stefan. There had been no contact since he had sent him to the address that Carter had given him. That meant he had likely been arrested. His man was well trained so he would not have used his firearm if confronted. The understanding was that if any of them got caught they would be looked after and a way found to secure their freedom. The large amount of money on the table bought silence and loyalty, something that was in short supply these days. He had checked news sites on his mobile but all he could glean was that a woman had been found dead in the building where Stefan had been sent. There was no mention of an arrest. Why not? If Stefan had killed her because he had no choice then he would have returned. He had not. That meant Stefan was either dead or under arrest. In either case, the press had not reported it. The obvious conclusion was that Carter's people had shut everything down.

He flicked the stub of his cigar into space and watched it spiral into a puddle in the yard. It sizzled and died. He looked up to where Carter was restrained on the third floor. JD admitted grudging respect for the man. Beneath the city banker veneer was an old-school toughness. Most would have cracked by now but after three days Carter had only drip-fed him information like any trained operative would do. He double-checked the chained gate and took a final look around the building. The extra man he had put in place before the ambush had acted as a nightwatchman. No one had breached the walls or gates. No suspicions would be raised. They were secure. This old factory gave them a good view of the surrounding area should anyone get too nosey.

Carter had decided to kill himself. He could not hold out any longer. He had bought sufficient time for his son to be safe, his family would have been protected and if fate had been kind Raglan was in London and had dealt with the gunman who had been sent to his flat. One down, how many others were there? The local man, the driver: he had not arrived wherever they were now, but a new man had been waiting when they drove through the gates and hauled him up three floors. Now they had left him unguarded. He had only minutes to end it all. Death was a better outcome than this agony: he would sell his soul to stop the torture. He had rocked the metal-framed chair until it fell backwards and pushed himself along the floor with what strength he had left in his legs. He left a blood trail across the wooden floor as he inched towards the glassless window frame. If he could get across the low sill the fall would kill him.

The effort was excruciating. A bloody mass of tissue where his left eye used to be wept and the pain squirmed in his head and neck. They had given him a local anaesthetic when they took his eye. One man sat on his lap; another gripped his head. When the scalpel came close he screamed and bucked, but they were too strong for him. As the first cut sliced deep he had passed out. Now he could take no more. He had to end it before he told them everything they needed to know. Carter whimpered with despair. He heard rapid footfalls as someone loped up the concrete stairs. The sound of the approaching man and fear of the torture that would follow gave him the strength to reach the wall. He wedged the chair's back against the wall and pushed with his legs; the chair frame slid sideways against the concrete. He pushed again, using what little strength he had left, found some purchase and felt the back of the chair scrape upwards. He was almost at the ledge. All he had to do was raise his back a few inches higher and his weight would tumble him into space. The room spun, the ceiling, the wall, the drop, and then he saw JD turn from the stairwell and race towards him. Carter shook his head, teeth gritted, but his legs couldn't give him that final push, and then JD was there. His tormentor pulled him upright and dragged him all the way back to the middle of the floor. Carter wept while JD got his breath back.

'It's not for you to say when, Jeremy... Those aren't the rules.'

At the end of the room, a cistern flushed and groaned. One of the gunmen came out of the toilet. He stopped when he saw JD kneeling next to Carter.

'I said watch him. Next time leave the door open,' said JD.

The man nodded sheepishly and took up his position at the window. 'It's fucked. The toilet.'

'Then we go back to a bucket. Organize it.'

JD wrapped a blanket around Carter and pulled the IV drip stand towards them, reconnecting it into Carter's arm. He opened up a medical pack and prepared a syringe, tapping out the air bubbles.

'We don't want you dying on us, Jeremy. Not yet.' He swabbed Carter's arm with as much care as a hospital nurse. 'Hypovolemic shock is bad news, Jeremy. Got to slow down the trauma or you'll be no good to us at all.' He squirted the excess out of the hypodermic. 'Now this bit of God-given relief is morphine sulphate. It won't help you survive for long but it'll do wonders for the pain. I know how too much pain scrambles a man's thoughts, but I need you, Jeremy. For a while longer at least.' He injected Carter, who winced. Even the slightest scratch now ricocheted through his damaged nervous system. 'And if for some unlikely reason I let you live, I'll make sure you're a junkie for the rest of your life. There's got to be some pleasure to be had from that. Now, what or who was at that address you gave me?'

Carter felt himself slipping away as the drug embraced him. 'Your man hasn't come back, has he?'

'What's there?' JD insisted.

Carter lifted his chin from his chest and settled his remaining eye on the man. JD's face blurred face was close to his.

'Everything,' he said.

27

The briefing was held at the Shepherd's Bush Police Station from where the search and investigation was being co-ordinated. The two-storey building was plain and functional but the meeting inside its conference room was being energetically directed by a ruddy-faced man, Detective Chief Inspector Liam James. He had spent twenty of his fifty years tracking down terrorists in Northern Ireland when he was stationed in Belfast. As the SIO running the investigation into the murders of Carter's driver and Raglan's neighbour he had full command of the resources available to him, though they were limited. The world wouldn't shift on its axis because of a couple of murders and a kidnapping.

The speed with which the police had swooped on Eddie Roman's known associates impressed Raglan. Little had been gleaned about the man – he'd said nothing to anyone about his involvement with JD – but a lock-up had been found where there was enough evidence to establish at least one car had been resprayed. They traced registration plates hidden behind a hardboard panel to a second-hand car yard on the other side of the city. With some hardnosed persuasion from the police, the owner admitted Eddie had bought two old turbo-charged Saabs for cash. One was silver, the other dark blue, but the respray showed they were now black. They passed this information to every officer on the street, along with JD's mugshot. The news channels and newspapers had not been given any information about JD in order to protect Carter for as long as possible.

It was obvious to Raglan, sitting with Sorokina and Abbie in the crowded room, that DCI Liam James was a man who cracked the whip. They had made good headway so far. Two key things needed to be established. How these men were moving across the city and where they might be hiding.

Investigation into Eddie Roman's stint as a hospital porter had yielded proof that someone had stolen an ambulance, which meant the killers were prepared to keep Carter alive and stretcher him wherever they planned to go next. The Met detectives knew that the stolen ambulance was one of the small estate cars used by medics to move emergencies quickly through traffic and not the box-sided ambulances everyone notices on the street. What they did not know was if it had been spray-painted or whether the kidnappers wanted to use its ability to cut through traffic using siren and lights. Now priority had been given to tracking down stolen cars and their number plates which might have been switched on to the Saabs. The teams had worked day and night scouring the city's computer files of cars being stolen over the past two months which was, DCI James admitted, a rough stab at how long it could have taken for the kidnap and murder to be planned. If he was correct in this assumption, this fallow period of time would have taken away any urgency from overstretched police officers to find the missing vehicles. Abandoned vehicles are towed to various police compounds and those vehicles without plates were traced to the owners through the engine numbers. The owners confirmed their cars' original plate numbers, which were being circulated to every officer and traffic cam operator. It had been a herculean task achieved in less than forty-eight hours.

Specialist firearms officers would be deployed from across the whole Metropolitan area, DCI James said. On the PowerPoint image behind him, he showed how the search areas would circle in ever-increasing and -decreasing sweeps from inside and outside of the London boroughs. Then he brought the briefing to a close by extending his compliments to their visiting senior officer from the Moscow CID who would ride with one of the armed teams.

As the crowded room emptied Raglan saw Maguire standing at the back. Raglan always remembered how, when he was a kid and he looked as if thunder was rolling around inside his head and the world was about to end, his mother would say *he had a face on him*. Maguire fitted the bill. Ignoring Sorokina and Abbie, he nodded to Raglan to follow him. When they were free of the crowded room he turned on Raglan.

'You're screwing the Russian?'

Raglan didn't care that Maguire knew. 'Why are you having me followed?'

'Because you don't stay where I put you. I gave you that safe house for your own protection.'

'I don't need it. I go my own way.' Raglan knew that Maguire would not have used his own people to track him. More likely the 'watchers' from MI5. They were the best surveillance teams in the world. Put fifty of them in a room and they would look no different than any member of the public.

'You know these Russians use anything they can against us. If you're compromised in this operation everything could go down the pan.'

'I'm off the books, remember? What I do to practise my Russian language skills is none of your business. Have a nice day, Maguire.'

He left the MI6 man to choke back his annoyance. Maguire had nowhere to go with this. Raglan was an outsider; he was a risk, but one worth taking. He strode over to where DCI James stood with two plainclothes armed officers and Major Sorokina. Maguire tasted the salt on his tongue. Lust was not something easily ignored. She was the perfect honey trap – if that was her game; but whether it was or wasn't he admitted to himself that Raglan had scored big time. Maguire wished he was still in the field: he'd also have taken her to bed, were she willing. He took a deep breath and by the time he joined the conversation his cloak of professional indifference was back in place.

Every police officer on vehicle patrol had a map of their own borough's boundaries where they were to start and spiral outward towards the next area. The search patterns would intersect each other and they would check any abandoned or derelict buildings. Trouble was there were a *lot* of derelict buildings. Some had been abandoned for over twenty years, their owners clinging to the ever-increasing value the land generated. Raglan sat with a map on his lap and pinpointed some of the known sites so that Abbie could use her knowledge to get them through the heavy London traffic by cutting back and forth through back streets. She was good. More than. When a building lorry blocked one street she expertly reversed, found another route and delivered Raglan to their destination. After two hours they had checked four sites which, given the weight of traffic, was a good result and all due to her skill.

'We're doing all right time-wise. We need to keep food going in whenever we can. Find a place to pull over when you next see a takeaway and I'll grab us something.'

She kept her eyes on the road. Secretly she was pleased that they had assigned the Russian detective to a different unit. She and Raglan were there on Maguire's say-so and not that of the Metropolitan Police. She felt a growing sense of satisfaction that she had been tasked to help the man next to her. He hadn't shaved for a couple of days and wore the same street clothes and still didn't say much, but the quiet confidence he instilled in her had boosted her confidence. Even knowing that he was armed no longer frightened her. She didn't know why she hadn't told Maguire about the gun when she reported finding the first location to him. In fact, she didn't know the answer to most of what she felt about the man. The confusion, she decided, was because she had never known anyone like him or anyone who did what he did.

'There,' she said, seeing the canopy of a small takeaway. 'Don't take too long. I'm in a no-parking zone.'

Her brusque order was met with a smile. 'Yes, ma'am.'

She sighed. 'I can't tell a traffic enforcement officer we're hunting a killer and needed a bite to eat.'

'Is that what they call them these days? Whatever happened to traffic wardens?'

'Lousy pay but enhanced work titles.' She shrugged. 'Tell me about it.'

'Preferences?'

'Food and water.'

As a matter of habit Raglan always checked the way ahead. Pure survival instinct never left him. Going to a takeaway counter was hardly threatening unless you considered the danger of food poisoning, but he was working in no man's land and right now the killers had the upper hand so it was prudent to expect the unexpected.

What he hadn't expected was London prices for a sandwich.

28

The Hammersmith traffic demanded patience. JD sat without complaint as the Saab's driver nudged closer to the address where the woman had been killed. What was so special about it? If there was still a chance to retrieve the information Carter had hidden there then risks had to be taken and that was why he needed to see the building for himself.

'Keep moving,' he told the driver.

'Barely,' came the response. The street was one-way westbound and it was clogged.

'It's enough,' JD assured him. 'But if we need to get away from here in a hurry then go down the pavement.' He studied the small shops and buildings as they edged closer to the target building. Now he could see the police officer who stood guard at the entrance. Blue tape was zigzagged across the door frame. The officer was a tall, bearded man who stood even taller with his raised bobby's helmet. His hands were tucked into his stab vest but there was a holstered weapon at his side. It was a small show of force not meant for the likes of JD, more for assurance or warning to the general public. 'Keep going,' JD said.

'Boss, the traffic is clogging up big time.'

'Take the first turn, let's get back towards the river.'

Fifty metres ahead traffic filtered off the congested Hammersmith shopping street. The taped door was four metres away from where JD sat on the passenger side. He looked up. There seemed to be two different apartments that faced the street. Four windows side by side separated by a party wall: two windows had floral curtains; the other two had American shutters. Had Stefan been set up by Carter or had he run into trouble on his way to the next-door apartment? Carter wouldn't have given him a false address; the consequences would have been too harsh. JD was satisfied that whatever had happened when Stefan went to the apartment, someone else, other than the dead woman, must have been involved. The police officer hadn't even looked in JD's direction. Mind-numbing boredom from standing on duty for hours on end allowed the mind to wander. The black Saab nudged forward and then disappeared around the bend.

PC Jimmy Norris gave the perfect impression of a man bored to tears, but after seventeen years on the street very little escaped his attention. He bent his head to his police radio, pressed the call button, mentally double-checked the car's description and registration number and called it in.

Raglan and Abbie had already finished their hurried food intake and were heading south towards the Thames when the alert came through. *Contact. Contact. Saab answering wanted vehicle description turned from Hammersmith King Street. Identified moving on to West Cromwell Road.*

'We're close,' said Raglan. 'Get us to where it's heading. He must have been taking a look at my flat. That means he hasn't got what he's looking for.'

Three minutes later Abbie swung the car south.

'He's going east,' Raglan said.

She was concentrating hard on finding roads with fewer cars than those facing her. 'I'll cut across.'

Raglan tugged the pistol free. She glanced nervously at it but Raglan was intent on the road ahead. Suddenly her hands felt moist. She took one from the wheel and wiped it on her jeans, then did the same with the other. Raglan didn't turn his head, but could feel her stress.

'Just concentrate. Patrol cars will pick them up before we do. There won't be any trouble. Focus on getting us there.' His voice was calm and unhurried, with no sense of urgency.

'Can't we get a helicopter to help?'

Raglan shook his head. 'Cloud base is too low.'

She changed gear and weaved the car through several side streets.

Another disembodied voice came through. The Saab had turned. The officer who had seen it was caught in the middle of construction traffic. Raglan prayed that the cops' enthusiasm to catch JD did not scare him off. They had been instructed to use a silent approach until he could be boxed in and armed police officers surrounded the vehicle.

Raglan remained silent. It was impossible to make headway with any speed. Only when a gap appeared did Abbie go faster. Raglan had no idea where they were but Abbie was muttering directions to herself, her mind already streets ahead of their current location.

Another traffic jam. She swore. Cut in front of an irate driver and barrelled across an intersection. She bumped the kerb. Frustration bordering on panic gave her voice an edge. 'Sorry, sorry…'

'It's OK. You're doing fine,' Raglan assured her but knew that if he were driving he would have made faster, more aggressive progress. He considered taking over and have her direct him but knew the time lag between thinking through a route and relating it to a driver took longer than a driver who was mentally attuned to where she was going.

Subject now on Edith Grove, the dispatcher's voice told them.

'He's going for the river,' Abbie said. 'We need to go another way. Bugger.'

She pulled up, spun the wheel, taking the car across the road, and then stopped in a side street. She closed her eyes. Raglan waited. Her lips were barely moving but he heard her sibilant whisper mentally checking a route. Her eyes opened. 'Got it.'

She accelerated.

A motorcycle cop was directing traffic around a minor accident. A patrol car had half blocked the road and one officer was dragging clear a boy's damaged bicycle while its owner sat on the kerb. A car was parked up as a worried motorist gave a statement to the second patrol car officer.

The Saab slowed. JD lowered the window and checked. 'It's nothing.' He tugged free his pistol and slipped it between the seat and his thigh. The accident scene looked genuine but this was not the time to take anything for granted. The motorcycle cop waved on the cars and as the Saab drew level the cop held out a restraining hand.

'Hang on there!' he called, looking at the driver, who tensed and put the car into first gear ready to roar past.

JD spoke quietly. 'Don't.' The officer had halted them to allow an oncoming car to squeeze through. Once it had passed they were waved along. The Saab moved away as JD gave a smile of thanks to the officer dealing with the snarl-up and then referred to the satnav screen plugged into the cigarette lighter socket. He checked his surroundings against the proposed route and then gestured for the driver to continue driving straight ahead. 'Two hundred yards go right.'

Raglan scanned the streets ahead. Leaning forward he peered along every side street they crossed over. They came to a set of traffic lights; as they waited for them to turn in their favour, a stream of traffic came into view on a filter light allowing the cars to travel across their path. Four cars back was an old black Saab.

'That's him,' said Raglan without raising his voice, not wishing to panic her. 'He's gone past. U-turn. Get across the other side.'

Abbie had no time to question him. She reacted quickly, swung the car out of the line of traffic and forced herself between the oncoming cars. Horns blared in anger but Abbie got the car facing the same direction as the Saab.

'Don't see him.'

'You're OK. He's a dozen cars ahead. Two men inside.'

She peered beyond the cars to her front and saw the black shape go around the slight bend ahead. 'Got him!'

'Don't let him see you. Keep back.' Raglan knew JD was 150 metres ahead of them. If he stopped for any reason Raglan could sprint and reach them. He was no Usain Bolt, but he could get there in under twenty seconds. But if the shooting started he knew JD would have no hesitation in targeting innocent bystanders to cause mayhem and impede any attempt to apprehend him. The manoeuvre to box him in needed to be done in the right place and then Raglan would deal with him. He saw the attack in his mind's eye. Shoot the driver to stop any attempt at escape, and then try and wound JD. That part was unlikely because JD would already be shooting. He would have to put JD down quickly.

Abbie gripped the wheel, concentrating as Raglan's soothing voice tried to calm her. 'It's all right. Stay at this speed. Not time to go yet.'

'He's going for one of the bridges,' she said, unable to keep the edge of panic from her voice.

'Just keep him in sight,' he insisted.

A Porsche sped past the car, forcing itself in front of her, blasting its horn and giving her the finger.

'Bloody cretin!' she shouted, slamming on brakes.

JD's driver, alerted by the horn blast, checked the rear-view mirror as JD turned in his seat and looked back. The intruding Porsche cut in and out of traffic and then roared past their car. He watched it go by. Nothing seemed suspicious, but instinct always played a part in his survival. He turned back again, and then looked at the wing mirror, checking the line of cars behind them.

Four cars back, a vehicle nosed out of line and then dipped back again.

'What do you think?' said the driver, who had seen the vehicle in his rearview mirror.

'Test them.'

The driver nodded, found an opening and put his foot down.

'He's on the move,' said Raglan. 'Steady. Stay with him if you can. He might be drawing you out.'

'I don't think so. He couldn't have spotted us,' Abbie said confidently.

Before Raglan could tell her to stay put she heaved the car out into the traffic, accelerated past one more vehicle than she should have and earned another reprimand from a car's horn. Abbie swore under her breath, knowing she'd made a mistake.

JD kept his eyes on the wing mirror. 'Maybe... maybe not... Let's not take any chances. Go,' he calmly ordered.

His driver dropped a couple of gears and floored the accelerator, eyes flicking between the road ahead and his rearview mirror, their speed forcing oncoming cars to avoid them.

★

Now Raglan's voice was urgent. 'They're on to us. Go!'

Abbie could never match the killer driver's skill. She changed down a gear, tried to find an opening, then cut into the blaring oncoming traffic.

'Red-line it!' Raglan said.

She panicked. 'What?'

'Second gear, foot down, push it into the red! Max the revs! Go on!'

Abbie obeyed; the engine protested.

'That's it! Keep it in the red! You need the power!'

The car ahead swerved left. A sudden violent turn of the wheel that slewed the car across the traffic.

'Stay with him! He's going for the other bridge!'

Abbie tried to turn left but was blocked by a lorry.

'Go straight! We'll get them at the Embankment!' said Raglan, keeping his eyes locked on JD's car.

Abbie was doing a decent job of keeping up, but the strain was showing. The car they were pursuing was moving swiftly through the gears and swung on to the bridge across the river. As Abbie tried to follow the snarled-up traffic blocked her. Raglan piled out of the car, tucking the gun into his waistband. He ran hard and fast towards the bridge. And then he saw what had brought them to a halt. A car had stalled at the mouth of the bridge and was refusing to start. JD was already clear and on the far side. Raglan clambered on to the bridge railings and balanced precariously, watching as JD's car was swallowed by traffic in the distance.

Raglan jogged back to the car and sat back next to Abbie. She was sweating, her hands still tightly gripping the steering wheel. 'He's gone to ground now.'

'Sorry.'

'It's all right. You did well. Most wouldn't have,' he said to reassure her.

Abbie nodded her appreciation. Odds were that anyone else would have torn a strip off her but Raglan hadn't berated her. Quite the opposite. And for that, she was grateful, though she could not shake the haunting thought had Elena Sorokina been driving the killers would now be captured.

'OK to drive?' he asked.

'Yes.' She turned the car sedately into the traffic.

Raglan relayed the information to Maguire. 'Narrow the search. He's south of the river.'

29

Rain fell heavily, dancing off the pavements, snare-drumming on car roofs. The downpour shrouded street lights as Raglan and Maguire hunched in a doorway watching Sorokina shaking hands with her police counterparts as she left the control centre at Hammersmith.

'So damned close,' said Maguire, shaking his head at the thought of how near Raglan had been to stopping JD.

'If it wasn't for Abbie we'd still be sitting in a traffic jam. And we got lucky. Can't ever write off luck. We just need a break.'

'What we need, Raglan, is to find out where the hell Carter concealed everything and why.'

'The why doesn't matter. Even the best field agents can feel compromised. He might have known JD and his paymasters were on to him after Qatar. Who knows? He could have been trying to get them to show their hand. They did and he wasn't ready.' Raglan saw Sorokina waiting in the building's entrance. 'When you brought me in on this you said I could have whatever resources I needed.' He took the umbrella that Maguire held. 'I need this.'

Before Maguire could protest Raglan had jogged through the rain to Sorokina, raised the umbrella and escorted her on to the street. Maguire watched him for a moment and then smiled. He'd had his own fair share of liaisons. As he splashed through the puddles towards his waiting car the thought crossed his mind that maybe it had been Sorokina who had wooed Raglan. When the car pulled away from the kerb Maguire spotted Abbie. She was parked with a good view of the police station and Raglan and Sorokina huddled arm in arm beneath the umbrella. Had Maguire been able to read Abbie's emotions he would have been surprised: he wouldn't have thought her capable of being so envious.

Raglan ordered the cab driver to take Sorokina to her hotel while urging her to use her contacts to narrow down any derelict sites south of the river. Then he made his way to the Hammersmith Underground Station and in less than ten minutes alighted at Turnham Green. From there he walked to Carter's house. The armed police were still on duty and once they recognized him he went unhindered through the armed cordon that still straddled the road.

'Anything?' said Amanda once he had stepped inside.

'We're narrowing it down.' He embraced her, feeling her initial resistance, as if being comforted might shatter her resolve. She relented beneath his strength and buried her head into his shoulder. He held her for a minute and kissed her hair. A few seconds later she gently broke away. He saw the glint of moisture in her eyes.

'You'll stay for dinner?'

'Yes, of course. What about the kids?'

'They've already eaten. Steve's with Melissa in there,' she said, nodding towards the lounge. She hesitated before asking, 'Jeremy bathes her about now. If I do that will you read to her later?'

'Sure.'

There was no need for her to thank him, her gratitude was written in her smile. He went through to the lounge where the children were watching television. Steve looked up, eyes begging for any news at all. Raglan gave a brief shake of his head as Melissa jumped off the sofa and ran to him.

'Hey, how you doing? What's this we're watching?' he said as he picked her up and spun her around.

'It's rubbish,' she said. 'Is Daddy with you?'

'No, sweetheart. But he'll be home soon.'

'I hope so because I've been doing drawings for him.'

'Can I see them?'

'Yes, you can, but don't tell Daddy because they're a surprise for him.'

'I promise,' he said, allowing himself to be led away by the five-year-old. 'Your mum's going to give Melissa a bath,' he said to the forlorn-looking teenager. 'How about we go on that run?'

'You don't have any kit,' said the boy, pre-empting the possibility of spending time with Raglan being rejected.

'I could use your dad's? We're about the same shoe size.'

Steve jumped up from the sofa, his grin wider than a moment before. 'I'll sort it,' he said.

Raglan tucked the semi-automatic out of harm's way on top of the antique wardrobe in the spare room and changed into Carter's tracksuit. Steve was more animated than before. It was time to get a break from the overwhelming emotions in the house. Raglan cleared it with the duty police officers. There was little risk of anything happening in the nearby streets for an hour's jog. He told the cops the route they would take and a time for them to return. They checked with their command centre and after a few minutes, once the higher-ups knew the identity of the man taking Steve Carter out of the house, permission was granted.

The two set off, jogging slowly and effortlessly, and then Raglan picked up the pace, wanting to force the boy to push himself harder. Exertion concentrated the mind. After twenty minutes, with his own lungs biting for air, Raglan slowed and began a gentle probing to uncover anything else that Carter might have told his stepson. Steve answered the query by increasing the pace again, running away from the memory. Raglan had no problem keeping up.

'Steve, ease up. All I am saying is that there might be something. A word, anything, that your dad said in the car that you hadn't remembered.'

The boy came to a sudden halt, anger flashing across his face. 'Why are you torturing me?' he shouted. 'I don't *want* to remember!'

Raglan grabbed his shoulders but he was strong enough to shake free. 'I thought you were on my side,' Steve pleaded.

'I am. I promise you. But I'm getting nowhere fast and I have to find your dad before it's too late. That's the reality so no matter how tough it is I'm willing to push you hard because you were the last person to see him. Your dad had only seconds to give you a helluva lot of information. Why do you think he shouted at you? He was driving it into your mind. The name Serval, the initials of the man JD, the place where the key was hidden, my address. Everything was pressure.' He took a more conciliatory tone. 'Steve, an action like that ambush probably takes less than thirty seconds from the time it kicks off. Your dad would have given you little more than instructions and names, one or two, maybe three words. He hammered them at you and your survival instinct lodged them in your brain.'

Steve sank down on his haunches and put his head in his hands. Raglan watched as the boy shook his head from side to side.

'Nothing. There was nothing else that he said. I told you everything.'

'Go back to the shooting. Your father grabbed you. He made you look at him. You were scared. You kept wanting to look at the men with guns but your dad made you listen. He forced you to look at him, didn't he?' said Raglan, knowing that Carter's years of intelligence work would have been concentrated into those few vital seconds. There had to be more than the boy remembered.

Steve nodded. 'He told me where to go. How long to stay in your flat. Gave me those initials – JD. He was shouting at me. I've never seen him scared like that...' His voice trailed off.

Raglan squatted next to the troubled teenager. 'Close your eyes. Look at his face,' he said gently. 'Look at it. You heard him tell you what to do. Now watch his lips. Can you see the words? What else did he do or say?'

Steve raised his head. He had tears in his eyes. Raglan could see him searching his memory of those final terrifying moments in the car.

'He... he pulled my face to his... said he loved me... Yes, he put his lips next to my ear... and... and said he loved me. Then forced me out of the car. That's when I ran.'

The boy's eyes were searching the image bank lodged in his consciousness. And the buried memory revealed itself as gently as a forensic archaeologist's brush eases away the grains of dirt from a buried corpse. He looked momentarily startled.

'There was something else... after he said he loved me... he said...' The boy looked bewildered. 'It was... the stars.'

Raglan took Steve back to the house and while the boy showered phoned Maguire. The message that Carter had passed to his son in those final moments meant nothing. They bounced the phrase around between them for a few minutes. A pub? Something to do with the Planetarium? None of it made any sense. All Maguire could do was to put his people on it. Then Raglan phoned Sorokina and asked her to check with her Hungarian contacts. He sluiced down in the guest bathroom and asked Amanda whether the word meant anything to her. It did not. Raglan went into Carter's study and went over old ground again. The desktop and laptop had been taken by the MI6 search team, so too had the phones, and they had not yet returned any other electronic device in the house. Amanda was dependent on the house's landline and it was a fair bet that MI6 would still be monitoring all calls in and out. Raglan's search turned up no further clues and he admitted defeat. He ate the meal Amanda had prepared but she did little more than move the food around her plate. An overwhelming sense of helplessness pervaded the house. Finally, she scraped the plate into the bin.

'Melissa is sleeping in my bed. Do you have time to read to her?'

'Of course.'

She leant on the sink, head bowed. For a moment he thought she had reached the end of her slender thread of courage.

'Mandy?' he said gently, stepping quickly to her.

She shook her head before he could embrace her. 'Don't,' she whispered, in obvious pain. She turned and faced him. 'Too much tenderness now might finish me off. Understand?'

He did.

30

He stayed longer than he wanted because Melissa demanded the story be read twice, and then it was obvious to Raglan that Steve needed more time too, so he could talk about the man who had assumed the role of his father. While he was giving the children time Raglan mentally pursued the clue given to the boy by his father. What the hell did the 'stars' have to do with anything? It was too vague and he could still make no sense of it. If Carter had expected him to work it out quickly then he had put his own life in extreme jeopardy. And Raglan knew that if he couldn't figure it out then Carter would eventually crack under torture. That's when the bad guys would win. Even the boy had been given the barest information. Always the professional, Carter had known that if his son had been captured then JD would not have gained anything more than the bare-bones clue he had planted in the boy's terrified mind. Carter had been prepared to die in that ambush and the boy he loved had inherited the secret.

By the time Raglan had comforted Steve there were no taxis and rather than take the Underground he strode homeward through the persistent drizzle that softened the city lights. A bus splashed through puddles and he caught sight of three or four people sleeping, heads resting against the steamed-up windows. Rough sleepers seeking a few hours of safety and warmth. There was no need for Raglan to skirt the building to double-check Maguire's people weren't watching him. They knew where he was and had more important things to do. As he walked through the night he'd kept thinking. And thinking. He phoned Sorokina.

'I've got it wrong,' he said. 'He went south across the river on the Albert Bridge. We were stuck in a jam. Now we've alerted everyone to look on that side. If I were him I'd have gone around the park,' he said, his mind's eye seeing Battersea Park on the map he had held on his lap while cruising the streets with Abbie. 'I'd have doubled back on Battersea Bridge. He's north of the river. Damned if he isn't. Everything he's done is this side. The ambush, the first hideout, using Eddie Roman – a local man who knew his own patch. They're still here. I've wasted time. Get your Hungarians back on track.'

He followed suit with Maguire. It was no good giving vent to the frustration of knowing that they had lost hours that might have cost Carter his life.

He was soaked by the time he reached his room. He changed into the spare clothes from his holdall and then settled down on the old bedstead and opened the only book he had brought with him from his apartment. Carter had used the Arabic book to show him that he had visited Qatar but was there more? The page that had been marked by the boarding pass was a section on tenth-century Arabic astronomy and showed a table of named stars and constellations. And that surely was where the clue that Carter had passed to his son in those final desperate moments would be explained. Raglan had spent months in the desert; there, he had not only depended on the latest GPS positioning but on celestial navigation, yet as he gazed at the book he couldn't work out what Carter meant him to see. There were two hundred stars and constellations listed. For the next couple of hours Raglan noted various combinations of the Arabic names on the pages and their meaning in English but by the time the street lights blinked off in the morning all he had for his efforts was a stiff neck and a sense of frustration that whatever trail Carter had left him went nowhere.

Morning traffic was already busy on the road below his window as he checked up and down the broad street. He saw Abbie waiting in her car on the nearside kerb. So Maguire had told her where he was staying. He would have preferred Maguire had kept that information to himself. Abbie was useful for navigating the busy streets, but she was Maguire's crew and he knew every thought he spoke aloud would go back to her boss. He tucked the semi-automatic into his waistband and decided that after the day's reconnaissance he would move rooms again. As he closed the small volume on the bookmarked page the dull light through the window showed the faintest of pencil marks, almost impossible to see unless the book was held to the light on a flat plane. It was enough. He ran down the stairs into the street, phone to his ear.

'Maguire, Carter marked up an Arabic-named star called Al-Nilam. It translates pretty much as a, or the, string of pearls.'

'What the hell does that mean?' the irritated voice demanded.

Raglan strode to where Abbie waited. 'I've no idea. This is your town, you figure it out.' He climbed into the car and covered the mouthpiece. 'Ever heard of anything called a string of pearls? A place?' he asked her.

She shook her head. 'Sounds like a pub.'

'Maguire,' said Raglan, 'get your people on to this and—'

Abbie placed a hand on his arm. 'Wait. The String of Pearls was some kind of millennium celebration. They opened up buildings for the public. Places you never usually got to see. I remember my father telling me.' She shrugged at the sparsity of the information she offered.

'Abbie's just told me it was something to do with

buildings being opened up twenty-odd years ago to celebrate the millennium.'

'Yes, I remember. Dammit, Raglan, how the hell do we trace anything that far back? There were dozens of places opened to the public.'

'Something will link Carter to one of them...' He heard Maguire covering the phone and shouting orders; then he was back listening. 'Whatever he was doing before he joined the service,' said Raglan. 'His university perhaps. His time as a lawyer? He spent years in the army. Those are the links. We're going on with the derelict sites but text me a list of places.'

Maguire severed the connection.

'Where to?' said Abbie, looking happy enough to drive to the end of the world if Raglan asked her to.

He unfolded the map and squared it off so the area he wanted was visible. 'We stay north of the river.'

She looked as though she was about to argue that the man they pursued had gone south, but stayed silent. If Raglan had decided otherwise so be it. She swung the car into traffic. For the next fifteen minutes, she navigated around bottlenecks and roadworks. The journey was almost leisurely. She drew in a breath and steadied the flutter in her stomach.

'My parents have invited you to dinner...'

He glanced at her.

She shrugged. 'You made an impression. Dad's never done that before, so...'

'It's a compliment,' Raglan said.

She nodded, her face flushing with embarrassment. 'I'd better warn you: it'll be one of his hot curries. I said you were busy so don't feel obliged. Honest. No big deal.' It was.

'That's very kind, Abbie, let's see how the day goes. I'd be honoured.'

She beamed.

His phone rang. Abbie could hear the Russian woman's voice.

'Something looks promising,' she said. 'I'm in a police car and heading for a place in East London. It's a derelict factory.'

Raglan pressed the phone to his chest and instructed Abbie: 'East London.'

She nodded. 'I heard.'

Sorokina was speaking to the two police officers; then her voice came back again. Raglan put the phone on speaker so they could both hear her instructions. 'You are nearest. It is an abandoned building in Commercial Road. My contacts tell me the building is used sometimes by film companies as a location. It was rented four weeks ago for cash but no questions were asked until I asked them. The film company does not exist.'

Raglan looked at Abbie. She shook her head. 'That's an hour away. Can they get an armed response vehicle from another borough?'

'I want to be there,' said Raglan. A hunter sensing his prey.

'But if we don't secure the area and the men you're after are there then they could be gone,' Abbie urged him.

Raglan nodded. She was right. He wished he could click his fingers and be instantly transported to the target. But of course he couldn't. He raised the phone. 'Get the local police to task ARVs. Deep cordon. No breach. Secure the streets and no sirens. Confirm when they get there. We're on our way. Elena, you follow.'

Abbie was already finding gaps in the traffic but irrational envy taunted her again when she heard Raglan call the Russian by her Christian name. She changed down a gear and floored the accelerator, more confident since she had pursued the black Saab.

Raglan kept his eyes on the road ahead but his mind raced. The armed response officers were top-notch guys who dealt with violent crime involving firearms, but if JD was in that building who knew how many gunmen he had with him. It was all too easy for a hostage to die in the crossfire. They needed a breach by trained assault troops or the Met's Counter-Terrorist Unit. They would be worth their weight in gold, except they had been stood down by their commander because JD was wanted for kidnapping and murder so this was a simple hunt for armed men led by the police investigation teams.

Abbie braked hard, avoiding a slow driver.

'Don't take risks,' Raglan told her. 'Find the best route you can, but we need to get there in one piece.' He smiled, wanting to offer her some comfort. 'We can't let your folks down. I haven't had a chance for a curry since I got here.'

31

As they approached the location Raglan saw the striped police cars angled across the near and far end of the road. The two yellow discs in their windscreens indicated they belonged to armed officers. One of them waved them down while his partner covered him, weapon tucked into his shoulder. Raglan wound down the window.

'Mr Raglan, sir?'

'Yes.'

'They told us you were coming. We got here twenty minutes ago; we secured both ends of the road.'

Raglan climbed out of the car, grateful that Maguire had cleared him. 'Stay here,' he told Abbie. He turned to the second officer. 'Make sure she does. No one goes forward.' Raglan glanced at the huge billboard that someone had erected. He smiled.

'Operational command lies with my assistant borough commander, sir,' said the cop, pointing to a uniformed senior officer at the second vehicle. Raglan nodded and strode towards the female officer.

'Raglan?' she said as he reached her. He nodded. She hadn't been at the operational meeting in Hammersmith. 'My orders are to give you every assistance.' She hesitated. 'Whoever you are.'

Raglan had no time for soothing bruised egos. A lie was easier. 'I'm a hostage negotiator. Keep your officers back. We don't know how accurate our intelligence is or how many men might be in there.'

She flipped open a tablet and brought up an aerial picture of the building. 'There's a canal at the rear with a towpath. We have two armed officers at each end of the building. The front is boarded up with one window clear top right that gives a view down the street, but I have my people behind that hoarding there,' she said, pointing out the high wooden walls surrounding an adjacent building site. 'So they won't be spotted. We have sealed off any approach road. We're telling people there's been a hazardous chemical spill from a tanker. We couldn't risk using a drone to check the place out, but my team got a pole camera above the rear yard walls. There's a black Saab visible and another similar-sized vehicle under a tarpaulin.'

'You and your officers have done a lot in a short time. My thanks.'

She nodded. 'The way in is from the canal side at the rear. Any attempt to break through the boarded-up windows and doors at the front will alert whoever's inside. I can't commit my officers to breaching the building and unless we have a terrorist threat we can't get armed counter-terrorism officers here.'

'I understand.' He turned as the police car bearing Sorokina arrived. Raglan raised an arm and beckoned her to him. 'You won't have to.'

Abbie watched the Russian shake hands with the female police officer. Raglan was showing her something, then pointing out the building. They bent over the tablet with the superintendent. Abbie's phone rang. It was Maguire.

'Anything?'

'No, sir. We're in Limehouse at an abandoned building in Commercial Road. ARVs are here but no evidence of anyone inside yet.'

'Keep well back, Abbie, this isn't why you are there. Understand?'

'Yes, sir.'

'Very well. I'm on my way. We've narrowed our search down on the String of Pearls information. I might need you back in town soon.'

'Sir, this isn't resolved here and Raglan might still need me.'

'You don't work for Raglan,' he snapped.

She didn't answer.

He sighed. 'All right. You've done well. Let's hope this is it. Tell Raglan to hold off going in until I am there. He's switched his bloody phone off.'

Abbie got out of the car but the burly policeman blocked her. 'Stay in the car, miss.'

'I have orders for Raglan. I'm only going to your boss.'

The armed officer looked across to the huddled three-some. 'Come on,' he said and accompanied her. When they reached Raglan and the two women he stood off from his senior officer. 'Ma'am? This lady has a message for Mr Raglan.'

Raglan looked at her. She smiled with a hint of embarrassment, but was secretly pleased to be drawn back into his world. She was about to deliver Maguire's message when he stepped quickly to her, took her arm and turned her away from the others.

'I told you to stay in the car,' he said quietly but firmly.

Realizing that he didn't want the others to hear what she had to say she lowered her voice. 'It's Maguire. He's annoyed because your phone is off. He thinks they're close to finding where Carter has hidden the information, but he wants you to hold off going in until he's here.'

'We don't even know if this is the right place. Time is against us. If Carter is still alive we need to save him. Get back to the car.'

'What do I tell him?'

'That you told me.'

*

Raglan watched Sorokina spread her fingers across the tablet's screen and enlarge the building's plans. 'This isn't the greatest target appreciation I've ever seen,' he said.

'It's all the Hungarians had.'

'Better than nothing, then,' he said. He pointed at the layout. 'It's a huge space. They're probably on the top floor for a good OP. That corridor, it runs right underneath to the back stairs. That's my way in.'

'You cannot do this alone. He is my prisoner; I will be there.'

'Have you been in a situation like this before?'

She hesitated and then shook her head. 'In training, yes, but I am not afraid. I have fought with guns before. I know the danger.'

'All the training in the world doesn't cover what happens. It's different. Especially the first time. Stay here.'

'We do not know how many men he has in there. I can be of use.' She peeled off her jacket and checked her pistol.

Since he first laid eyes on Elena Sorokina he'd been struck by her air of professional ability and self-confidence, and now having slept with her he knew she was forthright and liked to be in control.

'You don't move without my say-so. All right? Do what I tell you.'

She nodded. 'What about your Mr Maguire?'

'You want him breathing down our necks?'

'He will be angry.'

'It comes with the territory.' He turned to the assistant borough commander. 'I need two of your officers to come in with us and secure the entry point. They don't need to do more than that, but I need someone covering our backs.'

She nodded and popped the boot of her car and took out two body armour vests. Raglan and Sorokina pulled off their jackets and shrugged into them. 'Two of my officers are ex-paras. I won't put their lives on the line, Raglan, but if it comes to it they have the experience to clear rooms and secure your backs. But only as far as the entry point. Good enough?'

'More than. Thank you.'

The burly officer and his partner who had waved down Abbie's car followed Raglan and Sorokina. Raglan briefed them; they nodded their understanding, asking no questions. What Raglan asked of them was routine for the two ex-paras: their grins seemed to say: *Give us half a chance.* Raglan led them through a hole in the fence beneath the huge rectangular billboard that some church or crackpot organization had erected at the front of the derelict building. The printed message proclaimed boldly: *Judgement Is Coming.*

The rear of the building was in as much disrepair as the front. Bushes and weeds had seeded themselves over time, choking much of the lower-floor windows. The glass in the dozen or more windows thirty feet above their heads was mostly intact, evidence that vandals could not throw stones from the narrow angle offered by the towpath below them. It also meant that if the top floor was intact and JD and his men were there then it was unlikely they could look directly down and see any movement. Raglan bent and moved through a sagging door frame.

Inside the vaulted factory, steel girders supported gantries around the walls, a walkway for each of the floors. Rusted machinery was everywhere and looking at the underside of the first gantry that ran above their heads Raglan saw the green of mould on the wooden floor timbers. They might be too rotten to support a man's weight. As he edged forward peering up into the vaulted roof he saw the pitched glass was still intact. The low dark clouds outside weighed down even more gloomily on the interior. Pigeons fluttered on the high beams and somewhere in the distance water dripped into a puddle, its gentle splash echoing through the cathedral-like chamber. There was no other sound. No voices carried across the bare space. But there were men inside somewhere. The breeze through the broken windows wafted the unmistakable stench of excrement.

He turned, signalled the two cops to go left and right into the brick-walled rooms. They were good. Using hand signals they declared the areas safe. Raglan nodded, pointed with his forefinger to his eye and then to the door and passageway they had used to gain entry. One man was to stay to keep watch. Raglan gestured to the other to watch from another window's vantage point. The concrete floor was mostly clear of debris and the officer had no trouble picking his way tactically across it. His new position gave him a clear view across the ground and the immediate upper floors. If anyone came out from a hidden place behind Raglan and Sorokina then the armed officers would have a clear field of fire.

Raglan tested his weight on the first step that abutted the bannisters. If there was anywhere that would support them it would be here. The thick planking barely gave under him and as he turned on to the half landing he used the full width of the stair tread and looked up, checking the length of the gantry above him. He heard Sorokina's quickened breathing behind him. Both held their handguns at the ready, moving the weapon in the direction they were checking. More confident that the heavy timbers would support their weight, Raglan moved quicker, eager to get off the exposed stairway. Fifteen more steps. Five more to reach cover. Always ready for the unexpected.

A door opened on the next level up. A man's voice. His words were indistinct as he looked behind him to someone else in the room he had stepped out of. A complaint. He went to the edge of the balustrade and tipped a toilet bucket's contents into the void. Movement was a soldier's best friend or worst enemy, depending who was doing the hunting. Raglan froze, his arm stopping Sorokina from instinctively trying to hide. Raglan kept his eyes and his weapon on the man. It was a fifty-fifty chance whether he would have seen Raglan and Sorokina exposed on the open stairs when he tipped the bucket out. Turn right and he would be looking down straight at them. Turn left and his back would be to them. Raglan dared a quick glance downward. The burly cop had his weapon in his shoulder. He had read the situation. And waited.

Still complaining, the bucket man turned left.

Raglan took the stairs two at a time.

They reached the gantry, edging forward. An open shell of a room, three of its walls broken down, held crates and pieces of machinery. Huge chains used for lifting goods from the lower floors; sealed double loading doors which would have given access to the canal outside. His gaze swept the room, caught a glimpse of Sorokina with her weapon doing the same at his back, both covering arcs of fire. She was good.

It was barely noticeable but there was a slight change in the light from a broken window, then a pigeon clattered upwards, and a wooden pallet moved. Raglan swivelled, ready to shoot. A boy's wide-eyed face looked back at him. The kid's mouth opened and closed, fear restricting his throat.

Raglan snatched at Sorokina's gun hand, clamping it, forcing it down from the fire position as the small boy began to tremble. Her intake of breath told him her immediate instinct had been to shoot. The seconds it took for Raglan to separate the movement and the child's appearance whirled him back to the moment years before when he had shot and killed the boy in the cave. The thudding in his chest took his breath away. He shook his head to clear the image and steadied his hand. He gestured for the boy to remain silent, lowering his weapon to negate any threat the boy felt and within a half-dozen strides reached the frightened stowaway.

As Raglan reached the pallet he saw another boy huddled down, making himself small. They were only nine or ten years old. The wide-eyed boy was shaking, a pool of urine at his feet, his tracksuit bottoms soaked. Raglan smiled. 'It's OK. No one's going to hurt you. Understand?' he whispered. The boy nodded. 'Tell your mate to stay quiet. There are bad guys here? Yeah?'

Again the boy nodded. 'Mister, they weren't here last week... We play here... but... but we heard them and we hid...'

The second child had stayed low, hugging his knees, looking up to the bigger boy. Maybe brothers, Raglan thought. Older brother taking his sibling on an adventure. Raglan glanced at Sorokina, who had knelt and covered the opening.

'Listen, that lady is a cop. And there are a couple more downstairs. She's going to take you down but you have to stay dead quiet and you mustn't run. Got that?'

'Are we in trouble?' said the boy.

'No. I promise you. I bet even your mum and dad won't know you've been here.'

The look of relief on the boys' faces told him all he needed to know. The younger boy got to his feet, his voice barely a whisper. 'We heard someone make a noise, like he was being hurt.'

'Where?'

The boys pointed in unison. It seemed there was another staircase inside one of the derelict rooms that must lead up to another room.

'OK. Remember what I said. We don't rush and we don't talk. Got it?'

They nodded.

Raglan led the way to the gantry, peered down, saw the uniformed cop, who watched his every movement. Raglan pointed to the two boys. The cop nodded.

'Go down with them,' he told Sorokina quietly.

For a moment he thought she would protest but she recognized the seriousness of the situation and ushered the two boys towards the stairs and then led them down. The ex-para cop moved forward, still covering the upper floors, and knelt in cover behind a hulk of machinery. It would serve as a good fire position and a safe haven for the children before he passed them to his partner guarding the entrance.

Raglan watched Sorokina descend the stairs; when she and the children were near the bottom he turned and made his way into the room two doors along the open gantry. A broad iron stairway led upwards. He edged forward, waited, and calmed his breathing. It was darker here. The light did not penetrate these side rooms. He looked up and saw the faint glow of a gas lantern. And then the murmur of voices. The upstairs was blacked out, the windows most likely sealed.

Raglan took the first step.

Judgement Is Coming.

32

The attic room stretched across half the building. It was walled off halfway, before the glass roof could filter any natural light into it. It had once been a storeroom but now the windows were boarded, all except one, which had a panel cut out of it where a gunman sat on an old packing case keeping watch. From where he sat he could see the walled yards where the car and ambulance were parked and where the man they worked for would return through the double gates that led on to the side street. From the angle at which he sat he could not see the police blockade. And he was tired. They had been on the go for days and now they were nearing the end of the operation. He and the two other gunmen in the room would be gone by that night. The helicopter was organized; the rewards would be substantial. They would return to their homes and wait for the Russian's next call. And before nightfall they would kill the man strapped to the chair. He was tougher than anyone had imagined. The gunman reflected for a moment and doubted whether he or his companions, all ex-Spetsnaz men, would have withstood such pain. Everyone had a breaking point. He mentally shrugged. Who cared? He chewed the sandwich and rinsed the dry bread down with water.

'Pyotr. Make us a brew,' he said in Russian, turning to one of the men. They had made themselves as comfortable as possible. They might only have old sacking beneath their sleeping bags, but the small gas canister camping stoves gave them hot water. They had forsaken cooking in case the smell drifted, but sweet tea was a constant comfort. They had kept things basic: candle stubs gave them enough low light and the bucket in the corner a means of relieving themselves. They would usually shit in a bag and take it away but there was no need in this run-down factory. Pretty soon it would make no difference what was found here. Most likely in time a wrecking crew would discover the remains of their prisoner. The man, Pyotr, rose without demur and checked the water bubbling on the stove. Even when he moved the few paces to where the camping gas stove flared he carried his assault rifle. Such actions were ingrained.

Carter, barely conscious, raised his head as the shadow passed in front of him. 'He won't come back... or meet you... or whatever it is you've arranged... He'll take it all... You won't see him again. That's how he works. Trust me... I know...'

The man with the rifle, Pyotr, ignored him as he prepared the tea. The man at the window turned to look at the others. 'What if he's telling the truth?'

The others looked at him. Uncertainty could undermine everything.

'He'll come back,' said Pyotr. 'Don't listen to him. We kill him. Then we go. Relax.'

'You're fucking idiots,' Carter said. He was barely able to hold up his head but forced himself to gaze at the blurred image in front of him. 'Hey, Pyotr. All this way from home and... he runs out on you. Without him you're... stuck... You think your kind will help you here?' he grunted painfully. 'You're on your own.'

The tea-maker put a wicked-looking killing knife at Carter's throat. 'I'm tired of you. Enough now. Shut up.'

The third man rolled from where he lay and squeezed his companion's arm. 'Not yet... but soon. Be patient.' He grinned. 'We have to get going soon – we're running out of sugar.'

Raglan ascended carefully towards the opening above his head that in days past would have been a trapdoor. The flickering light illuminated the ceiling. Footsteps creaked across the floorboards. He stopped, controlled his breathing, urging his heart to stop thudding in his ears. He heard Carter and the murmuring of men's voices.

'He's... double-crossed you. He's not coming back. You... you don't know him... like I do.'

Raglan crouched and dared to go higher. He inched his face above the rim of the trapdoor. The floor area was dark, the candlelight throwing shadows against the walls. He saw Carter strapped in the chair. Three gunmen. One at the window. One spooning sugar.

One gunman crossed his line of sight carrying a mug in each hand, making his way towards the man at the window. Carter sucked up the energy in a desperate attempt to needle his tormentors.

'He's gone! With the information. I know him! I was his controller! YOU – STUPID – BASTARDS!'

Raglan controlled his shock at seeing his mutilated friend as the man spooning the sugar slapped Carter.

'Shut up! Or I kill you now!'

Carter slumped.

The gunman at the window berated him. 'Don't be stupid. We might still need him.'

The man with the sugar argued back: 'Look at him. He's finished. He won't last another hour. What difference does it make? Let's kill the bastard. I'm tired of all this.'

The men looked at each other. The man at the window seemed in charge. He nodded. 'Use your knife. We don't want noise.'

Raglan braced, ready to force himself into the room. The man at the window had his palms resting on the weapon on his lap. Window Man would react quickly; Raglan would kill him first. Knife Man's weapon lay on the makeshift table next to the tea-maker's. Tea Man would be the last man to die because he stood halfway across the room, with a mug in each hand: he was the least threat of the three. Raglan pushed himself up into the room.

Shadows jigged across the space as the gunmen saw a figure loom up through the darkness. Their moment's hesitation was all Raglan needed. He turned the handgun on Window Man as the other two rolled clear. No time for double-tapping shots: he squeezed the trigger again and again. The man's chest and head ripped apart. Knife Man grabbed for his weapon, but went down with multiple rounds in his neck, head and chest. Noise thundered in the confined space. Tea Man dropped the mugs and pulled a sidearm from his shoulder rig. He got off two quick shots that went wide as Raglan sidestepped, fired, half turned and fired again. He watched the man hurled down by the force of the rounds that whipped into his neck and jaw. He was dead before he hit the floor. The blurred moments of high intensity cleared as Raglan refocused and stood his ground, sweeping the room for any movement. His ears rang.

He didn't hear Sorokina call his name, but he sensed the movement behind him as she put her head above the floor level. He turned rapidly and in that millisecond as he saw it was her it was only his years of training and combat experience that made him pull up the barrel as he fired off two quick reflex shots.

'Elena!' He stepped to the trapdoor and peered down. She had fallen back down the stairs and was picking herself up, recovering her dropped weapon. She swore at him in Russian. There was no time to apologize. 'Get an ambulance!' He turned back to the room and kicked away the knife-man's body from where he had fallen close to Carter. He tugged a sleeping bag near the chair and, using the dead man's knife, cut the bonds around Carter's hands and feet. He lifted his battered friend from the chair and laid him on the sleeping bag, rubbing gently at his wrists where the ties had pressed into the flesh, calling his name.

'Jerry? Come on, man. Hang on.'

Raglan heard shouts from below, orders bellowed. Carter regained consciousness, his hand touching Raglan's. 'You... took your time,' he whispered.

It went quiet. Raglan knew the man was dying. His mutilated face and the wounds on his body told of unspeakable cruelty. Raglan raised a water bottle to the man's caked lips.

'The traffic was heavy,' he said gently.

Carter licked his lips. He sighed and nodded and managed a flicker of a smile.

'Knew you'd come.' He shuddered as his body's core strength began to dissipate. The low candles flickered and then went out. The shadows closed in. 'I'm sorry...

I... I couldn't take it any more...' Tears welled in his eye. Raglan gently wiped his cheek.

'Don't talk, Jerry. Help's on its way. We'll have you with the medics soonest.' He spilt water on a piece of rag from the floor and tenderly bathed the man's blood-caked face.

Carter wanted Raglan to understand his failure. 'I wasn't strong enough... The pain, Raglan, my God... I'm sorry...' He wasn't going to last much longer.

Elena put her head up. 'Maguire's here.'

'Keep him out for a few minutes,' Raglan told her.

She saw a man holding his dying friend in his lap, comforting him like a child. She went back down without saying a word as Raglan dribbled more water between his friend's lips. It revived him.

'I told him... told JD where the stuff is. An old... safe deposit box... He's got the codes and the money. I sent him to the money and the... codes,' he repeated. 'Did you... understand... the message in the book... did you see it?'

'The star? The String of Pearls? Yes. Maguire's probably found it by now.'

Carter grinned. 'Thank God... Well done, old friend... knew you'd figure it out... That's the first team list... the real players... I kept going as long as I could... JD's got the money... and the B team names...' He moved his head side to side. 'B team's not the jackpot... but... they won't know that...'

'Jerry, listen: where is it? Where did you send him?'

'Doesn't matter now, does it? He's got more men... had them here and there... don't know how many... maybe... two more... couldn't tell.'

'I've got to get him for what he's done – even though he doesn't have the main players on that list. Come on, where did you send him?'

Carter's mind cleared. His mission to live long enough and deflect the killer's intentions was completed: now he could think only of his family.

'Is Steve... all right?'

'He got to the flat. Jerry...?'

'He's a good boy... Oh God, Raglan... my baby... my Melissa... oh God...' The tears spilt on to his cheek again.

'OK, mate. We'll have you out of here ASAP. Where's JD?' he insisted. 'This is the last piece of the jigsaw. We capture him, we get a lot of information from him. The Russians want him, Jerry, he's a direct link through organized crime to the Kremlin.'

Carter shook his head. 'The money, blood diamonds for the black ops... let it go... No one knows... We're clean... the Service is clean... all of us...' He managed to smile. 'Queen and bloody country, Raglan. It dies with me... He's gone; I know it... heard them talking... a chopper... Isle of Dogs... somewhere... Christ... I'm scared... Don't tell Steve... I couldn't hold out.'

'No one could have got through what they did to you. I wouldn't have.'

'Is this... a confession?' Carter searched his face. Raglan nodded.

'Back then, after all those days of being tortured, I told them what they wanted to know. By the time my guys killed everyone the info was old. No one knew. Except me.'

Carter said something but Raglan couldn't hear. He lowered his ear close to Carter's cracked lips; Carter smiled and whispered, 'Your secret's safe with me.'

The man's final sigh brushed Raglan's face.

33

Police lights flashed in the night as Raglan ran out into the light rain. He signalled to the borough commander and her officers it was clear. The men who had covered his back led an ambulance crew inside. Maguire stood with Sorokina.

'Carter?' said Maguire.

'Dead,' Raglan answered.

'Did he say anything?'

'You mean other than worrying for his family?'

'Christ, Raglan, we'll do our grieving for the man later.'

'Did you get the Qatari paymaster's list?'

Maguire nodded. 'We hit three of the locations in the String of Pearls celebration that he was most likely to have any association with. The Inns of Court came up trumps. His old chambers from when he practised held them in their security vault.'

'JD's got the money and another list,' said Raglan.

'More names?' said a stricken-looking Maguire.

'Carter planted a B list with the money. You've got the prize – the A list. He was your man to the end, Maguire. Carter was innocent.'

'We'll see,' Maguire answered.

'You didn't deserve him. He wouldn't let the Service be seen to have dirty hands. He sent JD for your slush fund. He saved your neck.'

The chastisement washed over Maguire. 'Where?'

'Isle of Dogs and a chopper,' said Raglan. He glanced up at the clouds. 'Not in this though.'

'It's lifting,' said Maguire. 'We wanted a police search helicopter, but it's another hour or so before it starts to lift and even then it'll be minimum flying weather. If JD has a hotshot pilot waiting somewhere, then he can be gone.'

Sorokina raised her eyes and then scowled. '*B'lyad'!*' she spat, turned away and pressed a speed dial on her phone.

The corner of Raglan's mouth creased in what could be taken as a smile. Russian obscenities were unique and rich in their expression and not easily translated, but her expletive didn't need one. 'She swears a lot, but she has connections,' Raglan explained. 'It's how we got here. Maguire, listen. JD must have gone to wherever Carter sent him. That will have taken time. Then he had to get to his final location on the Isle of Dogs. More time. And he has to wait for the cloud base to lift. We can still get him.'

Maguire nodded and beckoned his driver. 'Perhaps, if we're lucky. There's a helipad on the Isle of Dogs – companies use it for bringing people into Canary Wharf and the Olympic Park.' His driver waited. 'Alert the police and get our people there. Shut it down.'

Maguire saw the borough commander making a beeline for him. 'Christ, Raglan, there'll be an inquiry into the shooting.'

'Tell them I took the weapon off one of the gunmen.'

'We're not above the law. They'll want to interview you and that's going to close you down. You're done here.'

'No. We're not finished yet, Maguire. We owe it to Carter,' Raglan told him, taking a step closer to the MI6 man, looking to where Abbie stood a respectful few paces behind them. Her pay grade didn't make her privy to what her boss thought or said unless he chose to share either with her. 'Get me out of here,' he said to Maguire, but with his eyes on Abbie, who barely concealed a grin at still being involved.

Maguire turned his back to the borough commander, who had been waylaid by one of her officers seeking clarification on something. 'Abbie. Take him home, do something with him, but get him off the streets until I can buy some time.'

'Yes, sir.'

Raglan followed her to the car, catching Sorokina's eye as she looked his way. He nodded. She understood. She wanted JD as badly as Raglan did.

Raglan looked at the folded map on his lap as Abbie drove the car away at normal speed so as not to draw attention to their escape. The map-reading lamp showed where the hunt for JD had started.

'Every step of the way he has been heading as far east as he could. He'll use the river to make his escape. How long until we get down there?'

'Fifteen minutes if we're lucky. But where? The helipad is right on the river.'

Raglan pictured himself on the run. If he had pre-planned this operation, a commercial helipad was not the place to make an escape. The Maguires of the world could shut it down with one phone call. Too obvious. 'Keep driving,' he told her. 'Ignore the helipad.' He keyed in Sorokina's number. She answered.

'Nothing yet,' she said without him asking.

He hung up and went back to the map. Nothing jumped out at him.

'If he gets a chopper out of here, he's low level down the Thames. Air traffic control has strict routes for flying over the city and the river is a good safety net if an aircraft goes down. That's where he'll be, down there somewhere. A fast pickup and he'll be across the Channel and gone.'

His phone rang. It was Sorokina. 'The Hungarians have nothing that far east of the city. It's a dead end, Raglan.'

Raglan stared at the map. And then he knew where to go.

'When these top-flight executives come to London, stress their way through boardroom wars and then comfort themselves with rich food, where are you going to take them when they have a heart attack?'

'Hospital,' said Sorokina.

'The Quayside Private Clinic is slap bang next to a dock. Plenty of safe flying through the high-rise buildings. There's a helipad on the hospital roof.'

He switched off the phone.

Abbie was already threading her way towards the financial centre. 'Five minutes,' she said.

They turned down the road leading alongside the deepwater dock. The six-storey glass-and-steel building that rose up on the next corner was dwarfed by its big brothers belonging to the world's financial powerhouses. Penis envy all round. Six storeys made sense. A small private clinic. Two operating rooms, two laboratories, twelve private suites over four floors. Ritzier than The Ritz. Dying in luxury an option.

Raglan wound down the window and looked up towards the roof. The clouds obscured the top of the taller buildings, but not the clinic's. If he was right, JD had even figured on the weather playing into his hands. The top floor of the clinic was in darkness. He pointed at the down ramp. Abbie swung the car to the barrier. Raglan took the ticket. Visiting hours were any time that suited. There were more spaces than cars. His phone beeped. It was Maguire.

'I have men at the helipad on the river. There's nothing scheduled at this time of night in these conditions. Whoever is flying in isn't using a London heliport. I have ATC tracking anything that moves. We're ten minutes behind you. Major Sorokina is closest to you with two armed officers. Raglan, that's a private hospital. You'll need uniformed police to effect a search.'

Raglan switched off the phone, pointed to a parking bay next to a concrete column. She glided the car forward.

'There,' she said.

Fifty metres ahead an old black Saab nestled in the shadows. It was empty.

He tossed the phone into her lap. No need to risk unnecessary distractions even if it was off. Damned thing could tempt him to make a call if the shit hit the fan.

'He'll call back the closer he gets. Tell him there was no time for me to wait. Get the car out of here. Stay with it until Maguire or the cops arrive. I can't have you running loose. You understand?'

She nodded, eyes wide with apprehension.

'Your word.'

'I promise.'

'Thank you. You've done a brilliant job. I couldn't ask for anyone better. It's almost over. Maguire will be here soon. Time for you to go home.'

He closed the door quietly behind him and then she watched as he jogged into the shadows. Abbie reached for the ignition key. What if Raglan got into trouble? What if he needed to make a run for it? She let her hand drop. She would wait. Just a little while.

The lift went from the garage to the roof with an obligatory stop at reception. Raglan took the internal stairs, hoping they would take him to the helipad, but as he reached the turn at the ground floor he met a set of one-way doors: a release bar on the other side to allow anyone escaping a fire, but obstructing anyone from going further without authorization. Raglan pushed through a second door on his left, which accessed the marble-floored reception area. There was no one at the desk. He leant over to check behind the counter in case the night receptionist had been attacked. There was no sign of disturbance. Venturing as far as he could down the dimly lit main corridor brought no joy either; the double glass doors were secured by a code pad and card swipe and led only to consultation and waiting rooms. Everything was closed. This clinic was not for 24/7 emergency care.

Raglan returned to the main reception area and checked the large glass doors of the main entrance. They were jammed closed. Someone had hammered a nail into the locks on the top and the base of the doors. No one was getting in that way. A sign showed that the clinic was operational only during daytime hours. A door was closed next to the main entrance. Raglan eased it open. It bumped against something on the floor. A nurse lying sprawled face down. He turned her over. Her name tag said she was Marjorie Chambers. The receptionist. The dead receptionist. Blood spilt from a wound where something narrow and pointed had been plunged into the base of her skull. Not long ago by the look of the wound. She had not died alone. An unarmed security guard lay crumpled, one arm beneath him, blood pooling below his body.

Raglan went back to the main area. Another door led to an outside fire escape. It was open to the elements and exposed to gunfire from anyone above. He pressed the lift button, but it held on the sixth floor. A larger elevator designed to carry trolleys was also held on the same floor. JD had shut the place down. In the corner of reception, a modern glass spiral staircase swirled upwards. Raglan took the stairs three at a time. The first floor had coded doors to the inner workings of the hospital. The only way was up.

He slowed his pace as he turned on to the final twist of stairs that would take him to the sixth floor. He crouched, weapon raised, looking up. What had been a pristine, brightly lit series of passageways on each floor below, with the occasional glimpse of a night nurse moving across a corridor from one room to another, became an unlit, unfinished area that resembled a vast storage room, the only light coming from the buildings outside. The sixth floor was not yet functional. Hospital beds, equipment, chairs, desks, mattresses, trolleys and wheeled medicine cabinets huddled against the walls like orphaned children in a darkened bomb shelter. The breadth of the building was boxed with room partitions ready to be completed as private wards.

Raglan inched forward. Those ahead of him had jammed the two lift doors open. He scanned the darkened area in front of him and edged along the wall. A window exposed the broad expanse of the concrete flat roof outside at the rear of the building. Beyond the flat area a galvanized ramp with a handrail led up several feet to the helipad where patients would be brought down the ramp on a trolley into the lift. He listened. There was no sound of a helicopter. There might still be time to corner JD. The bodies downstairs were freshly dead. The killers were still in the building. A shard of light flashed at the end of the corridor. A side passage door had been opened.

Raglan zigzagged through the detritus, then heard a hiss behind him. He whirled round. A crouching Sorokina flat-palmed him from the head of the stairs. She gestured that the two armed officers were downstairs. Raglan nodded. She made her way towards him. Just paces from where he stood she clattered into a medicine trolley. She gasped. Alarmed, Raglan half turned and instinctively pressed himself against the wall as out of the corner of his eye he saw movement from where the shard of light had been. Two rapid shots followed: Sorokina was hit in the chest. As she buckled Raglan returned fire at the half-concealed man. Rapid gunfire snapped the air around him. A piece of masonry shattered, and he felt a tearing in his thigh. A flesh wound. He heard a magazine being changed. Ignoring the burning sensation and trickle of blood down his leg he strode forward. The gunman dared to look around the corner, ready to continue firing and Raglan shot him twice in the head. He cut across to the other side of the broad corridor. A partition wall offered no effective cover, but it obscured him from anyone else who might appear from the side passage. There was no sound or movement. He looked back. The two uniformed officers appeared at the head of the stairs, weapons at the ready. They were the same two who had covered his back at the factory.

'One man with me! The other get her out!'

The men needed no further commands. They moved rapidly. One grabbed Sorokina's wrist and dragged her to safety; kicking aside the trolley that blocked the lift door, he pulled her inside. Raglan heard the incongruous dulcet tones of a female voice telling the passengers to stand clear of the doors. The second cop posted himself on the opposite side to Raglan, ten feet back, ready to give covering crossfire. Raglan felt the same shudder of anxiety and excitement that always embraced him at times like this. A satisfying gut feeling kicked in, seeing the experienced ex-army police officer ready to move forward into a kill zone. It served no purpose to give a thought to Sorokina.

Focusing on where the dead man lay, he stepped forward. The cop moved tactically, covering Raglan every step of the way. The soft squelch of his police radio sounded as loud as an alarm in the stillness following the gunfire, but it was too low for anyone outside the room to hear. Raglan paused, watched and listened as the man responded in a whisper, giving a quick sitrep, then listened to the voice in his earpiece. He moved to Raglan's shoulder and put his face close to Raglan's ear.

'The Russian's alive. Four ARVs outside, eight men. Surrounding streets being secured. Your boss has shut down the helipad on the river. He's en route. Orders are to wait.'

Raglan smiled. The cop shrugged, knowing full well they were in an operational groove and that forward impetus was in their favour. One gunman down. It lessened the odds. Time to press on. Raglan edged around the corner with his new fighting partner at his shoulder. Raglan held up a hand. They reached the corner where the dead man lay. The corridor was wide, without partitioned walls. To Raglan's left the plate-glass windows brought in light from the illuminated skyscrapers. The interior glass mirrored the image of a gunman waiting around the corner. Raglan shifted the weapon to his left hand, kept his eye on the image in the glass and fired around the corner. The thud of the bullet strikes was followed by the sound of the body slumping against a door. Raglan and the officer turned the corner. Two dead men now lay beneath their feet. As they went forward, he heard the distant but unmistakable sound of a twin-engine helicopter. If luck was on their side, there would be fewer men now to defend JD as he made his escape. Raglan stepped across the second crumpled body and then pushed through the door into the unknown.

Abbie had not done as Raglan instructed; she had stayed in her car. When Sorokina arrived at the clinic, the police car had pulled up outside the parking ramp to block any attempt at escape from inside the hospital building. They had tried to gain access through the front doors but retreated once they realized the doors were jammed. Two of the armed police escorted the Russian major down into the gloom of the parking basement. Abbie caught their attention and told them where Raglan had gone. Abbie waited and ten minutes later, when she saw Sorokina being dragged out of the lift by one of the policemen, she ran to help. Her heart caught in her throat at the violent reality of the situation. She helped take some of the unconscious woman's weight and couldn't help noticing the puncture marks in the Russian's body armour. For a moment she thought Sorokina dead until she heard the injured woman's rasping breath.

'She's alive,' said the cop. 'It's like being kicked by a mule. She'll be OK. There's an ambulance outside.'

'There are doctors here,' Abbie urged. 'It's a hospital!'

'We've locked down the place, love. No worries. She'll be all right in a bit.'

Abbie left them at the top of the ramp. Two police cars were outside with an ambulance, its rear doors open, anticipating casualties. There were no blue lights swirling. Everything was quiet. On the far corner of the block, well away from the clinic, she saw people going into a restaurant, oblivious to the drama unfolding on the upper floors. If any of them gave the police and ambulance a second glance, the scene might well have been dismissed as business as usual. After all, they were outside a private hospital.

Abbie suddenly remembered she had left the two mobile phones on the seat of the car. She ran back, leant inside and as she reached for them saw through the windscreen a movement in the shadows against the far wall where the black Saab was parked. A rough-looking man wearing a dark canvas jacket, boots and jeans had a phone pressed to his ear and was opening the boot of the car. He pulled out an assault rifle. Abbie's stomach clenched. There were more gunmen in the building than Raglan might know about. No sooner had the frightening thought crossed her mind than the man looked at her. Too late she realized the car's interior light had come on when she had opened the door. She jerked out of the car, keeping her eyes on him, but the man hadn't moved. He was alert but unconcerned. It didn't make sense. And then the man smiled and nodded. A rough hand smothered Abbie's face and mouth. Strong arms held her tightly. The gunman had an accomplice.

34

Raglan and the armed officer slipped through the double swing doors beyond the dead man. They led to an unlit passageway that connected the top floor of the clinic to the roof and gave access to the ramp leading up to the helipad at the far end. The corridor was like the converted loading tunnel for boarding aircraft at major airports, its non-slip floor led from the outside roof ramp and past the swing doors where he and the armed officer stood, weapons raised, searching for JD. The tunnel led downward and as far as he could see it then curved back on itself, sweeping around to the floor below. That was where patients would be trolleyed to and from the helipad. The sixth floor was not yet operational. If JD had put men on the working floor of the hospital someone somewhere would have raised the alarm. Killing an after-hours receptionist was not the same as subduing a whole floor. Raglan's senses were primed. Never underestimate your enemy. Especially an ex-intelligence officer.

JD had left three of his men with Carter. He had extra men in different locations. Eddie Roman was killed because he somehow got in the way. So far Raglan had killed six men. The man at his flat, three at the factory and two here at the clinic. How many more at this location? To get this far and make sure he could control a landing zone for a chopper, probably at least four. Lookouts, backstop guards and someone to cover when the chopper landed. Where were the others?

Raglan and the policeman stepped left into the empty tunnel. Now he could hear the helicopter in the distance, its variable engine pitch fading as it circled. Raglan put his shoulder against the swing doors and felt the cold wet air bite his skin.

'Go right and skirt the walls. We can cover the roof and any crossfire. I'll go this side towards the cooling ducts. If that chopper is called in whoever's going for it needs to step out in plain sight.'

The seasoned cop needed no further explanation. He went off at the crouch, searching the edge of the building. If either man came under fire, they had a good chance of retaliating. The helicopter was still out of sight, the cloud base stubbornly low, caressing tall buildings in a ghoulish embrace, suffocating their lights. There was a passenger jet descending for its landing at Heathrow Airport: its landing lights managed to pierce the fine mist-like rain in the night sky and its roar defeated the helicopter's growling impatience to land. The roar deadened, too, the sound of gunshots fired from near the cooling funnels. Mortar shattered near Raglan's head; fragments cut into his cheek and neck. He pivoted and saw the cop kneel and return fire with three rapid double taps. It saved Raglan from being targeted. He ran, pressing his back against the wall. A sudden thunder bombarded his senses as a searchlight blinded him. The chopper had swung around, laid off beyond the helipad and used its powerful front headlamps to highlight Raglan and the policeman.

As Raglan closed one eye, attempting to keep his night vision intact, a shadow loomed around the corner, levelling a handgun. Raglan rolled, his shoulder slamming into the wet roof, rapid fire crackling over his head. He threw himself forward, forcing the gunman back on to his heels, denying him an easy follow-on shot. Raglan kicked away his attacker's legs. The chopper swept away again, the pilot not being prepared to risk the conflict. As the spotlight veered off into darkness, Raglan's vision returned. He slammed his shoulder into the man, heard him grunt, knew he was agile enough to recover but Raglan's free hand had grasped the man's wrist as he brought up his knee into his groin. The man twisted, taking the blow on his thigh. He headbutted Raglan, catching him across the bridge of his nose. He heard it break, tasted blood at the back of his throat, but never released his grip on the man's gun hand.

The sudden intimate close-quarter fight brought the man's face into focus. JD snarled and tried to headbutt him again, but Raglan had thrown his weight against him, forcing the man's arm to bend or break. He heard gunshots behind him and as JD tried to regain his footing Raglan saw the cop on the far side of the roof shoot a man in a canvas jacket whose assault rifle flew high and wide. For a split second in time the man's body froze, head thrown back, balance gone, rifle leaving his fingers. It was a Robert Capa historic photo moment. And then the cop staggered back. He'd been hit. He went down, rolled, tried to get up, his left arm cushioning his wounds, determined to stay in the fight, but the impact had robbed him of his strength and despite his determination could only roll over on to his side and give in to the damage inflicted on him.

JD recovered, using elbows and feet to beat Raglan back. Raglan's grip forced JD to drop his handgun. Raglan kicked it away as he slammed the killer against the wall, forcing his head to snap back. Raglan landed two savage punches into his midriff and, as JD bent forward, slammed his chin back with the heel of his hand, a tooth-crushing blow. JD's head hit the wall again. Raglan pinned him upright, hands round his neck. JD's eyes glazed and cleared. The chopper held off again, hovering with its searchlight beam illuminating both men. JD's eyes widened as he recognized the legionnaire commando from so many years before.

'I'll be damned. You. You're a long way from the desert, my friend. I thought the ragheads had killed you.'

'And we all thought you had gone down in flames.'

JD gave a bloodied smile. 'That was theatrical licence.'

'Yegor Kuznetsov. The Blacksmith. Aka John Doe. You're a sick, dangerous bastard. You're going back home. In a body bag if I can make it happen.' He twisted JD around and held him bent over in an arm lock.

JD laughed and spat blood. 'Never gonna happen. You're out of your league. How did you find me? Carter? Did you find him? No, it wasn't him, he didn't know where I was going.'

'You're not as smart as you think. Carter is dead.'

JD sighed. 'I told them to wait before they killed him in case the bastard had sent me on a wild goose chase.' He snorted. 'You just can't find good help these days.'

'You tortured him so badly he couldn't hold on.'

'He played a raw-bone game. Isn't that what your kind called it? Strip it all away, tear back the skin and muscle. Get it down to the bone. A face-to-face kill. Suck up the pain and go through with the mission.' He snorted. 'I've got the money and the names, places, account numbers... Carter was very good. I've got it all and you can't do a fucking thing about it.'

JD was too confident. Raglan knew there had to be another man. Behind him.

'Drop it!' said a voice loud enough to be heard over the helicopter engine's roar as its wheels settled on to the pad. The pilot had seen the play unfold. It was time for the pickup. The downdraught bore down on them, the blades sweeping the rain across the pools of water on the rooftop.

Raglan turned; his stomach lurched. A big man held Abbie with one hand, a pistol in the other. The girl was terrified. Tears stained her face. The damp air settled fairy glitter on her beautiful dark hair. Game over. Raglan had no clear shot. He dropped his handgun and half raised his hands clear of his body. No sudden movements. No final desperate attempt to snatch at JD, who kicked away Raglan's weapon and bent down to retrieve a briefcase tucked against the wall. Pushing Raglan aside he ran towards the ramp, signalling for the man to bring the girl.

Raglan made a move forward but the man holding her pushed the gun muzzle into Abbie's head. Her wide-eyed fear hurt him. He raised a hand to reassure her and shouted, 'Leave her!' darting as close to the edge as he could.

'Raglan! Help me, please help me,' Abbie cried.

JD was at the helicopter's open door. He turned and looked at Raglan. A hard, cold killer's look. Eyes reflecting a soul that was damned. He put the briefcase inside the helicopter, grabbed the girl and let the man with him clamber inside. He stood triumphantly for a moment. Abbie looked disbelievingly at Raglan as JD hauled her into the wavering chopper. He forced her to sit on the rim, which gave him cover should any snipers be in place. Raglan had got as close as he could. A dozen fast-paced strides and he could lunge at the open door. But to do so would sign Abbie's death warrant.

He pointed at JD. 'I'll find you!'

JD grinned through bloodied teeth. 'You lost. The battle *and* the war.'

Raglan swore as the helicopter began to lift. 'Don't hurt her!' he begged.

He heard JD shout back. 'Why not?'

The gunshot cracked through the sound of the rotor blades.

Abbie slumped. JD let her lifeless body fall, tumbling down past the building. Raglan ran to the edge and saw it splash into the dockland water.

The chopper dipped away, soon gone from sight.

35

Maguire arrived soon after the killing.

Police had cordoned off the area, ushering away diners and late-night workers from nearby buildings. The clinic's skeleton night staff had remained oblivious to the gunfire on the roof and, being used to the sound of helicopters passing by, had ignored the battering rotor blades that came and went. It was only when armed police officers appeared on the floors demanding that they stay locked down that panic set in. Staff and those patients who could be moved were herded into a safe area while the police searched each floor. There was no need. The killers had fled or were already dead.

London's air traffic control attempted to determine the flight path of the mystery helicopter, but the pilot had used the Thames to escape, flying low and fast, following the course of the twisting river. Maguire waited with a bloodied Raglan as police divers dragged the dock. The night's chill rain added to everyone's discomfort but Raglan was impervious to it. His anger had settled into the dull ache of helplessness at being unable to save the girl.

Police floodlights illuminated the dock's wind-rippled surface. Abbie's body had plunged into the black depths. Falling from that height into water was like hitting concrete: her body would have suffered multiple injuries and might never be recovered if an undercurrent took it. There was no comfort for Raglan or Maguire in knowing she'd been dead before she hit the water. Raglan spat the taste of blood from the back of his throat.

'How's the cop who was on the roof with me?' he asked, keeping his eyes on the police divers' boat.

'Wounded but not life-threatening,' said Maguire.

'He saved my life. I owe him. They came up the outside fire escape. He was sharp.' He faced Maguire. 'I couldn't get a shot in time to save her.'

Rain trickled down Maguire's neck. He shook his head. 'Abbie was one of mine. My responsibility.'

'I left her in the car. She was supposed to leave.'

'She would have stayed for you, Raglan.' He hesitated. 'For whatever reason.'

A coroner's van pulled up in the street below and waited in the shadows.

'Sorokina's got a couple of busted ribs. Her body armour saved her,' Maguire said. 'The Home Office is all over this. Europol and the Met. IOPC will start an investigation before the paint's dry. MI5 has washed its hands of it. Deny, deny, deny is the best line of defence. I don't blame them. This wasn't their game to play. I've got a meeting with the PM tomorrow morning.'

'How will it play out?'

'Quietly. The Met Commissioner will give a press conference at the same time. An armed man attempted to break into the private hospital for reasons unknown. Armed police responded. One officer was wounded in the line of duty; they shot the suspect dead. End of story.'

'And the other bodies?'

'What bodies would that be?' said Maguire. They fell silent. The narrative was already written.

'What are you going to tell Abbie's parents?' said Raglan, remembering their pride in their only daughter.

'Car accident is best, I think, don't you?'

'Why not tell them the truth?'

'A need-to-know basis. And them knowing doesn't bring her back.'

'What they need to know is what happened to their daughter. She was part of this. She was shot, Maguire. Talk your way out of that one.'

'Her post-mortem won't show any record of that. Officially, a hit-and-run driver is already being sought.'

'When will you go and see them?'

Maguire shook his head. 'It should be tonight.'

'Let them sleep,' said Raglan. 'They won't be getting much of that for a long time to come.' Raglan wiped his sleeve across his face. His nose was bleeding. 'I've met them. I'll go and see them first thing. You can do the follow-up and give them all the usual official claptrap.'

Maguire nodded. 'All right. It's not an easy thing to do and you still have to see Carter's wife... widow. And the kids.'

The men in the water swam further apart, lights piercing down into the depths. It was a cold dark grave.

'Not the first time it's been my job. It's how I pay for my sins,' said Raglan.

Maguire's tone softened. The next few hours would push two families into their own personal vision of hell. 'Get that blood off your face, have the medics fix your broken nose and get a couple of stitches in that leg wound.'

'I don't need them. Ice packs and painkillers for the nose once I push it back into place. It'll be as good as new in a couple of weeks. I'll stitch the leg myself. I want nothing official being recorded here.'

'Between me and the police, you won't be drawn into it.'

'OK. I'll look after myself, Maguire.'

'But it's over, Raglan. Nothing more to be gained from this. Time for you to go home.'

A diver broke the surface and raised a thumb. They had her. He watched as the police lights caught a flash of white in the water. Two divers raised the ragdoll body to the surface. The white blouse was stained from the blood washed through its weave. Abbie's head lolled to one side. As they placed her in the recovery boat, the floodlights brought the dead girl sharply into focus. Her eyes stared at Raglan.

They would join others that haunted him.

He owed it to Mandy, Steve and Melissa to tell them that Carter was dead. He walked away from the place of killing. By the time he reached the outer police cordon he had changed his mind and decided to speak to Abbie's parents first. Mandy had endured loss before, Steve had escaped the terror and Melissa just wanted her daddy home. They would console each other, and grieve together, and no matter what pain they felt right now Mandy had a future with the children. That was their hope. Abbie was all her parents had.

By morning, when the crime scene officers gave the all-clear, the bodies had been removed and the police tape taken down from the cordon, Raglan was sitting in a taxi outside the Southall house. He had cleaned up and changed his clothes but his face still bore evidence of the fight on the rooftop. Would they believe the lie that it resulted from a car crash? A fatal one for their daughter who had been driving? A hit and run. He waited until the curtains were drawn back, picturing Abbie's mother making the first of many cups of tea for the day.

He paid the cab driver enough money to wait for him and went up to the front door.

Abbie's mother looked startled at the rough state of the man who stood before her. She ushered him in, clutching her dressing gown. He smiled regretfully. Her startled look was one of denial and disbelief. She knew; of course she did. The man who stood before her was about to tear their lives apart. She would need more strength now than ever before. Her husband would take it hard. Tears welled as she forced one leaden foot in front of the other.

Raglan sat with Abbie's mother and father. Two broken hearts cleaved in pain. After delivering the news he watched the man slowly disintegrate as his wife clasped his hand to her tear-streaked face. Raglan stepped forward and placed his hand on his shoulder. Jal Khalsa breathed deeply and settled his pain. He nodded Raglan away and regained his composure and dignity.

'I will deal with this matter, Mr Raglan. I can see that you were also hurt in the car crash. It was thoughtful of you to ignore your own injuries and bring us the news of our daughter's death. That cannot have been an easy duty to undertake,' Abbie's father said with quiet formality.

Raglan was ready to leave. 'A man will come and speak to you in a short while. He was Abbie's boss.'

'From the Department of Transport?'

Raglan nodded. The lie was the lesser of two evils. Maguire was right. The girl had kept her own secret intact – why unravel that with the truth now?

'And the man who caused her death?' said Abbie's father.

'I'll find him,' said Raglan. 'I promise.'

36

The government machine swung into action. The story neatly unfolded that a team of detectives, acting on a tip-off from an informer, had discovered where the kidnapped banker was being held. Armed police had rescued Jeremy Carter, but he died from the injuries inflicted by his kidnappers during his imprisonment. The men who died in the shootout with armed police were of Eastern European origin. No one said they were believed to be Russian. In a separate, unrelated incident at Canary Wharf on the Isle of Dogs, a single as yet unnamed man believed to be suffering from mental health issues broke into a private clinic and killed the hospital's 45-year-old receptionist, named as Mrs Marjorie Chambers, and the 36-year-old security guard, Alan Jessup. Their families had been informed. Once again armed police responded and were attacked by the suspect, who was shot dead. A full Independent

Office for Police Conduct investigation would take place.

Maguire, the Home Secretary and the Metropolitan Police Commissioner had thrashed out the denial of the truth in a pre-dawn meeting, which was then used to brief the Prime Minister. They decided that the heading on their briefing notes from Maguire, namely: *RBOC: Russian-Backed Organized Crime*, would not be brought to public or media attention. An international arrest warrant remained in place for Yegor Kuznetsov. They made no mention of the fact that the man had worked in the past for French intelligence and was wanted for the murder of four Moscow police officers. Given Kuznetsov's involvement in the past with the Russian state, the latter was suspected of being the main beneficiary of the attack on Carter and the information he held. None of that could be proved and it was deemed not to be in the public interest to air it. Eventually the Russian killer would resurface and when he did, Maguire hoped MI6 would be the first to know about it.

Raglan stood with Elena Sorokina at the airport while a Russian embassy official spoke to the airport security people. Her personal sidearm had been stripped and placed in a tamper-proof box that would be kept by the pilots in the cockpit. She had returned to the miserable hotel to nurse her broken ribs following the shooting while awaiting her final orders from Moscow.

'What about the Indian girl?' Sorokina asked Raglan.

'Dead,' said Raglan. 'He killed her.'

Her face creased with disgust. 'I have failed, Raglan. Where will you go now?'

'I'll stay with Carter's family for a couple of weeks, help them to deal with it.'

'No one deals with it,' she said.

'I know.'

The embassy official beckoned her. Sorokina extended her hand in farewell. 'Let's not pretend that our one night together means anything more than it did.'

He saw the cold look again and knew that she had retreated into her professional shell. It suited him, though her grip stayed in his for a moment longer than was necessary.

'Safe journey,' he said.

Raglan spent the following three weeks with Amanda and the children, his presence helping to temporarily fill the void left by Jeremy Carter's death. He took over household duties his friend would have managed, while the family's slow absorption of the stages of their grief bubbled to the surface. There were tears, and rage. They were angry at Carter for dying, for abandoning them. Bereft that there had been no final embrace or tender word. An agony of silence descended on the household. Raglan created a routine of running every day with Steve and telling Melissa a night-time story while fielding questions about her father. Following his investigation, Maguire finally reached the conclusion that Raglan's defence of Jeremy Carter, insisting that he had never diverted funds, had been correct. The family would receive Carter's civil service pension and the additional sum due to any serving field officer who died in the line of duty.

Amanda Reeve-Carter buried her second husband in the fourth week after he had been seized, on a bleak and misty October day. Muffled against the cold, she hugged her children to her as Raglan gripped her shoulder to ease her trembling. Maguire and several dark-suited officials from the Service attended, standing at a respectful distance from Amanda and her family at the graveside. The directors of the bank, ignorant of Carter's true role, muttered words of consolation and sorrow at his death. They seemed nervous of the anonymous, emotionless men watching them. They must have known they would soon be under the most intense investigation.

Maguire approached Amanda, and Raglan saw bitterness pull at the corner of her mouth. She was a courageous woman, unafraid to express her feelings towards those who caused injury to her family and he half expected her to slap aside Maguire's extended hand. She didn't; she simply ignored the gesture of greeting.

'Jeremy held out for nearly a week under appalling treatment and you dared to question his loyalty,' she said to Maguire.

'Amanda—'

Her arched eyebrow made Maguire backtrack from his attempt at intimacy. 'Mrs Reeve-Carter, I can offer no explanation that might lessen your distress. There are protocols in place that we must adhere to, as we did in the early stages of our investigation. I have spoken to the Prime Minister and made the strongest recommendation that Jeremy is awarded an appropriate honour for his outstanding courage and exemplary work for the Service.'

'I have enough medals given for death in the line of duty,' she said. She stepped away with her children; then she turned to deliver a final admonishment to the MI6 section chief. 'I know how this works. What you feed the press is one thing, what I want is another. Find the bastard who did this and kill him.'

As Raglan went to accompany her, Maguire caught his arm.

'We need to talk.'

'I'm leaving in a couple of days. I thought that's what you wanted. I'm the one person you don't need to be dragged into any more of this. Besides, what's left to say?'

'Your Russian girlfriend is back in town.'

37

Raglan took his time walking the hundred yards towards her. She was waiting on the Victoria Embankment, standing beneath one of the old-fashioned street lamps. The River Thames looked a muddier shade of grey than usual. Maguire had given Raglan the time and the place: obviously Sorokina was still distrustful of meeting indoors. The constant noise of traffic on the Embankment and the sibilance of the wind across the water would make it difficult for her conversation to be recorded. She wore calf-length boots over jeans with a three-quarter-length belted coat, its collar turned up against the cold. Her head was bare as she faced into the wind so that it blew her hair back from her features. He looked beyond her but saw no sign of any minders or cars parked under the pretence of being broken down. She was alone.

She saw Raglan approaching her. There was no smile of greeting. 'You are late,' she said icily. 'I thought your kind was never late. Being in the right place at the correct time can be a matter of life and death in your business.'

'Are you planning to kill me?' he asked, risking a smile, 'because if you are, I would rather be late for my own funeral.'

'This is something funny? I don't understand. Of course I am not going to kill you. Why would you think that?'

'It was my pathetic attempt at humour. Forget it.'

'Very well. There is no time for humour. Do you wish to take me to bed?'

Raglan considered the proposition for a moment. 'You came all this way for sex? What's happened to all the men in Moscow? Is the rumour true?'

She looked puzzled. 'What rumour?'

'That President Putin is gay and that all the men in Moscow have followed his example.'

She frowned. 'Are you drunk?'

'I'm beginning to think it might be better if I was. What is it you want, Elena?'

'I am here to propose to you.'

'You want to marry me?'

'No,' she snapped. 'Why would you think that?'

'Because you said you wanted to propose to me.'

'Then I have my words incorrect.' She thought for a moment. 'I wish to say I have a proposition for you.'

'Ah. That's me condemned to a single life after all. OK. I accept.'

'I have not yet explained what it is I have in mind.'

'I'm sure I'll find it pleasurable.'

She gazed at the madman who stood before her. 'You are a fool, Raglan. Perhaps we should speak in Russian so there is no further misunderstanding. I am here on business but I did not see any reason why we could not enjoy some pleasure as well.'

'Your last words to me at the airport were that we shouldn't pretend our night together was anything more than what it was.'

Finally, she smiled. 'And what it was, was pleasurable.'

The tourist hotel was an improvement on her previous one. The bed was bigger, firmer and quieter. The room was warm; it was comfortable to be naked. And room service was efficient and convenient for anyone not wishing to leave the hotel. Which they didn't.

Her broken ribs had left no visible sign on her slender torso; the wound on his leg was a narrow furrow with a few black marks left by the stitches. The bruising from his broken nose had faded. Sorokina's body was as firm as her unabashed desire for him was strong; though he was careful, just weeks after her injury, she was fierce. She winced in pain as he pressed too hard against her; she swore, ignored the discomfort but let him ease her into a more comfortable position. Then she laughed as her chin caught the tender bones around his nose and he gasped, tears in his eyes. They squirmed with care and then their desire overcame them.

After hours in bed and then sharing the tub bath, eating whenever they felt like it, she awoke to find him sitting at the small table by the window. He had pulled on a T-shirt and boxer shorts and was watching her. She glanced at her shoulder bag and small carry-on suitcase. Neither seemed to have been tampered with. She was uncertain. The wardrobe door that concealed the room safe was open, but the safe door was closed. Even Raglan could not have discovered the combination.

'What are you doing?'

'Wondering who sent you and why. We've had the pleasure; maybe it's time for the pain,' he said and tossed a brown Manila envelope on to the bed. She looked alarmed and glanced at the wardrobe again. He shrugged and lowered the tension with a smile. 'I'm nosey and I like to get a heads-up on what's around the corner.'

She was less angry than he imagined she would be. 'How did you open the safe?'

He tipped out her small shoulder bag and flipped open the small leather wallet exposing her identity card. 'First four numbers, last four, middle four. It was the middle four.'

'You should trust me, Raglan. I do not wish to cause you harm.'

'After the last few hours, I might have to disagree.' He smiled again. 'I didn't open the envelope. You're not armed this time. The hotel is booked and paid for by you. I checked. So whatever this is, other than being a time to reacquaint ourselves, it is not official.'

'In a way it is.' She sat up and tucked the sheet around her, hiding her nudity now. The envelope stayed on the bed. Raglan went to the coffee machine and gestured with a cup. She nodded. He slotted in the capsules.

'Are you in trouble? Did your bosses give you a hard time when you got back?'

'No, not really. They might even promote me to lieutenant colonel.'

He fiddled with the coffee preparation. 'Do I salute you now?'

'No. Later.' Now it was her turn to smile.

He handed her the coffee. 'You're a different woman when you smile, Elena. You should do it more often.'

'In the Moscow police if you smile too much they think you have big secrets and you end up in the frozen north in a police station that looks for stray dogs. Or that you are a village idiot. I did not get to be a major by smiling. I said I did not wish to cause you harm, but what I have in that envelope might even cause your death.'

'Then the sex was for a condemned man.'

She didn't smile. 'Perhaps, yes.'

He waited. Her seriousness told him he should stop the quips. Time to listen and find out the real reason for her unannounced visit to London.

'Nine days ago there was a show trial in Moscow. Without police knowledge, another internal security branch seized Yegor Kuznetsov. It was a mock arrest. My boss, General Ivanov, was not even involved. He had no cause for complaint because they prosecuted the man you know as JD for the murder of my brother and the other police officers. His arrest meant the international arrest warrant was no longer in force.'

She leant forward, now not caring that she exposed her breasts from beneath the sheet. She peeled back the flap of the envelope and slid out a folded newspaper cutting. She handed it to Raglan who unfolded it and saw a photograph of JD being escorted into the courtroom. Raglan could read enough Russian to understand the headline, which stated that the wanted cop-killer had been arrested and quickly brought to trial.

'It was...' She searched for the appropriate saying. 'A set-up. General Ivanov had no access to the information as to how Kuznetsov was so quickly found after his return from London. Obviously, it was arranged with the help of corrupt officials. It means we are no longer looking for him. The case is closed.'

'So if a deal has been done, then where is he?'

'We no longer have the death penalty in the Russian Federation. He was sentenced to life imprisonment in a prison colony miles from anywhere. We discovered that your JD is part of organized crime. The Russian mafia. He is protected.'

A dummy court case to protect a key asset who had delivered vital information to his backers. Organized crime acting on behalf of the Russian state, and state officials would not sacrifice someone as efficient as JD. He was too valuable to them.

'There are more press cuttings, but it was unnecessary to bring them. They gave General Ivanov and the Moscow CID full credit. Those who are protecting your JD made sure we could not challenge the arrest. He has been sent to a penal colony, but it was all part of the show trial so that the public's faith in our judicial system could be restored. He will be there a couple of months. No doubt with special privileges. And then – who knows?'

'They'll pretend to transfer him for health reasons to another prison, but they will give him a new life somewhere else so they can use him again.'

She nodded.

'And your General Ivanov told Maguire about JD?'

'Yes. But he said they could not involve the British intelligence service.'

'In what?'

'Sending a man to kill him.'

38

The bookshop in the narrow lane known as Cecil Court, in the West End of London, was a favourite haunt for anyone seeking signed first editions. It was a quiet store where a bibliophile could browse undisturbed. Two rooms up and two down meant there was always a quiet corner for a whispered conversation, words cushioned by wall-to-wall books.

Maguire pushed a hardcover book about the Hundred Years War back on to the shelf. 'A bloody period of our history. Killing was a far more straightforward business then. No passport required.'

'Why did you want to see me? Are you buying me a book for the trip?'

'Raglan, Moscow got in touch with me and I gave them a categorical answer. I will not involve us in this venture. We did our bit here in London. It's a done deal. It's over. If you do this because of some sense of personal loyalty to Carter's family then I am in no position to offer any assistance. If you're lucky enough to be captured rather than killed, we have no chance of reaching out on your behalf.'

'And you're scared to death that if I'm caught there might be an association between you and me.'

'In a word, yes. We cannot risk embarrassing Her Majesty's Government.'

'She didn't seem to mind when you brought me in from France. Surely you told Her Majesty I was in the country?'

'Christ, man, this is no time for bloody jokes. You're being asked to kill him.'

'He needs killing.'

'Not by you. Let me speak to Ivanov again. See if he can't use someone.'

'The Moscow police are stitched up. It needs an outsider. Why do you think she came to me?'

Maguire bid farewell to the owner behind the counter and stepped out into the bookshop-lined alleyway. He pulled on a pair of gloves and turned up his collar against the wind funnelling down the passage.

'Are you going to try and stop me? I need a clear run at this without your people picking me up at the airport,' said Raglan.

Maguire shook his head. 'You're on your own. Besides – and I don't care how many contacts you have from your Legion days – getting to him will be impossible.

You won't even get close, wherever he is. The people protecting him will have him squirrelled away. Going to Russia as a tourist is one thing, going to find one of their killers…' He shook his head. 'Raglan, I value what you did for us. I thought I would make a personal appeal to stop you. What's done is done. JD will resurface in the future. Here, Europe, the States, wherever, and when he does we'll get him.'

'Good luck with that, Maguire.'

Raglan turned down the lane. Time was short. The winter snow would hit Russia soon. Its bitter harshness didn't come close to what Raglan felt about the double agent. The brutal torture and death of Carter and Abbie's cold-blooded murder needed justice. If he was going to find and kill JD, it had to be now.

Raglan packed his holdall. Before she returned to Moscow Sorokina explained that despite corrupt officials forging documents for JD's trial and sentencing, she had others who had helped her. Cops don't forget their own being murdered: it was the same the world over. Given that her father was a judge whose detective son had been shot to death, she had skilled friends ready to help. And Raglan could help her to set the record straight.

Raglan checked the forged Russian passport Sorokina had given him. It looked as genuine as any other, even down to border stamps for Ukraine. It was sufficiently dog-eared and finger-smudged. Raglan's image stared back at him as its owner, now named as Daniil Regnev, was shown to have held the passport for five years, with another five to go before expiry. Sorokina had colluded with no one other than her boss, General Ivanov, and her father had in turn approached others in authority who wanted to halt the corruption infecting their beloved homeland. Once Raglan was in Moscow then wheels would be put into motion and they would help him reach his target.

At the Carters' house Raglan took Amanda aside and told her he had a tip-off about the man who had caused her husband's death. They sat across from each other at the kitchen table. Amanda stone-faced, drained from grief and tears; Raglan sipping a mug of coffee.

'What I said to Maguire at the cemetery, I... I shouldn't have said it. If anything happened to you I'd blame myself.'

'It goes beyond Jeremy. He also murdered the young woman who was here, at the beginning. She helped me.'

Amanda searched her memory. 'I remember her.'

'There's a score to be settled, Mandy. You'll manage now. Steve is strong and Melissa, well, she's very young, and as long as she has you she'll be OK in time. All of you will.'

She nodded and reached out with her hands for his. 'I've known you since we were kids. Longer than any love affair or husband, longer than anything else. I want you to be around for a lot longer.'

He smiled. 'That's my plan.'

'When will you tell Steve you're leaving?'

'I already have. He's OK with it, don't worry.'

A sudden look of alarm crossed her face. 'When are you going?'

'Now.'

Raglan sat at a bar on the upper level of London's St Pancras International Station watching the late shoppers and commuters scurrying along the concourse below. He had dropped into his conversation with Maguire that he would travel from an airport, a lie should Maguire have a change of heart and decide to try and stop him. All the same Raglan expected Maguire would not only have his people at the London airports checking overseas flights but would have covered his bets by having officers at St Pancras to watch international trains too. Providing they didn't try to stop him, there would be no trouble. If there was, Raglan would deal with it. There was a thirty-minute check-in for the Eurostar to Paris and he had ten minutes left. As yet he had only a half-formed plan in his head to get to Moscow.

He pressed the phone to his ear and heard the gruff tones of his old comrade. 'Raglan, you are fucking mad,' said Sokol after Raglan had explained where he was going and why. He had related the saga of JD while the Russian former legionnaire remained silent, listening. Raglan did not mention his time with Elena Sorokina.

'Bird, what do we know about the Russian mafia?' said Raglan.

'Enough that you shouldn't get mixed up with them,' said Sokol.

'Too late for that. I need to be seen as one of them. Not sure yet how that's going to happen.'

'If they're pond-feeder muscle then they'll have tattoos. If they're the bosses who sit at the top of the table they're the suits. Six-figure cars, trophy women, property in London. Which end of the scale are you?'

Raglan knew there was little point in trying to masquerade as a fixer for the Russian mafia; he didn't have the money available to buy the handmade suit or hire a luxury car. None of that would help find JD in a penal colony in the wilds of Russia. 'I'm working class. The muscle. I need tatts to prove it.'

'Can't be done in a hurry. You'll stick out like a painted tart at the officers' regimental dance. Wait out...' said his friend.

Raglan heard the rustle of a paper as if Sokol was turning the pages of a book. 'There's something here, maybe... or maybe not. OK. I will scan pictures of mafia tattoos. They all have a meaning. They denote your status.'

'No good. I'm on a burner which I'm about to dump. I'll pick up another when I get to Paris and phone you when I'm there. I need somewhere that can receive those scans. I'm heading for the train now. I'll be in Paris in a couple of hours. See what you can do.'

He switched off the phone, stripped it and threw it into the refuse bin. A man in a suit and overcoat who was sitting further along the bar with a good-looking girl stood up, picked up his briefcase and readied himself to leave. He pecked the girl's cheek but Raglan saw her eyes dart past the man's shoulder towards him. Raglan had seen them earlier walking around the concourse below him before they appeared on the upper level and sat at the end of the bar. To all intents and purposes, he was a young businessman going off somewhere and she was here to bid him farewell. She had no luggage and her casually smart outfit was offset with running shoes. Fashion aside, the scruffy trainers didn't gel with the rest of her outfit. If he was mistaken and she was nothing more than a city commuter wearing them for comfort then he'd soon find out. He had a bet with himself that she was wearing them for a fast pursuit.

There was only one way for Raglan to confirm his instincts that they were a team on the lookout for him. He stepped into the main bar area, making his way through to the restrooms. As Raglan entered the toilets the businessman was a few paces behind him. Raglan slammed the swing door into him. The man stood no chance of defending himself. Raglan hit him once and then dragged him into a cubicle, lifting him on to the toilet seat. He found his identification. Maguire's people were getting clumsy.

He locked the cubicle door and clambered over the top. When he got outside the young woman didn't disguise her look of concern quickly enough. Raglan winked at her and hurried towards the Eurostar platform as the woman hesitated a moment and then ran into the restaurant looking for her partner, her phone already pressed to her ear. When he had arrived at St Pancras Raglan had reconnoitred the station and estimated that Gate 28b was the nearest to where he would be sitting and that it would take him four minutes to get there from the upper level. He had made allowances for any interruptions. Ignoring the lift, he jogged down the stairs, made his way through the crowds and presented himself at the security gate.

The station clock told him it had taken three minutes and forty-three seconds.

39

The train was a safe environment. Things might change once he reached Paris but for now, he relaxed. The Eurostar, slow-moving across the southern English countryside, picked up speed on the continent. The dark landscape outside reflected his image in the window as he stared into the glass, running through in his head what Sorokina had told him of how JD might be found and how her allies had put together false documents to get Raglan close to him. A deal had been made with the deputy governor of the prison where JD was hidden. This deputy governor had endured half his life in the wilderness but if all went to plan he would be moved to a better prison nearer civilization. Everything was in place. Once Raglan had killed JD then the district police would move in. The investigative committee would have the deputy governor detained and questioned as a matter of procedure, but there was enough influence in place to see that he would be exonerated and then get the reward promised to him. The question was could Raglan get to JD before they moved him? Raglan would be on his own and no one had ever escaped from a penal colony in such a hostile environment. Imagining the worst could be fatal. He'd make a plan. Personal survival sharpened the mind. Like a condemned man facing the noose.

Every soldier knows to sleep when they can and he dozed until he heard the announcement of the train's imminent arrival. Before he had cleared the concourse he had bought a new phone and then stood at the entrance on the Rue de Dunkerque considering how to move on to Moscow. He and Sorokina had agreed on a two-day window for him to get to Moscow. If anything had gone wrong at her end then her enemies would likely be waiting for him at an airport, and it was now highly likely, too, that Maguire would have French *flics* watching out for him. They were all in the same old boys' club.

'I've got something,' said Sokol, answering Raglan's call. 'You remember Milosz?'

'He left the Legion three years after me.'

'Correct. Works security now. Set himself up as a small company, corporate protection, that kind of thing.'

'How can he help?'

'I'm not sure yet but he has a young brother in Warsaw. He's something to do with the film business, special effects or something. I can't remember his name. I'm trying to get hold of Milosz – I've left a message.'

Raglan knew that if he diverted from Moscow he could lose valuable time. 'I'll give it an hour. If he can help me somehow then I'll get a ticket there.'

'And Moscow?'

'Not sure, yet.'

'OK, listen, I've got a distant cousin who's a few hours outside Moscow. Some small village. I'll pay her a visit. Give you a chance to have a bolthole. Can't do any harm.'

'It looks as though we're still in the fight,' Raglan said.

'Never left it,' said Sokol.

Raglan added his own message on Milosz's voicemail and forty-two minutes later his phone rang as he quaffed coffee and devoured a ham and cheese baguette. 'You on a job, Dan?' said the gruff voice. He hadn't heard it for a few years but the length of time made no difference; it was as if they had spoken that morning. No need for a greeting or small talk.

'Milosz. I need help.'

'Where and when? I'm in Israel right now.'

Raglan explained what Sokol had said and that he was preparing to go undercover as a member of the Russian mafia.

'Don't do it. They'll spot you before you knock on their door.'

'I've only got one crack at this. Can you help?'

Milosz sighed. 'It's your neck. I reckon my kid brother can help. My family disowned him years ago because he's queer but I didn't, and anyone gave him a bad time I sorted them. So he'll always help me out. He's in the film business, does makeup. He's some kind of genius. The only one we've got in the family other than me. He's in Warsaw. Can you get there?'

'Yes, I'm in Paris now.'

'Bird told me. You have money?'

'Enough to get there. After that I don't need much where I'm going. Sokol can wire me some.'

'Don't, it's all traceable. My brother will give you what you need; he knows I'm good for it. I'll phone him now. The movie studio he works for is in Lodz; it's a hundred clicks from Warsaw. You can't get a direct flight there but I know he's between jobs. I'll get him to meet you in Warsaw. He'll sort something out. He does private work at home. Society women flock to him. They strip to the skin so he can work his magic. Doesn't that make you wanna cry? What a waste. Better you go there. Get on the next flight at Charles de Gaulle.'

'Got it. Talk to Bird because he needs to send scans through to your brother. Can you do that?'

'Consider it done. You always were a crazy bastard. If you live through this we need a reunion. And you're buying.'

Raglan ran for the train and the thirty-minute ride to CDG airport. The elements of a plan were coming together now. He felt the keen sense of anticipation. The gap between him and the man he hunted was closing.

A lean, tall man stood at the entrance to Warsaw's Frederick Chopin airport. He wore a tailored grey overcoat and his fashionably trimmed beard might convince a casual onlooker that he was one of the many successful younger entrepreneurs that modern Poland boasted. There was no physical resemblance to the hardened legionnaire that Raglan had fought alongside. The only way he knew he was Milosz's brother was the discreetly folded legionnaire's beret held at his side: better than any name board and more discreet.

Raglan walked up to him. 'I'm Raglan.'

The man extended a delicate hand, long fingers, hands that could play a piano concerto. 'I know.' He smiled without further explanation. 'I am Tomasz,' he said with a slight inflection to his English accent. 'I live in the city so do not drive myself, but I have a private cab waiting nearby and a meal ready for you at home. I hope you like traditional Polish food.'

Raglan smiled. 'That's kind of you, thanks. I lived alongside your brother for many years. Back then I had no choice about the food, but I'm certain you will improve on his cooking.'

'From what he said you need more than food. I hope I can help you. It's lucky I'm between films. You'd have been delayed further getting down to the studios at Lodz,' he said as they walked briskly in the cold air.

Winter in Eastern Europe was already closing in and the chill reminded Raglan that he could not linger here.

'But from what Milosz told me, I was afraid I would not have the materials here in Warsaw. I have sent my friend to the studio to get what I need. He will get there and back in four hours – he drives like a crazy man. By the time we have eaten I will have what I need and in the meantime, I will prepare you. The tattoo images you want take time.'

It took twenty minutes to travel the ten kilometres into the old town. The car turned down a narrow street, tyres rumbling over the wet cobblestones past burghers' townhouses painted in various hues. It stopped on a street corner which offered a fine view across a vast square towards the city's Royal Castle.

'Let me,' said Raglan, reaching for his wallet to pay the driver.

'It's on my account. I use them all the time,' Tomasz said, wishing the driver goodnight by name. He led Raglan through an ornate old door and upstairs to his apartment, which covered the top two floors of the four-storey building. His host opened the door on to polished wood floors, oriental carpets and the appetizing smell of a meal on the stove. An ornate marble fireplace dominated the high-ceilinged room furnished with an eclectic mix of antique and modern furniture. To one side of the mantel, a gold statuette stood with an official awards ceremony photograph of Tomasz receiving his Oscar. Raglan stopped to admire it. The inscription told him it was awarded for best makeup on a well-known movie.

The walls displayed what appeared to be select pieces of modern art. On the sideboard next to the fireplace were several silver-framed photographs. In one Tomasz embraced another man of similar age, probably his partner, Raglan thought. In another picture, Tomasz was laughing with Milosz. Pride of place went to Milosz in legionnaire dress uniform. A group photograph of Sokol, Milosz, Sammy and Raglan in combat fatigues, looking somewhat worse for wear, explained how Tomasz had recognized him at the station. And it was obvious that Tomasz hero-worshipped his older brother.

'Your room is through here,' Tomasz said, dropping his coat on the sofa and guiding Raglan through the spacious apartment. He plucked an envelope from the dining table as they passed. 'My brother said you needed money, dollars and roubles. But not too much. Enough for a few days. If this isn't enough let me know. I can go back to the bank,' he said, handing the wedge to Raglan. 'The train ticket to Moscow is in there; it leaves tomorrow afternoon and gets in at eleven in the morning the next day. My brother said nothing fancy, just a second-class cabin, no shower or toilet. You will have to share with two others. Is that correct? It's an eighteen-hour journey.'

Raglan smiled. 'He doesn't want me going soft.'

'I cannot help you with anything official like a passport and you know the train goes through Belarus so you will need a transit visa...' He caught himself in mid-sentence. His brother had told him enough about Raglan to suggest that he would not undertake such a journey unprepared. 'Except for anyone travelling on a Russian passport, that is.'

'It won't be a problem,' Raglan told him.

Tomasz nodded. He shouldn't have underestimated Raglan. 'Very well. Freshen up. Don't shower yet; wait until we have eaten. I'll explain why later. I'll get the food ready.'

Raglan thanked him. The room being offered would not have been out of place in a five-star hotel.

Tomasz smiled. 'Milosz told me just a few details of what you and he did together. I'm honoured to help. Now, let's eat. Then you can strip down.'

40

Raglan did as he was told. Once they had finished the meal he showered, dried off, pulled on his boxer shorts and returned to the main room.

'In here,' he heard Tomasz call.

Raglan padded the length of the room and saw another door that led to what appeared to be a small beauty parlour booth with a treatment table covered in a towel, raised up to waist height. Rows of bottles of beauty and skin treatments stood on a small table beside it, and a strong lamp with magnifying lenses. It was the makeup expert's equivalent of a mechanic's garage. All the tools needed to ply his trade. Tomasz wore a white tunic buttoned to the neck and his long delicate fingers were now clad in latex surgical gloves. He studied Raglan when he came into the room.

'Please stand there,' he asked.

Raglan stood, relaxed without being self-conscious, as his host walked slowly around him. His intake of breath was barely audible when he saw the scars from bullet, knife, shrapnel and torture. 'It's had some wear and tear over the years,' said Raglan. 'I could probably do with a retread.'

Tomasz came to his front and stood close to his face, gently tilting Raglan's head this way and that, studying his bone structure and the muscles that ran into his neck and shoulder. 'I am on the medical register here in Warsaw. I have helped people with disfigurements and injuries far worse than any of the scars you bear. I can work with what you have.' He smiled. 'These are the tattoos your friend sent through that I am going to give you,' he said, pointing to a computer screen discreetly concealed behind the door. It showed a selection of Russian mafia tattoos. 'I have most of the transfers from the studio. Anything smaller than these large ones I can draw and fix on to your skin by hand using specialist materials. No needles,' he added. 'And I wanted to do them tonight so that I can see everything is as it should be in the morning before you leave.'

The tattoos adorned ugly, broken-faced men. None had much in the way of head hair; most looked to have bad dental work; all looked as though they would happily cut out your liver and eat it raw. Raglan reckoned some of them had done just that.

Tomasz pointed out the men's various tattoos. Some were so crude in design it was obvious they had been inked in prison. 'These are the most significant and tell the world who you are in the hierarchy. How many people you have killed, your distrust and hatred of authority.' His finger went from one design to another, tattoo images that would go on Raglan's back, chest, arms, neck and hands.

'How do you know all this?' Raglan asked.

'The man, Sokol, who sent the pictures, he gave me a list. He was very knowledgeable about these Russian *vory-v-zakone*, but I have heard of these *thieves-with-honour* gangsters from a television series I worked on at the studio. Now. Face down, please,' said Tomasz. 'I need to prepare your skin. There must be no natural grease otherwise the transfers will not adhere properly.'

Raglan climbed on to the treatment table and felt the sudden warmth of the lamp on his back. Tomasz's fingers felt his back muscles. 'All right, I will explain what I will do. You can ask anything. There is no pain involved.'

Raglan felt a cool liquid being applied to his back. His muscles rippled as it stung the abrasions sustained during the fight with JD.

'I apologize. This is ninety-nine per cent alcohol to strip out the natural oils.'

'It's nothing. I need to know what I have to do to keep those things on me without them peeling.'

'They will not peel, do not worry. They will fade and once I get them on you then I will put a final seal on them and the alcohol in it will seep the pattern into your skin like an old tattoo.'

'Making them look as though they've been there for some time is good. Some of them can be more faded than the others. It'll give me street-cred status. You're sure they'll hold?'

'I put a water-based adhesive on the back of the transfer which will not irritate your skin. I use it for medical prosthetics. These are the tattoo transfers they use in the film industry today. You see those actors on screen covered in jail tattoos? They are fake. As fake as the Royal Castle across the square which was destroyed in the war and rebuilt exactly as it used to be. Fake can be made to look real. In your case only for a while.'

'How long?'

'If you sweat a lot, or if you shower every day, no more than eight or nine days and then they begin to fade quickly. It will be noticeable.'

'I need longer.'

'If you shower less, then perhaps I can do something. Let me see how I get on.'

Raglan kept his face down through the space in the treatment bed. His muscles flexed across his arms and shoulders, a blank canvas for the special effects artist. If Milosz's brother was as good as he seemed then in a few hours he would emerge ready to be seen as a Russian gang member, his tattoos a passport telling those initiated into their secrets everything they needed to know about the man who bore them.

Once he was satisfied that Raglan's skin was ready for the transfer Tomasz lifted the sheet of plastic-backed paper bearing the image. He cut out the shape from the clear protective plastic and then laid the fake tattoo face down on Raglan's back, carefully peeling off the paper backing. This would be the largest and most detailed of the tattoos and needed to be done with precision so that it lay perfectly flat on the contours of his back muscles. The complex image was a storytelling tableau. Across Raglan's shoulders there was now a castellated crusader fort, below his shoulder blades the strident image of a crusader slaying a victim, and where Raglan's back tapered to his waist there were now bloodied bodies.

'Now I must swab this with water,' he told Raglan. 'Do not move, please.'

Raglan felt a wet sponge pressed on his back, small rivulets running down his flanks to soak into the towel beneath him.

'I use only bottled water for this because there is chlorine in tap water,' Tomasz added with a note of professional pride. 'I will towel you dry when I come to the rest of your body.'

Raglan felt the delicate sensation of powder being

dabbed across his back. 'This takes away any tackiness,' said Tomasz, pausing as he changed procedure, 'and now another damp sponge with a final sealant.'

The application of the transfer and its fixing was done with the utmost care and without haste under Tomasz's delicate touch. 'All right, now I use a hair dryer's cool setting to dry everything off and make the glue adhere to your skin.' The expert waited until he was satisfied that the transfer was fixed. 'Now you turn over and we do the next big one.'

Tomasz adjusted the light and examined Raglan's muscled chest. He smiled. 'It will be like trying to lay a wet sheet across a mountainous terrain.' Then he said, with a hint of regret, 'Forgive me, but what I said about it being painless, that was not quite accurate.' He paused. 'Now we must remove the body hair.'

When Tomasz had finished his work of art and was happy that the tattoos looked as though they had been on Raglan's body for some years, he pulled a secondary set of plastic curtains around the room and had Raglan stand, arms outstretched. Pulling on a medical face mask he instructed Raglan to close his eyes and then he airbrushed him with a water-based foundation to match his skin tone. Then it was powdered, dried and, finally, the work was finished.

'Now, I think you must look at the man you have become.' He pulled back the curtain and opened a storage cupboard door that had an illuminated full-length mirror attached to the inside.

Raglan looked at the tattoos that adorned his body, arms, hands and legs. The most striking was the double-headed Russian eagle that spanned his chest with blood dripping from its heart. Military-style epaulettes on his shoulders gave him rank; a snake curled up one side of his neck. His hands bore small faded crude tattoos as if done with a needle and ink in prison. His thighs bore skulls on one and a snarling tiger head on the other. A blade with droplets of blood appeared to pierce the skin on one side of his neck.

Tomasz stood back as Raglan examined his transformation. He pointed to the dripping dagger. 'Apparently that means you are a killer for hire.'

Raglan gave him a questioning look. The artist took a sheet of paper from the side table. 'Your Russian friend sent through a list of explanations for what they all mean.' Raglan took it but was more interested in the adornment that covered him.

Tomasz stepped back into the apartment's main room and peeled off the gloves. He looked at the lean-muscled torso of the tall man who stared unsmiling at himself in the mirror; his dark, scowling eyebrows accentuated the vision of brutality.

'My brother taught me an English expression and now I understand what it means.'

'Which is?'

'You scare the shit out of me.'

PART THREE

RUSSIAN FEDERATION

41

Russian Federation
October 2019

The long journey across Poland, Belarus and into Russia was uneventful except for the amount of vodka consumed by Raglan's two travelling companions, who slept stacked above his lower bunk bed in the three-tier cabin. Friendships were often formed on long train journeys and Raglan used the time to let the language seep back into him so that his own words came more readily when he spoke. He questioned the men about Moscow, giving the lie that he had been to visit his sister who had married a Pole but that he was from Belarus and was travelling to meet a well-known businessman who had offered him work. He was not familiar with the renowned underground system even though Sorokina had briefed him on what to do once he reached Moscow. He had familiarized himself with the various metro lines using Tomasz's computer before leaving Warsaw but getting information from native Muscovites was valuable. They were happy to talk about their city, which they regarded as the greatest in the world even though they had never travelled further than Warsaw for their annual railwaymen's convention. Moscow was streets better than St Petersburg. Everyone knew that. The tsars and their gilded buildings? No, they insisted, St Petersburg was only for tourists. Real people lived in Moscow. If they were lucky at this time of year it could mean bab'e leto, and who wouldn't want an Indian summer when winter was just around the corner? The idea of late warmth brought a sense of cheer to the two men's mood. Raglan imagined them huddled in the biting cold of their small apartments, hoping for that late autumn fresh air when maple trees turned yellow and red. Nostalgia played its part even with the seasons.

His companions were older men and had plenty of stories to tell about the Soviet era. When they first entered the cabin Raglan had offered to give up his lower bunk to the older whiskered man, who quickly berated him for his offer of charity. Did he look infirm? he had demanded. But when he noticed the tattoos on Raglan's hands and the snake's head inching up behind his ear from beneath his collar, his attitude softened. Like most Russians, their goodwill and companionship were soon apparent and they readily shared their food and drink. The vodka soothed any trepidation they felt at sharing the confined space with a gangster.

The younger of the two, a swarthy man with dark stubble and wild curly hair who looked as if he could have been a wrestler in his youth, dared to suggest their cabin was as small as a prison cell. He had once been arrested, said the stranger, attempting to find common ground with his fellow passenger. He'd been drunk one night and his wife began giving him a hard time. He had slapped her to keep her quiet. The police were called and he punched an officer. He spent two weeks in a city jail and reckoned this carriage was luxury by comparison. The man introduced himself as Igor Voronin, and his older friend was Josef Naumov. Both of them were retired workers from the Russian railways. Raglan offered to buy extra food and drink from the buffet car, but no *vory-v-zakone* ever pays. The two men had the citizen's grudging respect towards gangsters, men who challenged authority, refusing to do anything that aided the state, living their lives according to their own law; their code gave these men a unique place in society.

By the time the train pulled into Moscow's Belorussky Station the two older men had spilt out their life stories. Russia was a modern country now, designed for those who could push their way to the front; it was not for the older generation. Tears had welled at the loss of the old Communist way of life and the travails they now endured under the new regime. But they had learnt nothing about the quiet man who had shared their journey. Between themselves, as they humped their cases on to the platform, they agreed that it was better not to know.

Raglan watched as they made their way towards the end of the platform. A younger man dressed in jeans and a sheepskin jacket came out of a carriage and appeared to accidentally bump into them and then quickly offered an apology. But the apology took too long. Igor and Josef shook their heads. They were being questioned. Josef was about to turn and look back towards the carriage where Raglan waited but the apologizer gently took his arm and turned him around to stay facing him. Then, without another word, he walked away. Igor and Josef hesitated and Raglan guessed they had decided not to get involved. He watched as they shuffled away. Their interrogator put a phone to his ear and half turned to watch the passengers streaming down the platform as Raglan stepped down out of the carriage with his holdall.

No doubt about it. Sheepskin Man was a cop. They had been tailing him since Warsaw. Elena's men had been alerted.

It was a few minutes' walk to the metro station. Raglan was not much interested in architectural design unless he was assessing ways to root an enemy out of a building, but he allowed himself a few moments of appreciation for the sheer beauty of the Moscow underground and the skill of the artisans who had built it. Admiring the art deco ceiling he deliberately missed his footing, dropped his holdall and used its recovery to glance back. Sheepskin Man was some distance behind and quickly lowered his head, blending in with the hundreds of other commuters who walked head down, gazing at their mobile phones.

Raglan caught the line to Mayakovskaya Station and seven minutes later emerged into weather that was definitely not that of an Indian summer. A cold wind threatened to bring rain from the leaden sky. He knew where he had to go and continued down Tverskaya Street. He was a couple of miles from the Kremlin but he was heading for somewhere less impressive in a side street that lay off the broad, well-paved road. It reminded him of Paris and, to a lesser extent, Regent Street in London. Classical buildings nudged more modern designs. High-end boutiques and restaurants offered their wares to the rich Muscovites, a multitude of them, given the number of expensive cars that poured along the broad highway. He ignored the stream of yellow taxis that caterpillared down the boulevard and ten minutes later turned down a side street and then a narrow lane to a small ten-room hotel. He stepped inside and asked for a room. At best this was a family-run one-star hotel, the kind of place that needed all the business it could get. A neon sign in the window confirmed it: there was a 20 per cent discount on all rooms. The receptionist was probably the owner's daughter as her level of front-of-house greeting was limited to asking whether he wanted to pay the 1,500 roubles in cash or on his card. Raglan paid cash and handed over his passport.

The small room was glitzy, an attempt to make it look smarter than it was. A gold-painted pine bed with a red cover clashed with the black diamonds on the grey carpet. He didn't care. He was going straight back on to the streets and wanted a shower before they came for him. Where he was going a shower would be a luxury. He decided against it. Better to stink than risk damaging the tattoos so soon.

42

Moscow Police HQ
Building 6
Petrovka 38
Tverskoy District, Moscow

They arrested Daniil Regnev on Mamonovskiy Pereulok Street barely two hours after he arrived in the city, just as Major Elena Sorokina of the Moscow CID had told him in London. It was carried out efficiently, especially the flurry of blows the cops rained down on him, knowing how much punishment to administer without causing serious damage. They snatched him as he sheltered in a doorway, pulling the collar of his jacket higher against the first cold bite of sleet. The police knew exactly where he was and held him in detention for twenty-four hours, where he once again felt the heavy hand of Russian police questioning techniques.

From one of the seven investigation departments of the Central Administrative District of Moscow, orders were issued for the prisoner to be taken directly to CID headquarters. The intimidating building had existed since the nineteenth century and served the city as a barracks and police station. As they drove Raglan past the front of the building he saw the bust of Felix Dzerzhinsky gazing out from a plinth facing the busy street. The father of the old Russian secret police and inspiration for the KGB represented the time of the terror under Stalin. The massive statue of him that had once stood outside the old Lubyanka KGB headquarters had been pulled down when Communism ended twenty-odd years before. Now there was a movement to have the old statue reinstated. Many Muscovite families had suffered the terror of Stalin's purges a century before. In those days the executions of enemies of the state often took place in churches or banks where solidly built basements deadened the sound of gunfire. The victims' bodies were then taken on trucks to Butovo on the city outskirts where they were buried in mass graves. That statue of Dzerzhinsky symbolized repression and fear. The self-same fear clung to many inhabitants of the city now, as surely as the winter fog clung to the Kremlin's domes.

Raglan was hauled into the rear of the building, up three floors and past dozens of closed doors. He hoped he had not fallen into the wrong hands. These drab painted walls were as thick as a bank's, more than solid enough to smother the sound of a gunshot. The corridors ran in straight lines along the length of the building and beneath its high ceilings footfalls echoed on old parquet flooring. By the time he reached the interview room and sat down opposite Sorokina the bleeding from the cuts to his lip and face had stopped. Raglan checked the walls. No sign of cameras.

She gazed at him for a moment, her back to the two-way glass window, and then lowered her eyes. 'You resisted arrest,' she said, examining the prepared documents in the folder that lay open on the table in front of her. Raglan looked at the old table's scuffs and scratches. Formica. How long had it been since anyone had a Formica table? The graffiti in the holding cell suggested the fixtures and fittings had been in place since Soviet days. Russian police station decor had not moved with the times.

'Of course I did,' he said, smiling through his cut lip. In fact it had taken determined self-control not to defend himself; had he done so he would still have been walking the streets and two of Moscow's finest would be lying crumpled and bloody in that doorway.

She was cold and businesslike, more so than he remembered. There had been warmth and sensuality in the Russian detective only days before when they slept together, but now she was playing a new role, looking every bit the part of a CID major in the Moscow Police.

He glanced around the stained green walls, the peeling paint the only hint of colour in the bare room. Old blood dries like ochre. Although he had determined that there were no cameras recording the meeting, without doubt though there would be hidden microphones. She studied him for a few moments, noticing the tattoos on his hands and arms and the coiled snake that seemed to slither from beneath his collar up on to his neck. He gave her a questioning look and she nodded to the two heavyweight cops, who hauled him to his feet and roughly pulled aside his shirt, exposing his torso and revealing not the usual thieves' spider tattoos, but Russian gangland symbols: the *oskal*, an image of a skull with bared vampire-like fangs that told the world that he bared his teeth at authority. The double skulls hovering over coffins proclaimed the man sitting before her was a murderer. For a moment she couldn't hide her shock at how his muscled body had been transformed. Then she nodded again and the two cops pushed him back down into his chair, checking that his manacles still restricted any movement and exited the room, leaving their senior officer alone with the man they believed to be a wanted killer. She lowered her eyes and glanced at the open folder with its falsified details.

'The fugitive warrant from when you escaped detention two years ago has now been executed. Your original sentence stands. Twenty-five years,' she intoned.

The proceedings were exactly as she had explained they would be when he had sat with her in the hotel room in London. The trumped-up charge was going to give him the opportunity to hunt down and kill JD.

She passed over a sheet of paper. 'This is the official court order for your detention.'

He glanced down at the typed sheet and showed no sign of surprise. It told him where he was being sent, and also that his target was there. She had arranged everything. Right under the noses of the FSB, inheritors of the KGB ethos, who would have happily slammed her and the whole Moscow CID into one of their internment camps had they realized what she had done. He was being sent to a maximum-security prison in the middle of nowhere, a prison inhabited by serial killers, rapists, child murderers and organized crime hit men. These pin-up boys for maximum sentence crimes were lifers in a place from which there was no return. She reached across and turned over the page, pressing her forefinger on to the sheet of paper. Read on, she was saying. Her prose was blunt. No frills. The where and the why. Cause and effect. The people who used the man he was after had to make a show that he was being punished, while at the same actually protecting him. He was hidden from view. And, just as with Raglan, the mountain of bureaucratic paperwork was deep enough to cover their tracks. How soon would it be before the man he hunted was released or moved to an open prison and then put back on the streets? How much time was there?

'You can see why you are being sent there,' she said, choosing her words for the sake of those who were doing the recording.

The final paragraph made it clear. The Moscow Police and a sympathetic judge – not necessarily her father but someone else in the judiciary as weary of the ongoing corruption and conspiracies within the state apparatus – had wrangled the paperwork and had the man known as Kuznetsov incarcerated in a place of *their* choosing, held long enough for whatever retribution could be inflicted on him. Those who controlled the killer believed it to be a safe haven while the heat died down, after which he would return to work for the powers-that-be. It was a hellhole, but he would only be there for a few months. If Raglan had any chance at all of getting out of that penal colony alive he needed at least one friend in place and that appeared to be the prison's deputy governor. Those he would share a cell with were unlikely to extend the hand of friendship.

Major Sorokina retrieved the sheet of paper, her hand briefly touching his. She tucked the sheet back into the government-issue folder and pushed back her chair. He thought he saw a flicker of emotion. 'I doubt I will ever see you again,' she said. He knew she meant it. She reached the door. 'It's a hard place to be sent to. It would be a miracle if you survived,' she said, her tone non-committal for the sake of those who listened.

And that time he definitely saw the look of regret in her eyes.

43

Penal Colony #74 (White Eagle)
Sverdlovskaya Oblast, Ural Federal District
1837 km east of Moscow

They bundled him into a secure cage in an old windowless Volga prison bus. The authorities' intention was to inflict sensory deprivation on any prisoner and ensure he had no awareness of the direction of travel, which helped quash any idea of escape. It was also a psychological ploy. Being trapped in a box like this was an introduction to a lifer's confinement in a cell five paces long and two wide, with a light on every minute of every day. A single iron-frame bed and a latrine bucket would be the only furnishing. The Volga had only the bucket. Get used to the bars, locks, cages and guards with dogs, the authorities were saying. This box is better than the coffin we will put you in. Better to be executed with a bullet to the back of the head. Then annihilation would be instant, not a lingering torture. Perhaps that's why they repealed the death penalty. To inflict a life worse than death.

Exhaust fumes seeped through the rusted floorpan as the bus thumped and rolled over the unkempt road. Raglan hunched his chained arms across his chest and withdrew deep into himself. This journey was going to be nothing more than a longer version of the enforced interrogation exercise when he had volunteered for the commando special forces in the Legion. The mind games needed to be controlled. Shut them out. Find a place in your head and stay there. Elena had told him it was going to take the better part of twenty-four hours to get to the prison. As the cold gripped his limbs he knew it was going to feel longer.

Every few hours the bus stopped; Raglan figured the guard and driver needed to relieve themselves and although he couldn't see them because of the steel walls on the cage, the sudden blast of cold air revived him as the men clambered down. He heard their feet crunch in frozen snow and smelt the rough cigarette smoke as the men lit up. He sucked in the refreshing air, forcing himself to stand and stretch despite the limitation of the chains. When the men got back into the cab the guard opened a flap in the door and pushed through a metal billy can with a lid that held hot watery soup with bits of potato and cabbage floating in the greasy liquid. Like any soldier, Raglan was immune to food being too hot and he drank the fluid, feeling its warmth creep into his muscles. He dug his fingers down into what had settled at the bottom of the can and pushed it into his mouth. Every time the bus stopped they fed him but as the journey wore on the soup became colder and greasier. His internal clock told him it seemed to be a fixed rotation, every five hours, and by the time he had swallowed the fourth offering, by now shivering from the cold, he knew he was only a few hours from the penal colony.

When they eventually arrived at their destination and he saw the desolation he knew Elena's final words might be prophetic. He was going to need a miracle to get out alive.

Shuffling between the guards, he moved as quickly as the manacles would allow. There was already snow on the ground, whipped up by the wind through mesh wire fences topped with rolled barbed wire. The wind's bite scratched his face like flying rusted barbs. It was less harsh when they escorted him through a solid wooden gate that opened when the guard rang a bell. He glanced back and saw the bus had stopped between a reinforced mesh wire fence and a high wooden outer wall. The lime-washed wall was pitted and grooved from the same punishing winds over the years. Telephone and electricity wires swayed precariously across the fences and walls.

His eyes watering from the assaulting temperature, he calculated there were four perimeter walls or fences around the complex. It was eighty-nine shuffling paces to the next sentry post. Another fifty to the next guard post. So far he reckoned 150 metres would take him from the first building ahead of him to the open space where the bus had stopped. There were obstacles to overcome, but if he ever got to where the bus had stopped there was only the outer palisade wall that stood between him and freedom on the road. It was a short run across the dispersal area to that wall. A run that would have him under the guns on the watchtowers that loomed on this side of the compound. Then he dismissed these first thoughts of an escape route. Once inside he would determine how to get out. They passed more guards as they took him through a succession of doors that led deeper into the buildings. As every door was opened and closed, the jangle of keys and the clang of metal taunted him with their echo.

Unseen by Raglan, the deputy governor, Anatoly Vasiliev, his shoulders hunched against twenty years of being stationed at Penal Colony #74, watched through the grime-encrusted window of his office. He drew cigarette smoke deep into his lungs. He was a religious man, strengthened by the resurgence of the Orthodox Church since the fall of the Communists, and he prayed that he would pass unscathed through the coming days or weeks. This new prisoner being brought into the prison represented great danger to him personally should anything go wrong. People in Moscow had planned the man's incarceration, and the earlier arrival of the other inmate. Neither were serial killers or rapists; they did not, as far as he knew, torture and kill children; they were professionals in their own right, working for people he had no desire to know about. But he had agreed to go along with the plan because his family would see a better part of the world than this frozen wasteland. As the rough tobacco's smoke bit into his lungs, he thought of a sheep being tethered as bait for a predator. The difference being that Kuznetsov was no docile creature being readied for slaughter – he was a wolf in sheep's clothing, more dangerous than any of the other violent inmates because he did not kill through drunkenness or insanity. Kuznetsov killed efficiently and without emotion. If this man shuffling in his manacles was to kill him then Vasiliev had to make sure that it would be only their blood spilled on the snow, and not his own. He would do everything he could to facilitate the desired result but with the power struggle going on in Moscow he would make sure he protected himself too. If the execution was successful then he would have to make certain that this man, Regnev, also died.

Inside the administrative building, the guards removed Raglan's manacles and ushered him into the deputy governor's office, itself hardly the height of luxury. A rug lay across the worn flooring; a wood burning stove offered warmth. From high above a bookshelf the President of Russia stared out of a framed photograph, his cold eyes saying, *Fuck you, scum.* Raglan stood looking over the head of the balding man who studied his case file. Raglan kept his eyes fixed on the wall. You don't make eye contact until you're told to. Ask any soldier brought up on a charge in front of a senior officer and he'll tell you the same thing. To stare with any kind of intent is called dumb insolence and always antagonizes. And this was not the time to piss off the man who held your life in his hands.

The deputy governor wore the same sturdy boots and disruptive pattern combat fatigues as the two guards who flanked Raglan. He tapped his cigarette on the rim of an overfull ashtray and sipped at a glass of clear tea. The small bowl of sugar lumps implied he was a secret sugar-sucker, with or without the tea. It might be the only pleasure in this godforsaken place, Raglan thought.

'Daniil Regnev, I am conducting this interview because Governor Lichevsky is on four weeks' annual family leave,' said Vasiliev.

Raglan heard the real meaning behind the words. The deputy governor was briefing him. *Information: the governor cannot be part of the conspiracy to kill JD which is why Raglan had been sent here at this precise time.*

'Do not think I am any less sparing in my condemnation of your crime. Do not expect pity or understanding from me. You are a murderer. You will serve your full time. Do not think of escape. There is nowhere to go. The nearest town is eight hours away. The nearest city fourteen. Forests surround us greater in scale than the country of Germany.'

Information: He's declared his neutrality and described their location and surrounding area.

The deputy governor rapped the end of his cheap pen on the desk. *Tap tap tap.* It was a summons to look at him. Raglan lowered his eyes. 'You will be in a dormitory of six. You will be given work.' He paused, his eyes full of meaning. 'You will be under constant guard as part of the forest detail. The weather will be clear for a short while longer. The nearby lake is already frozen and snow will arrive in days. In two weeks this prison will be cut off. Winter is earlier than usual. You will bring the felled timber to the yard and work under the orders of a long-term prisoner and trustee. Prisoner Yefimov.'

Information: there is only a brief window of time before the winter shuts down any chance to kill and escape. Yefimov might be friendly.

The deputy governor nodded and the two guards grabbed Raglan's arms, forced him to bend double and handcuffed him. Bent at the waist, he was marched along the corridor, arms pinned straight behind his back. The painful manoeuvre made any kind of resistance impossible. They pushed him into another room, bigger than any office, with a closed-off grille, exposed rafters and shelving where neatly folded dark grey uniforms were stacked. There was a woodstove in the corner, its pig-iron metal as pitted as the face of the guard who held his neck down. The warmth that seeped from it barely made an impression on the cold air in the hut. It must have been minus twenty outside.

One guard punched him in the stomach; Raglan wheezed out air and fell to his knees. They hauled him up and the second guard struck him hard in the ribs. The pain from the sudden flurry of blows doubled him over again. Best to try and stay on his feet because if he went down this time those stout winter boots could break his skull or put out an eye. All this physical exertion must be what kept the guards warm. Their intention was to weaken him and then remove the handcuffs. One of the guards gripped his neck, forcing his head on to the counter. He complied without resisting. Once he had been allowed to stand upright again a guard appeared on the other side of the hatch and without a word passed through a folded bundle of prison clothes. Raglan pulled them to his chest, using the effort to tighten his stomach muscles to help keep him upright.

If this was their welcoming committee he wasn't looking forward to the main event.

44

Muscle had cushioned his ribs but he could already feel the soreness that heralded bruising. At least the pain was not as severe as a broken rib: he'd had that before – this was a minor beating from guards who knew how to inflict misery without causing serious damage.

He yielded to the prison barber who sheared his hair to little more than a shadow, then stripped and changed into the dark grey prison clothing. He pulled a *feska*, the prisoners' black cap, snugly on to his shorn head. One of the guards pushed a card bearing Raglan's new name, crime and sentence into the clear plastic pocket stitched on the uniform's jacket, to tell the guards whom they were dealing with and remind them of the heinous crimes the prisoner had committed. These killers and rapists were not to be treated with respect or compassion. They were there to serve their time, their full term without remission.

The guards escorted him past the double-storey building that held the lifers, men who had been convicted since the death penalty had been repealed and who were kept in cells little more than an arm's width wide. Men who could not even join others in the fresh air of the compound. The only time they saw the sky was in a walled yard twenty paces long with a caged roof. The penal colony was harsh enough but the state wanted these prisoners to rot in a living hell.

Once he had been shoved into the dormitory, home to some of the men serving twenty-five years, the guards closed the doors behind him. The room was empty. There was only one vacant iron bedstead with a rolled mattress and blankets. He glanced around the room. The window frames were rotten, the glass as grimy as the deputy governor's. He unfurled the bedding; it was damp. He'd be sleeping fully clothed until the stove was lit and the mattress dried. But it presented little hardship to someone who had spent so many years living in every hellhole the French government had sent him and his friends to. Raglan stood in the centre of the room looking from bed to bed. At the side of each was a rough wooden cabinet with a couple of drawers. On one of the windowsills, an old radio stood wired into a light socket. It looked as though it had already served a life sentence. There was no point in checking for any weapons in the bedside locker. The guards would toss the dormitories and cells regularly. If a prisoner had a knife or anything that passed as a stabbing weapon, it would either be stitched into his mattress or hidden behind a loose brick or floorboard. And if a man wanted to kill another there were more opportunities to do so outside in the exercise or work yard.

Before he could give any more consideration to his new surroundings the door opened and a tall man, whom Raglan thought to be in his sixties, stepped into the room. In his prime he would have been a well-muscled pugilist, by the look of his broken features; now years of hard labour and harsh living conditions had pared down his weight and burnished his skin into a saddle-leather patina. He pulled off his feska and rubbed a hand across his white-cropped scalp. With a glance at Raglan, he retrieved a letter from his own bedside locker. The bed was the closest to the stove, denoting a privileged rank within the dormitory. Raglan stood where he was. He glimpsed the man's name tag: *Yefimov*. The long-term prisoner pocketed the letter and stared at Raglan.

'You're no Russian. You don't look Russian and I'll wager when you open your mouth you won't sound Russian.'

Raglan remained silent.

Yefimov grunted and took a step closer. 'We don't like strangers coming into our midst. It makes us nervous. We think the authorities have planted a spy.'

'Why? Are you thinking of having a secret birthday party?'

'Ah, a funny guy. That's all right. We like a joke,' said the older man without breaking into a smile.

Raglan stared him down: an age-old masculine tradition telling each other that neither was used to yielding ground. The old man wasn't fazed; he'd seen enough tough men come through these doors. Once they had spent a few nights listening to the banshee wind tormenting them, insisting that they would be unlikely to see their loved ones again, the toughness was soon knocked out of them. They became part of the herd, finding their place in the hierarchy until a hand of friendship was extended. It could be a slow process. But this Regnev was different. The deputy governor had told him to shepherd the man around. So be it. He'd get extra privileges. Perhaps extra phone calls to his daughter and grandkids. Anything else was none of his business.

'There are only a couple of hundred men here. It's better in a smaller camp like this than some of the others. You get to know who's who. I've been here thirty-seven years. Soviet and Russian time. They're no different. They gave me a double life sentence. It took me a long time to learn from my mistakes. I'll die in here. If they hadn't stopped the death sentence I wouldn't have had to endure this hell. You understand what I am saying, young man?'

Raglan saw that the man's tag denoted he was a multiple murderer. His measured demeanour also told him that Yefimov was one of the more dangerous prisoners. His life was already written off; at least others would serve their twenty-five and get out. Yefimov had nothing to lose except privileges if he killed again.

'I'm not here to cause trouble,' said Raglan. 'Not for you or anyone else.'

The older man nodded. This Regnev had learnt the first lesson quickly. Know who was in charge among the men. A shrill clanging sounded from outside.

'It's time to eat. Then I'll show you where you'll be working. Get used to this place quickly, Regnev. A man can lose his mind here if he doesn't.'

Raglan followed his guide across the snow-covered yard towards the canteen building. Seventy-four paces away. He was mapping out the layout of the camp.

'Some prisoners are allowed telephone calls to their families. Few have that privilege. It depends.'

Raglan didn't ask what such privileges depended on and Yefimov didn't expand. Most likely it was a reward for good behaviour or someone somewhere had sent money to grease the wheels.

'We are allowed three parcels from the outside every year. You have someone? Someone who will send you the things you need?'

'No.'

'Then you will have to trade some of your rations, or do someone a favour.'

'What kind of favour?'

'Whatever they need. Are you queer?'

'No.'

'Good. Homosexuals are ostracized. They eat together and no one accepts anything from them. Understand? No favours from them. No cigarettes. No food. Nothing. Them and the child-killers. We don't even shake their hand. They are not us. We call them "downcasts". They are tolerated because we don't want trouble in the camp.' Yefimov gestured left and right as they walked. 'We work at the saw bench and carpentry shop. You any good with engines? There's work in the garages.'

'I can fix things.'

'Good.' He made a vague gesture beyond one of the enclosed yards. 'Over there, when the snow clears, we grow vegetables. We eat well here. And that place past the wood yard? That's the barn where we keep pigs. Maybe you can kill pigs? Most of us refuse. They squeal. They scream as the knife cuts into their throats. Most of us don't want to hear such screams again. So, here's the canteen.'

Raglan followed him inside. Steam from the large pots of stew misted the windows. Men stood in line to be served two ladles of watery stew and a chunk of thick bread by cooks behind an open hatch. Tables with four or six men seated around them filled the room. Three long refectory tables split the room into informal sections. All the tables were covered with discoloured oilskin tablecloths. The line of men parted as they gave Yefimov a place of honour. He stepped in without acknowledging the gesture and took one of the stacked metal plates and spoons and handed them to Raglan, who understood that from then on he was being protected by the senior man in the camp. Yefimov nodded towards a table on the far side of the canteen.

'Downcasts,' he said. 'Remember their faces. Take and give nothing unless you need a blowjob. Then you give them a couple of cigarettes. That's as far as it goes. We even make them use their own plates and spoons. We are condemned men, Regnev, our souls are probably beyond redemption, but them… they burn longer in hell than the rest of us.'

The watery stew splashed into Raglan's plate. The food did not look appetizing but it was hot and something that looked like a piece of meat and a few cut vegetables floated in the murky water. There had been times when he had eaten worse during his time in the Legion.

'I see what you mean,' said Raglan. 'You eat well here.'

Yefimov grinned. 'You're learning already, Regnev. You'll have no trouble fitting in.'

45

Two weeks was barely enough time to find JD and make a plan of how to kill him, thought Raglan as he settled into his still-damp bed. Where was JD? There had been no sign of him in the canteen, no sight of him among the squads of prisoners being marched from their dormitories to their workplaces. There were 273 men in Penal Colony #74 and if Yefimov was in on the plan, then he had made no mention of the killer concealed among the murderers. And if he was incarcerated in one of the lifers' cells then he could not be reached.

Raglan only half slept, monitoring the unfamiliar noises that surrounded him. His mind tried to track the sounds, alert to anything untoward: the creak of a floorboard that shouldn't be there, the intake of breath from an assailant as the night air cooled, anything that would give him warning of a sneak attack. The old wooden building creaked, moaning with age and fatigue.

The wind found every gap in the planking and a constant cool brush of air wafted across his face. Yefimov had told him that by morning the weather would be clear and he would join the work party in the forest. The long-term inmates knew the vagaries of the weather in all its seasons, just as creatures of the forest did. The room stank of stale sweat and flatulence. Occasionally someone would moan from the depths of his tormenting dream. So far, nothing unusual about men sharing sleeping quarters. The meagre blankets offered some warmth, but until the wood stove was cranked up when winter descended and it was −45 °C outside, the chill never left the room.

The siren woke them in the darkness at five when it was still dark and Raglan followed the men from the dormitory to the ablution block.

'You're lucky,' said one grudgingly, 'we get hot water once a week. But you get it the day after you arrive. We stink after a few days cutting and hauling timber.' There was no attempt at greeting; no introduction. The men from his dormitory cast a glance his way every so often. Weighing him up. Waiting to see what tattoos he bore and what they revealed about him. A side room had rough wooden cubicles for the men to hang their clothes. The green gloss-painted woodwork was the only colour Raglan had seen inside the prison. Once they had stripped naked, they went into the room next door, which was furnished with half a dozen stands with buckets of steaming water and padded cloths and soap. A cistern hung from each side of the room with a rope release to sluice water over a soaped body. Raglan did as the others did, soaking the cloth and soaping himself. He uttered a silent prayer that Tomasz's temporary tattoos would stand the rigour of the hot water and soap. If the killing symbol of the knife stained into his neck seeped and ran, he would be dead before the day was out. *You'll be left standing with your dick in your hand and nowhere to run.*

He turned and bent to wash his legs so he could glance around at the others. Very few men bore gangland or prison tattoos. If they had been looking his way they quickly averted their eyes, all except for one prisoner. His muscled frame told Raglan he had stamina and strength and his body bore tattoos to rival Raglan's. This guy was a hard case. Russian mafia. Hitman. He too had inked epaulettes denoting he had held rank in a gang. Across his back were images of Russian church spires; his neck and arms sported knives piercing skulls. An *oskal*, a tiger's bared fangs, snarled from his right shoulder and a knight's shield smothered his flanks. All these symbols, interspersed with various stars needled into his flesh, declared him a man not in any way fearful of causing death, or dying himself. A tapestry of violence. He kept looking. Raglan turned his gaze away and sluiced himself off beneath the cistern.

Daylight ushered in a sky that shone so blue it hurt the eyes, the snow gleaming beneath the stark rays of the sun. Once dressed the prisoners stood in four ranks before the guard commander who barked out a roll call. Seasoned prisoners were given status even here on the parade ground. Those who had served the longest were called and checked and released from the ranks. They got to eat breakfast first. Yefimov was the first to be dismissed; Raglan the last. He looked across the ranks of prisoners but there was still no sight of the man he had come to kill. A momentary fear stabbed at him. What if JD was not here at all? Raglan might be imprisoned here longer than he thought. He pushed aside the doubt, convinced that the deputy governor had given him all the clues he needed to know that JD was here somewhere. By the time he reached the canteen, there was barely time to grab the tin mug of tea, find a table that still had sugar cubes and wolf down a wad of thick bread smeared with margarine and jam.

Another siren signalled work parties to gather. Raglan ran from the canteen and spotted Yefimov striding towards a group of men: most were from his dormitory and already issued with axes, saws and chains.

'You work with my group, Regnev. Take that,' Yefimov said, pointing to a long-handled axe. 'You'll clear the undergrowth while we chain up the cut timber.' Guards' whistles blew, gates were opened, and the prisoners formed up and trudged through the snow.

Their crunching boots broke the stillness; one of the guard dogs barked. That was the only sound. The rest was silence as they passed through the palisade walls and into the boreal forest that pressed up against the prison. If a man could get over a wall, or through a wire mesh fence, he was already condemned to a slow death in a forest that blocked out light and had no man-made tracks. They might as well not have bothered to build the walls, Raglan thought.

Seven hundred and fourteen paces took Raglan from the buildings across the work yard to the outer gate. So far he had determined that the prison had an outer palisade wall, then at reasonably equal spacing, in true bureaucratic and totalitarian discipline, a double wire fence topped with barbed wire, another wooden fence, then another mesh-and-barbed-wire barrier and finally the inner palisade wall that formed the first line of defence closest to the buildings. Glancing left and right he saw six watchtowers strategically placed, each manned by a single armed guard.

As the men passed through the gate, they crossed a road going left and right. To his right, the road disappeared into bleak nothingness. A single strip road leading away to infinity, ploughed snow piled high each side, frozen and grimy. The road dipped and rose again. Beyond the perimeter fence and to the left in the distance was a cluster of dwellings, a little hamlet with smoke rising from the houses' tall chimney stacks. He reckoned this was accommodation for the administrative staff and the guards and their families, little more than a kilometre away. Somewhere out of sight was the frozen lake which would most likely be the only open expanse in this dense forest. If an escape could be made that's where he would try to put some distance between him and pursuing guards. It was early enough in the winter for the frozen lake not to bear the weight of vehicles if he dared to cross it. And if he made it that far then he knew he could outrun the unfit guards. After that? He had no idea. Not yet. That would be a desperate time and desperate decisions would be made.

The work party struck across the clearing in the forest. Like rodents gnawing a cardboard box, the woodcutters had edged their way into the larch and pine over the years. After what felt like a thirty-minute walk across the harvested ground, their guard settled himself on a pile of stacked wood, laid his submachine gun down next to him, yawned, lit a cigarette and left Yefimov to organize what needed to be done in the clearing. Most of the men had already split up into their respective pairings.

'Regnev, you will work with him,' he said, pointing out a man of similar age to Raglan. Yefimov turned his face away so that the man could not hear what was being said about him. 'His friend's wife and daughter were abducted, raped and murdered by another family's sons. The family were Communists who had got hold of some easy money and bought influence. It's a well-worn story, Regnev. He got pissed one night and took revenge on behalf of his friend. He murdered seven people. The whole family. Did it nice and slow as well. Invaded their house, tied them up and spent the night killing each one slowly in front of the others. He saved the father until the end so he could watch his family go under the knife – or rather a meat cleaver, according to the police report. He's all right. He won't cause you any trouble. In fact he will be helpful to you, because he can already see that you are at my side.'

Raglan glanced at the man, who looked as though he could have been back-room staff in a supermarket. He was slender, with a receding hairline and wire-rimmed spectacles. Raglan doubted he'd have the strength to wield a pen, let alone clear land with an axe. He didn't bear any tattoos: he was simply an uncomplicated mass killer.

'Don't get him started on Communists, for God's sake. He has nothing less than a religious hatred for them. His name is Kirill. If he talks it will be about the Bible, Russia and Putin. Let him. Save yourself grief by not arguing with him. Not everyone here believes in God or Putin, but we have a few. They're a pain in the arse. You're my gift to him. It gives the rest of us a break.' Yefimov grinned.

Raglan snorted the droplets from his nostrils. The cold air was already stiffening his face muscles. He nodded. 'OK. One of the men I knew when I was in the army was

Vietnamese. He was a Buddhist.' He glanced to where Kirill was walking towards the undergrowth with his axe. 'I could offer him an alternative point of view to Russian Orthodoxy.'

Yefimov scowled. 'The hell you say. You want to start a religious war?'

He gazed at the stony-faced Raglan and then he realized.

'You're a strange one, Regnev. You had me going there for a moment.'

Raglan shrugged. 'Just something to pass the time.'

'Time isn't something we think about here. Get your arse over there and start cutting. We need to clear a way so that when we fell the trees, the horses can come in and drag them clear. We take a break in four hours.'

'And then?'

Yefimov glanced to where the guard was sitting, now facing away from them.

'Then I'll tell you about the shit storm you might have started and the man who would be happy to cut your throat before the day is out.'

46

Kirill proved to be a decent enough work companion. He had only served ten of his twenty-five-year sentence. He prattled on non-stop, which suited Raglan because he doubted his Russian vocabulary was broad enough to discuss the finer points of Vladimir Putin's desire to see the Russian Orthodox Church become a defining characteristic of Russian life. That Putin, insisted Kirill, is a good man. You'll see, he persisted without drawing breath. Putin will make Russia great again. He stopped swinging his axe, raised his eyes to the infinite heaven above, pulled free his feska, crossed himself and told Raglan that now the Church had a close relationship with the Kremlin, Mother Russia would be blessed by the Almighty and achieve great things in this decadent world whose cancerous values had spread from the West. The filth on television. The rise in prostitution. Russian women even selling themselves as wives in other countries. Self-respect and love for one's country had become diseased. It all needed to be cut out as a surgeon cuts out a tumour. Gathering the axe again, he swung it through the saplings and Raglan saw how a quick flash of anger had changed the face of the mild-mannered man. That look of rage might have been the last thing the murdered family ever saw. Kirill spat. Did his new friend know that during the Soviet era the priests and worshippers were persecuted? When those atheist Communist bastards had been in power they had torn down the Cathedral of Christ the Saviour in Moscow and replaced it with a massive swimming pool. Kirill shook his head in disbelief. He paused and wiped the sweat from his forehead. 'I only killed Communists,' he said by way of excusing his crimes.

'I told him I wasn't a Communist,' said Raglan as he joined Yefimov at the head of the queue where the men were being given a mug of what appeared to be steaming coffee. 'And that I wasn't a homosexual. He seemed keen to be sure about those things. Has he killed anyone here?'

He and Yefimov walked away from the others. 'If he had, he would be in the hell house. Locked up twenty-three hours a day, not allowed to sit on his bed during daylight hours. Christ above, that is a living death. No, he hasn't raised a hand, that's why we let him rabbit on.

Rage like that is better leaked like a broken pipe and allowed to dribble out little by little.'

'Then Kirill isn't the one who wants to cut my throat?'

Yefimov grinned. 'I thought you might wonder. I reckoned it might keep you on your toes with him. Listen, I've been told to keep an eye on you. Nothing is supposed to harm you in here. I don't want to know why, only that Anatoly Vasiliev ordered me to his office last week and told me you were being sent here. That I wasn't to ask any other questions. What he wanted was for me to watch your back.'

'I can look after myself,' said Raglan.

'You can. I see that. But here... you know, it is easy for a throat to be cut and made to look as though the man just fell in the snow and got caught on some old barbed wire. A pencil in the eye? Choking on a piss-soaked sock? Suicide. You see how easy it is. We would get a shakedown; they would send someone to the hole for a few weeks. It happens. Anatoly Vasiliev told me you would not be here long. I don't know what that means, but if it was said about me, I would think I was going to be a target. That they would kill me in here.'

Raglan weighed up the information. The plan was for him to kill JD and then make a run for it. If the authorities intended to kill him soon, then that would defeat the aim of the operation. So that ruled out Elena's involvement. But he knew there was a short-term commitment from the man running the camp in the governor's absence. If he was concerned about his own participation then he would most likely be the man behind the threat. Raglan kills JD and then the evidence is removed. The deputy governor's hands were clean. 'You think that's what will happen?'

Yefimov shrugged.

'Who might find out?'

'Kirill is a man who is useful. Maybe he is not a man, perhaps he is a ghost and his God has placed him among us for a reason. I don't subscribe to such nonsense but it does no harm to consider all possibilities. He watches and listens and you don't even see him there. I put you with him because once a week he goes down to those houses and works as a cleaner. Then he brings back a man's clothes for the laundry, a man who is not a prisoner, and then takes them back the next time he goes to clean. This man is not a guard; he is not a part of the prison staff. Who is he? Like I told you, Daniil Regnev, we dislike strangers in our midst.'

Raglan felt the relief of finally knowing where JD was being kept.

'And is he the man who wants me dead?' It seemed an obvious question. Perhaps JD had learnt of his appearance at the prison.

Yefimov studied Raglan for a few moments. He was wary of asking too many questions. Too much information could prove fatal. 'Did you see Kirill in the shower block this morning?'

Raglan scanned the images in his mind's eye of those in the shower block. The men had come and gone but he hadn't noticed the man he now knew as Kirill. 'I saw someone bent over a mop as he sluiced away the water on the floor.'

'I told you: Kirill gets cleaning duties. There's a prisoner from the hut next to ours. He's a torpedo. You understand?'

Raglan nodded. A torpedo was an organized crime hitman.

'So, Kirill sees you washing, he sees your gangland tatts, and then he notices this Spartak Matveyev watching you. Kirill is an observant man and now that you've let him talk about his favourite subject without interrupting you're already ahead of the game with him so he will also look out for you.'

'I noticed a guy watching me this morning. Is that the man? This Spartak Matveyev?'

'That's right.' Yefimov pressed a finger against Raglan's bicep. He wasn't surprised at the resistance his finger met; Raglan was well muscled but that muscle wouldn't stop a sharpened dowel honed to a fine point in the workshop, which is where the hitman worked. 'Here is where you have a tattoo of a wolf. The man who watched you this morning has a bear tattooed in the same place. You are from rival gangs. And several years ago a very important man belonging to the other gang, Gennady Dorosh, was kidnapped and tortured, his body dismembered while he was still alive. Your people mutilated him.' Yefimov sighed and tossed the cold dregs from his mug. 'You have brought a turf war into our midst. Now, tell me, how am I supposed to watch your back as the deputy governor has instructed me if there is a hitman out to kill you?'

'I don't intend staying long enough to cause you that problem.'

'Tonight, tomorrow, next week. Maybe he will wait for when the snow comes. It won't be long, Regnev, and hiding a body in the snow is child's play. You would be listed as an escapee.' He nodded towards the vast forest. 'And that's as good as dead. So, you won't be missed beyond that. Some paperwork and a reprimand for the guards. Shit, it's nothing.'

Raglan needed time. If he could find a way to get to the house where he now suspected JD was hiding then he would kill him and run, but he had to plan at least two days in advance. At least. Good weather and a clear run at it.

'Talk to Matveyev. Promise him whatever he wants. When I am out of here, I'll make sure you get the best parcel you've ever had.'

Yefimov grinned, shaking his head. 'You're a foreigner, I know that. You stumble over words. Many would think you are an uneducated hard man from the inner city, someone with no schooling. Maybe even Belarus. Someone who joined the Moscow gangs and made a name for himself. I don't know how much of that is bullshit and I don't care. It's a good enough smokescreen but you're not going to live long. Talk to a torpedo? He has nothing to lose. He won't care if he's put in the hellhole. His reputation will climb higher than that hawk up there,' he said, looking up at the dark shape circling high in the sky. 'To him, you're an honour killing.'

47

Raglan spent the next two days working in the clearing with Yefimov's crew but kept a wary eye out for any sign of Matveyev. If the man had any intention of trying to intimidate Raglan, then he was keeping a very low profile. Raglan had seen hard men take the intimidation route before: a constant in-the-face challenge until the man provoked struck out. That was a mistake. It gave the tormentor the upper hand. He has been waiting for it. His mind is detached. His emotions are under control. But Raglan didn't think Matveyev would try that tactic. The men in the penal colony were not yet subdued like circus beasts; they might have had years of incarceration behind them but that did not mean they would let one man get away with creating havoc among them. If Matveyev made a grandstand attempt to kill Raglan in front of the men, then that would draw in others, which could cause a riot. There had been no word on the prison grapevine that the torpedo was planning an assault, so it was possible he would come at Raglan when least expected. Somewhere out of sight. Away from the eyes of the guards.

Raglan saw Matveyev on roll call but the gangster avoided eye contact. On the second night in the canteen he saw him across the room at a table with some men who were younger than most of the prisoners in the colony. These were likely to be convicts who had served less than half their sentences so they still carried that look of street-toughness. Raglan's eyes met Matveyev's briefly but the torpedo continued eating and talking to the small cohort of inmates around him. As Raglan made his way to a table with Yefimov his peripheral vision showed the hitman watching him. He was biding his time. There would be a moment, probably by chance, when the two would collide. And then it would be settled.

Yefimov took pride of place at the table, his back against the wall, leaving Raglan the remaining chair, meaning that his back was to the killer. He would have preferred to be facing Matveyev, who could saunter through the dining tables and plunge the sharpened handle of a spoon into his ear, a favoured means for a quick kill when a blade was not available. On the other hand, Raglan realized as he stooped to spoon the broth, turning his back on the man was a sign of disrespect that signalled he didn't give a damn about Matveyev's status.

Raglan tore off a piece of bread and softened it in the hot liquid, glancing up at Yefimov. The old man seemed to be concentrating on his food but Raglan saw that his casualness was a practised nonchalance. The old sweat had command of the room. He had placed men from his dormitory on the tables in front of his own. If the hitman made a move, then his cronies would try to run a blocking game as he attacked, and if that happened then Raglan's hut companions, as old as some of them might be, would get in their way. No blame would be attached to them should Raglan then defend himself.

Raglan had other concerns too. The days were slipping away without achieving a target appraisal. He needed a plan of action; he needed to find a way to reach JD and make his own escape before Matveyev's impending attack. If Matveyev was going to make his move it was more likely to be when Raglan had fewer men around him than here in the canteen. All Raglan had to do was have a plan in place and stay alive. But neither was a given.

The following morning after roll call Yefimov led the men out of the compound into the clearing. Everyone knew the weather would change in the next few days. Men grumbled among themselves that their outdoor work would soon be curtailed. Raglan learnt that those on work detail were prepared to work twice as hard on any day that the weather cleared. The timber would be dragged to the yard, ready for cutting, then chopped and stacked for the boilers and woodstoves. The fresh snow made their work more demanding but the effort was worth it to get out of the barrack confines.

The men paired up as usual and set about their day's work. Kirill and Raglan edged further into the undergrowth and began cutting through the saplings and dragging clear last year's fallen branches. The horses were already pulling clear the previous day's efforts of felled timber. After two hours of listening to Kirill's right-wing views about Communism, the decline in women's sexual behaviour and the conspiracy of the West to undermine the Russian Federation, they had moved ever deeper into the gloom of the forest, which put them momentarily out of the guard's sight. As Kirill began extolling the virtues of returning the old Soviet satellite states into the bosom of Mother Russia, Raglan stepped quickly to him and tugged him a few further paces away behind the larch trees.

'Tell me another story, Kirill. Tell me about the man in the house you clean.'

The fanatic's eyes narrowed behind his wire-rimmed spectacles. 'You want I should tell you about him? Why?'

'I think it will be a good story and I'd like to hear it.'

'I have privileges now, you know that. I get to work in the house two days a week. I kept my nose clean and

I mind my own business. What I do and what I see is for me to know.'

'And for me to find out,' said Raglan, keeping careful watch over the smaller man's shoulder to where the guard would soon walk into view.

Kirill shook his head. 'I gave you and Yefimov information about Matveyev. That's enough.'

'And if Matveyev thinks you're spying on him—'

'I do no such thing!'

'I know that, but he saw you in the showers that morning, and he knows Yefimov protects you, and if he comes for me, he might come for you. He would have nothing to lose, would he?'

'But you would kill him if he tries, yes?'

'I'll try, but he might get the better of me.'

'Then the information about the man in the house would be of no use to you and I might be dead anyway. I see no sense in discussing the matter further.'

Kirill turned away but Raglan blocked him. 'I have something to tell you about that man. If it is who I think it is, he has information that I need and he is the kind of man that you would hate if you knew the truth.'

'Truth? He is a man staying in a house. What more is there to know about him? I don't care.' But Kirill looked uncertain; Raglan had planted a seed of doubt in the extremist's mind.

'Describe him to me.'

Kirill didn't answer.

'All right, let me describe him to you.' Raglan quickly gave Kirill an accurate description of JD. 'Is that him?'

Kirill nodded and looked even more sullen.

Raglan went on: 'I don't want to tell you too much about him because you will react badly, and when you see him again, you might find it difficult not to challenge him. And then you'll lose more than the privileges you have worked so hard for. He's a dangerous man, more dangerous than some of the prisoners here. So tell me where the house is and what it's like inside. I know and understand all the things you have told me over these past few days. But the man in the house is against everything you believe in.'

'How could you know that?'

'He killed a woman I knew.'

Kirill considered the information. 'Plenty of men here have killed women. It's not uncommon. Even I have killed a woman and her daughter. I am paying for my sins and God will forgive me because He sees I am repentant.'

'But from what I have learnt you delivered justice,' said Raglan, trying to find a connection that would make Kirill think he was sympathetic.

Kirill nodded. 'I did. It was necessary.'

'And what I need to do with this man is necessary.' Quickly, Raglan told Kirill a simple lie to bring him on board. 'He's a émigré Communist who lived in Paris . . .' Raglan painted a picture of someone who'd made himself rich at the expense of ordinary Russians. Kirill spat in disgust. The worse kind of Russian. A Communist who made money on the backs of the others.

The guard appeared at the head of the clearing and checked that the prisoners were working. Raglan quickly bent and grabbed an armful of cut undergrowth as Kirill swept his axe into the next copse of saplings. When the guard turned his attention away Kirell tugged free the crucifix on a chain around his neck and kissed it.

'Tell me what you need to know.'

48

The house was approximately a kilometre from the camp's main entrance and sat in a plot of land of about 1,500 square metres, with clear visibility all around. The two-storey house had a small kitchen and eating area, three bedrooms, a sitting room, an indoor toilet and bath and a small extension a metre square and two metres high with shelving used for food storage: an ideal outside refrigerator. Old, probably fifty years, and until last year the family home of one of the guards who had since been rotated elsewhere. Raglan asked about the structure of the house. Walls and floors were wooden and the building sat on a concrete base so there was no basement. Yes, said Kirill when asked, the floorboards creaked when you walked on them, but they had rugs scattered on them for additional warmth, which had some kind of felt tucked under each corner so they wouldn't slip. He knew this because when he was sent to clean the house he was obliged to pull back the rugs and apply and buff the polish with a manual buffer. Did Raglan know how much hard work that was? A block of heavy metal on the end of a pole with soft rags underneath. Raglan did. He had done much the same when he was a recruit in the army. He doubted JD's house would pass muster with the Legion.

The stairs ascended from the living room. On the first floor there was a bathroom and three small bedrooms. Which bedroom did the man sleep in, Raglan wanted to know. Front or back? It was the front. Outside, the wood store was on the south side of the house under an open-fronted shelter. From what Kirill told him Raglan estimated that it was eighty paces from the gate to the front door, half that from the back fence and half that again from the side walls. Kirill always went through a small gate at the back, past the pantry and in the back door, which was always locked. A small bell attached to a chain was used to rouse the occupant. Electricity was not always reliable, especially when the backup generators weren't functioning as they should, so it was not unusual on some days to find propane gas lanterns, the kind that campers used.

How did Kirill get to the house? Did he walk or was he driven by guards? He would walk on a good day, ride in a snowstorm. The guard dropped him off and came back for him at the end of the day. Kirill went in at eight and came out nine hours later. He scrubbed floors, washed and ironed the laundry, cleaned windows, hand swept and polished all the floors and laid out the food at mealtimes on the small table in the kitchen. What about the man living there? He never spoke. Watched television. Smoked, drank vodka to excess but never seemed drunk; he also drank a clear liquid that turned yellow when diluted with water and which smelt of aniseed. It's Pernod, Raglan told him. A French drink. And here it would be a luxury. So the man in the house is being well treated for his crimes. Raglan saw Kirill bristle. Every negative comment Raglan made about JD helped keep Kirill onside.

After painting the picture of the house's location in his mind Raglan decided that the blind side over a low fence between the house and the snow-banked verges seemed to be the best way in. Anything else to worry about? Raglan wanted to know. There was a vegetable garden once the snow melted and if the ground had been turned and left fallow in late autumn then it would be uneven underfoot and difficult to see beneath a snowfall. Easy enough to twist an ankle on the hidden, concrete-hard ground. Kirill described the house again, but Raglan didn't mind him repeating himself. The more the image of the house coalesced into a vivid mental picture the easier it would be to plan his approach and gain entry.

From the street, a path led straight to the front door. Anyone looking from any of the front windows would have no difficulty seeing someone approach. A neighbour had a dog run alongside the left-hand perimeter which gave the house added security. There were no guards. None were needed. Besides, the man was armed. Kirill didn't know what kind of pistol it was, but he knew it was heavy because he'd had to move it off a side table to wipe up beer rings; he thought it looked like the same sidearm as that used by the guards. Raglan knew it was an MP-443 Grach. Unlike lightweight western law-enforcement sidearms, this was all-steel construction. Typical unbreakable Russian manufacture. Carbon steel on the slide and frame and a stainless steel barrel. A bruiser. Its clip carried seventeen rounds, sometimes armour-piercing, and one in the chamber. It was the same weapon JD had used in London to kill Abbie.

'And when are you going to clean the house again?'

'The day after tomorrow.'

'So, if a burglar was crazy enough to try and get into this house how would he go about it?' Raglan said.

'How? He wouldn't be so damned stupid. Neighbours to one side, front and back. A lane at the back and the road at the front gate. Barking dogs over the neighbour's wall and not a tree in sight. As bare as a baby's arse. A burglar here?' He cleared his throat and spat.

Raglan did not repeat the question. He waited.

'What? Your mother drop you on the head when you were born?' Kirill surrendered with a shrug. 'The back gate and a short run to the pantry. There's a window. Climb through that window and once you're inside the pantry there's a mesh fly screen into the back entrance. It's like an inner hall. The back door is there on the right of that. It's solid. But if you got into the pantry you'd be inside the house.'

'What's below the window?'

'A cupboard.'

'High enough for a man to get his feet on to?'

Kirill nodded. 'There are a few glass storage jars. That's all.' The look of pity on Kirill's face said it all. He shook his head and turned away. He had seen plenty of men lose their minds in the prison but never one who had arrived without one. These gangsters. What a bunch of thick bastards.

Like the other men, Raglan stank by the time they returned, their clothes dried with the stale sweat from their efforts and made worse by the humid warmth in the dormitory. He didn't care about having to wait before they were allowed to shower again, because he had no idea whether the tattoos would stand up to another hot wash.

'How much longer before the weather changes?' he asked Yefimov when he came into the dormitory.

'Never mind that,' Yefimov said, sitting next to Raglan on his bed. 'Matveyev is making his move tonight.'

It was too soon. The torpedo was going to jeopardize everything. The narrow margin of time was too tight for additional problems. Raglan ignored the information for the moment. 'When is the weather going to change?'

'You heard what I said? Matveyev is going to try and kill you.'

'When is it changing?' Raglan insisted.

Yefimov sighed and relented. 'Tomorrow it starts, then the day after more snow. It will clear for a day and then the snow gets heavier.'

Raglan knew he had to deal with Matveyev, stay safe another day, then get to the house and kill JD on the same day as Kirill's visit. And then escape. 'You're supposed to watch my back. Tell the deputy governor what's going down. He'll stop him.'

Yefimov shook his head. 'No, Regnev, I'm no snitch. It would come out and no matter who I am I would end up dead in the showers with my wrists slit. Suicide is not uncommon. I was told to watch your back like you said, and I have done that. I have warned you.'

He got up to leave but Raglan held him back. 'Where will he try?'

'I don't know that and I am unlikely to find out in time. I called in favours to learn this much.'

'Where would you make the attempt?'

Yefimov settled again. 'I would have tried to kill you in the wood yard. It's easy to stage a nasty accident there with the bandsaw and chipping equipment. But not at night. No, it will be inside somewhere.' He thought it through a moment longer. 'The boiler room.'

That made sense. Raglan had been sent there soon after he arrived to help feed the furnace. The area was not only deserted at night but the approach was a narrow passage, barely two metres wide, its height restricted by ageing metal pipework; the low ceiling made it even more claustrophobic. Bare armoured bulbs that gave out little more than a dull glow were all that illuminated it. The end of the passage opened out into the room where the pre-war boiler and furnace themselves were located. The boiler provided the administrative offices with warmth and the prisoner ablution blocks and camp kitchens with hot water. The room was the warmest place in the camp other than the bakery, but being a boiler attendant was a double-edged sword. The heat sapped a man during their shift and then the outside cold withered him further.

'Who sets it up?' said Raglan.

'Word will come from his people.' He looked at Raglan. 'You cannot refuse, you know that. *Vory-v-zakone* never back down.'

'I need to see the place again before then.'

Yefimov nodded. 'We had better eat first.' He stood and looked down at Raglan. 'It might be the last meal you have.'

'If he kills me you're in the shit,' said Raglan.

Yefimov shrugged. 'I lose privileges is all, but if you beat him then you can't kill him, because if you do they will close the camp to investigate. Hurt him enough to put him in the infirmary. You ask me about the weather; you ask Kirill about the house he cleans. Whatever you're planning, it all ends if you kill Matveyev.'

49

There was one way into the boiler room and one way out. Raglan edged along the passage, his arms extended, hands touching pipes and walls of bare rock, remembering through touch. The pipes creaked from the pressure of the heat from the old boiler; humidity from the poorly ventilated cellar covered the walls with a sheen of condensation. He listened to the sounds from the clunking boiler, to the drip of leaking pipes, memorizing the sounds so he was familiar with them and would recognize any other disturbance caused by his opponent.

Twenty-four paces took him to where the passage widened into the room. Six metres by ten. Pipework was suspended from the ceiling with rust-collared joints that dripped; others had a necklace of green from the lime content in the water that sealed in any escaping leak. A bunker heavy with coal sat beneath a chute, its metal trapdoor above seeping light around the edges and allowing melting snow to drip in, giving the dark nuggets a glossy sheen. Next to the coal was a stacked woodpile. The old boiler and furnace sat in the middle of the room and the closer he got the more he felt the heat smother him. He knew that Matveyev would come armed so Raglan looked around for any potential weapon. A cut piece of lead piping, as long and thick as an old-fashioned truncheon, lay on the floor, kicked to one side against the base of the wall. He hefted it, feeling its balance and weight. A long-handled coal shovel stood next to the bunker. There was little doubt in his mind that if Matveyev beat him, even into unconsciousness, then the furnace door would be knocked open with the shovel and his body forced into the white-hot oven.

Raglan retraced his steps to the entrance, turned back and gazed down the passage. The light switch was on his immediate left. Propping the lead pipe behind the fins of a disused radiator, half covered with a canvas tarp, he edged backwards and focused on what he planned to do. Satisfied, he turned again and clambered up the steps to where Yefimov had been keeping watch at the top. The old man opened the door to the outside yard, the cold rush of air suddenly chilling the sweat on Raglan's face.

'And now?' asked Yefimov.

'Sleep,' said Raglan.

*

Raglan slept deeply, compartmentalizing thoughts of the fight so that his body could get maximum rest. It had taken a couple of years in the Legion before he had learnt how to switch off the unnecessary worry about approaching combat. Preparation was everything. What couldn't be determined about the target would be dealt with when the time came.

The dormitory door creaked open. Raglan's eyes snapped open. The lights from the compound perimeter cast shadows through the murky glass as a figure crept in and knelt next to Yefimov's bed. The old man whispered something and then, as the messenger left, he clambered up stiffly and made his way towards Raglan. His hand reached out to touch Raglan's shoulder.

'I'm awake,' Raglan said quietly.

Yefimov remained silent and shuffled back a step, his thick woollen socks whispering on the floorboards. Raglan had remained dressed, ready to move should the *vory-v-zakone* code of honour not be as honourable as it was thought to be. Standards had dropped everywhere these days. Professional killers always needed the upper hand and Raglan had half expected Matveyev to creep into the dormitory and attempt to plunge a knife into him while he slept. But Matveyev would never have survived if he had done so. His reputation needed to be enforced by killing Raglan one-on-one.

Yefimov led the way out of the dormitory. Men turned in their beds, and he heard one or two of them wish him luck. No longer just the new man sent to the colony, he was being accepted as one of them, who shared the same privations and dormitory. Raglan estimated it was about two in the morning as they slipped out of the hut, their boots crunching on snow. Small balls of light from the individual light bulbs were dotted along the perimeter wire. The watchtowers were manned, silhouetted against the dark blue sky. Stars glistened on the sparkling snow. Raglan hunched against the cold but had deliberately worn only his uniform canvas jacket. He would soon be warm enough and he needed to be agile. Once inside the building the old man made him wait at the top of the stairs while he went down to ensure it was only Matveyev waiting in the gloom. Raglan heard the heavy footfall approach as he returned. The old man nodded.

Raglan tugged free his jacket and handed it to Yefimov. 'Are you going back to the dormitory?'

'I wait here in case his friends show up. He has a knife,' he whispered.

Raglan nodded and turned down the stairs. He felt the same anticipation as when he had crept into the caves years before.

Raglan went down the steps on the balls of his feet and then waited, letting his heartbeat settle, wanting the thud of the blood being pumped through his veins to die down so it did not interfere with his hearing. As his eyes adjusted to the dim light, he listened to the sounds he had familiarized himself with. At the end of the passage, a shadow crossed the wall. Raglan let his fingers find the hidden length of lead pipe. He reached out and switched off the lights. There was an immediate grunt of surprise from somewhere in the boiler room. Raglan stepped forward, hesitating every couple of strides as he listened for movement. He rolled the side of his foot to minimize the sole of his boot scuffing the concrete floor. He took fourteen paces and then stopped. He was halfway. Once again he listened. Seven more steps. Pause. Three more. And then, as he was at the mouth of the room, he extended his stride.

He smelt Matveyev before he felt the rush of darkness. Raglan half turned, pressed himself against the wall for support and swung the low-held pipe upwards in a fast uppercut blow. It connected with Matveyev's arm. The torpedo cried out, snorting in pain, but by the time Raglan had spun on the balls of his feet and brought down the pipe in a sweeping cross, he found only empty air. He quickly corrected, stopping himself from losing his balance. Matveyev was breathing hard but had stumbled back towards the boiler.

Raglan crouched, peering up to where the coal chute's cover showed a barely visible razor-edge of light from the compound lamps. It was enough for him to see the dark form of the big man cross in front of it. The coal bunker was six paces from where Raglan waited. He went forward quickly, swung the pipe and felt it connect with the man's shoulder but Matveyev had the strength to absorb the strike. Raglan felt the killer's body twist away and knew the knife held in the man's right hand was already lunging towards his stomach. He turned his back into Matveyev's chest – he risked being held by the bigger man but figured that with a numb shoulder and his knife hand being brought to bear, the mafia killer would have no chance of grabbing him. He brought both hands together on the length of pipe; straightening his arms he extended it to block any blow and felt the man's wrist strike the pipe hard. Matveyev cried out. Raglan gave him no time to recover; snapping his head up he felt the pipe connect with the man's face. Matveyev cursed, found strength in his numbed shoulder and brought an elbow down hard. It connected just below Raglan's neck into the muscle that connected to his shoulder. It carried a lot of power and told Raglan that the killer could take pain and still have strength enough to deliver a crippling blow.

Raglan threw himself forward as the knife swished where his head had just been. He felt the hot tear of flesh as the blade caught his ribs beneath his raised arm. Barely a second passed before he tucked in his shoulder, rolled, recovered and stayed low. He heard Matveyev's wet laboured breathing; his nose had been broken by Raglan's headbutt and the killer was sucking

air through his mouth. Suddenly the sound stopped for
an instant as Matveyev threw himself into the darkness,
his own senses telling him where Raglan was. He had
not realized that Raglan had stayed low; his legs struck
the Englishman. One of his kneecaps caught Raglan a
hard blow on the temple and Raglan felt the darkness
swirl as Matveyev, spitting a curse, fell headlong into
the wall. Raglan slithered away, his head spinning as he
tried to orientate himself. Matveyev recovered quickly
and began kicking out wildly. The toe of his boot caught
Raglan's thigh, dead-legging the muscle. Ignoring the
stabbing pain he sprang to his feet and swung the pipe
back and forth in front of him. He heard the crack of
bone. Matveyev cried out and staggered back. Raglan
lunged and the man's sweat was in his nostrils. Both men
grunted with the all-consuming effort of staying alive.

The heat from the furnace intensified as they grappled
back into the darkness. Raglan's free hand gripped
Matveyev's wrist, muscles straining as he forced the
man's knife hand back towards the heat. The torn flesh
in his side felt raw and he used its sting to drive air into
his lungs. He snapped his knee up between the torpedo's
legs and the stench of the man's breath smothered his
face as the wind was knocked out of him. The sudden
excruciating pain weakened the Russian and Raglan
pressed home his attack, forcing the back of Matveyev's
knife hand against the furnace. The skin sizzled, the
knife dropped and Matveyev bellowed. The agony of

the burn renewed his strength and his headbutt caught Raglan on the forehead. It felt as though he had struck him with a hammer. His legs buckled and he rocked back on his heels, losing the slender advantage he had gained. Matveyev threw his weight against his assailant but Raglan was lucky: he twisted clear as Matveyev, already unbalanced from the headbutt, crashed into the heaped coal. Raglan sidestepped, felt the heat of the boiler on his back and swung the lead pipe low and fast with all his weight. It connected with Matveyev's leg. He heard the shin bone splinter. The burly Russian vomited, the spurt of bile telling Raglan where he had turned his head. Raglan stepped closer, struck down again and heard bones in the big man's face crack too.

Raglan sucked in air and tested his weight on the dead leg, ignoring its protest. He controlled his breath, half turning his head so he could listen to the other man's rattled breathing.

It was done.

Raglan dropped the pipe and reached under his arm and felt the wet shirt. He couldn't tell how deep the cut was but blood soaked his shirt and waistband. It was a cut, not a stab wound, so nothing vital had been injured. He guessed he was four or five paces from the mouth of the passageway. It took three and he banged into the wall like a drunk in an alleyway. He swore, turned left and paced out the twenty-four strides to the end of the passageway where he fumbled for the light switch. The dim lights cast their muted glow as he walked back and found Matveyev unconscious. His face was a bloodied mess and he could see bone from his leg pressing upwards into his trouser leg. He bent down and checked the fallen man's pulse. He was still alive. After a moment's search Raglan found the knife. It was a seven-inch workshop shiv made of sharpened metal, its handle tine welded and bound with tape for grip. He had no idea whether any guards had been alerted so it made no sense to risk it being found on him. He tossed it into the darkness at the back of the room; then he limped back down the passage and up the steps. Yefimov stood in the corridor with another prisoner standing opposite him.

'One of his,' said Yefimov. 'Had the same thought as me. Came to see it was just you and him.'

'He dead?' the stranger asked.

'Hurt bad,' Raglan told him. 'He needs the infirmary.'

The man nodded. 'Better you did not kill him. Better for everyone,' he said as he started down the steps.

'So I'm told,' said Raglan, stepping out into the snow. He bent and grabbed a handful and pressed it against his ribs. The snow quickly coloured red.

50

The four-inch gash on Raglan's flank needed stitching but it was obvious he couldn't report to the infirmary. One of the men in the dormitory was an ex-army medic who knew enough about battlefield wounds to clean and suture. There was no means of anaesthetizing the cut and Raglan knew that the men who gathered around his bedside watching the medic sluice the wound and then pierce the skin were waiting to see just how tough the tattooed killer was. Raglan winced as the needle pierced the raw skin, but kept his intake of breath shallow enough not to be thought a weakling. His reputation had already been boosted by winning the fight and the gathered men offered their cigarettes and tea rations as a gesture of admiration and desire for his patronage.

Raglan kept his head and torso turned away and prayed that swabbing the wound did not smudge the tattoo that crept up his side and on to his stomach.

The stinging nerve ends brought a tear to his eyes, and the men winced and grimaced in sympathy. The medic prisoner pulled Yefimov's hand holding the candle closer to where he worked on the wound. When the siren wailed for 'lights out' it was a literal command which meant that they switched the electricity off. The medic muttered about fighting in Afghanistan and looking after Russian soldiers in the field, telling Raglan that this cut, this was nothing. Barely a scratch. He dabbed the wound again with harsh disinfectant stolen from the kitchen and Raglan cringed from its sting. The medic grinned. If tough gangland guys like Regnev had ever served in a war, then he would know what being hurt was about. Raglan stayed silent. The Russian admired his work and bound the wound with a broad bandage, contraband from the hospital wing, which he wrapped firmly around Raglan's torso.

When he'd finished, the men drifted away and Yefimov sat next to Raglan. 'You have to stay on work detail; there must be nothing said of this. Matveyev's injuries will be noted and probably written up as a workshop accident. No one in authority wants to report unrest in a camp. A personal disagreement is acceptable to them.' He studied Raglan as he tugged out a bottle of pills from his jacket pocket. 'Antibiotics. You will need them for your wound. I traded for these myself.' He shook out two of the tablets and handed Raglan a tin cup of water. 'You'll feel shit for a few days but at least you won't die of blood poisoning or infection.' Raglan swallowed the antibiotics as Yefimov put the bottle next to him on the bedside table. 'Take them every day, *tovarich*. I am still responsible for watching your back and if you die of sepsis, then my dick is on the block.'

Raglan nodded his thanks and lay gingerly on the pillow. The wound hurt now that his body had rid itself of adrenaline. The battering he had taken would stiffen his muscles and slow him down. There was still much to do before he could escape and it seemed ever more unlikely that he would survive the attempt.

'You beat a man who was feared even among the murderers imprisoned here,' said his minder. 'Men will turn to you for protection now and you will be looked after. Extra food and rations will be given to you.'

'I won't be here long enough. You know that, don't you?'

'You're a fool, Daniil Regnev. No one gets out of here. They have dogs and trackers. They have vehicles that chew up the snow. By the end of the week, it will be waist deep out there. What chance do you have?'

'Not much,' said Raglan. His eyes closed, and he fell asleep. In less than three hours he would be expected outside for roll call.

Yefimov watched Raglan's breathing settle. He had to decide how much he would tell the deputy governor about the night's events. Whatever was going on between him and Raglan it all pointed to a business that Yefimov wanted to avoid being drawn into. As he considered his own term of imprisonment, he felt a glimmer of something that had died within him years before. If a man escaped and survived, he carried the desire and hopes of every man in the camp. Yefimov laid a fatherly hand on the sleeping man, then pulled the blanket over him.

Roll call was no different from any other day except that when Matveyev's name was called, the section guard told the parade officer he was in the infirmary following an accident in the workshop. The officer readily accepted the explanation. No one said anything different and the work parties formed up and shuffled out of the gate. Raglan's wound felt raw and the skin tugged at his muscles, insisting he bend into the pain. If he did that he would be noticed, so he forced himself to stay upright and let the nerve ends torment him.

Kirill began swinging the axe but edged deeper into the undergrowth. He brushed snow from a fallen tree and gestured for Raglan to rest.

'What about our quota?' said Raglan.

Kirill smiled. 'Rest up. We have ways of cheating. Come on, sit. No good you working today, you'll tear the stitches.'

Raglan glanced to where the guard sat in his usual place, now half obscured by brush and saplings. He leant his back against the log and felt the relief on his side. Kirill kicked aside cut brush and then tugged more branches free to expose a half-dozen logs ready to be dragged away.

'Some days we work extra hard, cut more than our quota. We keep it hidden for the days when we need to back off. Sometimes you're sick or just too pissed off to work as hard as they want you to. We've got enough here to knock off for a few hours. I'll do some brush clearing.'

Raglan nodded, pleased that there were shortcuts even in prison. He looked up at the sky: the clouds were settling low, laden with their burden of snow, borne down from Siberia and ready to dump it on the camp.

'Some today, more tomorrow and then a day of blue skies again. We live for a blue sky,' said Kirill as he rhythmically swung the axe, reading the fighter's thoughts. 'You'll see, the months of being caged in the near darkness kills men. Not many commit suicide, most of these prisoners are too tough for that, but it gets to some people. I don't find it so bad. In fact, I see it as beautiful. The snow comes, smothers the world and its sins; the blue sky follows like the archangel's light and the world looks pristine. You'll work in the yard tomorrow and cut these logs into planks. It's too early in the winter for anyone to put their arm in the bandsaw.' He shrugged. 'It happens. The shock usually kills them.'

'You're going to the house tomorrow?'

Raglan's question caused an almost imperceptible pause in Kirill's rhythm. He stopped and dragged a sleeve across his brow.

'That's right.'

'Do something for me,' said Raglan.

Kirill looked as though he was about to face a firing squad. 'What?'

'When you leave the house tomorrow night, don't fasten the latch on the pantry window.'

51

When the work party returned to the camp Raglan approached the section guard in a small end-of-corridor booth where he sat behind a wooden table, close to a cast-iron radiator. He requested permission to make a phone call. He was questioned as to the who and the why and the guard filled in an official camp form with Raglan's answers. Prisoner Regnev needed to contact his brother because their mother was ill and would soon be taken to hospital. It was a worrying time and, because of the distance from where his brother lived, almost impossible for him to receive any visitors.

The guard wasn't interested in why this murderer needed to talk to a family member and suppressed any comment expressing doubt that such a man even had a mother. He opened a shallow drawer, took out a rubber stamp and ink pad, laboriously pressed rather than stamped the official imprint on the form and then put everything back in the drawer. Perhaps the guards needed to kill time as well, thought Raglan as the man tore a piece of scrap paper and pushed it forward with a pencil stub.

'The number.'

Raglan wrote the area code and number and the guard lifted his telephone receiver and recited the information. The camp's switchboard operator must have repeated back the information as the guard confirmed everything with a few grunts. After he replaced the handset, he pointed to a room. Raglan stepped inside. It was unfurnished except for a bench close to a booth that had a thick glass window halfway up, set at a height to accommodate a prisoner sitting on the inside. When Yefimov had shown him around the camp he had told him that this was where the visitors sat. The prisoner was brought into the booth and communicated through the two-way telephone. A guard was always present. There was no privacy and no means of physical contact. And no matter how far the prisoner's relative had travelled they were allowed only one hour.

'There,' said the guard, who had followed him into the room, pointing to a phone on the wall. 'Wait.'

Raglan stood next to the phone as the guard settled himself in the chair by the door and pulled free a folded newspaper and began reading. Raglan stood patiently for ten minutes and then the phone rang once. He picked up the receiver and listened for the connection to be made.

'Konstantin, is that you?... Yes... Yes, it's me, Daniil... Oh, I'm all right... It's hard but they treat us well here...' Out of the corner of his eye, he saw the guard raise an eyebrow at his remark. It was always worth praising the pig-ignorant bastards who beat you. 'Konstantin, how is Mother... Oh... Oh... I see... Well... It's snowing here as well, in fact, tomorrow will be heavy but I'm told the day after it should be clear... Oh, you too?... Yes, you're right, after then I won't be able to be outside...'

Raglan knew he didn't have long. Turning his back to the guard he listened and nodded to what was being said on the phone. The guard folded the newspaper. Raglan spoke rapidly, obscuring his true meaning. The guard walked towards him. 'Yes, exactly as I have said, Konstantin. Take Mother to the lake while the weather is still good. Tell her my thoughts are with her and I will hold her hand and we will look at the blue sky together.'

The guard tapped him on the shoulder with the folded newspaper. Time was up.

'Konstantin, I have to go now. Give Mother my love and I hope to see you soon. Goodbye.'

Yefimov knelt, easing wood shavings into the dormitory's stove and as they caught from the match, he fed in dry offcuts from the carpentry shop, then patiently built the fire up with chopped wood. It was already dark outside and the silent feathers of snow swirled beneath the sphere of the camp's street lights.

Raglan sat on his bunk while the Afghan war medic unwound the bandage and checked the wound. 'What do we do tomorrow in the yard if it's snowing heavily?'

Yefimov stared a moment longer at his carefully laid fire. 'We chop timber and stack it in the wood stores. This place needs as much as we can get for winter. We've almost got enough, I reckon. And then, as usual, they'll cut back the meat ration because we won't be working as hard.'

The medic sniffed and jabbed the livid edges of the wound.

'Why don't you try and make it hurt even more?' said Raglan.

'Good,' said the medic, 'it's supposed to hurt. It's healing. Stay out of trouble and you'll be all right.' He magicked a fresh bandage and dressing from his pocket, tore open the sterile dressing and pressed it against the wound. 'Hold this.'

Raglan reached around his arm and did as the medic instructed, who then wound the bandage.

'Make it tight,' said Raglan.

'You don't want it too tight,' the medic answered, 'it'll press against the sutures.'

'It'll help me move better,' Raglan insisted.

The medic shrugged and did as he was bid. 'The Christmas dance isn't for a couple of months yet.'

'I have some heavy lifting to do tomorrow,' countered Raglan.

The medic got up from the bed and warmed his hands next to the stove even though there was barely enough heat from the freshly lit fire. 'If he does too much, he'll bleed. Who's to say the guards won't notice?' he said, addressing the older man.

Yefimov glanced up. He was now sitting on the edge of his bed, changing his socks. 'It's his choice. What am I, his fucking nursemaid?'

'I'm just saying, is all.'

'And I'm just saying to mind your own business,' Yefimov snapped back.

The medic raised his hands in surrender and left the dormitory.

'We need to eat,' said Yefimov as he finished lacing his boots.

Raglan buttoned his shirt and reached for his jacket, but as he went to pass Yefimov, the man stuck his leg out to stop him.

'Kirill tells me you want him to do something for you.'

'I thought he might keep such a thing to himself.'

'He won't blab, but he comes to me out of respect.'

'There was nothing I could tell you without implicating you and I didn't want to do that.'

The old man lowered his leg and laced his boot. 'Whatever you have planned, Regnev, I cannot help you. You work tomorrow same as everyone. No favours.'

*

The snow duly arrived the next morning as predicted. After roll call, the men tucked their necks into their uniform collars against the wet flakes and then peeled away quickly to the canteen for breakfast. The snow was not yet heavy enough to stop the work parties going out, but once breakfast was finished, and with Raglan's partner Kirill absent on his house duty, Yefimov kept Raglan in the work yard. A small group of men manhandled cut timber, two to a log. One man took the front, the other the rear, then they manhandled the log on to a set of steel ribs. At the other side of these ribs, two more prisoners waited next to a moving belt. The man at the front pressed a foot pedal and the hydraulic ribs hissed and clanked as they lifted and rolled the log down on to the belt next to the two men. As each man arrested the log's momentum against their thigh, they fed the log forward into the whirring blade. As a plank of wood was cut from the log, the first two men retrieved what was left of the sawn log and repeated the operation over again until the log-cutters had sliced the final plank. And then another log was fed to them. The slow, monotonous routine created a steady pace that would take the men through their workload under Yefimov's watchful eye. The watchtower guards cast only an occasional glance towards the work party inside the wire, their attention focused on those working at the forest's edge.

'You and him,' said Yefimov, pointing to another prisoner. 'Take the planks and you stack them over there. Can you manage that, tough guy?'

Raglan lifted one end of a plank and followed the other man's lead. The long plank was easily manageable and caused little stress on his wound. They settled the plank in an open-fronted woodshed that abutted one of the inner perimeter fences. After an hour's toil, the astringent stickiness of the resin stuck to Raglan's hands. Raglan's work partner saw Yefimov's nod of dismissal and stepped away to relieve himself against the side of the building.

'Here,' said the old killer to Raglan as he stepped into a woodshed. Raglan followed. Yefimov lit a cigarette and watched the smoke drift away. 'Wind's shifting from the east. More snow tonight. It'll get colder.' He glanced towards the watchtowers. 'It's a blind spot here.'

Raglan checked. The corner of the building and the low roof of the woodshed obscured the watchtower guards' view.

Yefimov stuck the cigarette between his lips, bent down and heaved free one of the broad slats from the wood store's wall. It was as wide as the planks that Raglan had been stacking. Once the first slat had been removed the one below it came away easily. Raglan saw that no one outside the woodshed could see the missing planks. A double-blind. Without being beckoned he stooped and pushed himself through the gap. Half a metre behind the woodshed the wire fence was loose enough to crawl under. He crawled back inside. Yefimov pushed the slats back in place.

'You would have to clear seventy metres across open ground until you reach the next fence. Did you see that workshop?'

Raglan nodded.

'If a man used those oil drums next to it to get on to the roof, then he could jump down across that wire fence. He would need a blanket to throw on the barbed wire and it's three metres to the ground. A man with an injury might not make it.'

'I think he would,' said Raglan. 'The bigger problem is that there's a dog run on the other side. I saw it when I was brought in.'

Yefimov nodded. 'They are silent attack dogs. They don't bark. They have had their vocal cords cut. The dogs would tear a man apart and only his screams would be heard.'

'I need a knife.'

'You think you can kill an attack dog?' He didn't wait for an answer. 'Da, of course you could. A killer like you would slaughter their own mother if it benefited them. No, Regnev, you don't kill these dogs, or in this case one dog. There's only one in that run. The first thing the guards see is blood on the snow and the crows fighting over its carcass. You want to buy as much time before roll call and have a chance to escape, you give it meat.

They are hungry all the time. Uncooked meat is better than human flesh. For a few minutes anyway.'

Raglan waited as Yefimov sucked the last of the cigarette's smoke into his lungs and ground out the stub beneath his boot. A few moments passed.

'I can get meat. Someone in the guards' kitchen owes me.'

'Why are you helping me?'

'I have my reasons.'

'Which are?'

Yefimov averted his eyes. The two men were still in the woodshed but he looked somewhere beyond the unseen horizon. 'One man escapes, we are all free.' He faced Raglan and tapped his chest. 'In here at least.'

52

Raglan slept until two in the morning. The years spent in the Legion had taught him to awake at an appointed time. He dressed in the near darkness, checking that his wound was still bound tightly. The stove seeped warmth into the barrack room but most of the men slept half dressed beneath their inadequate bedding. That night Raglan slept in his underwear, wanting to feel the benefit of his clothing when he faced the bitter journey to the house and the unsuspecting JD.

Yefimov was the only figure who moved in the gloom. He freed himself from beneath the blankets and pushed his feet into a worn pair of slippers. They scuffed across the wooden floor as he shuffled over to Raglan.

Raglan pulled on the extra shirt and socks that Yefimov had given him as another layer to combat the night's chill. He buttoned the jacket and rolled his shoulders to make sure he had sufficient freedom. The boots were tight with the extra socks but they wouldn't hamper him.

'The wind has dropped but it's still snowing,' Yefimov whispered.

Raglan nodded. 'Good. It will help dampen any noise.'

'I don't want to know why you are doing this, Regnev, but you cannot survive. If this is a gangland revenge killing, you should think again. Nothing is worth dying for.'

The darkness obscured the man's features.

'I'll send you a new pair of slippers when I'm back home,' said Raglan.

Yefimov grunted, 'Sure. Size forty-six and a half.'

Wooden slatted beds creaked as men turned in their sleep, curled against the insufficient warmth of their blankets. Raglan tugged free his own blanket – for the barbed wire.

'There's a haunch of pig in a sack in the woodshed,' said Yefimov.

Raglan's eyes adjusted to the darkness. He peered out of the window. Cones of yellow light spotted the ground, the fences and gates obscured by the falling snow.

'It will take me an hour or more to get to the houses. Time to go, Yefimov.'

The older man nodded. *Udachi, tovarich.*

*

Raglan squinted against the falling snow as he ran across the yard to the woodsheds. The breeze swirled snowflakes upwards as they fluttered moth-like towards the security lights. Raglan stumbled in the dark shed, his hands already seizing up from the cold and wet. Yefimov's good luck wishes did not ease Raglan's sudden uncertainty when he could not find the sack that held the dog bait.

He sank on to his knees and reached beneath the cut timber he had stacked the day before. After moments of scrabbling, his fingertips felt the rough hessian. Hauling it to him he felt the meat inside yield as he pressed. The loose wall planks came away effortlessly. He bent and squeezed through the gap, wiping his eyes against the flurrying snowflakes as he tugged at the wire mesh fence. The snow had already obscured the place where it was loose. He pushed and pulled the wire until he felt the slackness, then lay flat and pressed his shoulder and hip against the wire. He felt the tug of material as the bare ends of the mesh dug into his back but he squirmed through, dragging the sack and folded blanket behind him.

Scrambling to his feet, he peered into the night. The darkness and the falling snow obscured the workshop. He pictured where he had stood when he identified it in daylight and without further hesitation ran forward. The shadow loomed. He swept his arm across the top of one of the oil drums, clearing it of snow, and clambered up on to the roof. He looked towards the watchtower whose dim light flickered through the snowflakes. Unless the guard swung his searchlight along the dog run Raglan knew he would remain unseen.

He threw the blanket forward across the sagging old barbed wire that topped the mesh fence and then tossed the sack over. As he spread his weight on the blanket, rusted strands snapped beneath his weight, but the momentum of his rolling body carried him across without injury. He twisted free of the wire and like any paratrooper in the world instinctively brought his knees and ankles together, bending his legs for the impact of hitting the ground. The snow crunched and he rolled free, alert for the sound of the scuff of snow – warning that the attack dog was silently charging. Snow obscured everything except for a glimmer of light that gave shape to a shadow. Raglan yanked the haunch of pig free from the sack and threw it towards the unseen dog. He wrapped the sack around his left arm and hand, ready to offer it to the dog should it not take the raw meat.

He heard rather than saw the snuffling dog rip into the raw flesh. How long he had he didn't know, but he turned and, pumping his arms, raced for the end of the wire corridor. There was a pedestrian gate at the end, padlocked and chained so that the dog handlers could come and go, but, because it was not part of the perimeter fence, there was no barbed wire above it. Raglan was sweating. He counted his strides. When he had first been

brought into the camp he had estimated the gate was
150 metres or so from the building he now knew to be
a workshop. He strained to hear any sound of pursuit
behind him, but his laboured breathing drowned out any
chance of knowing whether the dog was at his heels.
Its crushing jaws biting into his leg would be the first
moment when he knew his escape had failed.

He unwrapped the sack and dropped it in the hope
his scent and that of the pig's dried blood would buy
him vital seconds. He almost ran into the mesh gate as
it loomed from the darkness. He threw himself at it,
reaching high for the top of the metal frame. In one swift
motion, he hip-rolled over and lowered himself down on
the other side. He crouched, fingers hooked into the mesh
gate as he slowed his breathing and stared, searching
for the dog. Nothing moved except the snow swirling
in the breeze. Raglan sighed with relief. As he blinked
away snowflakes caught on his eyelashes a massive
impact smashed into the mesh gate. He fell back on his
haunches as the attack dog lunged at the wire again in
silent savagery, its paws pushing its weight against the
gate, bits of meat still clinging to its bared fangs.

Raglan swore under his breath. Every soldier needed
luck on his side in combat, but looking at that dog so
close to his face Raglan reckoned there was a Russian
angel hovering over Penal Colony #74. He had overcome
two of the four fences that surrounded the prison colony.
The first at the woodshed had proved easy; the second

into the dog run had risked injury; the third alongside the narrow strip of dog run was impenetrable. The camp authorities had doubled the barbed wire on top and reinforced the mesh fence with dense razor wire. That would stop anyone if they survived the attack dog. The only way out was over the gate he had just climbed. Facing him now was the broad roadway sandwiched between fence three and the outer wooden palisade where the prison bus had brought him into the camp. There was no barbed wire on that wall, only the sagging overhead wires that fed the security lights swinging lazily across their poles. The open stretch was a fifty-metre dash in sight of the watchtowers whose searchlights swept across the exposed area. The falling snow obscured him but not enough – if one of the crisscrossing lights caught him the tower guards would open fire.

One more wall. He waited. As the first searchlight pierced the falling snow and moved away, the second swept across to take its place. Two beams of light courting each other. He realized it could not be done. Either searchlight would throw his shadow into sharp relief. Even the snow would not obscure him from their strong beams. Defeat stared at him across fifty metres. Turning back was not an option.

He thought rapidly, his mind piecing together the camp layout, desperately seeking another escape route. A gust of wind shifted the snow and the Russian angel took pity on the Englishman. The lights went out. He used the power cut to run across the darkened expanse of roadway and nearly collided with the palisade wall. It stood a little over two metres high. Raglan backtracked a half-dozen paces and ran at it, lunging for the top. Wood splinters pierced his hands. Ignoring the stinging slivers, he tipped himself over. He listened for alarms as he squatted, his back against the wall. A minute later the lights came back. Raglan was already running through the snow towards the man he intended to kill.

The silence was broken only by the crunch of his boots in the snow.

53

The little hamlet was picture-postcard pretty. Snow cushioned the roofs, softened sharp-edged fences and walls and disguised the house that Raglan sought. He stood uncertainly at the junction where the road curved away into the cluster of houses. The street lights glowed as dimly as those at the camp.

He turned back and saw that his footprints were already being covered. The hours before roll call were ticking away: then the camp guards would be mobilized and if he was to have any chance of escape, he needed to be away from here before then. He needed warmth. His clothes were wet from the constant snowfall and sweat – he had run hard to get here. The houses were in darkness and the dull light denied him any clear idea of shape or form. He turned into the barely discernible curve of the road. He remembered everything Kirill had told him, willing his mind to bring up the image, as though he had seen it with his own eyes.

JD's house had two storeys. It fronted the street but had a lane behind it. The neighbour had a dog run along one wall. Raglan stared into the night. Either side of the road showed only dark huddled shapes. As he stepped away from a street light, he saw a road going left from his direction of travel. The road separated the back of one house and the front of a double-storey house opposite. The double-storey was set back from the road. A length of garden ran from the street to the front door. Beyond the garden, he could just about make out a low wall separating the house from its neighbour. He peered through the falling snow. It looked as though this was the only double-storey house on the road.

He continued walking, keeping the house on his left until he saw a narrow passage running behind it. Was this the narrow lane Kirill had mentioned? Raglan crouched and made his way close to the house wall until he reached the back gate. It was no more than forty paces from the gate to the back of the house. There was a small extension to one side. Something glinted. A reflection of a street light on the road he had just turned from. Glass catching the uneven light. A window that was ajar. Raglan had reached his target.

Raglan squeezed himself through the window, cursing the pain it caused to his wounded side. It focused his mind. The handicap of the wound could make him careless. A flickering light filtered through the pantry's mesh door, enough for him to see the storage jars sitting below him on the top of the cupboard. The pantry had shelving each side of the window and along each wall filled with cans of food, enough to keep a man in hiding for a month or more. The room had high ceilings with a cross-beam studded with hooks, no doubt used for hanging meat. The only thing that dangled into the room now was a string of garlic. Raglan gingerly stepped down on to the pantry floor, his eyes adjusting to the dull glow from somewhere inside the house.

The fly-screen door squeaked as he teased it open. He was careful that the spring-loaded frame did not bang behind him. Now that he was in the small inner hall he stood and listened for any sign that he had disturbed the man he sought. The dull sheen of the wooden floor that stretched before him into the main body of the house was, he could see, broken by rugs. He shivered despite the warmth coming from an unseen source of heating. His wet clothing hampered him and he stripped off his jacket and the extra shirt. He unlaced his boots and peeled off his socks. Going barefoot through the house would give him some advantage – the wooden floor was less likely to creak than beneath the weight of his boots. Stepping forward, he entered the main living room and saw that the flickering light came from a muted television screen. Two chairs and a sofa boxed the flat-screen television while a wood-burning ceramic stove gave out heat. The remains of a meal and a half-empty bottle of vodka cluttered the small coffee table in front of the sofa. Raglan moved cautiously towards the ceramic heater and rubbed the cold stiffness from his hands. As his eyes adjusted to the room, he imagined the killer feeling secure in his safe house. Curtains blocked any light from outside and Raglan was grateful for the glow from the television. A cartoon danced silently across the screen.

He moved stealthily, searching the room to see whether JD had left the pistol in plain sight. He had not expected the professional intelligence officer to be so careless and as far as he could determine the semi-automatic was not in the room. He edged around until he found the curtain which covered the entrance to the galley kitchen. It was too dark to see if any of the kitchen knives were nestled in a wooden block. A fingertip search gave him a cutlery drawer; he palmed a four-inch serrated steak knife from it. The open-tread stairs descended into the other side of the sitting room. Raglan edged around the room, staying as close as he could to the walls to diminish any chance of the floorboards creaking. So far he had detected no movement in the house. Crouching, he brought his eyeline level with the stairs, using the glow from the television to illuminate the risers. As far as he could see there were no trip wires laid to alert the man who slept upstairs.

Grasping the bannister he felt the first step give a little beneath his bare foot. There were twelve risers narrow enough for him to go up two at a time. As he stretched forward the stitches in his side tugged. He laid his palm on the shirt but felt no blood seeping. He reached the landing and its darkness swallowed him. He remembered the location of the bathroom and bedrooms from what Kirill had said and oriented himself to face the front of the house and the bedroom where his target slept.

The door was ajar. Raglan rolled his foot to lessen his full weight pressing down on the floorboards and then reached out with his free hand to push open the door. The deliberately slow movement had reached its halfway point when he felt the almost imperceptible pressure of a cotton thread tripwire snapping. It's what he would have done. His heart pounded. He knew it was doubtful that JD ever slept in the same bed two nights running. By its next beat, he had gone down on his haunches, sensing movement behind him. The blow whispered above his head, his attacker's breath exhaling with effort, and then grunting in pain as his fist connected with the door frame. Raglan heard the metallic clatter as JD lost the gun that was in his hand. The man's weight fell against him, tumbling them into the bedroom. The killer rolled on to him, smothering his chest and scrabbling for his wrists, searching out any weapon that Raglan might have. An iron grip twisted Raglan's knife hand and a lucky blow from JD's knee slammed hard into his wounded side. The knife slid across the floor as Raglan tucked in his chin and headbutted the suffocating shadow on top of him. He hit JD twice, felt teeth break. JD spat and drew breath, but so far neither man had made a sound other than to gasp in pain. Attack dogs.

Raglan wrenched free one arm, tucked his forearm close to his chest and hit out with the heel of his hand. JD knew what was coming. He twisted his head, deflecting the killing blow aimed at the base of his nose. And then Raglan bucked and rolled, throwing the man clear. Raglan ignored the agony of the stitches tearing and the blood trickling down his side. He smelt the man's sweat and his garlic breath and heard him scrabbling for the fallen weapon. Raglan threw himself towards the sound, heard a thump of an impact as JD collided with a bedside table. A lamp fell and lit the floor, throwing a crazily skewed shadow, exposing JD's scarred and snarling face. He hesitated when he saw his attacker – seconds longer than he should have, his mind computing how it was possible that Raglan was in his safe house, deep in the Russian wasteland. Those vital seconds gave Raglan the advantage. Gripping the man's throat, he squeezed with his thumb, crushing the windpipe. Most men would succumb quickly to pain and the rapid loss of oxygen, but JD's fist swung hard, catching Raglan on the side of his head. An inch lower and his cheekbone would have shattered.

Stunned, Raglan lost his grip. He tried to get to his feet, but JD was quicker and delivered a kick to his ribs. Raglan fell back against the bedframe, doubled up in pain as the wound split. JD abandoned his search for the weapon and hauled Raglan up. Raglan used the pain to power strength into his muscles and as he was dragged halfway up, drove his fist hard between JD's legs. The man sucked air, folded and tumbled on to the bed. Raglan hit him, splitting the skin on his remaining eye. JD tried to wipe away the blood that blinded him but he had lost the ability to defend himself. Raglan pressed his weight down on the man's chest, gripped his windpipe again with one hand and shoved the pillow across his face with the other. He leant into the pillow. JD's legs thrashed, but Raglan's strength held him.

All Raglan needed was another minute to suffocate the life out of him but JD had seen Raglan's blood-soaked shirt and knew it was the one place Raglan was vulnerable. He jabbed hard and fast into his bloodied side. Raglan recoiled, fell back and tumbled to the floor. JD let his weight fall on to him, his knees slamming into Raglan's gut and chest. The stark shadow of JD's snarling face sprayed bloodied spittle on to Raglan, who tried to rise, but felt the cord from the fallen bedside lamp tighten around his neck. JD kept his knee forced into Raglan's chest and pulled the length of cord tighter. Raglan choked, his lungs wheezing for breath, dizziness claiming him. He was losing consciousness. He hooked a finger into the double-stranded lamp cord, one part of it easing free from the other. It wasn't enough. Raglan desperately threw his other arm wide, struck JD, but it had no effect. His fingers groped for anything he might use as a weapon.

'Carter squealed for his wife and kids. Now you can join him. You stupid bastard,' JD spat.

Raglan tugged the cord a fraction, reaching for the fallen lamp and thrusting it into JD's face. The bulb shattered. JD fell back, hands reaching for his torn flesh. Raglan loosened the cord from his neck. The room was in darkness again. He fell on to the squirming man, grabbed him by his hair and drew back his right hand, driving its heel hard and straight beneath JD's chin. Something cracked. The Russian's jaw broke. JD let out a muffled scream, but found the strength to get to his knees and try to make for the door. Raglan grabbed him again, pressed his knee into his back, reached his forearm under the man's throat and gripped his wrist with his free hand. JD bucked, but he was in a vice-like grip. His hands flailed but made no impression.

'I told you I'd find you,' Raglan hissed.

The deadlock forced his forearm against JD's throat until there was a gentle sound, like breaking eggshells. Raglan heard the breath leave the killer's body. A low whistling hiss signalled JD's death.

Raglan rolled free of the dead man and dragged himself upright, his hand searching for a light switch.

The ceiling shade was old-fashioned, faded roses that did not let much light through, but enough for Raglan to see his reflection in a mirror. The room was torn apart, as ripped and damaged as he was.

He put fingers on JD's pulse to make sure; then, satisfied that he had done what he had promised to do, he went into the bathroom and ran hot water into the sink. He peeled off his shirt and undershirt and washed the blood from his face. Then he bathed the wound, searching the medicine cabinet for any dressings. Finding none, he went back into the bedroom and tore the bed sheet into strips. He made a pressure pad and bound the wound. The pain was starting to bite, so he sat for a moment looking down at JD's body as he rolled up the rest of the sheet. No sense leaving a torn sheet for the cops to scratch their head over. Besides, he would need fresh dressings once he was on the road. There was no time to rest.

He rummaged in the wardrobe, spilling clothes from their hangers, found what he needed and dressed. The shirt, trousers and woollen jersey were a decent enough fit and the dry, clean clothes made him feel better. Small mercies. He dragged JD's body to the top of the stairs and kicked it down, watching it sprawl and tumble and then lie crookedly on the floor below. Raglan went down and spilt vodka liberally on the body and furniture. It might be enough for a local police force to see it as a drunken accident. After all, there was no sign of a forced entry. A violent drinking session with a drunk smashing a place and himself up in the process wasn't anything new. Raglan took a slug of vodka and felt it sting the cuts in his mouth. But it was warm, all the way down. He found a small rucksack on the floor below the coats in the entrance hall. He stuffed it with fresh food from the larder and tossed in a couple of tear-top cans. He didn't know how long he was going to be on the road.

He gathered his prison clothes and tied them in a bundle. He would toss them in the forest as he made his escape. He retrieved JD's handgun and brushed the curtain aside to see the clearing sky. The dawn's pre-light promised a clear day. It had stopped snowing and the night's fall lay several inches deep, covering his tracks into the house. It was time to leave before neighbours woke. He checked the street. There were no house lights showing. He opened the door a crack. The air was cold and he knew he had to push back the fatigue that was starting to make itself felt. He had to make a run for it now.

He stepped outside and turned to face the dead man lying at the foot of the stairs. JD's one eye stared up at him.

Raglan sighed, weary. That was one look of death which wouldn't haunt his dreams.

54

Deputy Governor Anatoly Vasiliev followed his guard commander to the wood store where two of the wall's slats had been removed. The nervous man blustered, promising punitive punishment for the dozy watchtower guards. Vasiliev listened patiently, scanning the distance. Yefimov had proved his intelligence and loyalty by not telling him that Regnev had escaped; instead, he reported the matter to the guard commander at roll call. By doing this he had not implicated the deputy governor. Vasiliev felt the comforting warmth of knowing he had played his hand well. Vasiliev could have given Regnev the exact location of where the other killer had been given sanctuary but by having the newcomer placed with the right men Regnev had discovered the information for himself. No one could ever point the finger at Vasiliev. He was safe.

'You're organizing patrols?' asked Vasiliev of the wary guard commander.

'Yes, sir. And I have been contacted by the local militia,' his guard commander answered. The man was old enough to call the newly designated local police by their former name.

Vasiliev raised an eyebrow. The flutter in his chest was one of anticipation. The police would only be in contact if they had caught Regnev, or he was dead. 'Report,' said Vasiliev.

'One of the guards was going home after duty. He saw footprints in the snow going into the back of his neighbour's house. He thought this to be unusual because the man who lived there never left the house. He went to the door and saw the man through the window. It looked as though there had been an accident so he forced the door. He called the militia because the man was dead. Militia say it looks as though the dead man had been drunk and fallen down the stairs. But they think there was someone else involved. There were too many injuries on the body. That, coupled with Prisoner Regnev having escaped, leads me to believe Regnev got that far and broke into the house looking for food or shelter.'

Vasiliev turned away, afraid that his usual inscrutability might fail him. It was a fitting end and one that would go some way to soothing his family's long-standing suffering at being posted to the White Eagle penal colony. Regnev was a professional killer hidden in plain sight among all the other murderers in Penal Colony #74 by powers in Moscow. An unseen authority had determined that Kuznetsov had to die. And Regnev had succeeded. Vasiliev had already thought through the scenario that would follow. His expectation of success had been met and now it was up to him to finish the assignment in a timely manner. The regional department would investigate the murder and question how a killer escaped from such a high-security prison and then there would be an inquiry conducted by the Federal Penal Service. The escape could not be as easily explained to the Feds as to the police, but no one on that investigative committee would wish to make public a weakness in the system. The matter would be drawn to an end; they would put new security measures in place. They would transfer Vasiliev as planned, seen by many as a demotion, yet hailed by him and his family as a reward. The snow would return and blanket the ground. And the truth would be buried with it.

'Regnev will run for the nearest railway line. That means he has forty kilometres to go. Lock down the camp. The men stay inside.' Vasiliev lit a cigarette and exhaled cold air and smoke towards the crystal-clear sky. It was cold. The temperature had dropped rapidly since the snowstorm had ended.

'Grigory,' he said to the guard commander. The man had shared the last twenty years at the camp with him;

it was worth playing on that personal connection. 'This will look bad for us. If Regnev is caught who knows what he will say about the security and conditions here. It would be better for us if his escape failed but... also that he did not return here.'

The guard commander did not respond immediately to Vasiliev's none-too-subtle order. He needed to be absolutely clear about what was being asked of him. 'Sir,' he said, 'are you ordering me to kill him?'

'Daniil Regnev is a brutal murderer. He is dangerous. He might be armed. I will not risk any of our men trying to apprehend him. Shoot to kill at the first opportunity you have.'

After the killing Raglan had walked away from the houses and when he reached the road leading from the hamlet, he began running at a steady, sustainable pace. The cold air felt like cut glass in his lungs. Pain shot through his side and his muscles complained at his injuries, but he ran through the hurt, mind focused on the destination he had to reach before the road was crawling with militia and camp guards.

The road was long and straight, wide enough for two vehicles to pass, and the dark forest pressed on to the verge on both sides. Heaped snow, ploughed from the previous winter, was still frozen and had become an even higher bank from the fresh snowfall. A set of tyre tracks had scored a channel in the middle of the road and Raglan had reasoned it might have been the weekly delivery truck to the camp that had passed before dawn. He was grateful that the tyre tracks gave him firm ground underfoot, a better alternative than trying to run in six-inch snow. If he could reach the lake, he had a chance.

By dawn, he had made good progress and in the clear dry air the faint sound of the camp's siren reached him. They had discovered his escape. How long did he have before a full-scale operation was mounted to hunt him down? He calculated the men being formed up, armed, briefed and sent on their way. Would they wait for the local militia? No, they would liaise by radio. That would allow the net to be thrown wide for him. He reckoned he had less than an hour to reach the lake. If he couldn't, then he would push as deep as he could into the forest. His training had provided him with all the skills he needed to survive in a hostile environment. But not for long in these conditions. Wounded and with few supplies, what he needed was as much distance between him and the men who hunted him. Raglan considered his chances. The deputy governor had been in on the charade from the beginning but Raglan reasoned that just because he'd been bribed to facilitate Regnev's safety in the camp didn't mean he wouldn't erase any link he might have to the killing. There was no way he was going to risk Raglan being captured. Blood oozed from his wound.

Raglan lengthened his stride and ran faster towards the rising sun.

The sniper lay in his hide. The unbroken snow smothered the low roof of fallen branches and old foliage that he had burrowed beneath and which gave no hint of his presence. His white oversuit obliterated his darker thermal clothing. He did not know how long he would have to wait for Raglan to appear in the distance but he had chosen his position carefully. He had a clear view of the road with the sun behind him and the frozen, snow-covered lake to his left added to the glare. No one coming down the road towards him would be able to guess where he lay.

His preference was to travel light. Deciding which weapon to use was determined by the mission. There was no sense in lugging a heavy-calibre rifle weighing ten kilos and a fixed barrel length nudging close to a metre when this job was a medium-range kill. For this enclosed environment where the killing range was six, maybe eight hundred metres, he had chosen a favoured weapon. The Dragunov was far from being the latest sniper rifle issued to Russian forces, but he had a soft spot for the weapon, which had proved itself reliable in theatres of war since the sixties. The hardened steel core 151-grain bullet would travel at 830 metres per second and its side-mounted optical sight gave him a rangefinder and compensation adjustment for the effect of gravity on his bullet over distance. The cold-weather battery case for the telescopic sight was clipped inside his clothing, its cord attached to the lug on the sight to stop it from freezing. Everything was ready. The waiting game would soon be over.

Raglan was slowing down as his body succumbed to the cold and his injuries. Tears from the effort of running in the icy air blurred his vision. He dared not stop. Keeping momentum was vital. To stop meant muscles seized and rising pain. But he was going to hit the wall soon and then all would be lost.

The sun had reached the top of the trees either side of the chill, sunless gulley of a road. Part of his brain promised him warmth as soon as he reached the lake. It would bathe the open expanse in sunlight. His laboured breathing muted the sound of the first vehicle whose headlights beamed from the depression in the road a couple of kilometres behind him. Instinct made him turn. Another vehicle was travelling behind that, its headlights weaving, ducking in and out of sight, eager to overtake the lead vehicle. To be the first in on the kill. Their appearance confirmed what he suspected. The deputy governor was tying up loose ends.

How many men? A dozen? Six armed men in each vehicle? Possibly more. What had he seen at the camp?

Snow-tracked vehicles and small trucks were the norm but now he saw a blue light flashing somewhere behind the first two vehicles. There were probably twenty men in pursuit. Two Ks and closing. They would have studded tyres for the compacted snow. Perhaps he'd be lucky and the drivers' enthusiasm to catch him would make them over-confident of their driving skills. Slow and steady was the answer in weather conditions like this. Studded tyres or not. There was ice beneath the snow and it took a skilful trained driver not to lose control. How fast were they travelling? Sixty? Yes, sixty max. Maybe less. He pumped his arms, his legs responding to the increased pace. He sucked in more of the cut-glass air, spat phlegm as he grunted with exertion. His pursuers were pushing hard. At sixty they'd be covering near enough thirty metres a second. He hoped they were going slower. There wasn't much in it. They would be on him in less than two minutes. He could not wait until they were within the fifty-metre range of the handgun that he now tugged from his waistband. They might slow if he fired a few shots towards them.

He turned, double-gripped the Grach, aimed at the lead vehicle and fired twice. The gunshots cracked the still air. The rounds had no effect but the lead vehicle must have seen him turn, aim and fire. Perhaps even heard the retort. The car swerved, the driver reacting to having a weapon pointed in his direction. Raglan had already turned his back to his pursuers and started running again. There was a brighter area three hundred metres ahead. Sunlight bathed a part of the road. Light no longer obscured by trees. It had to be the open area where the lake was. It fitted in with what he had learnt at the camp.

Behind him, the lead car had slowed the others. Braking too quickly, it had skidded and he heard the crunch of metal as one of the following cars tail-ended the vehicle in front. The over-revved engines told him they were inexperienced fast-pursuit drivers but it would not slow them for long; they were good enough to drive in snow and ice, just not at speed. Raglan had bought himself a vital minute. He still needed three minutes longer. He needed to slow them again.

He leapt over the snow ledge on the side of the road and ducked beneath the overhanging branches. A slender track channelled between the accumulated snow and ice on the side of the road and where the tree trunks barred his way into the forest. He heard the engines change pitch. They were slowing. He ran; branches caught his face; he raised an arm, brushing others aside. The men following would be more cautious. They wouldn't be able to see him or to guess where he was and they would be unwilling to drive too close for fear of him ambushing them. The cars slowed again, voices called, and a rattle of gunfire cut the air above his head. He cursed his own stupidity. By brushing the branches away from his face he had disturbed the snow lying on them and the fine powder left low on the tree had been seen. He ducked below the snow ledge and saw that the men had kept back by a hundred metres. He fired twice more, saw them scatter, but knew he'd get no hit at that distance. He kept running, ducking lower, avoiding the branches. The thwack of bullets hit the trees where he had been moments before.

And then he ran out of track with two hundred metres to go before reaching the lake.

The guards and militia had better firepower than the Grach. The unmistakable sound of bullets tearing the air made him zigzag. A sharp bite stung the side of his leg. A bullet had scorched his thigh. Another tore into his side. He could run no more. He fell and slammed into a tree. He needed a moment to draw breath. A flash of memory of what had brought him here. And then sounds of pursuit drawing closer.

He knelt, seeing that the men had dared to run closer as they had fired. He squeezed off four more times and watched the men scatter, but none took cover because they knew they were still out of effective range. Emboldened, they ran towards him. Raglan fired again. A double tap. Counting the rounds he had fired, knowing he had only eight bullets remaining. Two of the men dropped as blood exploded from their heads. Time faltered as the bullet strikes surprised him and his pursuers. And then the heavier report of a rifle echoed across the hardened landscape. Two whip cracks followed his own as two more men went down. Cries of alarm and panic set in. Four rapid shots shattered windscreens and engine blocks. A fifth man bellowed in pain as his leg was smashed. His comrades hesitated but then bravely ran forward and dragged him into cover behind one of the cars, leaving a trail of blood in the wake of the man's screams.

Raglan clambered to his feet and ran limping towards the lake. The air bristled from the whirring sound of three more bullets far too close for comfort. He broke cover into the open space between the lake and the road. The blinding glare from the expanse of sunlit snow dazzled him. On the bend of the road where the white lake nudged into the bank a mound of snow rose up. The sniper raised a hand, put the rifle into his shoulder and shot twice more. Raglan didn't have to turn to hear the men's screams.

As Raglan reached his old fighting comrade and friend, the white-clad figure took a few strides to one side and hauled back a snow-encrusted tarpaulin exposing a two-man snowmobile.

'I didn't think you were going to make it. You're slowing up in your old age. Christ, you look like shit,' Serge Sokol growled. 'Damned near froze my nuts off waiting for you to get your arse in gear.' The tough Russian sniper grinned and looked past Raglan as they heard the one undamaged car reverse and then crash its gears as the survivors made their escape. 'They won't bother us any more,' he said.

Despite his exhaustion and pain, Raglan grinned and threw an arm around his old comrade. 'Cheers, Bird. Militia will bring in a chopper to search for us now.'

'Not with the weather that's coming in. We'll be long gone. I have a four-by-four hidden and a route out with a safe house near the border. There's a doctor waiting. Knowing you, I figured you'd need help,' he said with a grin. 'Let's be ready to move and then get some fluids in you.'

Sokol secured the Dragunov in its weatherproof sleeve that ran along the snowmobile's footrest. After throwing Raglan's pack into the forest he tied down his own, which he had lived out of since getting Raglan's phone call to his non-existent brother, Konstantin. Lifting the lid of the storage compartment he took out a slender metal rod and clamped it on to the back of the snowmobile's frame. Then he expertly cut one of Raglan's sleeves with a short-bladed combat knife, tore open an antiseptic wipe packet and swabbed his arm. He tapped his cold skin for a vein and inserted a cannula. The storage bin yielded an IV bag that Sokol hung and adjusted on the clamped frame.

Raglan was shivering from shock, exertion and cold.

'Almost there, *mon ami*,' Sokol said tenderly to his wounded friend. Sokol pulled free a padded thermal sniper's suit that had zips allowing the suit to be opened fully. He wrapped it around Raglan, zipped in his arms and legs, swaddling him in its warmth, leaving enough material free to accommodate the cannula. Warmth flooded into Raglan's body.

'Thanks,' said Raglan.

Sokol nodded. He knew damned well that it had only been Raglan's strength and determination that had brought him this far. He turned the ignition key. The four-stroke engine purred into life. He turned the snowmobile's nose across the frozen lake.

Raglan glanced back and saw that the sun's beams had penetrated the edge of the forested road. Rivulets of blood, frozen veins in the hard ground, had seeped down from the ambush site. A sharp wind rustled the treetops, shaking flurries of snow. It made no difference that the strengthening wind would also scour the surface of the lake, erasing the snowmobile's tracks. By then they would be out of sight.

Sokol half turned to ensure his friend was ready. 'Helluva a long way to track that bastard down. Was it worth it?'

Raglan nodded and tapped his friend's shoulder. Sokol twisted the throttle.

'It was a necessary kill,' said Raglan.

НОВОСТЬ, РАЗМЕЩЕННАЯ НА САЙТЕ СЛЕДСТВЕННОГО КОМИТЕТА РОССИЙСКОЙ ФЕДЕРАЦИИ

ДЕКАБРЯ 2019 г.

Следственными органами ГСУ СК России по городам Москве и Екатеринбургу возбуждено уголовное дело по факту убийства гражданина Егора Кузнецова на территории Свердловской области Уральского федерального округа. Приоритетной версией является умышленное заказное убийство, совершенное организованной преступной группой по мотиву мести. Указанная группировка предположительно состоит из выходцев из Республики Беларусь и имела целью не допустить дачу г-ном Кузнецовым свидетельских показаний об их деятельности. Согласно сообщению Московского уголовного розыска при попытке задержания указанной преступной группы лиц охранниками колонии №74 (Белый Орёл) совместно с офицерами регионального ГУ убойного отдела МВД, преступники оказали вооруженное сопротивление и в ходе перестрелки, которая продолжалась несколько часов, все члены банды были уничтожены. Имеются также жертвы (4 офицера) и раненные со стороны сотрудников правоохранительных органов. В ходе расследования ФСИН по факту побега из заключения (колонии №74 Белый Орёл) был объявлен выговор и возбуждено уголовное дело в отношении заместителя губернатора области Анатолия Васильева, которому была избрана мера задержания в виде заключения под стражу в один из следственных изоляторов рядом с Москвой. Проводится углубленная проверка систем безопасности в колонии Белый Орёл. Тело заключенного №76590 Даниил Регнева до сих пор не обнаружено, и указанный гражданин числится пропавшим без вести. Предположительно указанный гражданин мог погибнуть вследствие суровых природных факторов в районе расположения колонии.

NOTIFICATION POSTED ON THE OFFICIAL WEBSITE OF THE INVESTIGATIVE COMMITTEE OF THE RUSSIAN FEDERATION DECEMBER 2019

Investigative bodies of the Federal Sledstvenniy Komitet for Moscow and Yekaterinburg have opened a criminal case into the murder of Yegor Kuznetsov, which was committed in Sverdlovskaya Oblast of the Ural Federal District. The priority version is the intentional contract killing committed by an organized criminal group with the motive of revenge. The said group is likely comprised of Republic of Belarus natives and their objective was to prevent Kuznetsov from testifying against their activities. As reported by Moscow CID, during the attempt to apprehend the said criminal group by the guards of the Penal Colony No. 74 (White Eagle), in cooperation with officers from the Regional Murder Investigation Unit, the criminals fought back and following a gun battle of several hours the outnumbered officers sought to apprehend the gang after their attempted escape. Moscow Central CID reports that all members of the gang were terminated. There are also casualties (four officers slain) and a further number wounded from the aforementioned law-enforcement authorities. In the course of an FSIN (Federal Penal Service) investigation into the escape from the Penal Colony No. 74 (White Eagle) a reprimand was made and a criminal case started against Deputy Governor Anatoly Vasiliev, who was detained in an investigative jail near Moscow. An in-depth investigation of the Penal Colony No. 74 (White Eagle) security systems is being conducted. The body of escaped prisoner No. 76590 Daniil Regnev has not been recovered to date and this citizen is considered missing, presumed deceased. It is likely that this citizen succumbed to the elements of the rugged, inhospitable environment that surrounds the prison.

ACKNOWLEDGEMENTS

I would like to express my appreciation for those who helped me in the research for this book.

Michael Walker in London took valuable time from his busy writing schedule to spend hours driving me around the congested, rain-soaked streets of Bedford Park, Chiswick High Road and Hammersmith, helping me discover the perfect ambush site in Weltje Road. Furthermore, without complaint given the difficult conditions, he then drove me further afield to point out possible escape routes and hideouts for my criminal gang. The time he spent was invaluable in helping me plan and execute the various elements of the attack and kidnap. And more besides. Thanks, Michael.

My first contact in seeking help for the Russian elements of the story was Olga Puchkova, whose name was given to me by my friend and fellow author, Kate Furnivall, who contributed her own recollections of

Russia. Despite being extremely busy, Olga patiently and kindly responded to my long list of queries, giving me insights into various parts of Russia and the way of life in that vast country. One of my readers, John L. Scott, volunteered his recollections of having worked for many years in Russia on behalf of USAID and then introduced me to a friend and former work colleague who lives in Moscow, Igor Troitskiy. If I have captured any essence at all of that city, no matter how slight, it is due solely to Igor's valuable input as a passionate Muscovite. I am greatly indebted to him for every comment he made and for translating the end piece into Russian for me. Any errors in the information offered are mine alone.

One of my colleagues, Emanuela Anechoum, and her father, Abdelalì Anechoum, ensured my Arabic text was correct, which was extremely helpful given my ignorance of the correct form to use.

It took some digging around for me to find a means of connecting the character Eddie Roman and the newspaper, but retired journalist Marilyn Warnick kindly put me in touch with John Wellington at the *Mail on Sunday*. He swiftly disabused me of my original idea which did not stand up to scrutiny but his ongoing comments enabled me to solve the problem.

There is a raft of information about RBOC (Russian-Backed Organized Crime) but I concentrated my key areas of research on documents published by the United States Department of State and its Bureau of Diplomatic

Security. The European Council on Foreign Relations provided a valuable insight into the role of Europol and Interpol and the role of Russian organized crime in Europe over the past twenty years.

David Gilman
Devonshire
2020

Website: www.davidgilman.com
Facebook: www.facebook.com/davidgilman.author
Twitter: @davidgilmanuk

ABOUT THE AUTHOR

David Gilman enjoyed many careers – including firefighter, paratrooper and photographer – before turning to writing full time. He is an award-winning author and screenwriter.